STARDUST

Second Chance AT L♥VE

CATHRYN LYONS

STARDUST

Second Chance
AT L♥VE

Stardust Playlist

There are a several songs that inspired me as I wrote: "Sanctuary", from the soundtrack of *Nashville*; "All I Want" by Kodaline; "Beautiful Things" and "Before You" by Benson Boone; "Never Enough" from *The Greatest Showman*; "Lose Control" by Teddy Swims; "Love Me Anyway" by P!nk and Chris Stapleton; "We Found Love" by Rihanna and Calvin Harris; and "Wi$h Li$t" by Taylor Swift, which came out during developmental edits with my own frienditor, Michelle, and beautifully captures Honor and Brinder. You can find this on Spotify at https://open.spotify.com/playlist/5aXTF5rX2EBpYhrVF8HrgC

You can't go back and change the beginning,
but you can start where you are and change the ending.

— C.S. LEWIS

PROLOGUE

HONOR

"No. No no no. This *can't* be real."

Honor's eyes locked on the paused video, heart racing. "I'm going to close my eyes now," she whispered to the empty room, "and when I open them, this will all just be a bad dream. Please, *please* let this not be what I think it is."

A sharp paradox to her current mood, bright morning rays beamed in through the windows of her sunroom. Normally her happy place, where she read, wrote, and generally grounded herself in things that were real—so necessary, given her background and career—today the glass-enclosed sanctuary was on the precipice of becoming the setting of a horror scene.

Honor dropped her head into her hand and breathed deeply, her other hand reflexively pressing the long-ago-healed incision on her sternum. She closed her eyes. "This cannot be happening. *Please.*"

Easing her eyes open, she scanned the frozen laptop screen in front of her as she mindlessly rubbed the faded scar visible above her sleep tank. The same scar that makeup artists hid on a regular basis. At the moment, Honor fervently wished for a life artist to hide the disaster unfolding before her eyes.

"It has to be an AI deep fake," she willed aloud, voice shaking.

And, yet...she knew. It was real. The freaking video was real. And she remembered the exact night it had been filmed—without her consent.

How did she know?

She'd been on top. Her bare back to the camera, the full globes of her tush clearly visible, resting on those legs she knew so well. Head thrown back in ecstasy.

The camera had been cleverly placed so it showed mostly her back. But a bit of her side—the profile of her chest and the D-cup breasts that hurt her back—was framed in the center of the tableau.

Honor slid into a thousand-yard stare, remembering that evening almost two months earlier. She'd met with her agent in London to discuss her upcoming role and iron out the last pieces of contract negotiations. That completed, her editor, Ross, had joined via Zoom, sharing the amazing news that her memoir had landed in the top ten on two different bestseller lists.

After the meeting, she'd met up with Crispin and they'd gone to dinner to celebrate. Honor would have loved nothing more than a romantic meal at home, but Crispin made reservations at a specific Michelin-starred restaurant in the heart of London. It was a celebrity magnet, and therefore a paparazzi favorite, so Honor preferred not to go. But he loved their steak and mashed potatoes with cilantro (or coriander, as he referred to the seasoning) and she truly did salivate over the curry halibut.

She'd conceded, as she'd usually done with Crispin. It was just easier than arguing.

Rather than traveling five-plus hours to her waterfront Pembrokeshire County home after dinner, they'd relaxed in her preferred room at the posh boutique hotel in Kensington she frequented when staying overnight in London.

She remembered the welcome flare of her arousal as Crispin kissed along her neck, slowly disrobing her and placing her on the edge of the king bed. And her surprise when he eased between her legs, whispering that bestselling authors deserved a treat. She'd even enjoyed the flush of a building orgasm, an ever-elusive experience for her in any circumstance.

She'd gently tugged him away, breathlessly begging him to be inside her—a practiced part of their encounters, not fully fake, but also not fully real for her either. Then her happy shock as he'd cocked a grin and stretched out on his back, guiding her on top of him.

Their sex life had been decent but...drab. Foreplay occasionally included oral sex, but it rarely lasted long. She was always self-conscious about her blow job skills. Crispin never said anything directly to her, but Honor had always gotten the sense that particular act was as unsatisfying for him to receive as for her to give. He usually pulled her off him relatively quickly when she did find herself down there.

Some of her friends raved about how sexy giving head was, claiming they could almost come from it, blah blah blah. When this particular discussion came up, Honor had the distinct feeling of being a stranger in a strange land and tried to fake her own experiences by smiling like the Mona Lisa keeping a secret. That always worked to keep the embarrassing truth from them.

And, of course, there was the flip side. She'd never come from someone going down on her. After many years of failure on that front, she'd become reluctant to add to Crispin's frustration when she couldn't come from his oral efforts. He'd often gotten upset with her, blaming her neuroses over her childhood heart surgeries for her inability to truly let go.

To keep the peace—his and hers—she would do what was necessary: apply her Oscar-winning acting skills to some epic faking. When Crispin would make increasingly half-hearted efforts in that direction, she'd feign passion and an intense desire to have him inside her. Then, missionary sex. Almost always.

He'd come—loudly—and then they'd snuggle, him kissing the top of her head before falling into a snore-ridden sleep.

But this time? He was giving her what she'd shyly requested the week prior—some variety to their intimacy. She loved him, and he'd often effusively expressed his deep love of her. So when he initiated a change of position, she'd been thrilled.

Their lovemaking had ended the same way, of course. But her

passion was a bit more real, the excitement of change zinging between her legs. When she threw her head back (the moment currently paused on her laptop screen), that had been *real*.

Ironic. How she could be so comfortable on screen. So at home. How the big screen had been her salvation and, once upon a time, her deepest joy. And now? Her unwitting title role was about to blow her world wide open. If it hadn't already.

She hit play again, hoping to desensitize herself so the painful shock would abate.

Other celebrity sex tapes she knew about were often grainy. But not hers. No. This was high-definition. Artfully lit. Black and white.

Dissociating from her personal humiliation, and applying her trained industry eye, Honor could admit it was actually beautifully framed. And exceedingly and increasingly nauseating. A private moment with her now ex-boyfriend splashed all over a tabloid site. And heaven knew where else.

As the video ended, the sensation of utter violation settled in her gut. Mortification flooded her veins as tears filled her eyes, blurring everything. She gulped a sob, reflexively running the tips of her fingers along her scar once more. Honor wasn't sure which was racing harder—her heart or her head.

The chiming alert of her cell startled her. It was her agent, Benoite.

A she-devil bulldog, Benny was terrifyingly intimidating when you first met her, or when crossed. But when you were "hers," she was the staunchest advocate. A mama bear. The most assertive, self-assured woman Honor had ever met. She definitely had a girl-crush on the forty-eight-year-old industry titan. Tall, with icy-blonde hair, pale blue eyes, and a slim build, Benny was a Swedish-American former runway model-turned-uber-agent. She was a force. And she was currently blowing up Honor's phone.

Honor picked it up as if it were radioactive. Eleven missed calls in fifteen minutes. And dozens of texts. Ross. Benny. Her parents. Her brother...

Oh, cripes. They'd seen it. Seen *her*. Mortification, and its mean-girl friend nausea, rose in her belly again.

Sighing deeply, she answered, putting it on speaker, her hand shaking too hard to hold the phone.

"Honor," came Benny's in-charge voice, carrying with confidence over the room. Just that one word, and Honor felt a bit (a very teensy-tiny bit) of relief.

"Yes," she croaked, answering her agent's unasked question.

"It's viral."

The confirmation of what Honor had already suspected made her lightheaded. She forced herself to take three deep breaths, filling her lungs and slowly exhaling.

"I had nothing to do with it, Benny." Her words wavered, tears thickening her voice.

"I know." Benny's succinct, stalwart response soothed her jagged heart.

"Do we know who—who filmed it? Who leaked it?"

Benny paused ever so briefly. "Early speculation would be a staffer at the hotel placed the camera while you weren't in the room. Maybe a maid. A new one started not long before you stayed there and then quit not long after, so she's being checked out. We've got a tech team working on tracking the video's origins. And the entire PR and legal departments are working on getting it pulled down and scrubbed from as many sites as humanly possible. We are on this for you, Honor. We will manage and mitigate this. I need you to breathe. This isn't good, but everything is being handled swiftly."

Benny paused and Honor could hear the faint sounds of cheering in the background. She was probably at her son's hockey game, likely tucked in a corner so no one would overhear. Her agent was discreet and dedicated to her, but also would not want to miss a moment of her son's game. That dedication to her family was one reason Honor loved Benny so much.

"Crispin's already called. He's very angry and is hollering for a lawsuit." Her agent cleared her throat. "And he's asking to see you."

"I don't—" Honor swallowed past the lump in her throat. "I don't want to see him."

"I figured." A long pause. "We're investigating him, too, Honor."

Honor's head spun even more at the thought of Crispin being

behind this mortifying treachery. She closed her eyes and did one set of box breathing. *Nope. Didn't work.* "I can't even think straight right now. My brain is tangled with so many thoughts."

It's ok. We're on it for you. Just try to breathe." Benny's voice softened, a sure sign of her worry. "Where are you?"

"My house. Sunroom," Honor managed.

"Are you alone?"

"Yes. I'd already given Grayton and Bauer the weekend off from their protection detail. I was planning to go see my parents later. But now..."

She trailed off, unease triggering the palpitations that always alarmed her, no matter how often her cardiac surgeon and family friend, Rahul Desai, told her she was healed and healthy.

Dr. Desai. Brinder's dad. Her heart skipped. *Fudge!* He and Lady Jane probably knew about it too. And what about Brinder, the Ghost of Heartbreaks Past, living his best life in the States. Had he seen it too? Was there no end to the horror?

"Honor, are you there?"

"I'm here," Honor heard herself respond. *Huh. So this was what an out-of-body experience felt like.*

"Honor, try to hang in with me here. Do not go to your parents. Do not leave your house. Stay put. In fact, make sure you are in a room with privacy windows. Your sunroom has those, right?"

"Ye-yes," Honor choked out. "Why?"

"You've got paps set up at your gate and on the water outside your property. I need you to lay low. I'm sending back-up security until Grayton and Bauer can get back. They'll be in a vehicle disguised as a delivery truck, but I doubt the vultures will be fooled." Benny's assertive voice filled the room, leaving no room for argument.

"Where am I going?"

"Virginia."

Chapter One

Honor

The Mid-Atlantic humidity always surprised her. It was late May, and technically still spring, but Mother Nature clearly hadn't gotten the memo. To an American who spent most of her downtime in Wales, the weather was giving off bowels-of-hell vibes.

Honor dragged a hand through her hair, feeling the natural curl trying to take over. She grabbed for the often-present elastic on her wrist, pulling her hair into a high ponytail, uncaring of how it looked.

After being whisked to a private airport via an Amazon delivery truck, flying eight hours on a Learjet kindly loaned by a sympathetic mega-model client of Benny's, landing at another private airport in Virginia, and then driven a relatively short distance via a town car with dark tinted windows to the outskirts of Charlottesville, Virginia, Honor was fried. Crispy fried.

It felt as if she'd been run over by the delivery truck—twice—rather than shuttled to safety in it. It was almost three in the afternoon Eastern time, and her day had started back in England at seven thirty that morning, when she'd risen early with the intention to work on her screenplay.

Honor was the opposite of a night owl, often in her PJs by nine thirty. She loved the soft light of morning. The quiet of the day's start. The mist over her property on the pale gray mornings and the patter of rain on her roof. Or, when the giant star in the sky won out, the peace of sunlight shafts dancing on her sunroom floor while she worked or read, sipping a latte from her favorite mug. And she always preferred to engage in her writing inspired by the break of a new day.

Now, her internal clock told her it was evening. Her stomach growled, and she was shaky, likely from low blood sugar. She'd been so upset, replaying the video in her head on an endless loop, she hadn't been able to eat anything.

And her outfit was...a travesty. She was still wearing what she'd thrown on that morning, eager to get to her writing. The soft leggings were her favorite pair, as evidenced by the hole that kept opening on the inside seam of one of the legs from frequent wearings. She glanced down and smiled. Her rudimentary stitching was holding fast. *Well at least I have that going for me today. Ha!*

She still wore her sleep tank, sans bra, and had thrown on her favorite old hoodie for the plane. It was far too big and swamped her tiny body, but she loved it like you can only love a well-worn-in article of clothing. (Never mind that it had belonged to...*him*. Completely irrelevant. Yep.) Her flip flops displayed the chipped nail polish on her toes, teasing her with their reminder of the pedicure she'd had scheduled. Darn. Likely her PA, Molly—who managed her life with impressive skill—already canceled it.

Benny had assured her she'd take care of packing and sending luggage, but a private plane was waiting with a tight turnaround timeframe. So off she'd gone, head ducked out of instinct to avoid the paps, even though the interior of the delivery van wasn't visible. Still, she could see the camera flashes through the windshield out of the corner of her eye, wincing with every burst and cringing at the cacophony of the parasites screaming her name.

Self-consciously, Honor folded her arms across her chest. Of all things in this nightmare of a day, she was lamenting the lack of a bra. As a petite woman, her D cups seemed even larger by proportion. She wanted to shed the hoodie, the afternoon heat beating on her, but she was frozen with indecision. And embarrassment.

The driver, who was somehow connected to her security team, had dropped her at a beautifully restored farmhouse, promising to be back later with the luggage—coming via Molly on a commercial flight—and her two private security officers, who couldn't get to the airport on time.

In the meantime, it was sweat in the old hoodie or let Ross and her husband see her tatas in their unsupported glory, including the headlights that always embarrassed her.

She reached for the scar, rubbing her chest to calm herself.

The instructions from Benny were characteristically brief, but thorough. Go to Ross's farmhouse. She and her husband, Xan, had a cottage on the property where she'd be staying for the foreseeable future. No paps should be able to find her. Honor's longtime private duty security team—two retired Army Rangers—would keep an eye on the property once they arrived. And under no circumstances should she answer her phone except for Benny, Molly, or her immediate family, who'd been fully versed by her agent and then reassured on a call with Honor during the flight.

Benny's plan was to speak on Honor's behalf, via a statement, indicating the video was filmed without Honor's consent, expressing outrage at the violation of her privacy, and not dignifying anything or anyone with a comment beyond that. Benny and the PR team believed it would blow over with the next celebrity scandal—which seemed to happen daily these days—and that a public comment or interview by Honor herself would only fan the flames.

The plan was simple: Rise above it...while hiding in the Shenandoah Valley apparently.

Honor sighed deeply. At least it was picturesque here.

She doublechecked the text that had come in from Ross while Honor was somewhere over the Atlantic.

ROSS

> Hey, you. I'm so sorry about this clusterfuck. We'll take care of you. Text me when you are 10 minutes out and I'll go to the front porch and wait. Then I'll help get you set up in the cottage. Just a heads up that we're holding Leah's baptism today, as well as my niece Grace's, and my godson, Augie's. If for some reason I'm not in the farmhouse, follow the stone path behind the kitchen to the barn on the edge of the property. It's just past the pool. You can't miss it. We're having a small celebration—don't worry, it's only my sister, her husband and kids, my bestie and her hubby, and our good friend. And Xan of course. But he's a vault. We all are. And the party may be over by then, given three infants who need naps. It's going to be ok, Wheats. 💋🖤

Honor looked at the house, which she knew had belonged to Ross's late grandmother. And where her editor-turned-friend lived with Xander—whom Honor'd met once—their infant daughter, and Petey, Xan's son from his prior marriage.

No sign of Ross. She sent another text, waited a minute, and sighed again, pushing her sleeves up as high as they'd go and flapping the front of her hoodie to create some air flow.

"Guess I'm going to the barn. Please, God, if you are merciful, let everyone but Ross and Xander be gone."

CHAPTER TWO

BRINDER

Heading out of the cool barn into the unseasonably steamy Virginia afternoon, Brinder pulled Tiercy into a goodbye hug. Once, he might have experienced a pang of longing—or perhaps of regret—for what they'd never be for each other. Now? The only sensation in his heart was the special tug of deep friendship. The kind that shares its own unique sense of love. The clarity he'd experienced as he'd emerged from the haze of infatuation for his best friend's widow was both welcome and yet troubling.

Welcome, because he realized he and Tiercy were never meant to be more than friends. But it was the latter emotion that shook him. The end of his infatuation with Tiercy was deeply troubling...because it also underscored that he'd only truly been in love once. And the woman who'd held his heart in her hands hadn't felt the same. She couldn't have, or she wouldn't have left the way she did, essentially disappearing from his life with scant explanation.

She was always there, though. On the covers of magazines in the staff lounge. An interview on the TV. Charming and quotable in red carpet junkets he stumbled across. (OK...*sought out*...because he was a glutton for punishment.) Her light brown hair tumbling down her shoulders. The tiny dimple in one cheek that appeared when she was particularly amused. Her sexy, petite body with its decadent curves. The sparkling brown eyes, so large in her heart-shaped face that even well into her thirties now, she often was compared to a classic Disney princess. (A comparison he knew from their very ancient history that she loathed as infantilizing and trite.)

Bollocks. Why were his thoughts stuck on her? She'd been on his mind nonstop for weeks now—ever since her memoir released. And... unbelievably...it turned out that Tiercy's best friend, Ross, was her editor.

Small. Fucking. World.

However, neither Tiercy nor Ross knew he and Honor had a shared history. Didn't know they had once been the best of friends. Didn't know they'd been so much more...

The sound of a throat being cleared—loudly—paired with a firm hand on his shoulder, had Brinder releasing his hold on Tiercy. Embarrassed, he turned to Cole, Tiercy's husband. Pale gray-blue eyes honed in on him, one eyebrow raised.

"Uh...sorry, mate. I got lost in thought there."

"Evidently." Cole's tone was dry, but there was concern etched on his face along with an amused half-smile. Brinder's emerging friendship with Cole had been a surprise byproduct of the past couple years. Supremely self-confident in the love of his wife, Cole had borne no grudges against Brinder for his former infatuation with Tiercy. In fact, Cole had befriended him, Brinder becoming the fourth member of a tight-knit group that included Cole; Ross's husband, Xander; and Ted, the husband of Ross's sister Gaby.

When Tiercy, Gaby, and Ross all realized their due dates were within about eight weeks of each other, the visits between them grew more frequent. Then, in March, Cole and Tiercy threw him a curveball when they announced their relocation to Charlottesville. Cole was opening a new location for Colburn Construction, allowing growth with a new client base. And, as Brinder suspected was an even greater motivator, moving Tiercy close to Ross.

While he was deeply grateful Tiercy was finally getting her happily ever after, the pang of loss had seared Brinder's heart. Tiercy, Jemma, and yes, even Cole, had become family to him. The distance between his restored brownstone near the Baltimore waterfront and the small town outside of Charlottesville where the Colburns had settled wasn't insurmountable by any stretch. But he also knew their time together would naturally dwindle.

It seemed like a touch of serendipity when Ben Lopez, Brinder's boss at Fellowship-Unity, flagged an opportunity for an interim chief medical officer position at St. John the Evangelist, a major academic hospital in Charlottesville. Brinder and Luke had both shared ambitions around hospital leadership, and after three years as chief of radiology at the Baltimore hospital, Brinder was now achieving the next step in that goal at Evangelist.

He'd moved into a spacious loft condo in a converted factory located about halfway between the hospital and Xander and Ross's farmhouse.

And with that, the band was back together.

Except, when the seven of them hung out, Brinder was definitely the odd man out. The others were nauseatingly happy in their coupledom, and the PDA could be a bit hard to take—especially with Ross and Xan, who didn't seem to want to leave the honeymoon phase of their surprise relationship.

Brinder had known Ross for years, and they'd even dated for a hot second ages ago, but they were much too alike to click. There was no balance. Instead, both he and Ross preferred (or, that is to say, she *used* to prefer) a robust social life with many surface level dalliances. Brinder never thought he'd see the day when Ross was contentedly "hubbied up." But he guessed anything was possible when you fell in love and that love was reciprocated.

Not that he knew what that felt like.

And...there it was. Back to *her*. That unavoidable shift in his mind was both exhausting and frustrating. It was as if the universe was torturing him. She was the human version of an earworm song. He could not get her out of his mind.

His Tish.

He still often thought of her by that special nickname only he used.

God, it was ridiculous how much he missed her, and it was half his life ago.

More throat clearing.

Brinder startled, pinching his nose in embarrassment.

"You good, brother?" Xan stood with his arm around Ross's waist, a tiny baby with a tuft of soft brown hair nestled in his other arm. Leah was making tiny noises, little whimpers and squeaks, and shifting her head in the crook of her besotted father's elbow.

"I'm good. Sorry I'm a space cadet today. Can't seem to get my mind off work." There. That wasn't a total lie. Especially after the shitty, unexpected showdown with his Board chair on Friday. Why did work crises always happen on Friday afternoons and Sunday evenings? What vengeful work god had humankind angered? And how was he going to respond to Clark's ultimatum?

Next to him, Ross eased Leah from her husband's arms, tipping her head up to receive a tender kiss from Xan, which quickly turned spicy.

"Guys"—Brinder ran a hand through his hair, which was getting too long—"get a room."

"We just might," Ross winked. "Or outside works. I always enjoy an al fresco assignation."

"Good SAT word," Tiercy chimed in, as was their bestie habit, shifting her own infant son to give Ross a fist bump.

"I need to get Leah inside, nurse her, and put her down for her afternoon nap." Ross frowned. "What time is it?"

Brinder consulted his Tag-Heuer, a gift from his parents after he graduated from university. They'd mailed it to him, as they couldn't be bothered to attend. Or, more likely, his father refused and his mother, wanting peace with her spouse, capitulated. "Almost three."

"That's weird. I was expecting her to call." Ross swayed back and forth, gently shushing Leah.

"Is this your client who's in crisis?" Brinder had only gotten the vaguest of explanations for this unplanned visit from her nameless client when he arrived at the church for the three-way baptism.

"Yep," Ross nodded, worry bracketing her face. "Babe, can you see if I left my phone by the cooler?"

"No problem." Xander loped back inside, where they'd stashed a cooler of water, juice drinks for the older kids—who had all long since escaped to the nearby treehouse to play, under the supervision of Gaby and Ted—and adult beverages for the grownups, except the nursing moms.

"Not here!" Xander called.

"Shi—ooot," Ross quickly corrected herself. "Sorry, baby," she whispered.

"Girl, it's in your back pocket." Tiercy slid a hand into Ross's pants pocket, retrieving the phone.

"Does this count as getting to third base, Tierce?" Ross waggled her brows. The best friends cracked up, bumping shoulders—gently, so as not to jar their babies.

"Oh fu—phooey!" Ross yelped, staring at her phone. "I missed two texts from Honor. She must be walking this way by now. Dam—er, dang it."

Brinder barely noticed Ross hustling toward the farmhouse over the roar in his ears.

Honor.

Did she say *Honor*?

Cole raised a brow. "Brinder...are you ok? You look like you've seen a ghost."

He blinked his eyes and turned away from Cole...where his eyes landed on the very rumpled, very shocked, very beautiful woman making her way toward them. The very woman who'd broken his heart twenty years ago.

"A ghost, indeed."

CHAPTER THREE

HONOR

Honor gasped, winded like she'd been punched in the gut. Hard. She had to be hallucinating from the stress of the day.

Brinder?

When Ross hadn't responded to her texts, Honor had reluctantly followed the path toward the barn as directed by her editor. "Peopling" was the last thing she wanted to do. Even though it was just a small group, Honor was in no frame of mind, or state of attire, to socialize. She'd hoped to see Ross and disappear quickly inside the cottage that had been offered to her as a refuge from the surreal scandal that had exploded her life out of nowhere.

Instead, just as she turned a corner, the barn less than a dozen yards in front of her, she ran into Ross scurrying along the path, a tiny baby in her arms. But it wasn't Ross who snagged her attention.

No. That would be too merciful in what was quickly becoming the worst day of her life—and that was saying something, considering she'd undergone two open heart surgeries before she turned seventeen.

Standing just past Ross, shock freezing him in place, was Brinder.

Her Brinder.

Eighteen years. That's how long had passed since she'd seen him—at least live and in person. Her internet stalking didn't count. Nope. Not at all.

And...wowza...time had been very, *very* kind to him.

He was always tall—over six feet the last time she'd seen him—but he clearly grew in college. Honor knew she was "snack-sized," and she was terrible at guessing heights. Honestly, everyone seemed gigantic compared to her. But he was clearly several inches beyond six feet... maybe even six-and-a-half. And unlike some tall men, there wasn't a gangly bone in sight. Instead, the lines of lean muscular legs were visible against his formfitting dress slacks, the pop and curve of defined biceps nudging the sleeves of his rolled up linen shirt.

And what the heck? Was that a tattoo sleeve winding down his arm to wrap around his wrist? Holy hotness.

Her eyes dawdled on his broad chest and wide shoulders. Shoulders that had easily supported her as they'd horsed around in the lake on her parents' property. He was long, lean, and muscled. Objectively, based on many years around Hollywood's most attractive men, he was easily the most beautiful man she'd ever seen.

She allowed herself to scan higher. The product of an "English rose" mother and a handsome Indian surgeon, Brinder had inherited the best of both parents. Smooth skin that looked perpetually tanned. High cheekbones. Hazel eyes the exact replica of his mom's. He'd grown his not-quite-black hair longer than he'd kept it in high school, the dark silky locks trailing almost to the top of his collar. It was a good look.

Honor swallowed past a lump in her throat, trying to form words. But nothing came out.

Ross pulled her in for a one-armed hug, clearly oblivious to the hum of torment sizzling through Honor at the sight of her "one who got away."

"Wheats, I am so sorry. I'd turned off my ringer in the church and I clearly forgot to turn it up when we got back here. Baby brain is real." Ross released her and then peered at her closely. "Honor? Honey?"

Honor tore her gaze from Brinder, who still hadn't moved and was watching her with wide eyes, his face pale under his warm skin tone.

Using all her acting prowess, she forced a small smile. That was the best she could manage.

"No apologies," she croaked, her voice sounding rusty. Well, it was, since she'd barely spoken since her pre-breakout conversation with Benny. Hopefully, Ross attributed her awkward behavior to the sex video scandal. "You're doing me a big favor."

"Not a favor. It's an act of friendship. Friends have each other's backs, and your back needs some protection right now." Ross smiled at her with kind eyes, jiggling her daughter, who was beginning to fuss.

"Big time," Honor whispered.

The shock of this bizarre day now included the astonishing appearance of her onetime best friend. Her first lover. The man she once thought she'd marry, and who broke her heart nearly two decades ago instead. A surge of anger quickly crested in her belly and Honor bit her lower lip to hold back her words, not trusting the tide of emotion roiling within her.

Unaware of Honor's connection to the man looming before her, Ross misread the newest emotion playing on Honor's face, apparently attributing it all to the current media scandal. "You poor thing. I know this sucks. C'mon, let's get you settled."

Ross put the baby on her shoulder and patted her back. "It's ok, sweetie. I know you're hungry and tired. Mommy's got you." Ross turned to another tall man who appeared at her side.

Xander, her husband. Good heavens, Honor felt like she belonged in Oz. She was a resident of Munchkinland compared to these people.

"Babe, would you get Honor's things and set them up in the cottage? I need to feed Leah."

"Uh, there are no things," Honor chimed awkwardly. "Not yet. My stuff is arriving later tonight via my PA. She was packing my bags for me and then flying commercial with them. I, uh...left in kind of a rush."

The heat of a blush of embarrassment climbed up her cheeks even as her eyes traveled back to Brinder, the need to see him as compelling as her need for oxygen. He was just staring at her.

"I am being so rude," Ross chided herself. "Honor, these are my friends. My best friend, Tiercy, and her husband, Cole." The elegant auburn-haired woman and the man beside her, who looked like a dark-haired Chris Hemsworth, nodded and smiled, sympathy radiating from them. They clearly knew her situation.

At this point, likely most of the people in the free world knew.

"And this is our friend, Brinder." Ross motioned to the man who filled Honor's dreams and her fantasies more than she cared to admit.

There was the briefest pause from him. And possibly a hard swallow, though it was hard to be sure as her eyes kept returning to the freaking tattoo.

"We...know each other."

Chills danced across her arms at the sound of his voice—deep, warm, and tinged with the British accent that hinted at his upbringing in London—momentarily superseding the gnaw of decades-old hurt and anger in her gut.

He moved closer. "Honor. It's—" She saw the bob of his Adam's apple as he swallowed. "It's good to see you."

His voice cracked a bit on the last word, but Honor firmly ignored the traitorous softening of her heart. *Mostly.*

"Wait!" Ross shrieked, and then winced as the baby fussed a bit louder. "Sorry, baby," she murmured. "You two know each other?" she whispered, mossy green eyes flared wide as they volleyed between Brinder and Honor.

"Yes." Honor found her voice. "His parents and mine are longtime friends. And we—we used to be too."

Suddenly the infant in Ross's arms began wailing, little arms flying, fists bunched.

"Fu—ooey. I need to nurse her. Honor, why don't you follow me to the house. You have some 'splaining to do. Xan, would you double check that the AC has cooled the cottage down and set out some filtered water and towels for Honor?" Ross turned to her, worry creasing her brow. "That ok?"

"Yes, lead the way. Let's take care of Leah."

"Indeed. We know who's in charge around here these days," Ross joked, kissing the top of her crying daughter's head.

Fleeing the scene for the second time in hours, this time at the behest of a screaming child?

Well, that was on brand for the day.

CHAPTER FOUR

HONOR

Within minutes of escaping the very unexpected, and unnerving, blast from her past, Honor, little Leah, and Ross were ensconced in Ross and Xander's bedroom. Ross nestled into a cozy chair, propping her feet on an ottoman as Leah rested in boneless bliss in her mother's arms, nursing contentedly at her breast. Honor was shocked at how the baby went from frantic crying to utter peace in moments. Ross's friend, Tiercy, propped herself against the headboard of the king bed, nursing her own baby.

"It's a veritable maternity ward around here these days," Ross laughed. "Sorry for the boobalicious welcome, Wheats. But when it's chow time, nothing else matters to these little nuggets." She motioned to the chair opposite her. "Have a seat. This won't take long. She's a voracious eater, but then she passes out into a glorious nap. Kinda like me in college." Ross giggled and Tiercy snorted from her perch on the bed.

Honor, who had been standing awkwardly by the door, laughed as she eased into the ridiculously comfortable chair, unexpectedly soothed by the balm of the friendship between these two women and the solidarity of sisterhood. There was nothing like the support of strong, kind women to ease a tortured heart.

"Ok, wait." Ross swallowed a gulp of water. "Gah, I get so effing thirsty when I nurse," she muttered. "You're friends with Brinder? What are the odds?"

"*Were* friends," Honor clarified. "Our parents were friends. It was actually his dad who performed my heart surgeries. We went to schools in the same town, but I haven't seen him in years."

"Oh my gosh. How did I never put together that the Rahul Desai you wrote about was Brinder's dad?"

"Probably because Desai is a common name, and you'd have no way of knowing that Brinder and I knew each other. I certainly didn't tell you."

"And neither did he," Ross grumbled. "Don't know who he thinks he is keeping stuff from us. I think he's dead to us, Tiercy."

Tiercy laughed. "No, he's not. You're just salty because your nosy self didn't know. You'll get over it."

"Good point." Ross chin-tipped at her friend and turned to Honor. "But your folks are still friends?"

"Yep. I just—haven't seen B-Brinder in a while. We, uh, grew apart in our late teens. He went off to college. I left to film my first role."

"Which I know all about since I edited your memoir. Well, the film, not you and Brinder obv." Ross grinned and winked at Honor, absently stroking the adorable pudgy hand of her daughter, which rested on the top of her breast.

From across the room came a loud, rolling burp. Tiercy laughed, cheeks pink, as she patted her son's back, kissing the shock of dark hair on his head. "Sorry! Augie's a mini frat boy."

"Augie's just like his mother after a couple rum punches," Ross teased.

"You aren't wrong."

After the besties finished their giggles, Ross turned her attention back to Honor, her smile fading, concern radiating. "You ok, Wheats? I am so sorry this happened to you. I was scanning the internet during Leah's middle-of-the-night nosh-sesh and saw the coverage. I texted

Benny right away. She'd already been alerted by her PR team and was working on a plan for you."

Honor released a humorless laugh. "Am I ok? Too soon to tell. All I know is it felt like a military extraction. One minute I was trying to absorb what I was seeing on my laptop, and the next thing I know, I was being smuggled onto a private jet." Honor motioned to her outfit. "I didn't even have time to change. I'm not even wearing a bra—hence the hoodie, despite the heat."

"You poor thing. I'd lend you one, but all I'd have in your size is a nursing bra, and I'm not sure you want that. Normally, I'm a B, but given that I'm a dairy cow now..." Ross shrugged her shoulders in self-deprecation, the satisfied smile on her face evidence that she didn't mind her nursing-boobs at all.

"It's fine," Honor waved a hand. "Your air conditioning feels great. But isn't it supposed to be spring?"

"Welcome to May in the Mid-Atlantic, where the weather—and the seasons—can change hourly. Yesterday, it was rainy and barely seventy degrees. Today, we're close to eighty-five."

"Maybe Gaby has something you can wear?" Tiercy suggested. "She's only a few inches taller than you, and her pre-pregnancy knockers are close to yours."

"Ugh, my sister does have the more impressive rack. Bit—*ingo*." Ross laughed. "Two and a half months, not counting her gestation, and I'm still trying to reform my potty mouth." She grinned. "Good plan, Tierce. I'll text her. She's probably putting Grace down." Honor's editor shook her head. "Somehow all our babies are on the same schedule. And not on purpose. It's bizarre."

Before Honor could reply, Xan strode into the room, his clothes damp and a frown deeply etched between his brow.

"What's with the frowny brow? And the wet clothes? If I'd have known you were doing the whole wet T-shirt thing, I'd have kicked the ladies out." Ross's smile fell as she scanned her husband. "What happened?" Her expressive green eyes flared with obvious concern.

"The cottage is flooded. It's not habitable." Xander pulled a clean shirt and a pair of shorts out of a dresser. "I'm so sorry."

The resigned tone in which he delivered the apology was yet another gut punch to add to today's impressive tally. "My cottage? I mean, the one where I'm supposed to stay?" Honor's heart flipped. How much more could she take before she dissolved in a puddle of tears? At this point, the thought of melting away in a salty puddle of sorrow and only reemerging when this was all over sounded pretty good.

Ross eased the now-satiated and burped baby into a nearby bassinet. "What? Flooded? What happened?"

Xander answered through the closed bathroom door, where Honor suspected he was changing. "Best I can tell, when we turned on the AC this morning before the baptisms, an HVAC pipe burst. It's been releasing water into the cottage for hours. The floor is a wading pool, the walls are soaked, the ceiling is bowed, and I'm worried about an electrical hazard." He emerged from the bathroom, throwing his balled-up wet clothes into a hamper. "Basically, there is no way Honor can stay there."

"Oh fu—ooey," Ross breathed. "Well, then that settles it. You can stay in our guest room."

Honor struggled to process this latest curveball. "Ross, you are still on maternity leave. You have a newborn. I can't do that. You don't need a houseguest. I'll—I'll find a hotel. It's fine."

"You can't do that. The paps will find you in minutes. You won't get a moment's rest. You'll be a prisoner in the hotel until this dies down."

"Maybe I can book an AirBnB?"

"Not secure or trustworthy enough," Ross pronounced.

"She can stay with me."

CHAPTER FIVE

BRINDER

Every head in the room turned simultaneously. The synchronization of it would have been hilarious...if one of those heads didn't belong to the most beautiful woman—inside and out—he'd ever met. The woman who set such an impossibly high bar, he'd ended up with a failed marriage bookended by a string of meaningless flings. Because no one had ever measured up to Honor. No one.

Honor's doelike brown eyes were flared wide, shock written on her face.

"She can stay with me," he repeated. "She's right about you all needing your peace. I have two empty rooms at my place, and I work long hours. Honor, you'll barely know I'm there." *Although I'd know you were there.* "It makes sense. We can't trust an AirBnB host not to reveal your presence. And there's no room anywhere else that makes sense. My place has security, and I can take you up the back lift."

He inhaled, trying to steady his racing heart. Was he really suggesting having her under his roof? Was he mental? Yes, yes he probably was. But after not seeing her in almost twenty years, he realized he couldn't imagine being parted from her again. Especially if she was in some kind of crisis.

He lowered his voice and softened it, directing his next words to her alone. "I'll take care of you, Honor. Please let me help you."

For a moment, he saw "his" Honor. A small smile of relief. Gratitude. And then...was that...a flash of anger?

Just as fast, her face slid into a mask of bland neutrality.

"I really don't want to be a cause of inconvenience. Let me call Benny and I'm sure we can—"

"You're not an inconvenience," he countered. "You need a safe space. I have that to offer. And our families would appreciate you being in the care of a friend while you navigate your...crisis."

"A friend?" Honor's voice was flat. "We haven't been friends for a long time, Brinder Desai. But right now, my need to land somewhere... anywhere...quite outweighs any reluctance to spend time with you." She practically spat the last part. "I'll call Benny from your place and see if she can come up with an alternative arrangement."

Why the anger? She was the one who left *him*. Honor was the one who abandoned their plans, leaving a cold, scrawled note of cursory farewell...and no explanation. She was the one who ignored every attempt at communication. Who fully iced him out. What the fuck?

And, yet, his heart tugged with the need to soothe her. *Alternative arrangement my arse.*

Every line of her body evidenced the weight she was carrying. Her shoulders, bowing under the strain of the day. The bluish shadows under those captivating eyes. The slight shaking of her hands. She might be upset with him for some mysterious reason, but she was still his Tish. And like it or not, he was going to help her. And then maybe he could get to the bottom of this brutal and confusing case of the cold shoulder.

Because, even though she folded her arms across the long-faded away logo, he recognized what she was wearing: his hoodie. The one she'd always "borrowed" when she visited him at school. The one she was wearing the night she disappeared from their shared graduation party. The last night he saw her.

Brinder saw the moment she clocked his eyes landing on the hoodie —the one from the travel basketball team he'd begged his father to allow him to join. She glanced down at the age-softened front and then quickly looked up with defiant eyes. And the stain of a blush on her cheeks.

Ross's eyes darted between him and Honor, then landed on her husband, with a shrug. "Oookaaay," she drew out, clearly unconvinced of his proposed solution given the awkward vibe between him and Honor. "That makes sense. *If* Honor is ok with it."

He hadn't taken his eyes off Honor, so when she nodded her assent—with clear resignation in her eyes—a powerful wave of relief surged through his body. He knew he'd been offered a rare gift. And he had to take advantage of this time to fix whatever had broken between them years ago. Sometimes shit happened, but shit could also fertilize a vibrant garden.

Ross tapped out a message on her phone. "Gaby's on her way with a couple shirts, a pair of sleep pants, and a pair of leggings." She opened another text thread and typed a bit more, consulting twice with her phone. "Even though they would be clean, I know it's a bit creepy to borrow underthings, especially belonging to someone you're only just meeting. Benny is Instacarting underwear and a bra in Honor's size to Brinder's place. That should keep you until Molly arrives with your luggage."

Honor nodded, her eyes briefly closing. And then Brinder saw it. The crack in her armor. Her tell that she was struggling: she was absently rubbing where the scar was on her chest. He recognized that gesture from their past, as if it had been mere days instead of many years. In that moment, he experienced an epiphany that almost took him to his knees.

A part of him still loved her. He'd fallen hard years ago, and that had never stopped. Only been buried. Now those powerful feelings had been unearthed. And he wasn't sure what it would bring—for either of them.

CHAPTER SIX

HONOR

The silence in Brinder's G-wagon could only be described as strained. How had two such close friends—and first loves—been reduced to this?

Ross had tucked Honor into the SUV, clucking around her like a mother hen and loading the car up with leftovers from the party.

Brinder had chuckled at the flurry of activity and the volume of bags. "I do have food at my place, Ross." He'd rolled his eyes as Ross glared at him, practically defying him to stop her. "And whatever I don't have that she wants, we can order. It's not like I live in the middle of nowhere."

But Ross, being Ross, won that standoff, leaving Honor sitting with a cluster of bags around her feet, including a bag of clothes from Gaby, whom she met briefly on the way to Brinder's vehicle.

And now? The surreal icing on the cake. Driving in Brinder's car. To Brinder's home. To hide from a sex video scandal.

Nope. She did *not* have any of that on her bingo card when she woke up.

Who'da thunk it? as her late grandfather would have said. It was his signature line from the movie series that had made him a household name, and led to the legacy of the Wheatleys in the acting world.

Thankfully, Brinder had the AC cranked to cool the air and combat the oppressive muggy weather. But the downside was that the car wasn't sporting the only set of headlights. She could feel the hardened nubs through her two layers. Still self-conscious without a bra, Honor kept her arms folded across her chest.

And, yet, as she discreetly checked out Brinder via her peripheral vision, Honor had to admit the cold air may not be the only—or main —reason for her body's reaction.

Because Brinder was...nothing short of physically stunning. His tattooed wrist draped casually across the wheel. The faint scent of his cologne in the air, not overly present or cloying, just subtly there. His hair, curling slightly at his collar. Long freaking lashes. And his profile— sharp jaw, clean-shaven, but with the start of a five o'clock shadow.

Honor forced herself to look forward.

"It's ok. You can check me out."

OK. So maybe her use of those peripherals wasn't as subtle as she hoped. Honor's cheeks burned in embarrassment. And anger.

"I wasn't checking you out," she bit out, more defensive than she had a right to be considering she absolutely had been.

"Yes you were." Brinder grinned, glancing quickly toward her before returning his eyes to the road. "But that's ok. Trust me, I've done the same with you. You look good, Tish," he offered into the silence, invoking his nickname for her.

He smiled gently at her, and when she didn't return it, it slipped as he let out a long sigh. "I know this feels awkward—" he began.

"Ya think?"

"I was just going to say that I'm sorry, really sorry, that you're having a hard time. But I'm not sorry that I'm here to help you. I'm told I have a good bedside manner during a crisis and magical skills to help ease worries."

"And do your magic skills extend to erasing a sex video scandal?" Honor snarked, the rawness of this entire experience eroding her ability to communicate like a rational adult, especially with the man who'd shattered her naïve heart so many years ago.

"A what now?" Brinder kept his hands firmly on the wheel, but his head whipped in her direction, the shock of his response slicing through the air. "Someone released a video of you?"

Honor watched the tick of his jaw muscle as he clearly gritted his teeth. "You didn't know?"

How was that possible? She imagined by this point that private moment between her and Crispin would be all over the internet. Plus, how did Ross not say anything to prep him? Then again, Ross would be discreet. She'd had no way of knowing about Honor's history with Brinder, so she probably was vague about the situation.

"Ross just said she had a client who was navigating a serious crisis. She didn't say who or what. And with the baptisms and the party, I haven't even looked at the news today."

Brinder eased off the road into a nearby parking spot. Taking a deep breath, he dragged his hand through his hair. When he faced her, he looked ravaged. "What the fuck happened, Tish?"

And there it was again. His special nickname for her, a result of their Addams Family-themed costumes for a Halloween party during their Upper Sixth many years ago. He'd called her Tish (and would often kiss his way up her arm, starting with her palm). And he was her Gomez.

Honor stared at her lap, furiously blinking away traitorous tears. As an experienced actor, she was well-versed in managing her emotions to achieve a result. But hearing him call her Tish...well...that was just salt in the serrated wound that was her heart right now. Emotionally, she could not handle. One. More. Thing. Today.

"Please don't call me that." It was barely a whisper, but at least her voice was mostly firm.

She risked a glance at Brinder. A worried frown furrowed his brow over the softest, kindest eyes she'd ever seen. Just being with him in that moment, she could feel that soothing bedside manner he referenced. Despite her efforts, his concern made her feel better.

"I'm sorry. Force of habit." Brinder started to reach for her and then stopped, heaving a sigh. "I'm sorry. But, what happened, Honor? Talk to me. You made a sex video?"

"Apparently." Honor pinched the bridge of her nose with the hand that wasn't rubbing her sternum. "But not with my consent. I'm not even sure of everything, since today has been a whirlwind and I've barely had a chance to speak with my agent. But, best we can tell, someone hid a couple cameras in a hotel room where I stayed. They grabbed footage, edited it to highlight all the most violating and graphic moments, and then released it to an online tabloid. I woke to an alert that led to the video. Before I could even absorb the entire freaking situation, I was whisked out of the country to the wilds of Virginia."

Brinder snickered at her droll comment. "I'd hardly call the burbs of Charlottesville 'wild.'"

"It's been a cruddy day. Cut me some slack with my artistic drama."

Despite herself and the very effed up nature of this entire situation, she cracked a smile. They caught eyes, and for one sweet moment, they were eighteen again, filling each other's worlds with all sorts of happiness and promises for the future.

But that was a long time ago. Before he callously ruined what they had. And even though muscle memory had her relaxing with him, she couldn't let her guard down. She inhaled deeply, filling her lungs with a cleansing breath, and faced her passenger-side window, giving him the back of her head.

"Was it your boyfriend?"

Honor whipped her head back to face him. "In the video? Yes, I was with my *ex*-boyfriend. A private moment between us was vilely captured and spread."

"Ex? I didn't realize you and arse-face broke up."

"*Crispin*," she accentuated his name, "and I ended things, somewhat amicably, about two months ago. A little more than a week after we'd been in London."

Brinder said nothing, his eyebrows lifted high on his forehead.

"He didn't do it." Honor wasn't sure why she felt the need to defend Crispin, especially after the fight they'd had when she told him their lives and their priorities were just not in alignment. To say the least. They wanted different things. Also to say the least. Crispin had been incensed at first, slamming her door so hard her favorite painting, purchased from a street vendor in Florence, crashed to the floor. That upset her almost as much as the ultimatum he'd given her.

Still, the next day he'd called to apologize, remorse drenching his pretty words. Honor had heard him out, accepted his apology, but stayed strong in the decision to break up, which had been shockingly easy to make.

She pondered the veiled accusation by Brinder. Crispin could be selfish. But no way would he stoop that low. Plus, he had already been in touch with Benny and her parents—who employed him as manager of their Cotswolds-based theater company—about suing the hotel. He'd be a fool to risk his prestigious job—one that gave him access to the cream of the acting crop and certainly positioned him well for his own dreams. On that point alone, Honor was sure he wasn't guilty of that horrible violation of their privacy.

"No," she shook her head. "Not him. Usually my security detail sweeps for recording devices prior to arrival, but this was a boutique hotel that's been taking care of me for years when I go to London. We should have had them do their thing, but..." She swallowed, remembering Crispin's seduction and her unfulfilled ache to lose herself in desire. Her hope as they'd moved through foreplay...*maybe* this time.

But Crispin hadn't accomplished that, once again failing to transport her to a place of orgasmic bliss—despite what the video showed.

Brinder nodded decisively. "We'll figure it out. In the meantime, I guess we're roommates."

We. It was once her heart's main desire—and his supposedly as well —to be a "we."

She wanted to argue with him, but suddenly she was beyond exhausted. "We can't sit here any longer. Ross's Orioles cap only offers me so much coverage as a disguise. People may notice me..."

Carefully checking his mirrors, Brinder pulled into the traffic lane, accelerating through the main street as if just realizing the precarious position she was in. If anyone saw her, she was fully and unavoidably effed.

She closed her eyes, resting her head against the window. Honor almost never cussed, but if she did, she'd definitely be dropping some serious f-bombs.

Chapter Seven

Brinder

He eased into the parking spot assigned to his unit and turned off the engine, looking over to the passenger seat. Honor was sound asleep, a cute little whistle accentuating her exhales. She'd closed her eyes after telling him about the sex video (*what the hell?*) and then promptly racked out.

Suddenly, his problems with his Board chair seemed minor.

Honor had to flee her home and hide in another country because some arsehole wanted to make money violating her privacy. The idea of it made him want to rage on her behalf.

He inhaled a calming breath, shifting in his seat to better see her. Other than those first moments when she'd stumbled upon them leaving the barn, and a few minutes in Ross and Xander's bedroom, he hadn't been able to indulge himself in a thorough study of her. He'd allowed himself a modicum of quick glances during the drive. And that's what it was—quick, intoxicating hits of her. He was an addict who hadn't been tempted in years, and suddenly he couldn't get enough. His eyes needed to trace her, to catalog everything new about her...and the parts of her that were still his Honor even after all these years.

Her light brown hair, pale blonde highlights woven subtly throughout, was pulled into a messy high ponytail. Long brown lashes, tipped in a lighter brown, rested on her cheeks. Her face was more angular, but she was still a curvy delight. Not overweight by any stretch, but blessed with shapely hips and a nipped-in waist, which he knew from innumerable Google searches over the years.

He'd been enraged by the less-than-flattering comments he'd read, jabs at her non-Hollywood-typical size (*ridiculous*!). She would never be a skinny wraith, thank God, and she always posed with the confidence of a 1950s starlet.

His eyes stalled on those luscious breasts. Brinder looked down at his own hands, swallowing convulsively at the memory of their soft weight resting in his palms, Honor's hitched breathy moans as they both discovered the pleasure of his mouth on her pale pink nipples, his tongue teasing the pebbled tips.

He pressed the heel of his hand against the semi building in his trousers, a weak ploy to control his inevitable physical reaction to her and distract himself from that dangerous train of thought.

Brinder took a sip from his water thermos, his arid throat another byproduct of the shocking presence of Honor in his car. Feeling lecherous, but incapable of not savoring this sweet moment of taking in every bit of her, Brinder's eyes snagged on her breasts once more...which were currently hidden beneath a hoodie. *His* hoodie. His twenty-plus-year-old hoodie. That had to mean something, right?

He continued his perusal, feasting on the sight of her like an oasis in the desert. Her tiny feet, curled up under her legs. She'd topped out at five one, something that used to frustrate her.

But her entire family—with the exception of Bash—was on the shorter end of the bell curve. Her dad had been a Hollywood heartthrob, and fans who saw him in person were always shocked at his shorter stature—a trick of the light and flattering filming angles. Not that Jock Wheatley cared. He was one of the most self-confident people Brinder had ever met. What he lacked in height, he made up for with sheer charismatic presence—which shone on the screen and on stage.

Something his daughter had inherited. In spades.

He'd tortured himself by going at least once, and sometimes more, to every movie she released—even that first one that had stolen her from him for good. Yeah, that sucked. And, yet, in some odd way, it also soothed his broken heart to see her thriving. Doing her thing, after battling her parents for so long about it.

He thought about how he used to tuck her under his arm, and how she'd fit perfectly nestled against him. He remembered the time they'd gone hiking and the sole of one of her well-worn boots peeled completely off in the mud, resulting in him carrying her about five miles. She had maybe weighed one hundred pounds, soaking wet.

He flashed to all the times he'd popped her on his shoulders as they frolicked in the lake. Her peals of laughter as he fell backward, dumping them both in the chilly waters. Her shy smile the first time he touched her, shocked and then massively turned on by her slick folds. Her dramatic shivers (and giggles) when he kissed her neck. And, of course, the perfect sensation of sliding inside her tight channel, knowing that they weren't just joined physically. That their bond went far beyond carnal desires.

His cock gave a kick in his slacks, clearly just as caught up in the memory of them. After all, she was his first. And would have been his only. If only...

Instead, he'd rebounded to the polar opposite of a single body count, sleeping his way through medical school, his residency, and beyond. Of course, there was his pathetic attempt at marriage with his ex, Kira—the result of an utter lack of self-awareness on his part, immaturity on both their parts, and some strange need to play for keeps. Because that would perhaps finally banish Honor from his heart.

Spoiler: It didn't work.

His ex knew, even without Brinder ever saying Honor's name aloud, that she was second to someone. And when Brinder wouldn't admit to it—wouldn't share what had his heart so tied in knots—within months of their marriage, his relationship with Kira unraveled instead of his knotty heart. Quickly. Spectacularly.

His parents had been massively disappointed in him. Hell, he'd been disappointed in himself. Honestly, he'd deserved all the horrible words hurled at him by his dad—whose default position with Brinder was disappointment. Even before their estrangement. His mother, a sweet but quietly fierce English rose, had just watched him with sad eyes.

Brinder puffed out a breath, scrubbing his hand down his face. The movement startled Honor awake. Her eyes flew open, and for a moment, sheer confusion played across her features. Then she looked around, seemed to center herself, and cleared her throat.

"Are we here?" she rasped, sleepiness from her hard nap still coating her vocal cords.

"Yes. We, uh, just pulled in." Ok, a tiny lie. He didn't want her to know he'd been examining her as she slept. Even though his intentions weren't creepy, instinctively he knew she'd receive it as yet another violation. And he wouldn't blame her.

"Why didn't you wake me?" She rubbed the sleep out of her eyes and began reaching for the myriad of bags Ross had thrust upon them.

"I was just about to." He opened the door. "Hang on. I'll come around and grab that stuff."

"An evil jerk took away my privacy, not my arms. I can carry some of the bags." Acid dripped from her words. She grabbed several of the bags, opened the door, and headed to the elevator right by his parking spot.

Brinder quickly scooped up the rest. "Hey," he called, trying to keep his voice low enough not to attract any attention. He didn't see anyone, but it was a busy underground garage for the loft condos. "I'm going to take you up the back way. Follow me?" He raised his brows and nodded to a diagonal elevator. "This is the service lift. We aren't normally allowed to use it, but I did a medical favor for the building manager, so I have a key fob. It's faster than the main elevator, and more private."

Honor smirked up at him. "For when you bring ladies back?"

Heat crept up the back of his neck, and he gripped it with his free hand, hanging his head. Somehow, after not seeing him for a couple decades, she had him pegged. He indeed had used the elevator for private and expeditious travel to his place.

And, yet, with her in front of him, exhausted, frightened, hurt...he'd never seen anyone more beautiful. He wanted to banish the memory of those hookups. To carry her—only ever her—to his place. Tuck her against him, and shut the world away while he rediscovered her. Learned her new facets.

Instead, he struggled to deescalate her obvious anger, which had stunned and confused him from its first appearance. After all...*she'd* left *him*.

Rubbing his forehead with his free hand, Brinder looked around, ensuring they were alone. "Look, we haven't seen each other in years. And I'd be lying if I said anything other than this...it is so bloody good to see you. Despite the circumstances."

He absorbed the play of emotions that crossed her expressive face, those big brown eyes widening in confusion, the lines of anger bracketing her pursed lips, and...heartbreakingly...the dip of exhaustion in her shoulders.

"And," he continued slowly, searching for the words, "we both seem to have some, uh, heartache about how things ended between us."

She rolled her eyes, stalling any cogent formation of words on his part.

Why such anger directed at him?

Brinder sighed, his physician mindset shifting to triage the situation. "Let's just get into my place, get you sorted, and you can crash. Or, if you want to talk, we can talk."

Honor didn't react. She strode wordlessly to the elevator, hesitating before the keypad. Brinder eased past her and tapped it with the fob on his key chain, feeling her eyes boring into his back the entire time.

For years he'd imagined (ok, fanaticized about) what a reunion with Honor would be like.

This...was not it.

CHAPTER EIGHT

HONOR

Riding up Brinder's booty-call elevator was far from what Honor's active imagination had woven in the mental screenplay of her fantasy reunion.

Thankfully, the ride was short, and after more strained silence, the doors opened into a back hallway. Brinder shifted past her—oh so careful not to touch her with even the barest of connections—leading the way to a massive, sunny vestibule. Despite herself, Honor loved the vibe of the restored factory he called home. It was very Brinder.

At least as she remembered him.

Four industrial-style doors peppered the walls of the vast space. Her childhood friend and first love walked to the furthest one, waving a fob that unlocked the riveted steel door. Honor quietly followed him inside, and then froze.

Brinder's condo was nothing short of spectacular. High ceilings. Exposed beams. Hardwood floors with thick gray rugs. It was open plan, with a huge chef's kitchen, a living room with two overstuffed leather chairs and a leather couch, a large screen TV, and a glass and wrought-iron table in a breakfast nook. Two sides boasted floor to ceiling windows, with exposed brick on the other two walls.

It was one of the coolest spaces Honor had ever seen—and she'd seen plenty over the years.

It was an appealing combination of cool, funky, industrial, and cozy. Somehow, he'd infused warmth into it. Throw blankets. Fluffy square pillows. Framed photos sprinkled throughout. And various drawings, clearly created by a small child, attached to the side of his fridge with what looked like hardened dough magnets. She wondered if the same hands that drew the pictures created those as well.

Brinder shifted behind her, and she turned to see him motion to the bags still in her hands. In unspoken acknowledgement of his offer, she transitioned the bags to him.

Their hands bumped in the process, and Honor had to forcibly hold in the gasp from the electricity that zapped her. No, this wasn't static— it was attraction, pure and simple.

And unwelcome.

The silence between them was deafening, but Honor couldn't seem to find any words. Instead, she shamelessly scanned her environment. Brinder's habitat. Absently, she wondered if he still loved nature documentaries. Still held onto those DVDs he'd brought to entertain her when she was recovering from her surgery. And if those DVDs ever graced the big-screen TV on his wall.

The man was such a study in a fascinating blend of characteristics. Ridiculously handsome—morphing from the cute but nerdy teenager all the girls crushed on to a devastatingly sexy man. One she hoped still harbored that appealing nerd inside. The one who'd once shared his "favorite" nature and animal DVDs.

Honor's problematic but physically healed heart tugged at the memory, and she found herself softening.

Flashing to the booty-call elevator, and then a long-ago memory of a shocking embrace, Honor reinforced her hard-earned protective barrier. Nope. No softening. No unwelcome attraction. He would never hurt her again.

As she took in the space, Honor's eyes traveled back to Brinder again and again. The play of muscles across his back as he moved the food from Ross into his massive stainless steel refrigerator. The flex of his forearms, including that sexy sleeve of graphite tattoos that traveled from the back of his hand, disappearing into his shirt sleeve. Pure arm porn. She wondered where on his body the art stopped.

Honor's mouth went dry. She'd never been into tattoos before. Her perusal skipped along the ink, drinking in the muscles and sinew rippling beneath. Yep, she was now.

Brinder turned, catching her staring at him. She fought the urge to raise her hands against the hot flush of her cheeks. Instead, summoning years of necessary media-training, she forced herself to make benign eye contact, not giving in to the desire to break into nervous babble.

He, however, clearly had not experienced that kind of training.

"Honor, I'm...um...really at a loss here. I know this day has been so surreal for you and you must be exhausted. But I—I have so many things I want to say to you. To ask you. But I also want to respect your wishes. And maybe feed you. Your stomach was growling earlier."

He'd heard the insistent bark of her belly back at Ross's? Honor knew her ears were now as pink as her cheeks—whether from embarrassment or something else. Self-consciously, she rested a hand on the offending body part, as if to contain it.

And...not shockingly...her belly rebelled, loudly, as if to say, "I will not be silenced! Feed me!"

Standing behind the island, gripping the countertop with those long fingers, Brinder broke into an alarmingly panty-melting smile. The very one that captured her adolescent heart so long ago.

"That still happens?" He grinned at her.

Despite her exhaustion, her frustration, and her well-placed anger—at the man standing in front of her *and* the faceless person who'd invaded her privacy—Honor laughed, dropping her head and patting the pooch of her tummy. The same one that had been the source of many a showdown with various directors over the years—only some of which she'd won.

"Yes. Unfortunately." She hazarded a quick glance at Brinder, and her stomach flipped. How could he be so familiar and yet such a stranger?

He chuckled, a rich quiet sound. "I never understood how such a tiny body could make such loud sounds." His cheeks pinkened. "I mean, just your stomach. Not"—he waved his hand between them—"uh...sounds that we...uh....made. Together."

Yep, inside that decadent manbody was the shy nerd she had loved.

And just like that, a piece of her barrier exploded into smithereens.

"It's worse when it happens in public. Or during an interview. Once, I was on Liam Blum's late night talk show to promote a film. I'd been ravenous, my then-stylist insisting I wait to eat so I didn't have food-belly for the appearance. So I didn't eat all day. Only drank water. By the time we filmed, I was almost dizzy with hunger."

Honor watched a range of emotions play across his handsome features, his body stiffening, hazel eyes darkening with...anger?

She chose to ignore(ish) his reaction, continuing the story, which ended up one of her favorite memories. She could smile about it now, but at first it had been mortifying. Not sex-video level mortifying. But one of her most embarrassing moments...at least until today.

"I was mid-response and my stomach just...started bellowing. No other way to describe it. Then it happened again, even louder, and Liam —in all his comedic glory—called out to his producer to bring nachos. My love of them at this point had been well documented—both in interviews and by the paparazzi, who liked to take the most unflattering post-nacho photos and add to the malarky around 'Is she pregnant or just fat?'" Honor shook her head. "Anyway, within ten minutes, we were chowing down on nachos and finished the interview as we ate. He still calls me Nacho to this day."

"I remember," Brinder whispered, and Honor's eyes jumped to his.

"You remember?" she whispered. Had he been in the studio audience?

"I saw it on TV. In the residents' lounge during my training. With Luke. He was my best friend and he was married to Tiercy until he—" Brinder halted, his Adam's apple bobbing fiercely in his tanned throat. "Until he died."

Hands still gripping the counter, Brinder hung his head. "We went to med school and did our residencies together. We were so happy we matched at the same university hospital. Anyway, he loved that talk show, and he had it on, trying to unwind from a rough ER shift. I heard a familiar voice and looked up...and there you were. On the screen."

Brinder came around the island toward her. Not so close she'd have to arch her neck to look up, or so close as to make her (or him?) uncomfortable. But close enough. If she reached out, she could touch him.

But why would she do that?

"I never told him. About you. Or us." Brinder pinned her with soulful hazel eyes. "It's one of my regrets. Among many." He sighed, started to speak again, but was interrupted by her insistent, empty stomach.

He quirked a grin, wiping his hand over the stubble that had emerged, causing a glorious scratching sound that traveled right to her ladyparts. Which responded to his...well, his *Brinderness*...as fervently as her stomach had to the need for sustenance.

"Let's get you fed."

"Please." Honor looked away quickly, hoping he didn't realize the flush on her face this time was from her arousal, not embarrassment.

Chapter Nine

Brinder

As Honor slid her plate into the dishwasher, Brinder tried—and failed—not to check out her ass. Sure, it was essentially hidden in the hoodie. His hoodie. But he had a vivid imagination...and a phenomenal memory.

That ass. Ugh. He turned to the island, scooping up more discarded dishes until he could get himself, and his twitching cock, under control.

Ross had dispatched them with so much food. Small sandwiches, salad, spinach dip, hummus and veggies, and tiny cakes. Even though he'd just put it all away, at the insistent racket of her stomach, he'd hurried back around the island and pulled the abundance back out.

As he'd pretended to check email on his phone, he'd watched out of the side of his eye as Honor had selected a sandwich, some salad, and hummus and veggies. Given the volume of the ferocious growls emanating from her, that wouldn't be nearly enough food. If this were eighteen years ago, he wouldn't have hesitated to grab her plate and load it up.

But it wasn't eighteen years ago, was it?

They'd eaten in silence, although not quite as strained as the elevator ride. Eventually, he'd caved to the disheartening quiet and asked Alexa to play some Velvet Smoke. According to the media coverage he'd seen, Honor was close friends with the frontmen for the band—Marcus Russell and Xander Barclay, who were also apparently some sort of royalty—and their wife, Evie.

Media coverage had been rampant, following Honor as she'd attended various concerts of theirs over the years. She'd even been pulled onto stage during a recent festival stop. He loved those videos, watching them countless times and losing himself in her sheer delight.

Yep. He'd never gotten over her.

Honor flitted short glances to him—a ghost of a smile on her lips, her relief evident in those huge eyes—as she'd continued slowly consuming the small portions on her plate. When they'd both finished, including his first plate and his seconds (abs be damned), they'd both headed to the dishwasher.

Honor stood slowly, turning to face him. She stifled what was clearly a mighty yawn, her eyes watering. Then laughed at herself.

God, he missed that sound. How many times had they laughed together? He used to delight in cracking her up, and she'd smack at his shoulder as she doubled over. He loved her laugh. Especially the belly laugh.

He remembered the first time he heard it—when she was recovering from the valve surgery. Putting on the Shakespearean nursemaid headdress he'd found in her closet, a relic from a costume she'd worn in a supporting role in one of her parents' famous summer playhouse performances, he'd created a one-man (boy, really) skit for her. It was impromptu...and terrible. But her haunting brown eyes had compelled him.

She'd been on the mend, but still so frail. And sad. He'd made it his mission to make her smile. And when she'd belly-laughed at him? Well, he could live a lifetime on that sound.

In fact, he had.

Being the leading man of his own, silly homemade show for Honor hadn't been his sole method of keeping her spirits up as she healed. He'd spent countless hours with her watching BBC nature documentaries. He still had them tucked away in his designated storage locker on the basement level. Shortly after starting his job, he'd stumbled on the box when he'd gone down there to grab some camping gear for a spontaneous solo trip to the nearby Blue Ridge Mountains. As if in a trance, he'd teased the edge of the tape that barely held the flaps together, sucking in a breath at the sight of Honor's favorite orangutan DVD.

In the years they'd been apart, he'd only watched it once—about four months after Luke died. Storms had come through Baltimore, washing out the hundred-mile bike race he'd signed up for. Bored, grieving, and at loose ends, he'd made an unwavering beeline for the packing box containing those DVDs, which he'd taken with him every place he'd lived. Within minutes, he was listening to Sir David Attenborough talk about baby orangutans.

It had been like a time warp. If he closed his eyes, he could feel his arm around Honor's slim shoulders. Hear her sweet giggles at the primates' shenanigans. Smell the citrusy bodywash she used to use.

By the time it ended, Brinder was lost in sorrow. Over Luke and over Honor. And he was at a loss as to which hurt worse. He'd haphazardly taped up the box and never watched them again.

Next to him, Honor captured another eye-watering yawn, startling him out of his reverie. She nodded toward the hallway. "I haven't had the grand tour yet, but I'm guessing the guest room is this way—"

"I'm so sorry," Brinder interjected, equally embarrassed by his lack of manners and his spacing out. "You are probably exhausted. I should have shown you that first."

"No worries. I had to feed the beast anyway or I probably wouldn't be able to sleep." She glanced at the metal analog clock on his wall that he'd picked up at Eastern Market in DC. "Brinder..." she began, and then halted, clearly searching for words.

She'd barely said his name since they'd been thrown back together, and it sounded like honey pouring from her beautiful pink lips. He tried not to be sad, and livid, at the weariness in her voice. Sad at the distance between them and the rift that had driven them apart. And livid at the asshole who'd mercilessly blown her world apart. God, she'd been through so much in so few hours.

She cleared her throat. "I know we have a lot to talk about. I'm thinking it's inevitable with me here that we'll deal with some ancient history. But...please...can we not do this tonight? I can read your thought bubble, and I know you want to diagnose whatever it was that happened between us...But not tonight."

The finality in her tone pinched his heart. But he'd never been able to deny her, and he certainly wouldn't start now.

"Let me take you to your room—er, the guest room," he stumbled. "And I'll keep an eye out for the Instacart order and your luggage."

A tiny, relieved smile played across her lips. "Thank you."

"My pleasure, Honor. It's my pleasure."

You have no idea how much.

Chapter Ten

Honor

Honor could probably count on both hands, with fingers left over, the number of truly surreal moments in her life. Waking in the post-anesthesia care unit after her valve surgery, disoriented, scared, and a tiny bit worried that she'd died because she couldn't get her eyes to open. The shared graduation party for her and Brinder...and the slice through her heart seeing him in the arms of her high school nemesis, Gwendolyn. The first time she walked a red carpet as an actress in her own right and not as a guest of her parents. When she'd gently cradled the Best Supporting Actress Oscar—handed to her by one of her favorite actresses—now resting on its perch in her sunroom sanctuary. Waking up to the screaming headline "Nepo Baby Bares All" and realizing *she* was the subject. And that millions had seen her in the midst of (mostly faked) passion with her ex.

And now? Lying on a sumptuous mattress in the guest room of her first love, burrowing beneath soft sheets clearly woven from the feathers of angels' wings, attempting to lick her wounds. *Surreal on steroids.*

Underpinning all of the surreality was a disturbing lack of

confidence over which wound was more painful: the video...or the reappearance of the man who broke her heart.

Helping settle her in the pink room—a surprising color choice considering the man who'd furnished it—Brinder had loaded her counter with supplies. Soap. New toothbrush still in the packaging. A travel-sized toothpaste. Towel and washcloth. And a huge glass of ice water, handed to her with a quirk of his lips.

A secret part of her relished the little tug of her heart that he remembered she always got thirsty at night.

After his assurances that he'd place her belongings just outside the bedroom door, so as not to disturb her if she fell asleep, Honor had closed the door and collapsed on the bed.

A frustrating ten minutes of lying practically inert on the bed later, praying for the sweet oblivion of sleep, she sighed and rolled over. She was twired—that bizarre place between tired and wired when your body just goes a bit haywire. It was barely six in the evening in this time zone, and after eleven back home, but her body was succumbing to physical and emotional exhaustion.

Her mind just hadn't gotten the memo.

Honor had been acting for almost her entire life. First, much to her parents' consternation and with their reluctant approval, at their celebrated playhouse in the English countryside. Later, on screen, beginning with that first movie at eighteen. But those performances paled to the one she'd been giving since this morning (or yesterday, according to her originating time zone and her very confused internal clock). Everyone knew the phrase 'fake it 'til you make it.' In the entertainment industry, it was an accepted mantra.

But today/yesterday, she gave the performance of a lifetime.

Honor shifted to sit, aggressively punching her innocent pillow to plump it. And, well, maybe release some pent-up frustration. She flopped back down, the hood of her sweatshirt forming an uncomfortable lump under her neck.

Effing hoodie.

Of all things for her to throw on in her rush to leave her home, she'd grabbed...that. She saw the moment he recognized it, meeting his gaze with the world's most faked defiance coupled with, she hoped, an air of calm indifference.

Honor hopped out of bed and yanked the hoodie over her head, catching it in her hair and freeing herself with a body distortion that would make her Pilates instructor proud. She stood, hands on hips, evaluating her situation.

She'd slid into bed with only a cursory face wash, taking a bit more care to brush her teeth. And now, she really wanted a shower.

But she also just wanted to collapse into that heavenly bed.

Honor let out a massive, frustrated exhale. Poised between the bed and bathroom, she'd have made an excellent still life. The artist would title it *Pathetic Indecision*. Shower? Or go to bed?

Maybe a hot shower would calm her spinning mind and relax the bunches of knots that had emerged in her neck and shoulders. She should also change out of her sleep tank and leggings. Her inability to indulge in even the basics of self care was perhaps the most shocking sign of her discombobulation. She, the woman of the eight-part nighttime routine, had fallen into bed with just the cursories completed and in stale clothes. Gross...

Heaving a sigh of resignation, she'd just stepped toward the en suite bathroom when she heard rustling outside the bedroom door.

Hoping it was her luggage, or at least fresh underwear à la whatever Instacart location Molly could find nearby, Honor yanked the door open...startling the man on the other side. And herself.

"Shidoobie!" she yelped, leaning against the frame and holding her chest, as if to contain the repaired racing heart within.

Brinder, his own chest clearly heaving with her unexpected and forceful door opening, dropped his hands to his knees and doubled over, wheezing a laugh. "Jesus, Tish. You scared the shit out of me!"

Ignoring the diminutive, Honor held out a placating hand. "I'm so sorry. I heard noise out here and I was just hoping for some fresh panties."

For the seemingly zillionth time since seeing him again, Honor's cheeks blazed. Why did she use the term *panties*? She hated that word. But saying *thong* would have been a million times worse. *Underwear* would have worked just fine. Or, if her stupid brain hadn't short-circuited, even the very benign and obvious *clothes*.

Brinder stood slowly, darkened eyes traveling a path down her body, pausing at her chest for a loaded beat, then dropping below her waist before snapping back to her face.

A tiny (truly itty bitty) part of herself smirked in smug satisfaction. Yep. Despite the way things had ended, she could still get a...rise...out of Brinder. Good to know some things didn't change, even if her boobs were nowhere near as perky as they used to be. (Gravity plus time were jerks, especially for women with voluptuous chests.)

Boobs. *Dang it*. She'd forgotten about the hoodie removal, leaving her in her thin sleep tank, sans bra. And Brinder clearly liked to crank his AC. Honor crossed an arm over her chest, awkwardly grabbing the back of the opposite bicep as she attempted to cover herself.

"Shidoobie, huh? You still try not to swear?" He cocked an endearing smile she tried not to drool over, reminding herself that, his dabbling in white knighthood notwithstanding, she was still angry with him.

Honor lowered her head in resignation and allowed herself a small smile. "I try."

"I always loved that about you."

Her chin rose, eyes colliding with his.

Loved. If he'd loved her, why had he shredded her heart so callously? And on the cusp of finally realizing their shared goals.

She chose not to acknowledge the giant *L-ephant* between them, instead making an obvious study of the luggage and shopping bag.

"Yeah, uh, not long after you went to bed, your assistant came by," Brinder continued, as if they hadn't almost fallen hard into the hurt of the past. "Ross must have given your agent my mobile number, and she texted me a heads up that Molly was on her way up."

Honor craned her neck past the giant in front of her. "Molly's here?"

"She was. She dropped this off and then had to turn around and head to Dulles for her return flight on British Airways."

Honor was momentarily speechless. And angry. "Why didn't you come get me?"

"I thought you were sleeping, Honor. I asked Molly and she insisted I not wake you."

"Why did she leave so soon? That's ridiculous."

"She said her twins were both sick and she didn't want to leave her husband alone to manage them any longer than necessary."

That tracked. So on-brand for Molly, who managed to put everybody before herself—including back-to-back transatlantic flights so she could personally deliver Honor's clothes.

"She said to apologize on her behalf for the fast turnaround and she'll text you tomorrow. That she would handle all your day-to-day, so not to worry about any of that. And that Benny...did I get her name right?" Honor nodded. "That Benny was on the case."

Benny. Her fierce protector and champion. It was well after eleven in England, and Benny had clearly been up since the wee hours, alerted to the crisis. And she was still at it. Honor made a note to send Benny chocolate-covered strawberries from her favorite chocolatery.

"Thanks," she breathed out on a sigh. It was a small relief in a tumultuous day to have some of her things with her. She was grateful for the generosity of Ross's sister, but nothing beat sliding into your own comfy clothes...unless it was your ex-boyfriend's ridiculously soft hoodie. "I'll just...head back in and shower. Sorry to scare you."

"No harm." He frowned, dragging a hand through his hair.

His wet hair. He must have showered while she attempted to fall asleep. She permitted herself a quick scan, noticing he'd also changed into athletic shorts and a gray T-shirt that hugged the muscles of his chest and arms.

"I know this is so weird. On multiple levels," he continued. "The video. Us. You staying here. I just wanted to say...I'll follow your lead on how you want to handle all this. If you want to talk, about anything, I'm here. If you want to sequester in the guest room, I'll make sure you're fed and left alone. I just...I want to make it better for you, not worse." He scanned her face with beseeching eyes that tugged on emotions deep in her belly.

And triggered other, even less welcome, feelings elsewhere. Because, let's face it, freshly showered and smelling of some kind of delicious spicy bodywash, thirty-seven-year-old Brinder was delectable. Like

Mother Nature had taken the raw potential of his teenage self and molded it into magnificent sensuality. And her ladyparts were here for it, even if her heart wasn't.

"Thank you, Brinder." She searched his face, stifling a traitorous urge to lean into his arms, losing herself in the warmth of his embrace. "I'll just bring these in the room and then hop in the shower. Then hopefully sleep."

"I can call in and then pick up something for you to sleep, if that would help."

"No thank you," she demurred. "I try not to take anything stronger than acetaminophen or ibuprofen."

"Gotcha. Let me just..." He waved toward the luggage. "I know your arms work," he added with a devastating wink, "but I am going to help you bring these in."

"Thank you. Again." She remembered to cross her arms again as he rolled the two massive suitcases and placed them inside her door, followed by a department store bag.

"Try to get some rest." His voice was so gentle. She marveled at the difference in intonation from when they were young. Where he'd once spoken with a posh British accent that evidenced his privileged upbringing, now it had shifted, tinged with a decidedly American cadence, hinting at his decades in America. Brinder's accent was the same, yet different. And so very appealing.

Then he shocked the heck out of her, bending down and kissing the top of her head. For a stunned moment, she froze. Then inhaled, her eyes drifting closed for a moment, yearning flooding her body.

She had loved him so much. Once upon a time.

The side of his mouth curved up in a barely there smile. *Shidoobie, shiitake.* Honor wasn't sure which of his smiles was the most potent, but she was resigned to the glorious ponderings.

"Oh, and I'll turn down the AC."

She frowned, feeling like she was missing the plot. "Why?"

His smile widened.

Wowza. That one was a contender, too.

"You're cold." His gaze snagged quickly on her sleep tank before he met her eyes again, desire all but painting the gorgeous planes of his face.

Shidoobie.

"Good night, Brinder," she barely managed, then spun on her heel away from him, dropping to her knees in a pretend effort to get to her things.

When the door snicked closed, she released the breath she'd been holding. Rocking back on her heels, she inhaled and exhaled to steady her breathing and calm her heart.

Honor looked down, almost expecting to see the pulse of her heartbeat in her chest and stomach.

Instead, what she saw may have been worse.

She didn't just have headlights. Her high beams were blaring.

Shiitake.

Chapter Eleven

Brinder

Brinder swallowed a massive yawn as he swiped his keycard to access the well-appointed gym installed at the converted factory. Where once the heaviest machinery for power and production were located, now a different type of equipment powered humans.

He glanced at his sports watch with bleary eyes. And no wonder. With Honor just down the hall, he'd had trouble relaxing his mind. She'd been safely ensconced in the guest room his five-year-old goddaughter, Jemma, had called dibs on at first sight. The room he'd subsequently painted bubblegum pink, much to Jemma's delight, and added a soft mattress and cozy duvet.

He hadn't been in the Charlottesville area long, but Jemma had already slept over at least three times, allowing Tiercy and Cole some quiet time with their newborn, Augie, and Jemma some special one-on-one time with her godfather. Her eyes were just like Luke's, and Brinder often experienced a sensation of Luke watching him through his daughter. It should have been creepy, but he found it healing. As it was with Tiercy, Jemma represented a link to the person they'd both loved, and the flashes of Luke via Jemma were gifts he truly cherished.

And now Honor slept in that bed. Honor. The woman who destroyed his heart and his faith in women. Who catalyzed metamorphic change in his life, and not all of it bad.

Brinder had tossed from side to side, ears straining for any sound from her. Unlikely, given the distance and two closed doors.

But still.

She was there. In his home. Back in his life under the most unexpected of circumstances. Cue the tossing and turning as he relived every moment of their time together—fixating on that last day.

Somewhere between midnight and one, he'd finally fallen into a fitful sleep, then rose by habit at five as his eyes popped open of their own accord. Sometimes Brinder loathed his strong circadian rhythm. This was absolutely one of those days. His body may have betrayed him, but even it wasn't immune to fewer than five hours of sleep. He knew he would have to tap into his physical and emotional reserves to get through the day—something every medical resident learned, often the hard way, and eventually became a critical survival mechanism.

Stifling another yawn, he popped in his earbuds and stepped onto the treadmill for a thirty-minute run to warm up his body before lifting. The gym was often quiet at this time of day. Most of the time it was just he and one other occupant working out peacefully, usually only chatting when it was time to spot each other.

He caught the movement of the door in his peripheral vision. Speak of the devil.

In truth, there was nothing devilish about John "Cole" Colburn, who had stolen the heart of and quickly married Brinder's late best friend's wife. He'd truly wanted to hate the guy. After all, he wasn't Luke. No one could be.

But it was impossible. Cole was a genuinely good person—one who deeply loved Tiercy and Jemma. He'd initially seen it on powerful display after a scary car accident Tiercy had been in a couple years ago. And resented it. However, after that initial resistance on Brinder's part, he and Cole had fallen into an easy friendship.

Now, most weekday mornings before the sun was even a tease in the sky, Cole—also a gym rat—would join him. Since Cole's construction firm had rehabbed the factory into the upscale industrial condos, he had honorary privileges. It was perfect, as it was situated between Cole and Tiercy's new home and Cole's recently established Charlottesville office.

Cole waved gamely at Brinder, mouthing 'morning' with a smile, then pounded the last of what Brinder knew was a very strong Americano. He tossed the empty cup in the trash bin on a perfect arc, then hopped on one of the other treadmills, leaving an empty one between them. Because...gym etiquette. Sort of like urinals and bathroom stalls. You never used the one right next to someone else unless you had no other option.

Brinder nodded back, trying not to resent Cole's bright-eyed—and well-rested—vibe. He clearly hadn't missed any sleep last night, even with an infant in the house.

Brinder ran gamely, praying for an endorphin rush that never came. Eventually, with ten minutes remaining on the timer, he smacked the stop button. Possibly a little too hard. Cole didn't miss it. His eyebrows flew up as a frown emerged on the face Ross had often compared to a dark-haired Chris Hemsworth.

Cole pulled out his earbuds. With a deep sigh, as he stretched his tight calves at the base of the treadmill, Brinder did the same.

"At the risk of sounding like Ross"—Cole smirked—"what the everloving fuck is up with you?"

Cole even had Ross's cadence down pat, tugging a reluctant smile from Brinder.

He pinched the bridge of his nose, trying to clear the whirlpool of thoughts that had been swirling in his head ever since he'd emerged from the Graces' barn only to see *her* there.

"That bad, huh?" Ice blue-gray eyes that should have been cold, given their color, scanned him with what Brinder had to admit was warmth. Kindness.

Something in that look unlocked the vault of the emotional distress that had flooded him since the double whammy of his Board chair's tirade on Friday and Honor's appearance yesterday.

Slowing his own treadmill to a stop, Cole tilted his head toward the weight bench. "How about I spot first and you lift. And spill it."

Now Brinder released a much-needed chuckle. "You really do sound like Ross."

"Scary, right?" Cole ginned. He motioned to the bench again. "Get to it. I have an early meeting and a long day ahead."

Brinder loaded the barbell with his preferred weight plates, grudgingly accepting that whatever he put on there, Cole would likely double. Dude was a beast. He settled on the bench, pulling in a deep inhale—both to lift the barbell and to fill his lungs in preparation for what he was thinking might be a bit of a confused word vomit. Because that was exactly what it felt like.

"Today," he paused and grunted as he lifted the heavy bar—the first and last lift were always the worst—"has the potential to be a shitshow. I'm dreading it."

He could see the confusion on Cole's face. His friend had likely been expecting him to start with Honor. But Brinder needed time to work into that topic—sort the jumble of his thoughts.

"Does this have anything to do with why you seemed so off on Sunday? Even before Honor's arrival. And"—he pinned Brinder with a penetrating gaze—"never tell me that you both were *just friends*." Cole made air quotes around the last two words. "According to my wife last night, who got it from, and I quote, 'the Fairy Rossmother'—"

Brinder snickered and then inhaled for another lift.

"—there were definite relationship vibes between you two."

Brinder lowered the bar with slightly shaking arms, then wiped his face with one of his many Georgetown-themed hand towels.

"Ross needs to mind her own business," Brinder grumbled, next drying his sweaty hands so they didn't slip on the bar.

"That'll be the day." Brinder was pretty sure Cole's smirk mirrored the one on his own face.

"There is a story there. A long one. I'll fill you in. After I sort my thoughts. Or, more likely, Ross will yank the story out of Honor, and then share it with Tiercy—with Honor's permission of course—who will, in turn, tell you."

Cole snickered at the well-known and very effective friendship grapevine.

Brinder closed his eyes for a brief moment, and Clark's assholish, irritating face appeared behind his lids. "But, surprisingly, I also have another big issue on my hands." He finished his last rep and sat up.

Brinder took his time cleaning off the bench while Cole loaded more plates on the barbell. Bastard. Cole settled on the bench and Brinder stood above him, ready to intervene. Cole was known for pushing his body to exhaustion with his lifts, making a spotter critical.

"It's a bit of a long story. You sure about this?"

Cole nodded with a grunt as he heaved the bar up.

"OK, but remember, you asked for this." Brinder took another breath, and promptly spilled his guts. "On Friday, I had an unexpected and unsettling meeting with Clark Kenrick, the board chair of Evangelist. Clark had been a staunch supporter of mine, and he offered hearty approval for me as the interim chief medical officer during the executive interview process."

Cole sat up and guzzled water, then wiped down the bench for Brinder, even taking off the exact number of weights with a sly smile. "*Had* been?"

"You caught that, huh?" Brinder rolled his eyes—as much at his friend's attention to detail with the weights as with his words—and settled in for his next set. "Over the last few weeks, Clark had even been making comments about shortening the interim period." Cole already knew that arrangement had been offered in lieu of an immediate long-term employment contract because of leadership's skittishness following the scandalous departure of his predecessor. Brinder didn't know the full story, but sensed it was tawdry.

"And then Clark dropped a bomb on me Friday afternoon." Brinder was still reeling from the subsequent explosion of said bomb. He grunted, lifting the weight and noticing the increased shaking of his arms. Lack of sleep and stress were definitely not his weight-lifting friends this morning. "You sure you want to hear all this?"

Cole rolled his hand in a "keep going" motion.

"During my lengthy interview process as I was being vetted for the role, I—"

Brinder halted and Cole read his body language, helping to rack the bar. His arms were noodles today. And his brain was cooked too—not to mention his heart. After the requisite prep, Cole dropped back onto the bench, patiently waiting for Brinder to continue.

Eventually, Brinder managed to corral his thoughts, trying to frame it for Cole—and himself—in a way that would make sense. In truth, perhaps speaking about it aloud would help him to better process what had transpired and come up with a way through this bloody fucked up situation.

"I, uh, hooked up a few times with a woman I met in the bar of the posh hotel where the hospital had put me up. On my first trip, Laurel and I had a pretty sizzling encounter."

"I'd high five you on that, brother, but I strongly suspect this isn't a high-five situation."

Brinder briefly closed his eyes and nodded his assent to that understatement. "On my next two visits, we ended up in my hotel room bed." And floor. And shower. And bathroom counter. "She'd texted me repeatedly between visits, and I definitely got clinger vibes."

Laurel had referred to him as 'Babe' and 'Honey,' yet they definitely weren't at terms of endearment status. He noticed she'd also posted several pictures of them on Insta, calling him 'My Boo.'

Ignoring his tingling spidey-senses, he'd continued to sporadically sleep with her after he landed the job. When their schedules aligned, they'd go to dinner and then get busy. She seemed well-matched as a lover—enjoying being edged, lightly bound, and spanked...all things that revved his engine.

Brinder left out those details. He and Cole were friends. But no way was he sharing what happened in his own sex life, just like he didn't want to think about Tiercy and Cole. Brinder shifted to free weights and Cole leapt up to the pullup bar with surprising grace.

"About a month ago, Laurel conveniently placed a wedding magazine on my coffee table," he paused for effect, "with an article on engagement rings dog-eared."

Cole let out a long, low whistle.

"As you could imagine, I hit the back-up button fast. I'd known her barely three months, and you know I'm definitely not in the market for anything but a low-key situationship." He ignored the sudden memory of Honor, curled up in the front seat of his car—and the feeling of rightness that came with her presence in his home.

Brinder had thought he was clear on the status of things with Laurel. Sort of friends-with-benefits, but he'd never actually been friends with anyone he'd slept with. Maybe his first wife, but even that felt more expedient than anything. Not that the women who'd graced his bed hadn't been amazing humans. It was just...he didn't feel the need to deepen any connections. And he wasn't particularly inclined to explore the emotional barrier he'd placed between sex and friendships.

He just had a good sense of his own needs and expectations. It'd been his long experience that if you were clear and honest with them, women took it as the intended sign of respect. And he'd thought Laurel had been on board.

Apparently he'd thought wrong.

Although he loathed the term, Brinder accepted that he'd been deemed a "playboy." And it wasn't the first time something like this had happened. He knew who he was: a decent-looking doctor making a good living, who was both single and focused on being a generous lover. During his residency, staff even started calling him Dr. Desiiigh behind his back (and once, boldly, to his face by a particularly persistent X-ray tech). Over the years, there had been a few dramatic scenes, crying women who thought they could "change him" with their love.

He knew, and they needed to accept, there was no *changing* him. He enjoyed sex. He liked beautiful women. And he absolutely loved hot sex with beautiful women. But with one failed marriage under his belt already, he had no desire to add to the tally.

So when Laurel burst into hysterics, weeping about his broken promises to her...he was stunned speechless. Had they been in the same situationship? Or was she in a parallel universe where a not-jaded Brinder pledged some kind of feelings for her? Because in this life, he most definitely hadn't.

More likely, she was simply a drama queen.

"I tried to be gentle, telling her I'm just not built for relationships." He blinked hard as Honor's huge brown eyes and sexy, curvy body danced in his memory.

Cole winced. "The old 'it's not you, it's me.'" He released the bar, his routine of fifty pullups clearly complete. "How'd that work out for you?"

On anyone else, that comment might come out as sarcastic. From

Cole, who had a reputation as a bit of a ladies' man himself prior to meeting Tiercy, the sympathy of a once-kindred spirit was clear.

"About exactly as you'd imagine. I told her she was lovely and I enjoyed being with her, but there wouldn't be more than that."

He'd stared as she dive-bombed from distraught tears to flaming rage. Briefly, his mind wandered to the lesson in medical school on the Kübler-Ross phases of acceptance. Laurel had shifted quickly from denial to anger...and then stayed there, throwing her clothes from the night before into her overnight bag and grabbing the toiletries he'd only just realized she'd left in his bathroom. As she stormed from his condo, she'd screamed, "You'll regret this!" and slammed the steel door, practically shaking the rock-solid factory walls.

She'd continued to send a barrage of texts over the next several weeks, alternating between pleading and vitriol. Once she'd even shown up at the hospital, but his fierce and fabulous executive assistant, Amani, came to his defense, politely blocking Laurel's entry to his office while weaving an impressive extemporaneous lie that he was tied up handling a small crisis.

"So it didn't end well."

"Understatment of the century," Brinder muttered under his breath. "A few weeks later, Clark called me into the boardroom. He had this weird look in his eye. Every vibe was just...off. It was so confusing at first. He started talking about his daughter, how proud of her he was, how she was the light of his life and center of his world. How she was smart and would make an amazing partner for someone one day. And how someone had led her on, painted a vision of a loving future, and then recently and callously broken her heart, and, by extension, earned enemy status in Clark's eyes. Mate...the unblinking stare in his eyes was" —Brinder shook his head—"it's something I can't get out of my mind."

"Oh, fuck," Cole breathed, his eyes wide.

"Oh fuck is right." Brinder chugged his water, appreciating the drips that slid down his overheated body. "He asked if I wanted to see a picture of his daughter. At first, I was just praying that maybe Clark was asking me to take his daughter out to help soothe her wounds." But, somewhere deep in his gut, Brinder had known this was bad.

Really bad.

Swallowing past the lump in his throat, he'd nodded his assent.

Clark opened the gallery on his phone and passed it over with a steely glare.

Fucking fuck.

Laurel.

"It doesn't take a rocket scientist to figure out that my hookup…was his daughter."

"Christ," Cole breathed, racking the dumbbells he'd been using and fixing his full attention on Brinder. "That's so fucked up. I'm sorry. What happened after that?"

He'd tried to stammer an explanation, but the Board chair had only snatched back his phone, and motioned for Brinder to follow him down the hall to the president's office. There, Agnes Greco-Martin—his new boss—waited, arms folded, a not unkind set to her face. Brinder took heart from that, hoping he wasn't about to be fired by the president.

"He practically perp-walked me to my boss's office, where Agnes was waiting with my contract. She'd highlighted the morality clause. I remembered reviewing it when they'd sent their offer, but hadn't really given it much thought."

Why would he? He might have been a bit of a player, but his activities with the fairer sex were always consensual and he was a straight-shooter. He wasn't perfect, but he for damn sure wasn't immoral or unethical. He knew from his pre-hire discussion with the HR vice president they'd added the clause in response to the kerfuffle with the prior incumbent in his role. At the time, it barely registered.

Now? He felt like a wildebeest on the savanna, staring down a lion's gaping maw.

"Agnes went on to explain that, while my early work performance thus far had been stellar, they were concerned about my lack of judgment with relationships."

"What?"

Brinder found himself slightly heartened and very validated by the force of Cole's shock.

"Then Clark chimed in. Cole, he was practically sneering. I thought for a minute he was going to throw a punch. He was shouting that I better clean up my act. Or else. They put me on probation. One screw up...and I'll be out."

"That's just fucked up. His psycho daughter clearly misrepresented everything to her father."

"Right? But it felt tone-deaf and inappropriate to try to explain that to them."

No matter the injustice of Laurel's twisted version of their situationship, arguing his version felt...tacky. And he certainly didn't want to say anything negative about the chair's daughter. Even if she was a psycho revisionist clinger. He didn't speak ill of anyone he'd slept with. It was just bad form. No good could come from that. Instead, he'd taken it on the chin, sure that he could turn this around.

Cole nodded his agreement.

"Honestly, my head was just spinning."

"I can imagine. What did your boss do?"

Brinder sighed. "Agnes can be a tough read. Honestly...never play poker with her."

"Noted."

"But I got the sense that she wasn't really all-in on this. Agnes doesn't show her emotions much, but there was something in her eyes that seemed to convey support. I can't describe it. She was saying the words that Clark expected, and every single one felt like a punch to the gut. But I didn't get the sense she was fully supportive of putting me on probation."

He'd driven home from the confrontation robotically. As he'd pulled into the garage, he'd blinked several times, realizing he didn't even remember how he'd gotten there. He'd been in a haze, autopilot kicking in to get him home.

Now here he was, three-days post come-to-Jesus with his boss and his Board chair.

"Enter Honor." Once again, with only a couple words, Cole conveyed an innate understanding of the situation.

"Aaaand...curveball."

Right as he was preparing to begin the frustrating campaign to rehabilitate his Laurel-maligned image, his former girlfriend reappeared in his life. But not just any former girlfriend. The Oscar-winning daughter of two equally famous actors, from a famous acting family. And the subject of a recent sex video. Taking shelter under his roof.

Racking his own weights, he shook his head in a vain attempt to clear it. He was covered in sweat. Apparently talking through all this fueled enough energy to support what ended up being a vigorous workout.

"There's more to the story there."

"Much more." Brinder glanced at his watch. "Stay tuned for part two of Brinder's Sordid Tales of Woe." His lip tilted up in a self-depracting smirk. "But right now I need to head upstairs and get ready to face the day."

Face the day.

"Fuck," Brinder whispered to the gym ceiling. Somehow he had to protect Honor, while also ensuring Clark didn't find out and use her as ammunition against him. "Bugger," he sighed out again.

"What happens next?" Cole's eyes were sympathetic as he held open the gym door for Brinder.

"I wish I knew, mate. I wish I knew."

CHAPTER TWELVE

HONOR

The clanging crash of metal startled Honor out of her non-restful sleep. "Cripes! What the heck!"

For a moment, she was completely disoriented. Her exhausted body ached and her stressed mind spun, trying to sort itself into clarity. She scanned the room, taking in her surroundings. This was not her bedroom on the Welsh coast.

Oh...right.

She wasn't at home. She was in Virginia. Hiding from a sex video scandal. At Brinder Desai's, of all places.

Honor blew out a breath, cringing at the odor, which corresponded with her dry mouth. She quickly guzzled the remainder of the water Brinder had given her, then shuffled into the bathroom to relieve her bladder and brush her teeth. She tried not to dwell on why Brinder had extra toothbrushes. Thoughts of any revolving door bachelor pad antics would not help the headache forming at the base of her skull.

At least she'd finally managed a shower before falling asleep and was wearing fresh pajamas—a tank and shorts set that was similar to what she'd worn the night prior. She'd always run hot in sleep. Crispin had complained she was a furnace, often stomping off to sleep in her guest room when he spent the night. After missionary sex, of course. And a faked O on her part.

Honor started at herself in the mirror, noting birds' nest hair, bloodshot eyes, and a crease across her cheek from the pillowcase. The paps would have a field day if they saw her like this. And, yet, deep down, she trusted that Brinder, Ross, and her agent would protect her. She was safe. And they would figure this out. The scandal would die.

Eventually.

And...time to face the *other* unexpected shock that had flash-banged her world in the preceding twenty-four hours.

Honor exited the bathroom, grabbing the hoodie. It was either that, or highlight the goods for Brinder. That didn't seem quite the thing to do. Especially after last night's Nipplepalooza.

She trundled down the hall in her bare feet, following the mouth-watering scents of something cooking...and coffee. Turning into the kitchen, she froze. For long moments, Honor stood motionless, the only movement of her body the jig her ovaries were dancing at the sight in front of her.

Brinder stood facing the range, his strong profile to her, wearing nothing but a pair of workout shorts. Sweat glistened on his back and shoulders, and his hair was damp and curling at the ends.

Holy. Tomatoes.

Honor was tempted to unleash several much stronger words. Because if anything was cuss-worthy, it was half-naked, ripped, sweaty, tattooed Brinder cooking in his kitchen.

She wasn't sure, but she might have just gotten pregnant by osmosis.

And, she'd gotten her answer. An intricate series of tattoos wound across his hand, around his wrist, and up his forearm, where it traveled to the muscular knob of his shoulder.

He turned to reach for the Himalayan salt and startled, eyes wide with shock at her silent appearance in the kitchen.

"Honor," he rasped. "I'm so sorry. I hope I didn't wake you earlier when I dropped the frying pan."

"No, you didn't. I was already awake," she lied, unsure why she felt the need to hide the truth.

"Good." He offered her a gentle smile. "Sleep ok?"

"Mostly," she lied again, returning the smile.

Ok, this was awkward.

He motioned to the stove. "I need to head out for work soon, but I thought I'd make you an egg sandwich. I was planning to leave it with a note and some coffee for you."

"That's really kind of you, Brinder."

Good lord, so stilted and polite.

She remembered a different cadence to their conversations—easy, free, laughter-filled, raucous, and often tender. Nothing like this uncomfortable exchange, the discourse of strangers thrust into the same living space.

Because he was that to her. A stranger.

No matter how much her heart might disagree.

"OK. Well, I'm just going to head to work..." he trailed off, moving around the far side of the counter.

"Um, like that?" Honor bit her lip, fighting a smile.

"Huh?"

She waved her hand at his naked torso, forcing her eyes not to look (very much) at the tempting bulge in his shorts. Crispin had been averagely appointed (she guessed, based on her bodycount of three), but Brinder...*holy heck.* It didn't take a sexpert to recognize he was more than adequately endowed.

He followed the movement, eyes widening as he took in his own state of undress, and then shook his head. "Damn...right. I mean, I guess I'll shower. Yeah. Then, you know, head out. Good catch, Honor."

Honor stepped into the kitchen toward the coffee, pressing her lips together to contain the laughter that was fighting to bubble out of her. Behind her, she heard Brinder let out a massive exhale. Trusting her emotions were under control, she turned back to him, trying to keep a neutral face. But when she saw the amusement glittering in his eyes, a giggle slipped out. Then another.

Soon, they both were laughing. Gosh it felt *soooo* good to laugh. It seemed like years since any emotion but horror, worry, trauma, and mortification flooded her system.

Brinder grinned, shaking his head in self-deprecation. "Well, that was embarrassing. But maybe not quite as embarrassing as if I'd made it to my car, only to realize I'm just in my shorts. I keep a change of clothes at work, but probably still not a good look to arrive like this." His brow furrowed, smile slipping. "Especially now," he muttered.

"Sorry?"

He must have read the confusion on her face. "No, I'm the one who's sorry. Just work stuff. Politics, et cetera. I'm navigating a bit of a tricky situation."

"Oh," Honor replied, not sure if she should press or just turn back around and pour some much-needed coffee. The juxtaposition of being in her teenage boyfriend's condo while she avoided the public—along with her phone and any messages about the scandal—was more than a little overwhelming. The last thing either of them needed was more awkwardness than the situation already warranted. "Well, I'll just pour my coffee and get out of your way."

He nodded, eyes serious. "Your breakfast sandwich is on the counter. I'll clean that all up when I get home."

"I don't mind helping."

"Honor, you are here as my guest, not my cleaning service."

Honor's overactive imagination wandered to a sexy maid in a barely-there costume flitting around Brinder's loft condo—his bedroom, in particular—and perhaps replied a bit sharply because of it. "Fine. It'll be harder to clean, but suit yourself."

She poured her coffee, and then wandered toward the living area as Brinder moved down the hallway, the soles of his sneakers tapping on the hardwoods with each step away from her.

"Shewwww." She heaved a sigh. "Good times."

Like Ross, Honor relied on copious amounts of coffee to kickstart her day. In fact, they'd bonded over it. Ross was so different from her in many ways, but their working relationship had quickly morphed into trusted friendship. Honor took a sip. *Whoa, that was tasty.* How bizarre that her ex and her editor were friends, and living near each other to boot.

As she downed the decadent java of the gods and welcome caffeine flooded her system, Honor pondered the randomness of life. Her mind searched her memories of various meetings with Ross, in person and virtually, over the past few years, trying to recall if Ross had ever mentioned Brinder. Honor was sure she hadn't. Brinder wasn't a common name, and she was quite certain if Ross had ever uttered those two syllables, Honor would have taken immediate notice.

Heading back into the kitchen for a refill (that first cup had gone down fast), she wondered if she'd ever slipped and referenced Brinder. She closed her eyes, picturing the working session with Ross as they went back and forth with edits on the chapter where Honor had detailed her impetuous decision to go behind her parents' backs and take a role that had been privately offered to her by a rising star, and now Oscar-winning director. Firmly squelching any temptation, Honor never allowed herself to reveal her relationship with Brinder in her memoir, *Nepo Baby*, or to Ross—the habit of not talking about it still deeply ingrained.

Surprisingly, the media never managed to sniff out the teenage romance—likely due to the skill of her parents' PR team and a precious time prior to the advent of toxic social media. She'd been given the gift of a first love, and first heartbreak, without seeing it splashed and twisted all over the internet and the tabloids.

Speaking of that first love, he was still in his room. Honor peered at the funky metal clock. It was seven in the morning, noon her time. No wonder she'd perked up relatively quickly.

Pondering the coffee, she made the extraordinarily selfless decision —as only a java addict would understand—to pour the last of it into the travel mug sitting upside down on the drying rack. The mug was adorable. It clearly had been personalized for him—likely on an Etsy-style store—and featured a drawing of a small girl with way too many fingers on each hand and crayon-yellow hair, a taller person with black-crayoned hair, and a big heart around them. It was signed JEmmA, with a mixture of upper- and lower-case letters.

A loud growl filled the room and her stomach gnawed along in harmony. "Time to feed the beast." She reached for the sandwich and took a huge bite. "Unggg...yum," she moaned, swallowing and taking another bite, then moaning again. "Sooo good."

Chapter Thirteen

Brinder

Well, that was a sound he wasn't expecting—Honor Wheatley moaning in ecstasy in his condo.

That said, he heard it, and so did his cock, which immediately stiffened, wanting to get in on the action.

Brinder pulled on his suit coat, buttoning the jacket enough to hide —he hoped—the evidence of his body's reaction to a beautiful woman, who happened to be the girl of his dreams, making sex sounds in his kitchen. He'd remove it before getting in the car, but for now, it was camouflage.

Turning into the kitchen, he was treated to the site of Honor's shapely legs dangling from the counter, where she sat polishing off the last of the egg sandwich he'd made her, empty coffee mug discarded nearby. She licked her fingers and he'd never been so jealous of a set of digits.

He gave an involuntary groan, and her eyes flew to his and she gulped a swallow. God, he hoped she'd chewed that last bite well. Last thing either of them needed was for him to have to perform the Heimlich on her. Now, mouth to mouth...that was another story.

"I'm so sorry," she gasped, blushing prettily.

"No apologies necessary. Though I will say...I'm impressed with myself." He cocked a grin at her, knowing she'd take the bait.

"How so?"

Yep. Hook, line, and sinker.

"I mean, I know I've got skills. But I've never brought a woman to completion with just my egg sandwich." He tilted his head, appreciating the bloom of embarrassment...or was that arousal...flushing her neck and cheeks.

Her mouth dropped open. Then she did the most magnificent thing. She burst into a cascade of laughter, holding her hand over her mouth and giving in to the giggles. It was exactly like the times he'd shocked her into gales of laughter all those years ago.

He drank it in like a starved man, unable and unwilling to contain the reflexive smile breaking across his face.

Eventually she composed herself. Still shaking her head in amusement, she motioned to the recycled glass and cement countertop. "I shouldn't be up on your counter. That's awfully rude and presumptuous of me."

He waved her concern off. "I'm glad you're making yourself at home. Although"—he scanned the distance between where she was perched and the floor—"I'm wondering if you had to take a running leap to get up there."

"Hey! Not funny to short-shame." Her admonishment was laced with giggles.

"It's sort of funny." He grinned back at her. He'd left his room filled with dread for the coming day, and any potential Clarkfrontations—his term for the blindside courtesy of his Board chair. Now, dopamine flooded his veins, care of the sexy sprite giggling on his counter, easing him into a better mood. "Need a hand down?"

"Noooo," she dragged out, rolling her eyes. Honor gave a little shimmy and then hopped off the counter.

Unfortunately for Camouflage Cock, that maneuver caused her full breasts to sway under her hoodie. *His* hoodie, he noted with what was likely unwarranted satisfaction. More blood rushed south, and before he could even move, his barely controlled semi was rapidly on its way to… very much not controlled.

Honor, apparently oblivious to his carnal needs, shyly handed him his travel mug. "I gave you the rest of the coffee. It doesn't quite fill the mug, but I can make more if you have a moment. You looked like you could use some caffeine earlier."

Surprise ran through him, followed by another emotion. Gratitude. Here Honor was, barely twenty-four hours into a media firestorm and hiding out in Virginia, and she was trying to take care of him. No one did that for him. Not since he left England—much to his father's ire—for undergrad at Georgetown. Not even Kira when they were at their best.

He reached for the mug, brushing just the tips of his fingers over hers. By accident on purpose. "Thank you, Honor. That was really thoughtful."

"I, uh, I don't know how you take it. When we"—she fluttered her hand between them—"were together last, neither one of us drank caffeine other than soda. Well, I wasn't supposed to have caffeine, but you used to chug Mountain Dew." She shook her head. "I'm sorry I'm so awkward around you. I'll get past it. Promise." She hurried on. "Anyway, I kept it black and then figured you could doctor it." She half-rolled her expressive brown eyes. "Sorry…pun not intended."

Brinder debated lying to her, but something about those doe-like eyes stopped him from even the smallest prevarication. It was like they were on the precipice of something new, even if only friendship, and he didn't want to start it with an untruth. "I actually drink tea. English mother and Indian father. It's hard-coded." He shrugged, eyes pinned to hers. He couldn't manage to look away. He didn't want to.

"Of course," she murmured, holding his gaze, a slight tinge of pink to her cheeks. "I should have thought of that. Should have asked. I'm sorry."

"Please don't apologize," Brinder croaked, his voice coated with something that sounded to his own ears suspiciously like longing.

He placed the travel mug on the counter, reaching for her hand, only belatedly realizing that was probably not the best idea. And, yet, the sensation of her delicate hand nestled in his—and the still-life art of his larger hand cradling hers—was surely a core memory being created.

Brinder waited a bit, if only to ensure his vocal cords, which seemed to be as paralyzed as he was at the moment, would properly participate. "It's the thought that counts, and it counts for a lot with me."

They just stared at each other in silence, long moments accompanied by the tick of his clock.

Eventually, Honor cleared her throat and turned away. "If you show me where you keep your tea, I'll make you some before you leave."

He put a staying hand on her arm. "Not necessary. I keep what I need in my office." He looked at his watch. "And I should be heading out."

"Right. Ok."

"But please make yourself comfortable. And definitely finish that coffee. You can even drink it out of my special travel mug. Just don't steal it. Like you did my hoodie."

Her eyes flared in shock. Then she burst into laughter. "Busted. I wondered if you were going to say anything."

"When is a good time to confront a diabolical thief?"

"Diabolical?" Honor threw her head back and laughed. "It's a hoodie, not a cache of gems."

"Value is in the eye of the holder. And I loved that hoodie. It was hard-earned on the basketball court."

"Oh, I know exactly when you got this."

"And when you stole it..." he trailed off, taking great pleasure in this exchange. It was so them...circa twenty years ago.

"You gave it to me!" Honor laugh-yelled, her balled fists planted on her hips in mock indignation.

"Lent. Verbs matter."

She opened her mouth to offer some rejoinder, and released another sunny cascade of laughter. "Well, possession is nine-tenths of the law. And I bloody love this hoodie."

They grinned at each other, Honor having to tip her chin up given their sixteen-inch height difference.

Then her smile fell, her eyes suddenly serious. "I just—I just wanted to do something to show my appreciation. I know this is a bizarre, hideous situation, and...well...I'm just truly grateful you were there and offered to help. Nothing against Ross, but I'm told little Leah is a bit of a night owl. And I'm not."

"I remember." His voice was barely a whisper. "And it's not hideous to be with you. I—I've missed you, Honor."

"I missed you too." Her eyes searched his face. "But I'm also still angry at you."

His phone buzzed with a poorly timed work reminder, sidelining her anger as a mystery to be solved later. In the meantime, he offered the best medicine he could—compassion.

"Right, well, we can talk all about that. But in the meantime, you just rest...and try not to check the internet." He rubbed his hand over his freshly shaved face. "I have a medical staff dinner meeting, but I'll be home around eight thirty."

Honor whistled. "Long day."

"You know it. But please make yourself at home. There is a ton of food, but if you want to order, Ignacio—who staffs our security station here—will bring any orders up. Mi casa, et cetera et cetera, yeah?"

She nodded back, and Brinder tried not to think too hard about how disturbingly easy it felt for her to just...slide into his home and his life.

"Don't get into trouble," he teased. "And no house parties."

"Shoot," she clucked her tongue, shaking her head slowly back and forth. "Now I have to text the guys I met online last night and tell them the orgy is canceled."

Brinder's eyes flared, and something that hinted of jealousy coiled in his belly at the thought of Honor with someone, much less a group of someones.

"Be good." He wagged a finger.

She waved a hand, grabbed his travel mug, and took a huge gulp of coffee. "What trouble could I get into here?"

Chapter Fourteen

Honor

She was drunk. Utterly rat-arsed, as her English friends would say. There was no other way to describe it. But it wasn't her fault. Nooooope-aroni. It just sort of...*happened*...

After Brinder left for work, leaving behind only the trace of his mouth-watering cologne, Honor's day continued as benignly as this shiitake-show of her life allowed. She'd checked in with Benny, who assured her the official statement was well-received. The court of public opinion was weighted in her favor, with many of her industry colleagues offering support and voicing their indignation over the gross violation. She'd called Molly to thank her for the above-and-beyond efforts to collect and deliver her things, and to clear her calendar for at least the next week. Reviewed security with Grayton and Bauer, who had set up a 'field office' in an empty condo on another floor. Texted her brother, Bash, who hadn't replied. But he was also deep in a South American jungle, filming a comedy of all things. She didn't expect to hear from him until he got back into proper cell service, but she knew he'd be freaked out about his baby sister—which he still referred to her as to this day. After that, a FaceTime with Ross, who, like Benny, advised her to continue to lay low for at least a couple more days.

Ross relieved another worry, confirming that the paps hadn't yet discovered her location. Her frienditor (*frienditor*...look at her all smart and stuff, making up new words) also invited her and Brinder over to dinner, just to keep her from going stir crazy in her Super Secret Mortification Lair. When Honor shared that Brinder already had plans in place for that evening, they settled on the following night.

Then she'd (reluctantly) called her parents, who (expectedly) expressed a mixture of worry for her, anger at the situation, and freaking out.

Because...you know...her whole once-defective heart thing.

She didn't give them the opportunity to freak out about Brinder. In fact, she intentionally kept that detail absent from their discussion. It would have to be revealed at some point. Just... not yet.

For now, she'd limit their freaking out to their neverending worry about stress on her literally twice-repaired heart—once as a newborn and the other at sixteen.

Tetralogy of Fallot. That was the term for the congenital heart defect that could've ended her life before it barely started.

She'd been just a few hours old when a nurse noticed the bluish cast to her skin, particularly around her lips and tiny baby fingernails. That prompted an appearance by the on-call pediatrician, which led to being seen by a pediatric cardiologist. And that resulted in successful open-heart surgery, performed at a top London hospital by then-rising cardiac surgery star Rahul Desai. Her ex-pat American parents hadn't yet purchased their estate in the Cotswolds, but during her mom's pregnancy with her, they'd moved to London for her dad's acting residency with the Royal Shakespeare Company at the Barbican.

The other result? Her mom and dad whirled around her like parental Black Hawk helicopters.

Honor rubbed the slightly raised scar that ran the length of her sternum. The surgeon-turned-family friend had assured her parents she would be able to live a long and healthy life with few-to-no restrictions. Their expectations had been managed for the likelihood she'd need a valve replacement surgery at some point, which ended up happening right before her sixteenth birthday.

Before and after that second surgery, her parents had buzzed around her, always seeking to prevent any unplanned heart episodes by buffering her from...well, from life. To say they'd been protective was an understatement. If they'd referred to her as "medically fragile" one more time—their words, not Dr. Desai's, or "Mr." Desai, as surgeons were confusingly referred to in the UK—she would have exploded. Instead, she ran away and filmed a movie. Then built an award-peppered career.

And then...scandal.

Being her stubborn self, she full-stop ignored the strong admonitions of Benny, Ross, and her parents to stay away from the interwebs. Honor had never been particularly adept at following instructions when her emotions were running high. Like they were now.

So, yeppers, with a level of determination that was largely a façade, she'd opened up her socials. As she'd been told, there were many messages of support. Her PR team, acting as "her," had graciously responded.

And theeeennnn...the colossal mistake—reading deeper into the comments on her feed, as well as on those of her industry colleagues. Then she went down the toxic rabbit hole of various entertainment sites. Cue an emotional skid into a dark, vicious place. The negativity and recriminations directed at her—amplifying a trending theory that the entire scandal was self-made to drive memoir sales—were a painful blow. And patently false.

A particularly vile reality star, with more plastic in her than a Target toy aisle, went so far as to "analyze" how Honor had clearly framed and videoed the entire thing like a feature film, ensuring a good angle for the...well...the "display." You know...of her naked body.

It just went downhill from there. So much so, that Honor—who rarely drank more than a glass of champagne, and usually only on special occasions—stormed over to Brinder's industrial-style liquor cart and poured herself a heaping glass of...something or other...from the decanter. She had no clue, but thought it was scotch or bourbon or whiskey or one of those brown liquors that always confused her. She'd thrown back a massive gulp, gasping at the vicious attack on her esophagus.

But that hadn't stopped her. The brown liquid was as diabolical as the lies being hurled about to smear her name, and she'd been determined to at least win the battle with Brinder's booze. Ignoring her singed esophagus, she'd brought the glass to her mouth again and again, waiting for any kind of numbness to kick in.

Tired of standing—ok, her legs were starting to malfunction, wobbling in the most annoying way—she stumbled over and collapsed on Brinder's glorious couch, a fair amount of Brown Acid splashing her leggings. Honor pondered the wet patch, ignoring the fact that focusing her eyes was beginning to feel like an X Games sport. Should she suck out the liquid? It would be a shame to waste.

Honor huffed a laugh as she waved a dismissive hand at the damp spot. Shame seemed to be the name of the game these days. She'd just finish off what was in the glass and pour more.

"Sordid effing—*hic*—underbelly," she slurred, tilting her head back, then lifting the empty rocks glass over her and shaking it to force the last of the brown liquor into her waiting mouth. "Grnmn," she grumbled nonsensically in frustration, staring at the glass until inspiration hit, then licking deep inside, where she finally captured the last elusive drops. "Victory!" she shouted, throwing her arms in the air. The glass slipped out of her hand, bounced on the leather sofa cushion behind her, then gently ricocheted onto the blanket balled up next to her.

"Nice save, Mr. Couchie!" Honor shifted her body and planted a little kiss on the butter-soft leather upholstery. "You're the bessss, Couchie. You're a...ninja! You might have to come live with me in—*hic*—Wales. Or Shat—Shata—*Shaturn*," she emphasized, finally conquering the tricky pronunciation of the planet's name. "I bet thass the only jerkless place in the universe. I could—*hic*—colonize it."

The room darkened, and Honor closed one eye and looked around. "Did I pay the light bill?" Then she remembered. "Waaiiittt... This is Brinser's house. Oopsie!" *Wow...his name was actually kinda hard to pronounce. Why hadn't she realized that before?* "Did he pay the bill?" Honor blinked hard a few times, then patted herself awkwardly on the back. "It's a ssstorm, shilly! You figured it out! Shmart you, Honor."

Outside, the sky had turned a dark, menacing gray—matching the gloom around her since her assault-by-internet a-holes. Honor heard a buzzing noise. Ha! She knew that one too. It was Bad Phone.

"Where are you, Bad Phone?" she admonished, patting the cushions around her, taking care to avoid Glassie, which was still nestled on Blankie, which was wadded up on Couchie. "This place is ssssuper friennnly."

The buzzing continued and, as proof of her impressive alcohol tolerance—she really wasn't very impaired at all—she remembered throwing Bad Phone across the room in a fit of ire at a particularly bad edit of the video. One set to Salt-n-Pepa's "Let's Talk about Sex."

Spying the offensive device, which had no place among her new friends, Honor tried to stand. "These things aren't working." She patted at her legs. Stared at them. But they didn't want to lift her off the couch.

Honor, however, was nothing if not smart, as proved by her good taste in new friends and the way she figured out the whole dark-is-from-the-storm thing. Tucking to the side, she rolled gracelessly off the couch.

"Ooof," she huffed as she landed sprawled on her back. "Couchie, you are tall. Juss' like Brinser." Hey, his rug was reeeeallly comfortable. "Ruggie, you can come with Couchie and Blankie to my house. As soon as this shtorm stops making everything spin." Honor closed her eyes, but the spinning worsened so she opened one. "Oooo! Pretty ceiling!" And then she got sad because she couldn't figure out for the life of her how to get Mr. Ceiling to her place as well. "Fudge and phooey," she cursed, then giggled.

Ruggie really was comfortable, but she was also really thirsty. She eyed the liquor cart, which had to be at least six miles away. How many kilometers was that? She'd never managed to figure out the conversion to that dastardly metric system. Thankfully most Brits she'd met used miles, because as her Cheltonian friend Hannah had noted, "Who the heck knows kilometres?"

Sighing at the extreme distance, she rolled onto her knees and then crawled to the cart, impressing herself with her crawling skills, which she'd clearly retained since infancy. "Smart and an athle—*hic*—tic specimen. Who needs acting, anyway?"

Staring up at the high rise of the cart, Honor summoned a deep breath. "Heave ho!" she bayed and hoisted herself up. There, right in front of her, was a second glass. "Glassie, I found you a friennn too," she called to her new buddy on the couch. "Lemme juss pour some of this."

Tongue pressed between her lips, slightly sticking out—because *everyone* knew that's how you concentrated on a tough task—she assigned Other Glassie to one hand, the decanter of Brown Acid in the other. Impressed with the steadiness of her hands, she poured the last of the evil, yummy liquid, this time barely spilling any. Ish.

Lightning flashed.

"Preeeetty," Honor sighed, turning and staggering the couple steps to the expanse of windows. Inspiration struck and, shoulders shaking with a blend of hiccups and giggles, she opened her mouth, then pressed it on the glass and breathed out, puffing out her cheeks. "Pufferfishie," she sang, endlessly pleased with her impersonation.

The buzzing started again. Oh yeah. Bad Phone. Now where had it landed?

"Eh," Honor waved her hands in dismissal, again barely spilling any Brown Acid. "You can't be in our frienn group, Bad Phone." Turning her attention to Other Glassie, she drained the remains of its contents. "Tasteeee—*hic.*"

A door slammed, followed by an alarmed shout, startling Honor, who promptly threw Other Glassie in the air, screeched, "Aliens!!!" at the top of her lungs, and then ducked and hid next to the cart.

CHAPTER FIFTEEN

BRINDER

His pulse raced. The medical staff dinner and meeting wrapped earlier than planned. He'd tried to call Honor to let her know he'd be back by seven and to see if she wanted him to pick up anything for her to eat. She hadn't answered, which by itself wasn't a cause for alarm. She could have been napping. Or in the bath. It had taken a concerted effort to keep his mind from imagining *that* particular tableau.

A department chair then bent his ear for a good thirty minutes. Finally, swinging by his office and grabbing his bag, he'd tried her again. And again. He texted her too. Nothing.

He didn't have contact information for her security detail, but based on this, he was rectifying that immediately. He didn't want to call Ross or Benny. But if Honor didn't answer soon, he was going to panic.

He'd been trained not to panic during times of crisis. But this was different. This was *Honor*.

Even after all these years, she mattered to him. More than he cared to admit.

The entire drive home, he'd had Siri call her over and over. No answer. He called Ignacio, who assured him that Honor had not left the building and no one had been let up to his condo.

By the time he slammed through his front door, making a bull in a china shop look dainty, he was a mess. A million scenarios played out in his frantic mind.

Even though he knew from his father's expertise and his own medical education that a heart incident related to her Tetralogy of Fallot would be highly unlikely, he still pictured the worst—her collapsed on the floor, still and pale...and gone.

No. It couldn't be. Not when he'd just gotten her back.

He called out her name, trying to temper the panic in his voice. A screech pierced the air, then the sound of breaking glass, and a loud thump.

Brinder launched himself toward the sound, scanning the room for some kind of weapon, and grabbing the stone and mosaic statue on his entry table before charging into the family room.

"Honor?!"

In all the scenarios his addled mind embroidered, *this*...was not one he'd been prepared for. Honor, tucked in a crouch next to his bar cart, eyes wild, a spray of shattered glass around her.

The unmistakable smell of whiskey permeated the room. He quickly scanned the space, eyeing his decanter, which had been three-quarters full and now held barely a quarter of liquor. *Bugger. Honor'd had half a bottle of whiskey? Not good.* His pillows were strewn about the hardwoods and a fluffy throw blanket was balled up on his couch.

What the hell had happened?

"Shiiishke, Brinser!" she cried out, waving an arm forcefully enough that she tottered forward, landing on her hands and knees, just missing a large shard of lead crystal.

Brinder dropped the statue on one of his leather chairs and rushed toward her, heaving her into his arms like a bridegroom with his beloved.

Honor smacked at his chest. "What're you doing, Brinser? You scared the kittens out of me—*hic*!"

The kittens out of—? What the hell did that even mean?

His heart slowly settling into a civilized cadence, Brinder moved them toward the couch. As he shifted, and his senses came into focus, Brinder caught a whiff of her. It was hard not to. "Honor, are you trollied? You smell like a distillery."

She huffed. "It'snotdrunkifyoucanwalkorrollandirolled." The slurred pronouncement was accompanied by a giggle. "Thass how I roooolllll," she sang, her offkey singing even more pronounced given her obvious intoxication. Then she slapped a hand over her mouth, full out laughing as she mimicked him, impressively given her current state. "Trollied," she repeated, nailing both his stern, admonitory tone as well as his somewhat-faded English accent.

He eased her onto the couch and sat next to her, mind spinning with triage. He needed to confirm how much whiskey she'd ingested, flood her with water, and keep her on the couch while he cleaned up the shattered crystal.

"Watch out for Blankie and Glassie," she screeched, unfortunately right into his ear, which was now ringing.

"Who?" He looked around, confused.

He tried hard not to focus on her ass, swaying invitingly, as Honor crawled over the couch and cradled a glass within the blanket, rocking it. "My new frienns. Couchie," she patted the back of the leather sofa, "Ruggie, who is so soft—*hic*—and Glassie. Oh!" she cried, eyes filling with tears, and then started to scramble off the couch.

Thankfully, unlike hers, his reflexes were sharp. Brinder eased her back to a seated position, blocking her from touching the floor where glass could be anywhere.

"What's wrong, Honor?" he asked gently, stunned by the tears swimming in her beautiful brown eyes.

"He's gone."

"Who's gone, baby?"

"Other Glassie...and we were—*hic*—friennss!" she wailed, rubbing her face against the blanket and pressing a tender kiss to the glass.

Ohhhkay. She'd clearly consumed half the bottle. *Nope, not good at all*.

Making a quick judgement call, he shifted her back into his arms, tucking her in his lap.

"Be careful—"

"I'll be careful with—Glassie." Brinder shook his head in disbelief that he was referring to inanimate objects in his house by pet names as if they were sentient beings.

"And Blankie," she sniffled, tucking her head against his chest and breathing deeply.

"And, uh, Blankie," he confirmed, easing the blanket a bit further away.

"Thanks, Brinser." Honor offered him the sweetest weepy smile—then rubbed her runny nose against his dress shirt.

Ah well. Much worse had been smeared on his clothes over the years at work.

As the storm flashed around them, he allowed himself to bask in the sensation of her in his arms, her tiny, curvy body tucked against him. She wasn't wearing his hoodie this time. Just a different pair of leggings and a sports bralette that wasn't doing much to contain things, but definitely was doing a lot for him. In fact...too much. The curve of her full ass rested right where he wanted it, his dick trying hard to punch through the meager layers between them.

Not happening, buddy. One, he didn't ever mess around with women who were under the influence and couldn't consent. Two, things were way too complicated in his life and Honor's to add any sexcapades to their time together.

Sadly, his cock was *not* getting the message. Persistent chap.

Time for a change of scenery.

"Ok, Tish," he shifted one arm under her legs, "let's get some water into you."

"I'm not thirshty. Had plenny to drink," she mumbled against his chest.

Brinder rolled his eyes and summoned his best physician voice, temporarily ignoring the tenderness welling in his chest. "Water, Honor. Not booze."

She mumbled nonsensically in response. The only word he caught was acid. Whatever that meant.

"Why do you always smell—*hic*—so gooood?" she sighed.

Brinder was glad she couldn't see the smile that broke out on his face. It had been a very long time since he'd seen a drunk Honor—and never to this level—and he appreciated the truth serum element that particular five-hundred-dollars worth of whiskey afforded. Of course, she couldn't have grabbed the forty-dollar bottle next to it. Nope. His girl went for the premium stuff.

His girl?

He brought her to the dining room table, then eased her into a chair. He didn't trust her not to slump off the chair, or, worse, run after her dearly departed Glassie. Waiting a moment to be sure she didn't topple over, he hustled into the kitchen to pour a large *plastic* cup of water—including a lid and straw...he was no rookie. He wondered what Jemma would think if she knew a movie star was using the sparkly pink unicorn cup he kept on hand for his goddaughter, who was prone to spills.

Carefully, he wrapped her hands around the cup, and then lifted it to her mouth. "Small sips, Tish."

Honor complied, then whimpered.

"What's wrong, baby?" he soothed, stroking the snarled mess of her still-beautiful hair with his free hand, while also trying to prevent his body from reacting to the sight of her plump lips wrapped around the straw.

"I miss Other Glassie. We—*hic*—bonded. I miss hiiiim," she wailed, tears coursing down her cheeks.

Brinder had the distinct sense that her tears were less about *Glassie* and more likely a delayed reaction to the stress and turmoil of the last forty-eight hours.

Operating on instinct and not wanting to risk her stepping on glass, he once again pulled her into his arms, along with the cup of water, and headed back to the couch. Offering small shushing sounds, he cajoled her into small sips of water, which turned into large gulps.

"Easy now."

"I'm thirsssy," she insisted and took a deep swallow from the straw, hollowing out her cheeks until the straw gurgled in the classic signal that her cup was empty.

Nope. He would not, *absolutely not,* imagine those hollowed cheeks in another scenario.

Brinder placed the cup on his coffee table and then banded his arms around her waist, tucking her head under his chin.

Hic. Hic...hic.....hic.......hic. Slowly, her hiccups spaced out, then subsided.

Reluctant to move for many reasons, only one of which he'd acknowledge—not wanting to disturb his drunken houseguest—Brinder contented himself with the peaceful moment. They stayed like that for long minutes, accompanied by only the sounds of the thunderstorm and their breathing.

Eventually, after about twenty minutes, his leg started to fall asleep. He peered down to see if she'd dropped off to sleep and was surprised when she shifted back to face him, eyes less wild, but still sad.

"I had a bad day," she whispered, sounding a bit more like herself.

"I'm sorry," he said, and meant it. Not just about her bad day, but the last eighteen years of radio silence.

"I have to pee," she sighed, swatting her hand toward the cart. "Too much Brown Acid."

Brown—? Brinder chuckled. He guessed that was as accurate a description as any.

"Let me get you out of the 'spray zone' for the glass, since you're in socks."

"I was skating on your fun floors," she offered with a happy smile. "I like your hardwood." She burst into raucous laughter, clearly delighting herself with her unplanned double entendre.

Shaking his head imagining her sliding around on his hardwoods, and wishing he had security cameras in his main area so he could watch the replay of The Honor Show, Brinder carried her over to where the hallway to the bedrooms began, setting her down with great care, as the precious cargo she was. "You think you can walk from here?" He eased his arms away from her, keeping them loosely caged around her as she wobbled.

"Non c'è problema," she announced in slurred Italian, almost falling over as she saluted him.

He steadied her. "Easy there, Tish."

"Steeeady as she goes!" called Honor, lurching out of his hold and down the hall.

He waited, rooted to the spot as he watched to be sure she wasn't going to fall, almost going after her when she gently caromed off his walls—twice—giggling the entire time.

"Don't lock your door!" The last thing he needed was a drunken Honor locking herself in the room. Although, he did have one of those multipurpose keys to open the door, which he'd secured prior to Jemma's first visit to his home.

"Aye aye, captain," she answered from somewhere in the guest room.

While she took care of nature's call, Brinder carefully cleaned up the mess. He'd found her phone resting against the large base of a potted house tree. Having pocketed that for safekeeping, he turned to the rest of the Brown Acid crime scene. There were crystal shards everywhere, and he knew from past kitchen accidents that glass traveled far and to random places. Peering down the hallway periodically, he ran the vacuum, used a wet mop, and then deployed his hand vacuum.

Satisfied that he'd gotten all the glass, he placed the cleaning tools back in his closet. He was just closing the door when several loud thumps from the direction of Honor's room had him sprinting down the hall.

The sight greeting him was...something to behold.

In nothing but her barely-there strappy sports bra and a pair of boy shorts, Honor was hopping around, one leg half out of her leggings while the fabric from the other pants leg tangled around her foot. "Bleeding, flipping clothesies that won't. Get. Off. My. Body!" She punctuated each word, even her made up one, with an emphatic hop and an ineffectual leg yank.

Amused, he leaned against the door to watch her leggings dance, ready to intercede if needed.

Deciding on a different technique, Honor stepped on the bottom of one legging, then lifted the opposite leg, trying to pull her leg out. "Gaaaah!" she yelled. "We won't wear these when I live on Shaturn!"

Shaturn?

Now she switched legs, lifting the other one even higher—and before he could get to her, tipping over and falling backward. Thankfully onto the bed.

Honor's eyes flared with shock, surprise, and then she released a peal of laughter that made a smile spread across his own face.

"Here, baby. Need some help?"

Honor had thrown her arm over her eyes and her hiccups started again.

"*Hic.* Yes—*hic*—please." She stretched her legs out, as if to help him, then peeked out from behind her arm. "I had an—*hic*—accident." She lowered her voice to barely more than a whisper. "I spilled Brown Acid on my leggings." The eye that he could see was sad, her tone mournful and embarrassed. "It went through to my undies."

Stifling his amusement, he shifted into caregiver mode. A role he knew well. "It's fine, Tish. It happens. I'm going to get you out of these leggings, ok?"

She nodded her assent, still half-hidden behind her arm.

He tugged them the rest of the way off, wadding them up before tucking them under his arm. He'd launder them, and the whiskey-infused knickers, later. Speaking of...this was a pickle. She clearly needed fresh knickers, but he wasn't sure she could manage to remove one pair and don another.

"Honor, baby? I'm going to look for fresh knickers for you. But first I'm going to carry you and sit you on the loo, just in case you need to go again." *Or get sick.* "Can you get your dirty knickers down without any help?"

Another wordless nod of assent. In fact, other than her periodic hiccups, she'd said little since returning to the room, which meant she was probably moving toward passing out.

For the third time in that bizarre evening, Brinder scooped her into his arms. This time, however, he tried not to be too distracted by the fact that she was barely clothed, her bare legs brushing against his arms. "I'm standing you right in front of the loo, Honor. Can you sit down and then remove your undies? While you do that, I'll find you new— wait until I leave!" he yelped.

Honor had plopped down, shimmying out of her panties in a remarkable feat of coordination given her level of inebriation.

He turned away, but not before he caught a glimpse of...*oh fuck me...* perfect pale pussy lips. Brinder scurried out of the bathroom, simultaneously pledging to himself that he would not add that to his wank bank, while acknowledging that, indeed, he would.

She clearly hadn't bothered to unpack her suitcase—probably hoping this would all blow over quickly and she could head home. Brinder knelt on the floor and, careful not to disrupt what was clearly Molly's impressive organization, searched for fresh knickers.

Ah...double fuck me.

He'd found the knickers. And they weren't just any old knickers. No, a designated travel pouch inside the suitcase contained a plethora of silky, lacy panties. Boy shorts. Thongs. Some plain, but still sexy. And others...well, he wasn't sure what her assistant thought Honor would be doing while she hid from the paps, but she'd certainly packed for some good times. Either that, or thirtysomething Honor had developed a taste for sexy lingerie.

Swallowing past a massive knot in this throat, and pushing the heel of his hand to his very interested cock, he selected the most basic boy shorts he could find, then eased up, casting a careful glance in the bathroom. Honor was sitting on the loo, elbows on knees, head cradled in her hands.

"Tish? Here's some fresh knickers for you, love. I'm going to hand them to you and then you slide them on. When you're ready, call for me and I'll come get you."

He grabbed the discarded pair and hurried out of the room, tossing both soiled articles in the washer hidden behind a barn door. Then he refilled her water cup.

"Brin?"

"Coming, love."

Seized with inspiration, he skirted the island and grabbed the blanket, then headed to her room. He found her in just boys shorts and a bra, taking mincing, swaying steps toward the bed.

"I brought you Blankie," he offered, feeling only marginally ridiculous for using her drunken pet name for the item. "Let's get you wrapped in this." He set her water down on the nightstand and tucked the throw around her.

"Honor Burrito," she giggled, bringing another smile to his face.

"Up we go, Honor Burrito." He hoisted her back into his arms, and then gently deposited her on the bed, laying her on her side. It was still unmade from the morning, so he tucked the sheet over her. She sighed and snuggled in, eyes drifting closed.

Brinder brought in a bin from the loo and set it next to her, staying to observe her for long moments, debating. Worry that she might get sick and aspirate on her own vomit gnawed at him, and it only took moments to decide he was going to stay in there and keep watch.

He climbed onto the other side, careful not to jostle her, and stretched out on top of the sheet, his legs crossed in front of him.

A long curl was strewn across her cheek and he reached over and gently tucked it behind her ear, then pressed a kiss to where he knew a dimple hid. "Goodnight, Tish," he whispered.

"Goodnight, Gomez," she murmured. "I love you."

His heart stuttered.

I love you too, Tish. I always have.

CHAPTER SIXTEEN

HONOR

Her head throbbed. Honor reached up to hold it in place, as it was clearly about to roll right off her shoulders. Her throat was as parched and dry as cracked clay earth in a heatwave. Honor attempted to swallow, grimacing past the stale taste of her mouth. She needed water.

But that would involve actually opening her eyes and moving...the thought of which caused her battered head to pound harder. Honor groaned and rolled to her back. "Shidoobie," she rasped past the Sahara of her vocal cords. She craved water. She needed to be still. But...more than that, she needed to use the loo.

Heaving herself into a sitting position, she untangled her legs from the blanket. A memory flashed. *Blankie.*

Honor grimaced, memories from yesterday crawling out from the alcohol-saturated crevices of her mind.

The slicing ugliness of the internet. The decanter of brown liquor. *Brown Acid.* And...yep...Brinder coming in and finding her utterly schnockered. Him helping her change her clothes.

Honor's cheeks burned as she examined herself, busting out of the sports bra, the edges of the boy shorts riding up the generous expanse of her bum.

"Oh...drat," she whispered, flashing to a blurry recollection of her emptying the contents of her belly into a trash can—which was no longer by the bed—Brinder holding her hair and rubbing her back. Then giving her some water to rinse the nasty barf tang from her mouth. Him putting her back on her side and tucking in behind her. To keep her from rolling over onto her back, he'd whispered, as he anchored his arms around her.

Honor wrapped her arms reflexively around her body, as if to re-create the soothing comfort of being cocooned in Brinder's warmth.

She dropped her head to her chest. "I am never, ever drinking again," she mumbled. "Except water." And that...she desperately needed. Right after she visited the loo. Her bladder was full to bursting.

Easing herself from the confines of Blankie—could she ever refer to it any other way?—she stood slowly. The room spun a bit and she slammed into the nightstand, tipping the lamp over, knocking off her phone (*Bad Phone*), and banging her kneecap into a drawer knob.

"Son of a monkey!" she hollered, doubling over and rubbing her knee. "That'll leave a mark," she sighed.

Brinder flew into the room, sliding on socked feet and reminding her so much of the iconic Tom Cruise *Risky Business* move that—despite her aching head, her arid throat, and now her smarting kneecap—she released a gravelly laugh.

"Are you ok?" Brinder rushed over, gentle hands grasping her by the shoulders as he scanned her face and then her body in a clinical manner.

Honor didn't even want to examine the tug of disappointment deep in her belly at the lack of heat in his assessment. On the other hand, if she looked like she felt...Honor was quite sure she resembled something scraped from the bottom of a rubbish bin.

She pulled herself together. Ish. "I'm fine." She waved a dismissive hand. "Just whacked my knee on the nightstand."

A frown creased Brinder's brow, and Honor had to fight not to trace her finger in the sexy divot. *Cheese and crackers.* She must still be a little drunk.

"Here. Let me see it." He nudged her to a seated position on the side of the bed, which didn't take much effort given the rubbery composition of her legs this morning. Brinder ran a hand along her leg, brushing his thumb across the abused knee cap. He straightened and bent her leg, pressing oh-so-carefully on the injury. "Nothing broken, I don't think. But based on the coloration already emerging, you'll have a nasty bruise. And it may hurt a bit to walk."

Honor was frozen in place. It was like a forcefield held her immobilized. Brinder looked...scrumptious. He was wearing a different pair of athletic shorts, and his white T-shirt was plastered to his chest by sweat. His hair was damp and waving at the hair and necklines. Long, sexy fingers wrapped loosely around her leg. His elegant hands were so large, the span of his grasp so wide, his thumb and index finger practically touched. As he crouched, quad muscles bunched invitingly, she noticed the hair on his deliciously thick thighs was more dense than in high school.

Heat pooled where he touched her...and elsewhere. He'd always done it for her, but now in sexy doctor mode? *Whew!* Brinder was a human aphrodisiac.

Brinder lifted his gaze to meet hers, as if the force of her examination tugged his attention to her face. He scanned her again on the way up—this time with heat that shouldn't have thrilled her but did—stalling momentarily on her barely concealed breasts, and then halting on her face.

She relinquished herself to the sensual decadence of his study, the touch of his eyes landing on her lips and then moving up to her eyes, where he stayed...just watching her. Pinning her with hazel eyes that had appeared in her dreams over the years way more than they should have.

Years ago, Honor read an article about the powerful intimacy of prolonged eye contact, and that it was thought to release oxytocin. The love chemical. Nature's own bonding drug, it created a sense of connection, trust, and attraction. She'd always considered it hyperbole, especially after attempting it once with Crispin. Unsuccessfully. They'd both just stared uncomfortably at each other and then released awkward laughs after less than a minute.

And yet, right now, she believed it. *Knew* it to be true.

With one unexpected, unplanned interlude of gazing at each other, the warmth built within her, further thawing a part of her soul that had iced-over almost two decades prior.

No awkward laughs. Just the staccato beating of her heart.

And the growling of her stomach.

The forceful rumble startled them from…whatever this was. Cue the awkward—*relieved? Disappointed?*—laughs.

Brinder stood, joints popping, and grinned, holding out a hand, the invisible imprint of which still burned on her leg. "Need an assist?"

Gratefully, she took it, allowing him to tug her to standing.

"Ok to walk?" He towered over her by well more than a foot. It could have felt intimidating, but instead, it had always made her feel safe. Protected.

"Ok," she rasped.

"I did a quick workout and am just about to get ready for work. But I made you a smoothie. It's in the fridge. I'll get it for you." He turned to head out of the guest room.

"Brinder. Wait," she called, ignoring the up-tempo of her heart when he gracefully pivoted back toward her. "I—uh, just wanted to say I'm sorry I got so"—she shook her head and covered a mortified smile—"*trollied.* Some day I'll look up the origin of that random term."

"I bet Ross would know," he offered, eyes crinkling in a knowing smile.

"I bet she would," Honor replied, her face sliding into a matching smile. "Anyway, I'm really sorry. And I broke—"

"No apologies." He hadn't moved an inch, but somehow, it was as if his words caressed her, like he was whispering gently in her ear. "You had a bad day, as you mentioned. It happens. And I suspect you needed the release." He motioned to the bathroom. "I also suspect you need another kind of release—the loo kind—and that a shower would be medicinal."

"So says Dr. Desai," she murmured.

"Right. Doctor's orders." He grinned. "You go take care of things, and I'll leave the smoothie on Bad Nightstand."

Honor chuckled at his teasing, but then her smile faded a bit, weighted by her hangover and soooo many confusing feelings. "Thank you, Brin," she whispered. "For everything. For opening your home to a disgraced celebrity. For taking care of me. Holding my hair while I puked..." She cringed at the memory. "And for just...being you."

He said nothing. Just nodded, an unreadable expression on his face.

"I'm going to take that shower."

"You do that. I'll be in the other one. But don't worry, tons of water pressure here. Cole's firm designed this place, and it's top notch all the way." His eyes flitted across her face, as if trying to read her as well. "Your smoothie will be waiting." Brinder moved through the doorway, then paused. "And Honor?"

She cocked her head.

"You're not disgraced. It's the person who did this to you who is disgraceful. You...are perfect."

Then he walked away, unknowingly taking her bruised and battered heart with him.

Chapter Seventeen

Brinder

He listened for the sound of the shower, then hurried back into Honor's room—the realization he'd unconsciously transitioned to referring to it as Honor's space causing him to lose a step. Just like when they first met, she once again seamlessly fit in his life.

He took a steadying breath. He needed to slow his roll—on her behalf and his.

Guardrails in place—at least temporarily—Brinder placed a smoothie-filled Yeti tumbler on the nightstand next to a fresh glass of water and three ibuprofen. The last thing he needed was for Honor to come out, sans clothes, while he was in there.

Brinder wasn't sure he'd have the necessary self-control in that scenario. Because, even hungover, rumpled, and reeking of stale whiskey with the faintest traces of vomit...Honor Wheatley was stunning.

Tiny. Curvy. The most beautiful eyes he'd ever seen, so large and so expressive. Her hair, even tangled from her run-in with Brown Acid— he chuckled at her apt terminology for a non-enthusiast—may have been several inches shorter than she wore it years ago, but...it was the perfect length to wrap around his fist.

Aaand...that was his cue to get the hell out and prepare for work. Brinder hustled out of *her* room, taking care to firmly close the door, lest it shift open and reveal something he didn't want to see. Or, more accurately, *somethings* he wanted to see very much. Too much.

Brinder glanced at the clock. Six-thirty. After Honor had vomited in the middle of the night—Brinder beyond relieved that he'd been there to both help her and ensure her safety—she'd passed out. He was surprised to find her up so early. Perhaps she could take a nap today. On Couchie. With Blankie.

Brinder stepped into the shower, unable to wipe the smile from his face. Less than forty-eight hours, and already Honor had left an indelible mark on his condo.

The rainfall shower poured down, side jets pulsing to ease his aching muscles. He needed a massage. The stress of the Clark-Laurel dynamic, plus normal work stress, and now this Honor situation, had him tied in knots.

Tying knots. His mind wandered to a fantasy of Honor on his bed, gently trussed, her legs splayed open, writhing in pleasure. As his mind wandered, so did his hand, grabbing the shaft of his cock, now hard and begging for attention.

He'd been so good the past two days. He'd curtailed to a frustrating zero what was normally at least a once-a-day need to rub one out. Yesterday morning in the shower, he'd instinctively reached between his legs, his dick already stiff and waiting. But when the only thing he could imagine, even given his extensive spank bank, was a well-worn memory of the first time he'd ever kissed her sweet pussy...he gave up. Instead, he'd moved his hands far from where he needed them, fighting to distract himself by citing random animal facts from his favorite David Attenborough wildlife documentaries on the BBC.

It worked then...but it was most definitely not working now. No, not when he'd seen those lips, bare except for a light brown landing strip. Not when he'd felt the fullness of her breasts pressed against him as he carried her around. Definitely not when she'd nestled her arse into him so many times in the last twelve hours that he'd been walking around with a half-stiffy for most of his waking moments. The hard-on that had spurred him out of bed this morning—out of the warmth of her snuggled into his embrace—that *had* to be dealt with.

He'd done an aggressive workout—this time without Cole, who was home dealing with a sick family. Now it was time to work out in another way.

He stroked his shaft from base to tip repeatedly, squeezing hard and imagining it buried in her tight channel. They'd taken each other's virginity, and he would never forget that first slide inside her. She'd choked him with her untested walls. And, to his utter lifetime shame, he'd exploded into the condom within two thrusts.

He jerked his cock more ferociously, need spurring him on. Yes, he'd been a two-pump chump that first time. Later, he'd made it up to her, youthful stamina winning out along with the beginnings of what he knew was practiced skill between the sheets. But he always struggled with the worrying notion that she'd never been as undone by their endeavors as he had.

Brinder propped himself against the wall with his free hand, aggressively working his shaft. His balls drew up as his mind flashed to an image of Honor in her own shower right now, water sluicing down her indecent, delectable curves. He imagined her hand, snaking down between her legs. Her fingers sliding inside her, then pulling out and rubbing the stiff nub. Her other hand pinching the tips of her rosy nipples, peaked in arousal.

Brinder groaned. Fantasy Honor leaned against the shower wall, legs opened, pelvis tilted and thrusting. Head dropping back, she tensed. Then, smacking her pussy the way he longed to do, she exploded, the force of her orgasm bringing her to her knees. Where she looked up, mouth opening to take him in—

Brinder barely contained his shout, cum shooting out, painting the wall and his hand. He bowed his head, left arm still propping him up but now shaking from the effort and his release. *Fuck*. That...was hot.

He wanted to feel guilty about the fantasy, but couldn't. His persistent cock hadn't even fully deflated, as ravenous for Honor as he was. Brinder shook his head to clear it. Now was not the time to get hard again. Or let his mind wander too far.

No. If he let himself, he'd get sucked right back into her world—a place she'd made clear by her actions and her absence she didn't want him. Plus, he needed to get to work.

And...that was enough to deflate his boner.

Brinder sighed and mechanically continued his ablutions, forcing Honor from his mind and prepping mentally for the workday ahead.

Chapter Eighteen

Honor

After long, stunned moments, Honor managed to unfreeze herself from where he'd shocked her motionless, and shuffle into the bathroom. He'd called her perfect.

She stared at herself in the chrome-edged mirror, forcing her mind to accept the truth her soul already knew. Despite it all—the betrayal, the pain, and the thousands of days apart—she still loved him.

Shiitake.

After a very relieving loo session, *literally*, Honor gulped down two large glasses of water from the basketball-etched glass Brinder had placed on the bathroom counter her first night. She turned on the shower, smirking at all the handles and fixtures that had confused her before her first shower in his fancy condo. If the guest bath was this swanky, what the heck did his bathroom look like?

Honor eased into the steamy spray, the pulsing jets soothing the aches of her body as the rainfall showerhead slowly rinsed away her hangover. If Brinder was in the other shower, he was one-thousand-percent correct on the excellent water pressure.

Her traitorous mind betrayed her, wandering to images of Brinder in the shower. Honor had watched Crispin jerk off before, and it had never done much for her. But the idea of secretly watching Brinder engage in self-pleasure? Her mouth watered at the idea, her imagination quickly embroidering details. Brinder's biceps popping as he grasped his cock. Long, muscled legs leading to a firm ass, clenching as he jerked off in a primal rhythm. The flex of his right arm, the tattoo playing across the corded muscle.

Her hand joined her mind, betraying her too, as it slipped between her legs to press against the ache that had been building since her first night in Brinder's condo. Honor masturbated sometimes. But—as she'd discovered over Pimm's and charcuterie during a girls' night—not with the frequency her friends said they did.

Intent on relieving the ache tormenting her, Honor slowly rubbed her clit, pressing in the circular motion that often worked best. Truth be told, she wasn't very good at orgasming. With Crispin, it had never happened. Not that he'd ever have known—she was, after all, a world-class actor. Sometimes, alone in her room after reading a particularly suggestive novel passage, she'd feel the tell-tale ache of arousal and bring herself to a shuddering completion. But a scream-out-loud, grasp the sheets orgasm? Never happened.

Perhaps it was her mended heart. Or maybe her overactive mind. Or perhaps she was just incapable. Regardless, she could rarely relax her mind, and subsequently her body, enough to achieve an explosive release.

This morning, however, something was different.

Perhaps it was the leftover whiskey still humming through her system. Maybe it was the glorious sensation of the shower jets hitting the sides of her breasts, her ass, and—she shifted to test out a theory... *yessss*—her clit. Honor dropped her hand and tilted her hips so the focused spray pelted her in. Just. The. Right. Place.

Inhaling a shaky breath, she stepped closer to increase the force of the spray. "Aaah," she exhaled, the tension rising between her trembling thighs. Fast...faster than she'd ever experienced...her body amped. She clenched her muscles, gasping at the power of the steady pulse of water.

Reaching up, she pinched her nipple. She'd never done that before, always assuming they just weren't an erogenous zone for her. But, this morning? *Shiitake.* She tugged again, the movement sending a current to her clit, which was hardened and aching for...more.

She pinched and tugged her nipple again, panting as her body strained for release. Brinder's face flashed across her mind. The look in his eyes as he'd scanned her body. It had been many years, but both she and her body remembered the sensation of his hard cock sliding through her folds. She tilted her hips infinitesimally...the pressure so intense her body shook...and pictured his mouth. The pounding water became the suck of his lips, the unrelenting pressure of his tongue.

She clenched hard...and then shattered, a soft scream slipping from her lips—almost, but not quite, forming his name—as she slumped against the wall.

"Damn," she whispered, heart practically leaping from her chest.

If fantasies of Brinder Desai were better than her vibrator...

An actual encounter with him might just wreck her.

CHAPTER NINETEEN

BRINDER

He heard the cry as he passed the closed door of her room, started to rush in, and then thought better of it. Pausing, calming his mind the way he was trained to do in times of stress or high intensity, he listened at the door. The shower was still running. There were no additional sounds of distress, calming the ever-present worry that had encircled his heart since she'd catapulted back into his life.

Then what had caused her to yell out—?

Fuck me.

Brinder rubbed his hand down his freshly shaved face. He knew the tenor of that sound. She was doing what he had just done...and imagined *her* doing.

Had he manifested it?

If that was the case, he should go in there and give her another two or three. And then take her to bed, where he'd give her at least three more. Bring her to an explosive peak again and again, until her body was sated and limp, moaning his name in blissful relief.

Brinder shook himself out of that fantasy. No. More likely, after the stress of the past two days, she probably just needed physical relief. No different from him after a long day.

With one last yearning glance at the door, almost wishing for x-ray vision, he forced himself into the kitchen, where his tea steeped in his Jemma-decorated travel mug. It was now close to seven, and he needed to head out. It wasn't a very long commute to work, but he liked to be at his desk by seven-thirty at the latest. It was his most productive time of the day, before the majority of the administrative staff filled the suite. Some days, he'd arrive earlier, chatting with the surgeons in the lounge before morning cases and visiting with nightshift staff as they left.

From the moment he'd stepped on the hospital campus, he'd felt at home. Hospital employees smiled at him, and almost all greeted him with a friendly hello. The culture there was warm and inviting, and he'd wanted to be a part of it.

The feeling only intensified after he met with the charismatic young president. She wasn't even forty, and she was a powerhouse. He wanted to partner with her. Learn from her. Build something even more special for the patients and families who needed them.

Now, the specter of his much-aggrandized tryst with Laurel threatened to implode it all.

He had one month to fix it. One month to rehabilitate his image and reassure hospital leadership and the Board he was trustworthy, ethical, and stable.

Stable. That word had rankled. He was nothing if not stable. Yes, he had an active sex life. But it was always safe. Always consensual. And his discretion was as well-known as his love of giving pleasure—something he didn't brag about, but apparently his various partners had. Now, ridiculous lies by a well-connected clinger were shoving him toward a scary cliff. He had to fix this.

Movement in his periphery caught his eye. Engrossed in her phone, Honor halted just before crashing into him. Instinctively, he reached out to steady her, hoping she wasn't reading some of the rubbish posted about her online.

Her eyes flew up to him and darted away, her cheeks flushing bright pink. She could barely look him in the eye. Was she...embarrassed? A treacherous, amazing thought wiggled into his brain. Maybe she'd been thinking of him while she—

"I'm so sorry," Honor gasped. "I— thought you were gone."

Brinder reluctantly tore himself from that fantasy, which was next to impossible. Because now, all he wanted was the chance to make her scream his name over and over. After removing her very short denim shorts and that tiny top that tied behind her neck. Maybe with his teeth...

She continued with an almost nervous chattering, eyes landing everywhere but his face. "I was looking at my phone and not watching where I was going. I almost flattened you."

Brinder barked out a laugh, causing her huge, brown eyes to fly back to his face. "Honor, it would take a lot more than a bump from a tiny thing like you to flatten me." He tried not to think of how the curvy, wee woman in front of him had once managed to flatten his heart and crush his soul.

"I could take you down." She lifted her chin defiantly.

He raised his brows.

"I could," she insisted, poking him in the chest. "I had to learn Taekwondo for a film role, which then led to a small obsession with martial arts. I'm a red belt now, and if I'm ever able to show my face in the dojo again, I'm close to earning my black belt."

"Honor, that's incredible and impressive." Brinder held out a fist for a bump, which she returned, not gently. Ah, shit, he'd offended her. He offered an apologetic smile. "You're a badass. I saw that film. *Junbi.*"

Named after the term for ready position, the film was about a woman who inherited her grandfather's ramshackle dojo and turned it into a training center for female abuse and assault survivors. Honor had led the field for best actresses, winning both a Screen Actor's Guild and a BAFTA award before losing to a legendary octogenarian actress at the Oscars.

The tension in her body eased. "You saw it?"

"Yes, twice. With Tiercy, when Jemma was an infant and she was desperate for something to take her mind off...everything. And then, uh," he shifted, somewhat embarrassed, "on a date."

Honor titled her head, curiosity shining in her deep brown eyes.

"You and Tiercy are close. Close enough to be Jemma's godfather, right?" She motioned to the mug, with its precious drawing and the childish scrawl spelling 'godfather.'

He swallowed and glanced at his watch. Seven-fifteen. He was running late, and this was most definitely *not* the time to go over the ancient history of his now-extinguished infatuation with Tiercy. But he would at some point, just to be on the up-and-up with Honor.

"Yes, good friends. Cole too. I often think Luke reached out from the heavens and picked him out for her."

"That's...sweet. And heartbreaking." Honor's eyes glistened with unshed tears. Teenage Honor had always been in touch with her emotions, likely the result of a lot of therapy insisted upon by her parents given both their fame and her health challenges.

"She's happy now, and Jemma has an amazing father in Cole. That's what matters." He grabbed his mug of tea. "And you know what else matters? Me getting to work." He winked at her.

"It's so weird to think of you with such a grown-up job."

He snorted. "What? Did you have me working as a pool lifeguard or some other classic teen job?"

She grinned back. "No, we both always knew you'd be a doctor. It's just...strange...to see Grown Up Brinder in his work clothes headed to the hospital." She frowned. "Don't you wear scrubs?"

His smile broke across his face. "Sometimes. Only when I'm doing an interventional procedure. Why? Do you want to see me in scrubs? Or...out of them?" Brinder gave her his most exaggerated lascivious smile partnered with a silly eyebrow waggle, causing her—as intended—to crack up.

She swatted him. "Go to work!" And then she turned to rinse out the Yeti, but not before he saw the pink creep back into her cheeks.

CHAPTER TWENTY

HONOR

Honor hadn't seen the "writing cottage," as Ross referred to the stone and clapboard cottage where Ross's home office was located, and which had been initially offered as her safe haven. Now, taking in the spacious, sun-infused warmth of Brinder's condo, Honor couldn't imagine refugeeing anywhere else.

Truly, Brinder's place was incredible. It reminded her a bit of her glass-enclosed sunroom sanctuary at her Pembrokeshire home. The beautiful Welsh coastline spoke to her soul...and the two-and-a-half-hour distance from her parents' estate was both lengthy enough to discourage regular visits and close enough to get to each other when needed.

Now, they were an ocean away. Not that her mother seemed to notice. Texts were coming in with expected regularity, her mother's casual tone not in any way disguising her worry. Sighing, she answered the latest, assuring her mom that she was doing well and that she'd be speaking with Molly, Benny, and Ross within the half hour to get the latest updates.

On her *situation*.

If she cursed, she'd call it a *shituation*.

Honor rolled her eyes, well into the anger stage of this saga. If she ever found out who did this, she'd go after them with both barrels. Take them for all they were worth. And then donate that money to one of several battered women's shelters she regularly supported through anonymous donations.

She tried not to have a vindictive personality. In her industry, rising above all the attacks, both large and small, and not allowing retribution to prevail, was essential. The knot of anger would eat away at her soul if she wasn't vigilant about restraining it. That said, she permitted herself an internal evil smile and villain's hand-wringing at the thought of leaving the perpetrator as financially tattered as her reputation was, as well as sending a message to anyone else stupid and vulgar enough to try something like that again.

She stood and stretched, finally managing to pry herself from her cozy nest. She'd snuggled in with a coffee and the script for her upcoming film shortly after Brinder left for work. *Couchie and Blankie.* Honor giggled. They truly were ridiculously comfortable. And, unlike the prior day's booze-riddled afternoon, she was clear-headed and focused on how to make the best of an untenable situation. The muttonhead who did this to her would not scare her from her life. She was going to grab it back with both hands.

Speaking of grabbing with both hands...

She'd been trying—and failing—to ignore the insistent low ache of desire pulsing within her for the better part of the morning. She'd flash to her orgasm in the shower, where she'd almost called out Brinder's name. Her mind would wander to thoughts of his mouth on her. Of him inside her. Or her lips pressed to his. The caress of his tongue.

She sighed, frustration and worry now mixing with inconvenient arousal. The unwelcome emotions stemmed from her ongoing concerns about her upcoming role. They seemed to magnify every time she reviewed the script—which was currently resting on top of Blankie, open to a particularly troublesome sex scene. She'd be playing a high-end sex worker who falls in love with a socially awkward and reclusive client who relies on her employer's discreet service to meet his physical needs. Her character—a sexually aware, confident siren who offered her client smoldering sex—eventually gains his trust...and his heart. And he hers.

Honor sighed again...much deeper. Even before the scandal, she'd been reluctant to take the role. She'd never shown more than side boob in a film, and maybe the top of her butt crack. This film, directed by an incredibly talented colleague with tons of awards on her shelves, would require a fair amount of skin to show.

They'd agreed to a body double for certain scenes, but that wasn't the fly in the ointment. No, what really concerned her was her ability to convincingly convey unbridled passion.

As an actress, there had been a myriad of times when she'd had to learn a new skill (hello, Taekwondo) or pull from an emotional state not typical of her own personality. But for this film, she had to make audiences believe she was swept away by passion. That she was a sexual savant, experienced and talented in the bedroom.

In other words, the exact opposite of Honor.

She had only been with three men, and none of those had resulted in the kind of earth-shattering sex that could help inspire her transformation into this character. Her first partner was Brinder. They were young and inexperienced, with a fair amount of lust-soaked awkwardness. But there had been a hum of energy between them in their teenage intimacies that had hinted at the potential to explode into something...powerful.

Honor never found out, because just as they were getting into the rhythm of each other's bodies, their lives diverged.

Number two was a brief fling with a co-star on set in New Zealand. The sex had been drug-addled (for him), which led to less-than-satisfying results (for her). She couldn't speak for him, although he'd certainly moaned and bellowed and thrashed about with great vehemence.

And then Crispin. Uninspired, ordinary, sometimes-tender sex that really wasn't worth talking about with her friends. They thought she was just being discreet, when in reality, she was embarrassed at the nature of their couplings. And what was likely her own shortcomings (ha...non-comings!) in the bedroom.

How was she going to convincingly play this part?

And now even filming that role was up for debate, given the firestorm it would likely reignite if—no, *when*—they resolved this freaking video situation.

Honor was saved from further negative thought-spirals by the shrill chirp of her computer, reminding her of the Zoom call in five minutes. She quickly used the bathroom, refilled her coffee, and logged in.

Benny's stunning face filled the screen within moments. She was like a Viking warrior goddess, and Honor couldn't help but feel like an undersized, mousy troll next to her. Then Ross joined, with her dark brown hair and arresting green eyes. Also taller than her (but who wasn't?), Ross could batter even the most beautiful woman's self-esteem. There was just something charismatic about her—big personality, bigger heart, goofy laugh.

Honor caught a glimpse of herself in the small video box. Messy hair in a slapped together high ponytail, circles under her eyes, simple halter top. No makeup. No jewelry.

Yep. Channeling an ogre today.

"Honor." Benny smiled, encouragement and concern in her eyes, but her tone was no-nonsense. "How are you doing? Do you need anything? How is Brinder's place? Are you sleeping ok?"

Honor laughed. "Whoa, there! One at a time." Benny smiled at her and mouthed a 'sorry' with a not-sorry shrug of her shoulders. "I'm doing ok. Better today than yesterday." *That* was an understatement. "I don't need anything but some fresh air. Being cooped up in here is starting to get to me. I miss being outside."

The area around her property was perfect for long walks, chilly swims in the Bristol Channel just beyond the beach on which her home sat, and leisurely bike rides through the countryside.

She missed her home. And the peace she'd had there. Before.

Honor could almost hear her therapist reminding her to focus on the positive. She closed her eyes, reaching for one good thing. The first thing that popped into her head was Brinder's condo.

And Brinder himself.

She hadn't seen Ross's cottage, so she couldn't with full certainty say she wouldn't have loved staying there. But at least being where she'd wound up provided the comfort of Brinder. It was bizarre how natural it was to be with him—given the way things had ended.

Perhaps it was muscle memory. Somehow, being there just felt... right.

Of course, she couldn't say that out loud. Ross would be all over her in an instant. Honor searched for a benign statement to assure Benny and Ross she was fine at Brinder's place, while not tipping them off to their off-the-charts chemistry.

"Brinder's place is actually...really nice." *Yep. Nice and benign.* "And, yes, I slept ok last night." *If you count passing out from the excessive intake of Brown Acid as 'sleeping.'* "The mattress filler in Brinder's guest room is clearly gently harvested from pegasus feathers."

What did *his* bed feel like? More importantly, what would Brinder feel like on top of her...or under her...in said bed?

Ross interrupted that dangerous mind-wander with a snorting laugh. "Oh, I'm sure the beds at Casa Desiiigh's are *very comfortable.*" She snickered.

"Desiiigh?" Honor parroted as her curious mind battled with her wary heart to learn the origins of the nickname. Wary heart because she suspected she only needed one guess, which caused an immediate churn of unnamed feelings in her gut.

"Oh, you haven't heard that one yet. According to Tiercy, it's what all the ladies at his last hospital used to call him. Dr. Desiiigh." Ross purred dramatically. "Sort of like Fellowship-Unity's answer to George Clooney in *ER* and Patrick Dempsey as Dr. McDreamy. Except they are just characters, and our Brinder is the realio dealio."

Yep. Guess accuracy confirmed. No sooner had Honor processed that little tidbit from Ross that her last couple words sunk him. "Did you— have you—" Honor started haltingly, unable to ask the question past the rough knot of jealousy in her belly.

"Ha—no. We went out on a date years ago, back when Tiercy and Luke were first dating. We started to mess around, and about halfway into it, busted out laughing. Never even removed our dainty intimates. Zero chemistry. Which is a shame, because he is *such* a delicious morsel of a Hottie McHot Pants. But that's ok, because I ended up with the very hottest, very best Hottie McHot Pants."

Honor couldn't help but snort an appreciative giggle. She was familiar with this Ross-ism, having heard her describe her own husband that way many times, always with stars in her eyes and a satisfied grin on her face.

And yet, as if Honor's confidence wasn't shredded enough by the horrible online comments about her cellulite (it was what it was. She liked her shape, even if it wasn't the industry norm) and her non-perky boobs (you try holding up these Ds for thirty-seven years and see what happens), now she had the troubling image seed planted of Ross and Brinder all over each other...even if it hadn't been a *complete* encounter.

"Anywhoo," Ross continued, oblivious to the flash-bang she'd just lobbed into Honor's mind, "after we talk through sitrep—I'm reading a lot of Brittney Sahin and Charissa Gracyk military romances on my maternity leave—we'll coordinate an exfil to my place for an evening out."

"Things are well-contained on the video front," Benny chimed in, all business. "Our investigator is running down a couple leads on who might have planted the camera. People leave digital footprints they don't even realize. This'll be over soon. We just need to manage the media frenzy and the comments from the bottom half of the internet."

The blood drained from Honor's face at the thought of those comments and how ugly people could be when hiding behind their keyboards.

Benny must have seen her blanch. "It's all going to work out. And even with the vocal asswipes out there, public opinion remains strongly in your favor. But," Benny hesitated, "we need to get you some controlled exposure."

Honor choked on her spit as she started to speak. Nothing said 'classy, capable woman' like almost dying on your own inhaled saliva. When she'd cleared her windpipe and taken a sip of her coffee (because coffee always soothed life's small miseries), she managed a reply. "Controlled exposure? Haven't I been exposed enough?"

"I'm not asking you to streak through the streets of Charlottesville, Honor," Benny replied drily.

"Although, given the right social lubrication and enough privacy, that could be fun," Ross added with a wink.

Honor couldn't see but definitely sensed Benny's amused interior eye roll. Her agent was tough-as-nails, but she adored Ross. In fact, Benny had been the one to put her in touch with Ross when they were discussing the idea of her memoir.

"Lovely, Ross," Benny continued, not missing a beat. "Honor, we were correct to tuck you away during the initial maelstrom. But now, forty-eight hours later, we need you to be visible. Go out, in a controlled way, with your head high. You have nothing to hide."

Honor's heartrate kicked up. A public appearance? Surreal how something that was her bread-and-butter now made her palms sweat.

"Something small. Go out to dinner with Ross. Pop into a clothing boutique. Smile and wave at the cameras. But," Benny narrowed her eyes, "do *not* talk to the vultures. Don't respond to their questions. We'll just script a seemingly extemporaneous comment from you that you're visiting an old friend in Virginia. But you won't even mention the V-word."

"Vagina?" Ross chimed, smirking.

"*Video*, Ross. For fuck's sake," Benny sighed, shaking her head as she rubbed two perfectly manicured nails across her brow.

"Ah," Ross nodded, a shit-stirring smile on her face.

In that moment, Honor realized what they were doing. Benny was the straight man, Ross the comic relief. They were trying to distract her and spoonful-of-sugar this down her throat.

They needn't have worried. She was going to take control of this effed-up narrative. By the throat. And make it her...well, her bitch.

Somehow, even though she said it in her head, she heard her very proper maternal grandmother, who'd been raised in the Bible belt, cringing at the 'filthy' word. Her mother's mother had been a sweetie. But very religious. And brought up in a place and time where classy women didn't use vulgarities. Given that she'd stayed with Granny as a kid on the semi-regular occasions when her parents were on set together —either both in the same feature, or one just with the other for support —she'd been well-trained on how to express herself without curse words.

But sometimes the 'filthy' word was indeed the best word. Like *penis*. She stifled a grossed-out shiver. Somehow that word icked her out more than *cock*, which had always seemed like a solid, non-filthy word to her. And bitch was ok in her mind too, as long as she used it about a situation and not a person. There were better ways to describe a woman who needed an attitude adjustment.

And she *would* make this situation her bitch. Honor smirked. And then maybe she'd make sex her bitch too. She just needed to watch more porn. Well, really any porn other than the snippets on Reddit she'd watched with fascination.

"Wheats?" Ross's head tilted in curiosity. "You having a moment? Something you want to share with the class? Or maybe you're having a small stroke?"

Now Benny did give an epic eye roll. "Not helping."

"Oh, I'm helping," Ross retorted, her grin spreading across her face. "You see, I know this woman. And for an actress, in real life, she has an exceedingly readable face. At least for an expert in certain human behaviors, like me." She flung her hair dramatically over her shoulders, à la Galinda's 'toss toss' in *Wicked*.

"Oh, please, do share"—Benny waved her hand in a circular 'let's go' motion—"since I know we won't be able to finish our actual work conversation until you do." Benny's tone was brisk, but the half-smile on her face clearly conveyed she was amused by the editor.

"Weeell," Ross began, dragging out the syllable, "our Honor here went into the Bedsport Zone."

Honor cracked up, succumbing as always to the randomness of Ross. "Bedsport Zone?"

"Mmmm, yes." Ross nodded sagely. "It's the happy place where one's mind wanders when one has been, shall we say, tempted by the fruits of another."

"Great, now I'm going to be singing that," Benny muttered.

"And," Ross continued blithely, as if Benny hadn't even spoken, "methinks I know the source of said Zone, Mini-Wheats. You see"—she held up an explanatory finger—"all was normal with your face. Until I started talking about a certain person. And then Benny mentioned the plan to have you seen in public. Then I mentioned naked shenanigans— which are the very best kind, I might add—and you drifted off somewhere. But your cheeks got really pink and you bit your lower lip."

Honor reflexively touched the offending body part as Ross continued, "And you had a certain smile. The sly smile of a woman who knows what, or rather *who*, she wants, and has a plan to get it."

"I don't have a plan to get Brinder—"

"Aha!" cried Ross. "J'accuse! I never said Brinder's name! You're having dirty bedsport thoughts for Brinder Desai!"

"I'm not!" Honor's face flamed.

"You're a lying liar who lies, Mini-Wheats," Ross pronounced with a smug smile.

"Children," Benny interjected. "Whether or not Honor has the hots for Brinder—"

"I do not!" Honor interrupted.

"Do too!" Ross snorted.

"—is immaterial to the topic at hand," Benny continued smoothly as if Honor and Ross weren't acting like bickering siblings.

"If that's your story..." Ross singsonged.

"Ross." Benny's eyebrows went up, giving her patented 'stop now' look.

"Sorry," Ross responded. "Not sorry," she added on a whisper.

Benny hung her head for a moment, hiding her face, but her shoulders were clearly shaking. Ross had finally cracked her. And even though it was at Honor's expense, it was amusing to watch.

"Good Christ," her agent sighed. "Ross Beaufort-Grace, may we please finish?"

"I bet Honor wants to help Brinder finish." Ross snorted again and then burst into giggles, clearly unable to control it any longer.

Ross's laughter was contagious and Honor joined in, the release of a belly-laugh filling her body with much-needed endorphins.

After a few moments, Benny's eyebrows went back up, the agent clearly better able to control her own mirth. "You both finished?"

"Affirmative." Ross drew her hand down in front of her face, forming an exaggerated neutral face.

"Sorry, Benny," Honor replied, trying diligently not to picture Brinder...finishing.

"I have a hard stop in five minutes for my next meeting—"

"She said 'hard,'" Ross offered, sotto-voice.

"—and we need to finalize the plan. Ross will connect with Brinder today to confirm what time he's finished with work. He will then bring you both to Ross's place, so you can enjoy a nice evening out, get some fresh air, and be among friendly faces."

"Thank you," Honor whispered. "I appreciate the support."

"All good, Wheats," Ross replied, all traces of teasing long gone. "We've got your six."

"At Ross's, you will brainstorm an easy-peasy, low-key appearance to occur sometime in the next couple days. Then, one or both of you can run it past me, and I'll pressure test it with the PR team."

"Easy peasy lemon squeezy," Honor muttered, trying not to cringe at what she knew would be a phalanx of screaming media with blinding camera flashes.

Chapter Twenty-One

Brinder

With Grayton in the town car following from a distance, they pulled into the long drive leading to Ross and Xander's farmhouse shortly after six that evening. Besides his most recent visit, when his world fiercely and unexpectedly shifted, Brinder had been there quite a few times—first for Ross's thirty-fifth birthday last summer, and several times since his move to the area. It was a twenty-minute drive from his condo, and also close to the home that Tiercy and Cole had bought and were renovating four miles away.

Every time he turned down the lane and the farmhouse came into sight, he experienced a deep sense of peace. The land surrounding it was gorgeous, and he understood why Ross and Xander settled there, and then Tiercy and Cole had joined them.

He cast a quick glance at Honor, legs tucked under her as she took in the view through her window. He assumed on her first drive to Ross's, as well as the drive to his place, she'd been too stressed to appreciate it. Understandably. Now? A soft smile touched her lips. He wished he could drink in her expressive eyes, but much of the top half of her face was hidden behind the large-framed sunglasses and oversized hat she'd ordered and had delivered as her "disguise."

Since there hadn't been any indication the paps had figured out her location (nor even what continent she was on), it was probably overkill. But, she was a famous actress, and even in the sleepy Shenandoah Valley towns through which they'd driven, she'd be easily recognized.

Honor shifted in her seat, letting out a long sigh.

"You good?"

"Yes." She nodded, turning to face him. "I'm just glad to get out in the open. These lungs were meant for fresh air, and I don't think I can take one more minute indoors."

"I get it." He really did. For as long as he'd known her, which was basically since the start of secondary school until their graduation, Honor had loved the outdoors. At Cheltenham Ladies College, she'd been known for being a charming, outdoorsy classmate, who was down to earth and loyal. If you didn't know her name—that she was a *Wheatley* Wheatley—no one would have guessed that her parents were the mega rich stars whose family name was synonymous with acting.

A hint of nostalgia assailed him, and he realized he missed Jock and Clementine Wheatley as much as he missed his mom.

An image of random acting awards littering Honor's parents' family room, where her dad would arrange them in silly tableaux to her mom's endless amusement, sprang to life in his memory. It had been Jock Wheatley's version of Elf on the Shelf, and absolutely hilarious.

Now, Brinder's dad on the other hand...he hadn't had an actual conversation with him in years, and they'd not been under the same roof since he came home and announced he'd been matched with Georgetown for his residency. And that while he wasn't sure exactly where he'd specialize, he was quite sure it wasn't cardiac surgery. His father had been livid and stormed from the room.

"Where'd you go?"

Brinder blinked at the sound of her voice—American, but with a lilt of something British from decades spent in the UK. The opposite of him, he realized.

He looked around, taking in their surroundings. Before disappearing into old memories, he'd stopped the car at the end of the driveway, which led to the wraparound porch at the front of the farmhouse.

"Sorry," he replied. "Lost in thought."

"You don't say?" she teased, then glanced toward the house, where Ross was descending the porch stairs, her daughter snuggled in her arms. Petey, a towheaded little boy who looked just like his dad, hopped down them behind her. Honor propped her sunglasses on the top of her head, turning back to Brinder with concerned eyes. "You ok to be here? I know you said things are stressful at work."

You don't know the half of it. "Yes, fine. All good. Glad to hang out with the Graces."

"Even if you just saw them a few days ago?" Honor's smile lit up her face, her eyes sparkling with laughter...and the promise of fresh air.

"I can handle a double dose of Xander and the kids. Now Ross..." he trailed, causing her to giggle.

"I'm sorry Tiercy and Cole couldn't make it."

Tiercy had texted him and Ross earlier that Jemma was running a slight fever, so they'd opted to stay home out of an abundance of caution. Brinder allowed his mind to wander to a time when he'd imagined a future with Tiercy. Now, with the clarity of hindsight, he could recognize a stark truth. Tiercy was never the woman for him. She, Cole, and Jemma immediately fit together, like lost-then-found puzzle pieces.

No, Tiercy wasn't his future. But...*what if*...fate, or God, or the universe, or happenstance, or whatever you wanted to name it, brought him a gift? A chance to explore with Honor what could have been. What could still be.

A flash of conscience seared through him. *You have to be honest with her about your past. And your present. It's the only way to build a future.*

A future? With Honor.

Yes. And *yes*.

Something in his heart clicked into place. He was a physician. Knew the biological workings of the human body intimately. And, yet, he was at a loss to explain how a heart-shift that felt so inherently right could just happen. In a snap...his world changed.

Maybe it was the reemergence of muscle memory from the years during his teens when he'd been deeply in love with her. Maybe it was something completely new. Or perhaps a glorious amalgamation. All he knew was...in this moment, everything was different. New. Full of possibilities. Even given the cluster-fuck at work, he was suddenly... hopeful.

Honor's clear voice cut through his thought-dance.

"Brin? Did you hear me? I said I was bummed the Colburn family couldn't make it." She cocked her head, concern radiating from her mesmerizing eyes. "You ok?"

He caressed her lovely face with his eyes, when really he longed to do so with his fingertips. His lips.

Soon. But, first, they would clear the air. Lay old ghosts to rest and then move forward. Together.

He couldn't help but break into a wide smile. "I'm better than ok. You ready for this?"

Honor's face shifted from worry into a gorgeous smile, more beautiful than he'd seen on any magazine photo. "Beyond ready."

And, he realized, so was he. For anything and everything she'd give him.

Chapter Twenty-Two

Brinder

Honor opened the door, throwing her arms wide. "You must be Petey! I'm Honor. I work with your mom. I've heard so much about you."

To his credit, Xander's son—and soon to be Ross's by adoption—didn't miss a beat, stepping into her arms and returning Honor's warm hug.

Brinder held in a chuckle when he saw that Petey, at six, wasn't much shorter than Honor.

Honor released Petey and then leaned in to kiss Ross's check. "Thank you for saving me."

"Hey!" Brinder yelled, in mock indignation.

"Not from you, Brin. From my almost-solitary confinement in my Super Secret Mortification Lair. I'm stir crazy." She inhaled deeply and exhaled. "It smells so good here!"

"That's the honeysuckle. It's in bloom now, and Petey and I have had an amazing time tasting honeysuckle nectar."

"I can show you," Petey offered Honor with a wide smile and

earnest eyes. Brinder had the distinct notion of a childhood crush blooming along with the honeysuckle.

"That would be lovely, Petey."

"Why are you glad to be outside?" he asked, sticking like glue to her side. Brinder understood the attraction. *Same, kid. Same.*

"I've been stuck inside for a few days, and I was climbing the walls."

"I didn't know Dr. Brinder had a rock-climbing wall."

Brinder grinned. "No, buddy. It's just a phrase for when you have to be inside a lot and you're double extra bored."

Petey nodded, but clearly was deflated at the lack of the rock-climbing wall. "Why'd you hafta stay inside for a bunch of days?"

Ross, shaking her head, put a restraining arm on her inquisitive, possibly infatuated child. "Let's just say some people were being bullies, so Honor is staying in Virginia for a while until they can be taught a lesson."

Petey crinkled his nose. "Bullies are jerks. We'll take care of you, Honor." He reached for her hand. "Here, I'll show you where Mom set out dinner on our patio."

Brinder turned his head to catch Ross's reaction. Petey's birth mother had abandoned Xan and her son before Petey was even walking. But it was clear Ross had smoothly shifted into the role over the last year, filling empty spaces for each of them.

Ross brushed away a few tears with the heel of her hand. "Effing pregnancy hormones. My body is still out of whack." She grinned, clearly unashamed of her love for her bonus son, and his for her. "Let's follow them or he's gonna steal your girl."

"My—" Brinder froze.

Ross offered a wicked smile. "Don't even try to deny it. You're positively oozing pheromones and hanging on every move she makes." She winked. "Oh, and it's obvious you both were waaaay more than friends all those years ago."

Brinder just stared at Ross and said nothing. What could he say? That she'd been his once, and somehow—and he still didn't know how —he'd blown it? Or maybe his love hadn't been enough to keep her happy? Suddenly his newfound hope took a deep dive into his belly.

They'd have to clear the air soon. He had to try, for both the eighteen and thirty-seven-year-old versions of himself. Even if it meant fresh heartbreak for him.

Resolved, he slid into step next to Ross, watching a full-of-beans Petey chatter at Honor, his hand tucked in hers.

Holy shit. This kid was six, and he already had smooth moves. Xan and Ross were in for it in another decade.

Dinner had been an informal, leisurely affair. After, Petey had dashed across the property to play with his cousins at their nearby house, leaving the adults relaxing in the warm summer evening. Yesterday's storms had broken the early season heat wave. Ross and Xan were sipping whiskey sours, while Brinder—as the driver—drank water, and Honor (who'd turned a bit green at the mention of whiskey) was sucking down sweet tea. Baby Leah was sleeping in the main bedroom, a video camera monitor on the table showing her stretched out on her back in her bassinette.

Brinder's eyes kept returning to the infant, who had drifted to sleep in Honor's arms prior to being relocated. She was a natural with Leah and Petey. Not for the first time, Brinder wondered why she'd never married and had children.

"So how's the new gig going?"

Xander's question was innocuous, and hardly unexpected. And, yet, Brinder couldn't help his sharp inhale.

In the midst of a conversation with Ross, Honor whipped her head around to face him. "What was that sound?"

"What sound?"

"You did this weird inhale thing."

"I just took a breath."

"No, you definitely did a weird inhale thing." Xan smirked at him. "The females of Evangelist going after the fresh blood? Dr. Desiiigh is quite the catch, I'm told."

Brinder rolled his eyes at that nickname, which somehow seemed to follow him to his new hospital.

"Leave Brinder alone." Ross whacked at her husband's arm and then leaned in to kiss his cheek.

Relationships could be so weird.

Brinder suspected if Xan knew the real reason behind his reaction, he'd regret his teasing. "No. Just some political BS. I got stuck in the middle of something dodgy, and I'm just trying to sort it."

Honor frowned at him. "Dodgy? What happened?"

Truly not wishing to spoil the beautiful evening, Brinder evaded. "Just something with the Board chair. It's under control."

"Is it?" she pressed. "Why don't I believe you?"

"Honor, really. It's fine. Things just went a bit pear-shaped with him, and now I'm not his favorite person."

"Pear-shaped. Brit lingo for something went wrong," Ross announced dramatically—and quite unnecessarily, in Brinder's opinion—then downed the last of her drink before pouring another from the small pitcher on the table.

Brinder took a deep gulp of his water, trying to create a pause in the conversation. A moment for him to get his bearings.

"Went pear-shaped how?" Honor nudged again.

"Good lord, woman. You are relentless."

"And this is a surprise to you?" Honor's brow quirked. "Now tell us what happened. Maybe we can help."

Before he could stop himself, Brinder barked out a sarcastic laugh. "Now that would be interesting. You striding in to read Clark the riot act about his daughter."

Bloody hell. Why had he said that? He hadn't expected to be grilled, and clearly his words got tripped up between his exhausted brain and his mouth.

Honor's eyebrows flew high on her forehead. "I'm assuming Clark is your Board chair?" At his nod, she frowned. "And his daughter. Did something happen between you two?"

Brinder dropped his head back on the high-backed mesh of the patio chair. He'd stuck his foot in it, for sure. But hadn't he earlier acknowledged their need to be transparent?

"Damn," Ross murmured. "Spill the tea, Brin." Her tone was teasing, but her eyes were understanding. Ross, of all of them, knew the perils of clingers. Before Xan, she'd been an avowed commitment-phobe, and Brinder had heard dozens of tales from her and Tiercy about Ross's strange dates and minorly obsessed exes.

"Fuck it." He gave in.

"Sorry, baby." Ross reached over to cover the monitor with her hands, winking.

"Hilarious, Ross." Brinder shook his head, a smile breaking its way through the vibrating stress of Honor's inquisition.

"Stop stalling and spill it," Honor ordered.

Hell. For such a tiny thing, she sure was a force when she put her mind to something.

Brinder met her unwavering stare and sighed. *Guess that transparency starts now.*

"When I was interviewing for this job, I met someone at the bar. We, uh—" He looked at Honor briefly, suddenly uncomfortable with his previous extracurricular activities "We hooked up a few times. I came back for several interviews and tours, and every time I did, we met up."

"And?" Honor prompted, clearly focused on getting to the heart of the bollocksed-up mess.

"And we also, um, got together a few times after I was hired."

"You slept with the daughter of your Board chair. Repeatedly." Honor's tone was flat, but he could make out the grip of her hands on the armrests.

"I didn't know who she was at the time."

"But after, you still slept with her."

"No!" Brinder hadn't meant to raise his voice, but the whole thing just felt tawdry—both living it and talking about it to his friends. To Honor. "Sorry. It's just...the whole situation is so messed up. When we started, uh, hanging out, I told her I wasn't interested in anything serious."

"What's with the 'hanging out?'" Xander grumbled, emphasizing the end of his question by air-quoting those final two words.

"Sore subject with Xan," Ross whispered sotto-voice. "It's a phrase I used to use, back in the day." Ross patted Xander's hand.

"It wasn't even a year ago, Ross," he groused.

Ross leaned over and kissed him between his brows. "Your frownie line is out, Xan. Put it away. I love you, and only and always you."

"If you two are finished, might Brinder get back to his story?"

Brinder blinked at the sarcastic comment that Honor bit out. Was she...jealous? For some bizarre reason, that seemed to calm his unsettled belly, motivating him to continue. At least she'd know his time with Laurel had been about casual sex and nothing more.

"Bottom line? She got clingy."

"Hated that," Ross chimed, and then slapped a hand over her mouth.

"She left a wedding magazine on my coffee table with engagement rings flagged."

"What the everloving heck?" Ross cried from behind her hand. "What?" she asked in response to their confused faces, a half smirk on her face. "I'm trying not to curse in front of Leah and Petey. I'm evolving."

Honor snorted a laugh into her sweet tea, then quickly switched gears and pinned him with a glare.

"Obviously, she had a different notion of the nature of our situation. So, I ended things, as gently as I could. She cried. It was a bit of a scene. And then it was over. Or so I thought."

He hesitated, frustrated for the umpteenth time since the rug was pulled out from under him that he'd let the situationship with Laurel get so out of control. How had he missed—or at least ignored—the obvious signs of her clinginess? His anger at himself far exceeded his anger at Clark and Laurel. And that was saying something.

Now he was reliving the havoc aloud for the second time in nearly as many days, spilling it into the space between his friends, hoping for understanding. Or was it clarity? Forgiveness?

Transparency.

He shook his head. Better to just rip off the band-aid. Give Honor the whole story. Even if it made him look at worst like an insensitive jerk, and at best thoughtless and careless. Which, apparently, he had been. This was his doing. He knew better, and he'd allowed his cock to think for him at the worst possible time and leading to the worst possible situation.

Inhaling deeply, he barreled on. "A week or so later, I was called into a meeting with the Board chair. Who accused me of immoral and unethical behavior unbecoming a leader of the hospital."

"What the everloving fuuuuck." Ross breathed, apparently forgetting her potty-mouth rehabilitation.

"My sentiments exactly, Ross."

"Apparently, my predecessor had been quite a dick, and was removed for some severe transgression, or set of transgressions, that were never shared with me. My contract includes a morality and ethics clause, which I thought nothing of at the time of signing, given that my career has been pristine."

Honor snorted again, this time not with laughter.

He paused, doing his best to examine the poker face Honor had adopted. It was placid. But her eyes...they had always been the window of her soul. Based on the storms he was seeing, her soul was...seething. And quite possibly plotting his imminent demise.

Nothing to do but continue. Better to be hanged for a sheep as a lamb in the Court of Honor Opinion.

"Look," he responded, his defenses on the rise, "I may have had my fair share of bed partners, but I've always been respectful, straightforward, and honest."

"And?" Honor probed.

"And....technically, my boss, the hospital president, could have terminated my contract. But, she respects me and I respect her. I also get the sense she knows more about Laurel than she's saying. So instead of outright losing my job, I've been put on probation."

"For real?" Ross asked, taking another healthy swallow of her cocktail.

"Yes. I haven't had a chance to talk with her one-on-one. And I'm not even sure what she'd admit to knowing at this point. But, Agnes is incredible. She's smart. Talented. And I want to be on her team more than anything I've ever wanted professionally."

"Sounds like Agnes has the hots for you," Honor snarked as she swirled her tea in her glass and avoided his eye contact.

"Doubtful," Brinder retorted. "Her wife of ten years would probably take exception to that. As would I. I don't cheat."

Honor snorted again, derision written in every line of her body.

"Keep that up and you'll get a bloody nose from snorting so much," he snapped, out of patience and tired of being under the microscope for this messed up situation. And being under the Honor Microscope was infinitely worse.

"Ohkaay," Xander chimed in. "So the chick went sort of *Fatal Attraction*, imagined a fantasy life with you, and then went crying to daddy when it went tits up."

"Precisely. Now I have one month to rehabilitate my image or I'll lose my job."

Honor's eyes widened in the soft outdoor lighting that Xan had installed. "Son of a nutcracker," she whispered, all traces of her anger gone. "I can't stay with you," she continued, wringing the napkin in her hands in a clear sign of distress.

"What?" He knew she'd be offended—maybe even livid—about his carelessness with Laurel, but it seemed a bit out of proportion to have to up and move out, especially considering the related logistical nightmare. Besides, he and Honor hadn't been in a relationship in a very long time.

"I can't stay with you, Brinder," she repeated, her knuckles white on the napkin.

He ground his teeth, fighting to contain his anger at Laurel possibly fucking up another thing in his life. Ok, more accurately, fighting to control his anger at himself. "Why? Because of Laurel?"

"Because Brinder, you're supposed to be showing what an upstanding hospital leader you are, not harboring a sex video star."

Chapter Twenty-Three

Honor

For probably the millionth time since this fiasco had begun, Honor's stomach twisted and knotted, bile burning its way up her throat.

"I can't stay with you," she repeated a third time, unsure if her roiling insides were the result of sudden uncertainty of the immediate future, or the possibility of not staying with Brinder.

Because even if it had been barely two days, she was comfortable there. The upheaval of her mind and life quieting as she and her team prepared a battle strategy from the safe confines of Brinder's condo.

"Of course you're staying with me." Brinder's tone brooked no argument.

Honor glared at him.

I absolutely am not. "Of course, I'm *not,*" Honor rejoined, this time aloud, infusing her voice with a defiance she wasn't feeling inside. In fact, her insides were...wobbly...at the thought of leaving Brinder right now.

She summoned more false but necessary resolve. "Being seen with me right now would be terrible for your professional image. And if the paps find out I'm essentially living with you? They'd splash your face on every tawdry site, along with a twisted take on our relationship." Honor twisted her fingers, fighting not to rub her thumb along her 'emotional support scar.' "It would be career suicide for you. I'm not even sure the best PR team in the world could spin it for you in a way where you'd end up looking good."

"Honor, I'm not going to leave you hanging. You're safe with me. And we'll work double time to keep it that way." He trained those earnest hazel eyes on her—the same sincere, sweet, yet intense gaze that had melted her insides all those years ago, capturing her innocent, teenage heart.

She had loved him so much once. And even though he'd hurt her heart more than any congenital defect ever could, Honor couldn't allow him to place his career, and a job he clearly loved, in peril for her.

No. She couldn't do this to him. Wouldn't. She was going to have to find somewhere else to ride out the storm.

Honor ripped her eyes from their current immobilization in the Brinder forcefield, casting a pleading look to Ross. "I know the cottage isn't an option. Is your barn habitable?"

Ross shook her head with a small smile. "No, it's good for family activities, but there's no way you could sleep out there."

Honor sighed in frustration, but also got the sense she could see Ross's wheels turning.

"Please tell me you have some other hidden cottage for me," Honor implored.

"I'm so sorry, Honor. I wish I could make one materialize for you." Ross's eyes were sympathetic as Xander wrapped his arm around his wife, tucking her head against his shoulder. Honor had seen Ross and her husband together once before—in New York when she was prepping for a press junket for her memoir. Then, as now, she was struck by a deep sense of longing for finding her 'person.' Someone who cherished her, made her laugh, and who put her first and allowed her to do the same for him. Oh...and if he was a beast between the sheets, that would be helpful too.

"Listen." Brinder's crisp accent cut through her musings. "There isn't a magical cottage—"

"But that would be *fun*!" Ross interjected, clapping her hands in excitement. "I want my magical second cottage to have bottomless whiskey sours, unlimited romance novels, an array of sex toys, and—of course—soundproof walls."

"—and you aren't staying in a hotel," he continued, ostensibly ignoring Ross, except for a small gleam of amusement in his eyes.

Honor once again was struck with something that felt too much like jealousy when she thought of Brinder hooking up with the sexy and charismatic Ross. She swallowed past the knot in her throat, her mind whirring like a hamster on a wheel.

"You stay with me, Tish. That's the plan, and we stick to it."

"Plans change, don't they?" Honor challenged, and deep inside, she knew she wasn't referring to her current quandary. No, she'd regressed to their shared plans from a lifetime ago.

"Hang on a second." Ross held up a finger, clearly cutting off what was likely going to be a stubborn response from Brinder. "I actually think we can make this work for both of you, and Brinder's little peccadillo—"

"I don't even know what that word means," Brinder groused good naturedly, "but I don't think it's flattering for me."

"Transgression. Wrongdoing," Ross replied professorially.

"Nice SAT word, Principessa." Xander gazed at his wife from his perch right next to her.

"Thanks, baby." Ross nuzzled back into him.

Again, Honor's insides twinged with longing. Once upon a time, Brinder had been her Xander, filling her heart and her world with his caring, attentive love. It had shredded her to let him go, and it hurt worse now to see grown-up, amazing Brinder—and realize the unlikelihood of them ever being together. In some ways, it almost hurt worse to have him so close and yet so unreachable.

"You want to continue with your thought, Ross? Or maybe you two need to just get a room." Brinder's weary voice interrupted her spiraling thoughts. Thank God.

She couldn't help but feast her eyes on him. Brinder rolled his eyes and quirked a grin at Honor. Forty-eight hours with him was enough of a tease to remind her how special their connection was—and couldn't ever be again.

Now it was Ross's turn to interrupt her gloomy thoughts. "Right. Sorry not sorry." Ross returned Brinder's smile with a bigger one. "Anywhoooo, Benny said we need to create careful and controlled public appearances for Honor. Having her hiding isn't helping her reputation. She needs to go out, head held high. Effuse warmth and..." —Ross searched the sky, as if looking for the words she wanted—"a goddess-like demeanor. You," she intoned assertively, pointing to Honor, "are far above this tawdry situation."

"You want me to be a goddess." Honor shook her head, suddenly feeling beyond defeated.

"You *are* a goddess," Ross retorted. "Have you seen you? You're stunning, you're engaging, you're kind... You are this incredible mix of sexy and cute, and people love it."

"Um, Ross, something you want to share with me?" Xander teased.

"What? Can't a straight woman appreciate the attributes of another woman? Although, if I were going to take a swing at the other team's plate, Honor'd be a good choice."

"Would you please finish your thought, Ross?" Brinder rolled his eyes again, this time with frustration, but not before Honor saw him take a quick scan of her.

Everywhere his gaze touched blazed with the caress. Welp, that was... inconvenient.

"Honor needs to be seen in positive and wholesome situations," Ross continued. "And so do you." She waved a finger at Brinder. "Of course, the media doesn't know you both have a connection from your youth."

"Connection. That's one way of phrasing it," Honor muttered, ignoring Brinder's eyes on her.

"But that gives us the advantage. We can both leak it and spin it to our advantage. You can help each other." Ross tapped her finger on her lips. "We tell them you're old friends who met up again by chance... which is sort of true."

"More than *sort of*," Honor grumbled, starting to track Ross's train of thought and not liking its destination.

"We say you're dating, picking up where you left off many years ago. People love a second chance romance. It's catnip for the romantics. Your fans will eat it up."

"How did you—?" Honor's mouth dropped open in shock.

"Figure out that you two used to be an item? Let's just say that Fairy Rossmother sees things. Just like the instant whammo-bammo attraction between Tiercy and Cole. Maybe I'm just super sensitive to pheromones," Ross pondered theatrically.

"We were teenagers. It was a lifetime ago," Honor managed.

"And you and I both know eighteen years can be both an eternity and a minute." Ross's eyes were sad and knowing.

Honor realized Ross was referring to the long-ago tragic passing of her own parents, and the resulting now-healed estrangement with her sister.

Brinder took a long gulp of water and then carefully rested his glass on the table, his moves slow and measured. "You want us to fake date?" The frown on his face was almost as disheartening as the entire situation.

"Try not to look so horrified," Honor grumbled.

Brinder shifted to face her, his entire focus on her. "I'm not horrified." His voice was velvet soft, a caress in and of itself, and exactly what her abraded heart needed right now. For a moment, Honor had the sensation of them being the only two people in the world.

"Not horrified," he repeated, earnest hazel eyes scanning her face as he carefully placed a gentle hand on her arm—as if soothing a skittish animal. "Just trying to sort this in my brain."

"No sorting needed, Brinder," Ross interjected, shattering Honor's fantasy of aloneness with Brinder. "Honor is a highly regarded actress. She doesn't engage in tabloid-fodder behavior—"

"Sex video aside." Honor still had trouble believing this had happened to her. Ross wasn't wrong. Honor had always been so careful. In a world of twenty-four seven news, and the proliferation of entertainment sites and online forums, Honor always tried to carefully manage her actions and her public reputation.Then, in one brutal blow, the internet had turned on her. Sure, her defenders were out there and vocal in their support. But it was shocking to read the vitriol that oozed over social media.

"No, you see, I think that could even help. While your statement stands, you show by your behaviors that you are still your classy self. We set up some wholesome, public dates for you and Brinder. No flashy PDA."

"As if," Honor rolled her eyes, trying hard to ignore the frisson in her ladyparts at the mention of PDAs and Brinder.

"I still don't see how this helps. The paps will figure out she's staying with me, and it'll look like we're shacking up. Then we both look bad."

"Nope," Ross popped the p. "We make it clear that you are exclusively dating. That you'd reconnected a month or so ago—so it's clear we are talking post-Crispin."

Brinder's eyes narrowed at the mention of her ex. "Are we sure that twat didn't leak the video?"

"Yes," Honor insisted. "All other faults aside, he wouldn't do something like that."

"We say that you both had been talking nonstop and you'd been planning a visit," Ross continued, undeterred. "When someone tried to tarnish your good name, Brinder here"—she waved her hand at him— "was your Sir Galahad, offering his place as a sanctuary. The two of you are old friends reigniting an old flame."

"'Reigniting an old flame,'" Brinder parroted.

"Yep." More popping ps from Ross.

"It's not a bad idea," Xander mused and then caught himself, smirking a half-smile at his wife. "I mean, it's a *fantastic* idea. Tons of merit to it, Principessa." He cast comically flared eyes to Honor, who was trying too hard to corral her scattered thoughts to return Xander's gesture, which seemed to be an attempt to distract her from the obvious chaos of her brain.

"I think it's a stretch." Brinder's arms were crossed, head down and shaking back and forth.

"Not really. The best fake premises are based in the truth. And the truth is that you were teenage sweethearts. Anyone who's read your memoir knows your dads developed a friendship after your first surgery. It won't be a tough sell that you two once dated. In fact, I'm pretty ticked at myself for missing that little tidbit all along. Looking back, it's so obvious, but I never put together Rahul Desai with *Brinder Desai*." Ross aimed a glare at Honor, which quickly morphed into a knowing glance. "To add to the believability, there is definite chemistry between you kids."

"I don't think—" Honor started, fully aware her cheeks had bloomed a riotous pink.

"Don't think. Just do. Honor, you are an incredible actress. Brinder, you are motivated to make this work. So sell it."

Ross turned to Honor, compelling honesty in her eyes. "You were going to be in the U.S. anyway in a few weeks to start your publicity tour for the new role while you also continue to promote your book. We'll spread the 'insider information' that you two reconnected long distance, and are now exclusively dating." She pivoted her attention to Brinder. "Making sure, of course, the timing doesn't overlap with your Laurel shenanigans."

Honor saw the wince from Brinder out of the corner of her eye as she watched Ross animatedly describe the scenario.

"Just picture it. You two are madly happy together. Pair that with some staged appearances of a loving, stable, nurturing couple...and Bob's your uncle," Ross pronounced.

"And when we inevitably have to break up?" Brinder challenged.

Honor ignored the cramp of her belly at the blunt question, instead focusing on the drag of her sandaled foot back and forth across the flagstone.

"You'll be classy and amicable, saying only amazing things about each other. Gracious, complimentary, et cetera," Ross replied, clearly talking herself and them through it.

The thing was...it did make sense.

At this point, Honor's choices were limited. If she agreed to Ross's plan, she'd have a chance to control her own narrative, help Brinder, and maybe...*maybe*...get some much-needed closure to the end of their teenage romance.

"I think we should do it." Brinder's pronouncement stunned her—both the calm assurance of his voice and the use of the word 'we.'

If they did this, she and Brinder would be a 'we' again, even if it was just another role for her to play.

The thing was...would her heart recognize the difference?

Chapter Twenty-Four

Brinder

"In all seriousness, that actually is a solid plan," Xander said, shifting to tuck his wife further under his arm.

"One...don't sound so surprised, hottie hubby. Two...I'm a giver. What can I say?"

Brinder ignored the Graces' blatant flirting, giving his full attention to Honor. She sat next to him, stress radiating off her in waves he could practically see.

"You think people will fall for it?" Her brown eyes lifted to his, worry etched on her beautiful face.

"Why wouldn't they?"

"We'd have to tell my family the truth. They'd see right through it. There's no way my parents wouldn't recognize it for the ruse that it will be."

Brinder tried not to be hurt at the accurate, but still unsettling, description of a relationship with Honor as a ruse. "Why would your family see right through it?"

"Because they know how much you hurt me all those years ago," she replied, so softly he wondered if he'd heard her correctly.

"How much *I* hurt *you*—" Brinder couldn't contain the shock. "You left me!"

"Because—because you *made out* with her!" Honor shot out of her seat, hands visibly shaking.

"*Who?*" Brinder stood too, backing up so he wasn't looming over her. The tremors in her hands were like daggers to his heart, and he fought the urge to hold them. To stroke and calm the tremors, even if they matched the ones in his own heart.

But his feelings didn't matter right now. Honor was clearly vulnerable and scared—her entire world turned upside down. And unlike him with the Clark-Laurel situation, her life's upheaval was through no doing of her own.

He stifled the shudder that threatened to vibrate through him, focusing his attention on Honor, who was clenching her fists and growing even more visibly agitated.

He'd do anything just to pull her into his arms. To hold her. To calm her body...and her heart. To forget the last eighteen years ever happened and pick up as if nothing had ever torn them apart.

Instead, he took another careful step back, sensing Honor's temper about to blow.

"Gwendolyn!" Honor sneer-shouted, bringing him back to his confused question, and not even trying to moderate her voice. "I saw you two, all wrapped up in each other."

"I don't—"

"At our graduation party."

"I didn't—" Confusion poured through his mind, propelled by the adrenaline rushing through his veins. He wracked his brain, finally unearthing an interaction with a classmate that was so unimportant he'd forgotten it until now.

"Babe, do we have popcorn? I want to see how he gets himself out of this," Ross chimed to Xander from across the table.

Brinder fought the urge to grab Honor caveman-style and march her out of there so he could explain. Without an audience.

"You did. I saw it."

"No, Honor. It took me a minute to figure out what you're talking about. That's how meaningless of a situation it was—"

Honor snorted. "Meaningless to *you*, maybe—"

"It *was* meaningless. What you saw was Gwen plastered on me. She was completely trollied."

"Love that word," Ross whispered, miming eating popcorn.

"Gwen came on to me. *She* kissed *me*."

"Semantics!" Honor threw her hands in the air, disgust written all over her face.

"Wait just a hot second," Ross interjected, suddenly sounding slightly more sober. "Some chick just shoved her tongue down your throat? Seriously...who does that? That's assault, period. If the shoe had been on the other foot..."

Brinder paused to focus his swirling mind. First on Ross's excellent point about Gwen's sexual aggression, which had never occurred to him. And then on Honor's anger, which still appeared raw after all these years.

This was why she'd been so furious with him? A meaningless encounter with Gwendolyn Parker? Christ. All this time. If he'd only known...maybe they wouldn't have lost all those years. Ridiculous to think one irrelevant moment for him could shatter their future together.

Brinder fought to catch his breath, his mind whirling. He had to de-escalate this. Had to get her to understand.

"Honor...I didn't kiss her back." Brinder swallowed down his frustration, gentling his voice, all the de-escalation training he'd received at work kicking in. "I didn't kiss her at all. She tried to press her tongue into my mouth as she climbed all over me."

"He is built for the climbing..."

"Ross...seriously?" Brinder glared at her and turned back to Honor. "Nothing happened. I unpeeled her from me and told her I wasn't interested. That you were my girl and nothing would ever change that." He shook his head. "Or so I thought."

"I heard you. I heard you say, 'It's not as serious with Honor as everyone thinks,'" Honor seethed, defying his attempts at soothing her.

"Oh snap. I hate it when mom and dad are fighting. But my money's on mom here."

"Ross!" Honor and Brinder both snapped.

"Sorry," Xan chimed apologetically. "My wife is pumping and dumping for the first time and I think the two whiskey sours are hitting her. Her tolerance must have reset to preadolescent levels in the last year."

Ross grinned, "Speaking of hitting things..."

Brinder ignored Ross, understanding dawning across his face. "Honor, I did say that—"

"I know!"

"—but I didn't mean it the way you interpreted."

Honor just started at him, arms crossed in defiance, her foot tapping an impatient tattoo on the flagstone patio. "This should be good," she spat.

"What this will be is the *truth*, Tish! Gwen was talking about your health. About rumors that had been flying after you fainted."

"I'd been out for a run. I was dehydrated and hungry!" Honor erupted.

"I know, baby. I know."

"Don't *baby* me, Brinder Desai. I am most definitely *not* your baby."

Brinder dropped his head and blew out a sigh. "I'm sorry. Old habit. It won't happen again." He took a breath, trying to return to the thread of their misunderstanding. "Please understand... Not by me, but at the time, you were seen as—"

"If you say 'fragile', or any synonym for that, I'm taking Blankie, Couchie, and Ruggie with me and heading for Wales, paps be damned."

"Oooo...she *cussed*," Ross whispered, eyes wide. "Also, why is she taking the mice from *Cinderella* to Wales?"

Xander chuckled. "That's Gus-Gus and Jaq, Ross," he murmured, tugging her to a standing position. "Let's get you some water and give them some privacy."

"Oooh, privacy. *Maybe* I'll even let you make out with me, Hubby Hottie."

"*Maybe* when you sober up, Principessa..." Xander's voice trailed off as he herded his slightly intoxicated wife into the house.

Brinder waited until the door to the kitchen gently slapped closed. He hadn't stopped watching Honor, her gaze intense, pupils wide in her brown eyes. "You *were* seen as vulnerable." He held up a hand. "Let me finish. Again, not by me. You have to admit, it was unusual for a classmate to have a major surgery like you did. And before, as your valve was failing, you couldn't miss the blue tinge around your lips and your lack of breath. Most of our classmates, as you know, were excellent and supportive. But some students were...less than kind, and a few were downright mean."

"Including Gwendolyn Parker." Derision dripped from her voice.

"Yes, including her. She was jealous of you, Honor." Brinder paced back and forth, struggling to both contain his emotion and remember details of a forgettable interaction so many years ago. "Of any attention you received, from me or anyone else. Gwen was jealous of who your family is, of your last name."

"And of the scar down my sternum?" Honor practically screeched, then took a deep breath, rubbing her temples. "I'm sorry. I just...she was always a nasty cow to me, and when I saw her in your arms...and heard you say that...I thought you were cheating on me. I thought you told her *we* weren't serious."

"I would never cheat!" Brinder shouted, and then took a deep breath himself, pinching the bridge of his nose between his thumb and forefinger before continuing, his heart feeling almost...bruised. "I'm sorry I raised my voice. I just can't stand the thought of you thinking I cheated on you. That this has been weighing on you for all this time." He sighed, grabbing the back of his neck, which was now coiled with tension. "I never told her *we* weren't serious. I was saying that your health situation was no longer serious."

"She kissed you," Honor whispered, decades-old agony filling her eyes and tearing up his heart. "She wrapped herself around you, Brinder."

"Like a toxic anaconda, yes." Like a magnet drawn to its mate, Brinder stepped toward her and gently grasped her by the shoulders, practically bending in half to peer into her eyes. "Tish, I never cheated on you. Would never. I loved you. And when you left, without a word... I was devastated."

"I got a ride back to campus from Kitty St. John. She was sober."

"I didn't know where you'd gone. It took me an hour or so to realize you were no longer there. I thought you were off with your boarding house mates. I tried calling you and it went to voicemail. I didn't think much of it because you were always letting your battery drain. I checked with Hannah and she hadn't seen you either.

"When I ran into Kitty much later, she told me you were feeling sick—remember, you were just getting over bronchitis?—and that she had taken you home. That...tracked...and I didn't question it. I was going to ask Kitty to drive me to your place, just so I could check on you, but I didn't want her to have to make that drive again."

He paused, running his hand through his hair. "Honor, early the next morning when I came to see you and your place was empty...I freaked out. I called your parents in a panic, and when they said you were gone.... I thought they meant...*gone*." His eyes started to fill at the memory and he tipped his head up, blinking his eyes rapidly to stay the tears that threatened to drip down his cheeks.

"Oh, shit... Brinder..." Honor whispered.

"They were shocked that I didn't know where you were and did their best to calm me down. Honor," he croaked, "I was beside myself. I couldn't figure out where you'd gone and why you hadn't said anything. When I caught my breath, they told me you had accepted a film role and you were leaving the country."

Brinder shifted a bit closer, unable to resist the draw to her, even as they argued. He pressed his lips together, trying hard to ignore the distress mixed with anger churning in his belly. It had been eighteen years. How could this feel so raw?

"How did you even audition for that part without your parents knowing? Without me knowing? And how did you get away with hightailing it to London?"

A small smile crept across Honor's heart-shaped face. "The director had contacted me via the head of the theater program at Cheltenham. They were friends. She's a Cheltonian herself."

"Abby Marshman."

"Right. Abby scouted me for the role. She had a vision for me in it. I'd privately auditioned at someone's home near school over Christmas. Abby knew Mom and Dad were not supportive of me entering the family business beyond roles in their summer stock plays. When she offered the part, I dragged my heels for weeks, until finally she told me she needed a decision. They had a strong second choice identified. The idea of someone else taking that role...it made me ill. It fired me up. I wanted it." Honor inhaled and then released a shuddering sigh. "I had to tell her by the night of our graduation party. I was coming to talk with you when I saw the whole Gwendolyn thing."

"Then what happened?"

She took a long swallow of her sweet tea. "Kitty didn't know what to do. She kept asking if I wanted her to call you. No way was I letting that happen. After I threw some clothes into a suitcase, I begged her to drop me off at the train station. I knew catching a cab would take a while, and I didn't want to risk running into you."

Honor took a deep breath, looking away from the abject hurt Brinder couldn't mask in his expression.

"I took the last train to London. When I got there, I called Abby, who picked me up at the station and we drove to the Four Seasons. We reviewed the script again and I told her I wanted the role. She secured a suite for me at the hotel, along with a promise I'd connect with my parents in the morning. She wasn't stupid. She knew landing on their wrong side would be a poor career move. She also offered to meet with them.

"The next morning, I called my parents and broke the news that I was, against their wishes, taking a part in a movie. And that I'd be leaving the next day."

"Why didn't you tell me? We always talked about everything. Or at least I thought we did." Agony ripped his heart, tearing past old scars.

Honor shook her head, her eyes a study in sadness. "Brin, you'd been accepted to Georgetown. I knew you really wanted to go, to escape the shadow of your father. But when you and I both got into Cambridge, I knew you were settling so you could be with me."

"It was never settling to be with you, Honor." He reached for her closest hand and gently gripped it in his. To his relief, she allowed it.

"OK, Brinder, speaking of talking about everything, you never directly told me your first choice was Georgetown. I obviously knew you'd applied and been accepted. But you never said how much you wanted to go there."

"How—how did you find out?"

"I overheard you talking with Julian Davies after a rugby game. About how you requested a grace period to give your decision."

Brinder dropped his head. "I, uh, I actually had committed by that point."

"You what?"

"I was going to tell you, Honor. I just...I needed to find a way to reassure you that even though we'd be apart, that I would fly home to see you whenever I could. I was working up the courage."

"When were you going to tell me?"

"After the party. I just—I didn't want to ruin that night for us."

"So you always would have gone to Georgetown."

"And you always would have chosen to make that film instead of entering Cambridge."

"I guess," she whispered. "I mean, Gwen was the straw that broke the camel's back. I had been vacillating about telling you from the moment Abby contacted me. My whole life has belonged to other people. I wanted to keep this just to myself. Only for a while. Then I learned about you and Georgetown. I got the part. Then the Gwenaconda thing happened." Her lips tilted in a teasing smile that didn't reach her eyes.

"But I don't understand, Honor. Why wouldn't you ever take my calls? Answer my emails?" Brinder tried to calm the shaking in his voice.

"I was hurt. So hurt. And angry. You have no idea what it looked like to see Gwen in your arms. Your lips on hers. It...it broke me, Brinder. And it helped clarify a decision I really needed to make for myself. I had to see the audition through with Abby, but as long as you were in the picture, I knew I'd never be able to walk away. When I saw you with her, I took it as a sign from the universe to take the role."

She closed her eyes, a lone tear snaking down her cheek. Brinder instinctively caught it with his thumb, causing a few more tears to cascade. "I had to make a clean break. I knew if I talked to you, I'd change my mind."

"Would that have been such a horrible thing, Honor?" He swallowed past an enormous lump in his throat.

"Yes. It would have. Because you and I would have put our dreams on hold for each other. Think about it, Brinder. Think about all you've done and accomplished. Think about what I've accomplished!" She inhaled a shaky breath. "Gwen may have been the catalyst. The trashy catalyst," she added on a snarl, "but one we both needed. No matter how much it hurt. And it did hurt so much to see that, Brinder. Imagine if the roles had been reversed."

Jealousy seared his belly, as it always did when he saw pictures of Honor with Crispin and others.

She gave him a sad, knowing smile. "By the time it faded to a more manageable type of pain, I'd learned you had eloped."

"Honor, that was four years later!" Brinder dragged his hands through his hair, shock and sorrow blasting through his veins. "It took you four years to even contemplate giving me a chance to explain? After all that we were to each other?"

"You hurt me, Brinder!" she cried out, tears brimming in her eyes. "What I saw...what I heard...with you and Gwen—it *pummelled* me in all my insecurities."

"I would never—" Brinder dropped his head, defeated. "I would never."

"But I didn't know that then. I was eighteen, confused, scared about the decision I wanted to make, and it all just...happened. So I left. I knew if I talked with you, I'd cave. And in my gut, I knew we each needed to follow our dreams. When I learned you'd gotten married, I just figured you hadn't felt things as intensely as I had all those years ago."

"Honor," he whispered. "You broke my heart. Kira—she—we didn't even last three months. We didn't truly love each other. Not the way life partners should."

Not the way I always loved you.

"I didn't hear about the breakup until a year later."

"That's because I didn't tell my parents about it until then. My father probably told your dad."

"Who told me, probably not realizing how much that hurt."

Honor's eyes were huge in her face. She blinked and another lone tear trailed down her check, breaking his heart anew. Once again, Brinder reached out and brushed the tear away, fascinated by the softness of her cheek.

"I am so sorry," he whispered.

"Me, too." Honor's voice shook.

The darkening night sky surrounded them, the only sound the soft, soothing hum of katydids chirping. Brinder could almost feel peace settling into his bones. After all this time, he finally had his explanation for what happened.

In some strange way, her teenage rationale made sense. Even if it shredded his heart that she could ever think him capable of cheating on her...or anyone.

After long minutes of silence, while they watched emerging fireflies dancing in the early twilight, Honor grabbed his hand and squeezed it. "Ok, Gomez. Let's do this. Let's put the past in the past and help each other's futures."

CHAPTER TWENTY-FIVE

HONOR

Honor and Brinder quickly cleaned up the dinner dishes and then greeted Petey, who arrived in a rush from the other side of the manicured backyard, announcing breathlessly that he was exactly on time for his eight o'clock school-night curfew. In less of a rush, Ross and Xan emerged from the primary bedroom, with Ross looking like she'd taken a restorative shower.

Honor examined them, curious about their jealousy-inducing couplehood. According to a classic Ross overshare, she'd been cleared for sex by her doctor, and she and Xander hadn't wasted any time resuming that part of their relationship. But right now, there was no sign of sexploits on them, only the happy exhaustion of new parents.

After hugs goodbye, including a sheepish apology from Ross for her tipsy, runaway mouth, they headed back to the condo, her security detail trailing them. And once again, they ascended via the booty-call elevator.

Only this time, Honor was less focused on who'd been the prior lucky, uh, *riders*. Instead, as she watched Brinder from under her lashes —subtly, she hoped—all she could think was...she'd been wrong.

So very, very wrong.

About what happened. About Brinder. About how she'd handled it.

And yet, here, in the midst of madness, was the mercurial universe gifting her a chance to mend the broken.

As with their drive back, they continued wordlessly into the condo. Habitually, Honor headed to the couch, tucking into the corner and pulling Blankie onto her lap, even though it was still eighty degrees outside. Because everyone knew it didn't matter what the thermometer said...a cozy blanket was always in season.

Brinder dropped onto the chair across from her, raking his hands into his hair as he sunk back against the cushions.

Honor tried hard not to trace the bulge of his biceps with her eyes, and then gave up, fighting the flash of fantasy to run her tongue along his tattoos. She wondered for the zillionth time since she'd first seen them what the symbols gracing his arm stood for.

As he stretched out his long legs, crossing them at the ankle, his shorts rose a bit and tugged across his—

Honor coughed. *Holy tomatoes*. He really was a Hottie McHot Pants.

His eyes snapped up to hers. "You ok? Pollen level is high right now. I can get you an antihistamine."

Yes, that was it. Pollen. Yep. Ha! More like ballin'! Honor covered her snicker with another cough. "Yes, uh, definitely. I bet that's it. Pollen."

Brinder unfurled to his full height, a small frown between his brows. "You sure you're ok? I'll get you some water and leave a tablet for you in the kitchen."

Honor gave him her best neutral smile. The Mona Lisa had nothing on her. "Just some water would be great. Thank you."

She watched him prowl into the kitchen, in all his long-limbed muscled glory. *Shidoobie*. Memories of her shower sent a shiver racing down her spine.

"You cold? I can adjust the air."

Of course he'd been watching her. That was Brinder—solicitous and thoughtful. Always attuned to her. In fact, now that she really paused to think of it, with the emotion of the situation fully drained, it had been completely out of character for Brinder to kiss Gwen. Hindsight punched all sorts of holes into her decades-held theory of that night.

"I've got Blankie," Honor winked, tugging it up higher around her chest and then chuckling. "Poor Ross. She was feeling her drinks, wasn't she?"

"She was." Brinder smirked and then raised a brow. "But even that performance couldn't hold a candle to yours yesterday."

Honor had the good sense to look away as she flushed, embarrassment over her intoxication infusing her with unexpected shyness. If she looked at him right now, she'd probably curl up in mortification. And that was saying something, given the reason she was even there in the first place.

"Hey," Brinder came around and knelt in front of her, handing her a glass of water. "I was just teasing. I didn't mean to upset you."

Honor took a deep draw of water, using the action to camouflage her discomfort and steady her racing heart. He was so close to her. And he smelled so. Freaking. Good. Given their height difference, all she needed to do was tip forward oh-so-slightly and she could press her lips against his.

After a second swallow, she reached around Brinder to put the glass on a coaster.

"You good?"

She nodded and he rose, her eyes pinned to the roll of muscle in his thighs.

Gah. Now his cock was eye-level. *Mouth* level.

Honor had never honed her fellatio skills, Crispin always too impatient and often critical, but suddenly Honor had a battle underway. Tightly fisting her hands in her lap, she fought against the very real desire to unzip his shorts. To reach in and grab his cock, bringing it to her lips and sucking until he exploded in her mouth—which also had never happened with Crispin.

"Honor," Brinder whispered, startling her out of her fantasy. "You can't look at me—like that."

She tilted her chin up—way up—to look him in the eye, and was gratified to see a small vein pulsing in his temple as his throat convulsed on a swallow.

"Like what?" she asked, all innocence.

"Like you want to eat my dick," he growled, voice scratchy as tires on gravel.

"But what if I do?"

Shidoobie! Where had that come from? And, yet, she was no longer embarrassed.

No. She was aroused.

Her core was throbbing.

Suddenly, she had the best idea. The *very* best idea. While she helped him with Project Stability, he could help her with a project of her own.

"Honor," he groaned, turning and sitting back on the chair, resting his arms on his thighs, his hands clasped between them. "What are you doing?"

Honor sucked in a breath. *Here goes nothing.* "I need a favor."

He tilted his head, looking nothing more than confused. "Anything, Honor. Just say what you need and I'll do everything I can to make it happen."

Honor squeezed her hands to keep them from shaking. It was an audacious request she was about to make. And once she said it, well... there was no unsaying it.

"What do you need?" His gravelly voice held a note of promise that amped her even higher.

She closed her eyes, sure if she looked at him a moment longer she'd lose her courage. Leaned forward. And...heavens...caught a faint whiff of his cologne that pushed her over the edge. "I need you to screw me senseless. I need you to try to make me scream. I need you to tutor me in all things steamy sex. Help me to be able to channel a sex goddess. I need to know what a non-self-given orgasm feels like," she rushed out, then dropped back against the cushions, folding an arm protectively across her body, her other hand finding and worrying her scar.

She opened her eyes slowly to find his intense, unreadable gaze pinned on her. If he said no, Honor was sure this would unravel the tentative reknitting of their friendship. And the idea of losing him again was as scary as the idea of actually seeing this proposition through.

For long moments—way uncomfortably long moments—Brinder

just stared at her, pupils blown wide in the hazel eyes she'd adored from the first time she saw him at Cheltenham.

"You...what?" he managed eventually.

Honor sucked in another breath, her nerves steadying now that she'd said it aloud. "My next role requires me to convincingly play a high-end sex worker." Brinder's eyes flared. "But, uh, the thing is...I'm not sure I have anything to draw from." When he didn't say anything, she continued haltingly. "I'm worried I'll look like a farce. That everyone will laugh at me. That they'll be able to tell I've never really been deep in the throes of passion. Heck, I've barely waded in the shallow waters."

"You—" he started.

"I want you to be my sex tutor."

"Your sex tutor," he repeated slowly, woodenly, still staring at her.

Now she was getting embarrassed again. And a touch mad. Why was he making this so difficult?

"Yes," she snapped. "I'm grateful for everything you've done for me these past few days, Brinder. But, now, I really need...I need Dr. *Desiiigh*. Please."

His jaw dropped and he shook his head, never breaking their eye contact.

"I—I need to have real-life experience to draw from. Experience that I don't have. Brinder, I know this sounds bananas—"

"You think?"

"—but it's the perfect solution. We fake date. You help me hold my head high through this mess. I help you secure your dream job. And I... get some lessons."

"Some lessons," he muttered, then dropped his head into his hand and let out an incredulous laugh. "Honor, are you seriously asking me to seduce you, to *fuck* you, to make you scream?"

"And also teach me how to make you scream," Honor added, her heart thumping madly in her chest.

"It's a terrible idea," he said, almost as if to himself.

"Maybe. But...maybe not," she whispered. "Brinder. I need this."

"You," he choked out, dragging his hand down his face, "you've never..." he motioned with his hand.

"Had an orgasm? Not one given by someone else," she clarified, and then swallowed, realizing he would connect an important dot. "No. Never."

"Never," he whispered, blinking rapidly, his eyes darting across her face. "You mean, not since we—"

"Not even then," she cut him off, wincing at the look of shock on Brinder's handsome face.

"I know we were young, and had only been intimate for a few months before everything...but I thought..." he trailed, shaking his head.

"I know. I was a good actress even then."

"Honor, you're killing me. Why would you"—he scrubbed his face—"why would you fake it with me? We were both inexperienced. I would have learned with you. I would have learned what your body wanted. Would have shown you what it craved."

Honor tucked her legs under her, watching the shake of her own hands as she repositioned the blanket around her. "I always liked it. Well, except for that first time."

Brinder cringed. His *rapid* performance their first time had always been a sore spot with him.

"Liked it? Honor...way to damn it with faint praise." He closed his eyes.

"I'm not going to sugarcoat it, ok? I've never had amazing sex. Even with you. There. I said it."

"What about your ex?"

Honor scoffed. "No. We had strengths as a couple, but between the sheets wasn't one of them."

She briefly flashed to one exchange when she expressed a desire for him to toss her over his shoulder and have his way with her. At her diminutive height, Honor was still dwarfed by Crispin's five-eight, slight-of-build frame. She thought what she'd hoped was a sexy request was doable. But Crispin had merely grumbled that if she wanted him to 'fling her around,' she needed to lose some weight.

After she'd licked her hurt feelings—Crispin seemingly oblivious to the dagger he'd hurled—they'd had their same-old missionary sex.

"Well, that's part of your problem right there," Brinder commented, jarring her from what was truly an ugly memory.

"What do you mean?"

"If you were only ever doing it between the sheets"—his eyes gleamed with something she'd never seen—"you were missing out on a lot of other prime locations."

"Oh," she managed. "I—I didn't enjoy sex with him most of the time. Especially later in our relationship. I, um, I used to fake that I was asleep so he wouldn't touch me."

"You're a European common frog."

"Pardon?" she yelped, sure she'd misheard.

A sage nod from Brinder. Then she registered his lips twitching in clear humor. "Female European common frogs fake their own death to escape unwanted mating."

Honor giggled. "Really?"

"I never lie about wildlife facts from Sir David Attenborough, Honor," he deadpanned, then broke into a wide smile.

"I still like you, Brinder Desai," she whispered.

"I still like you too, Honor Wheatley."

For a moment, they just stared at each other, smiling like loons.

"So," he said, suddenly all business. "Sir Twatwaffle. Was he an in-bed, at-night, lights-out, missionary lay?"

"Ye—yes," Honor choked out, stunned by his accuracy as much as the change in subject.

Brinder clucked his tongue. "His loss. And yours." He held out his hand to her. "But there's still time for you."

"Wh—what are you doing?"

"Against my better judgment, I'm giving you what you asked for."

Chapter Twenty-Six

Brinder

His heart beat a ferocious tattoo in his chest, and his body ached like he'd been ten rounds in the boxing ring. First, the shock of her request. Then the unexpected blow to his self-esteem that he had never actually brought her to orgasm. That the bliss he'd experienced between her legs all those years ago was largely one-sided. That the times he'd put his mouth on her sweet pussy, soaking up her sexy aromas and licking her musky, sweet arousal...she'd just been *acting*.

And that was enough to spur him into action.

Never mind that every part of his brain was screaming *Stop*!!!

Never mind that his head was rapidly cataloging all the ways this would be disastrous.

Because now...he wanted a do-over.

Wanted her back in his arms with a desire so fierce it took his breath away.

She'd never experienced a proper orgasm, forget the sheer bliss of multiple orgasms, and he was going to ring at least three out of her before the night was over.

He tugged her to standing, pulling her toward the glasstop table next to the swath of floor-to-ceiling windows.

"What are you—?" she started, gasping when he lifted her easily and seated her on the edge of the table.

"Lesson one, baby. You might be a famous actress out there"—he motioned past the windows—"but in here, I'm in charge. Your orgasms, and there will be many, belong to me. And for that to happen, you need to let go, relax, and listen to me when I tell you something."

Honor's eyes widened, her pulse point fluttering rapidly.

"Can you do that, baby? Can you listen to me? Can you let go?"

She nodded, her throat bobbing on a stilted swallow.

Brinder examined her, taking note of her short, panting breaths. Her enlarged black pupils. The flush rising up her chest, making the faded raised scar more pronounced.

"Good girl."

"Oooh," she breathed out. "You're good."

"Sssh." Brinder stepped up to her. "Do you trust me?"

Honor nodded.

"I'm going to need words here, Honor."

"Y—yes, I trust you."

He could barely hear her over the thrum of his own heart. And his cock...well, that was hard enough to pound nails. Or pound something —or, more accurately, *someone*—else.

"Good girl," he said again, allowing a small smile to indicate he liked her reaction to those words. "And are you ok with me touching you? With me putting my mouth on you?"

Again she nodded, eyes flared, chest rising and falling rapidly.

He could practically smell her arousal. What she didn't know, but he was eager to teach her, was that the lead up to foreplay and sex could be as exhilarating—*almost*—as the actual act.

"Words, baby," he whispered, framing her heart-shaped face with his hands, stroking the line of her jaw with his thumbs.

Her eyes fluttered shut. "Yes. Touch me. Put your mouth on me, Brin." She let out a shaky exhalation. "Please."

It was the *please* that did it. Because he loved a good girl in bed.

There was nothing like the exhilaration of control being relinquished to him, trust placed in his hands.

He let out a low growl, blood heating under his skin. "Take off your top, Honor."

"My—?" Her eyes flew open, her hand frozen in the air.

"Your top, Honor. Off. Now."

She blinked several times, then raised a shaky hand to the ties that held her top together behind her neck. When she'd first appeared in that tiny halter, his fingers had twitched at the temptation to tug hard and release the straps. Now, she pulled the ties, slowly, letting go as the stretchy cotton triangles that formed the bodice dropped down.

Revealing the pale, soft globes of her breasts.

"Fuck," he whispered.

"It has a built-in bra," she offered, her chin raised, making no effort to cover herself.

"I see that."

He took her in. Full breasts. Perfect pink nipples puckered into mouthwatering nubs that practically screamed for his mouth.

"Fuck," he whispered again, dropping into the chair in front of her. "Honor, if you don't want this, tell me to stop now. Otherwise..."

Her voice rang out, strong and sure, more confident than he'd heard all evening. "I want this. I want you."

And that was all the permission he needed.

Chapter Twenty-Seven

Honor

Oh...*shiitake.*

Her first lover—the one she never truly got over—lunged forward, pulling her hips to the edge of the table. Before she could even take a breath, his mouth was on her breast. He cradled it in his hand, lifting it higher, and started teasing the edges with his tongue.

Honor held her breath, torn between the ecstasy of the mind-blowing sensations he elicited within her core and the fear of moving, lest those sensations dissipate. She was way too familiar with that.

He reached for her other breast with his opposite hand, rolling the nub between his thumb and forefinger and then pinching.

A current zapped between her nipple and her clit, and she felt a rush of arousal between her legs. "Breathe," he murmured, his breath tickling her straining peak, and she released the pent-up air on a shuddering exhale. He sucked her other nipple deeper into his mouth, flicking the tip repeatedly with his tongue.

"Ah...Brin..." she gasped, leaning back on her hands as her eyes drifted closed against the sensual assault. "That feels..."

"How baby? Is it making you wet?"

"Yes," she admitted, pressing her chest against him so he'd begin again. *Keep going, Brinder. Don't let it go away.*

He chuckled against her. "Relax, baby. Tell me how wet your pussy is right now."

"It's—it's so wet," she panted, inhaling sharply as he sucked and flicked again while gloriously assaulting her other nipple with his fingers.

"What's wet, baby?"

Her eyes flew open, and he looked up. Honor was struck by the raw eroticism of his mouth connected to her nipple by a string of his saliva, her other nipple straining against the measured flicks and pressure of his thumb.

"My, um..." She blushed, knowing what he wanted her to say. It had never been easy for her to express her sexual feelings, or use what Granny had piously called 'dirty words.'

"Say it," he murmured and then sucked hard. "Say it!"

"My pussy," she moaned, clenching her legs against the rising waves of arousal.

"That's my good girl," he said and then slayed her with a wicked smile and a wink. Honor was pretty sure her panties had melted off. "Do you know what good girls get, Honor?"

She shook her head, even though she was pretty certain she knew the answer.

"Good girls get to come. Repeatedly." He shifted back. "Shorts off. Now."

This time, Honor didn't hesitate. Keeping her eyes trained on him, she unsnapped her shorts and then slowly drew down the zipper.

Brinder shifted his hands under her hips. "Tilt up, baby."

She complied, and he slid her shorts down her legs, leaving her in nothing but a white, lacy thong.

"Fuck, Honor," he breathed out, and she reveled in the warm exhalation against her bare skin, chills erupting down her arms.

He buried his nose between her legs and...inhaled deeply. Honor squirmed, embarrassed by how she might smell down there. Crispin rarely went down on her, and only after they'd showered.

Brinder anchored her hips in his large hands. "Easy, baby." He inhaled again. "Christ, you smell fucking delicious."

Honor whimpered, torn between the rising rapids of desire she'd never experienced before, and her own discomfort at this act.

He looked up at her, fixing her with his earnest hazel gaze. For a moment, she was transported back to her eighteenth birthday—four months before their graduation—when they'd finally given themselves to each other. How he'd held her gaze as he slid into her, having done his best to get her ready. His soft, sympathetic whimper as he'd reached and then broken the barrier of her innocence. The gasp of pleasure—his and hers—as the initial pain disappeared into a strange and magical fullness. The sensation of him throbbing within her, answering the ache of her own desire. And the pulse flitting in his neck as he gave himself over.

"Tish?" he murmured, reaching up to stroke the side of her face. "You ok?"

Honor broke into a big smile. "Ok doesn't even begin to describe it. Put your mouth on me, Brinder."

CHAPTER TWENTY-EIGHT

BRINDER

irvana.

He buried his face in her sweet pussy, grinning against her soft lips as her legs instinctively wrapped around him. He dragged his tongue in a long lick, overtop her knickers, stopping at her clit and pressing down with his tongue. He was rewarded with a shuddering sigh from the tiny, curvy goddess stretched out on his table.

Honor dropped to her elbows, her head hanging back. "Brinder," she moaned, canting her hips up.

Brinder recognized that sign of approval and reached up, hooking his fingers on either side of her thong and tugging. She lifted her hips and he pulled them the rest of the way off.

And there she lay. Legs parted. Chest rising and falling rapidly.

"You're beautiful," he whispered.

And then did the thing he'd fantasized about for so many lost years. He pressed an open-mouth kiss to her pussy lips, running his tongue from her opening to her clit, which was stiffening in anticipation.

"And you taste like heaven." He gave another long, luxurious lick, watching as she squirmed. "Feel good?"

"Yessss," she moaned. "More. Please."

"Sssh...relax and let me eat this pretty pussy."

"Brin," Honor panted, rocking her hips as he alternated between lashes of his tongue and leisurely sucks of her clit. Her body knew what she wanted. And so did he.

Carefully, he slid a finger into her, his eyes rolling back at the soft, slippery decadence of her channel.

"Mmmmm," she moaned again. "More."

He slid another finger in, widening them and stretching her. He wasn't small, and he wanted her to be so ready, all she felt was sheer bliss.

Her arousal coated his fingers, and he pulled them out, bringing them to his mouth and tasting her.

"Brinder!" she choked out, shocked and blushing.

"Hmmm, just tasting my new favorite treat."

She lay on his table, fully naked, illuminated by the bright May moonlight. He gazed at her, stretched out, panting, waiting. Ready.

"You want my fingers back, Honor?"

"Yes," she replied, reaching for his hand and guiding it toward her center.

"Bold," he chuckled. "I like that."

He slid both fingers back in, then added a third. On her gasp, he leaned back in and flicked her clit with his tongue.

"Oh!" she called out, writhing against him.

"That's right," he murmured, working her over with his tongue and fingers. He flicked and sucked, working his fingers in and out, mimicking the action his cock would eventually make.

"Oh...Brinder...oh...*god*," she panted, reaching down to press his face against her. He could barely breathe, and he'd never been happier.

Her thighs clenched against him, and the squeeze of her walls against his fingers gave the signal. Brinder curled his fingers and pressed, sucking hard on the bundle of nerves.

"FUCK!" she screamed, shattering in his arms. Her hips rocked as she settled into nonsensical groans.

"That's my girl," he whispered, gathering her into his arms and carrying her into his bedroom.

CHAPTER TWENTY-NINE

HONOR

Brinder brought them to his bedroom in a handful of long, determined strides. As her once-faulty heart struggled to regain a calmer cadence, Honor gave herself over to the delicious sensation of being naked in a fully clothed Brinder's arms.

Why was that so sexy? And why hadn't she done that before?

Well, that was easy. Because she'd never experienced anything like this. Not even with the teenage version of the man currently holding her.

She tried, and failed, to feel self-conscious about her nakedness. About the fact that she'd full-out screamed the f-bomb. About the pulsing, throbbing heat between her legs.

He'd made her come. And that orgasm was far, far, *far* better than anything her bedside clit-sucker could induce. Also, as she'd suspected, better than her solo Brinder Fantasy Orgasm courtesy of his luxe shower

Still...her body ached for more. There was an emptiness, and she yearned to be filled. By him.

At the side of his bed, he set her gently on her feet, and she placed a shaking hand against one of the four simple ebony-stained bedposts to stabilize her wobbly legs.

He reached for her and tipped her chin so their eyes met. Great Scott, he was tall. And so sexy.

A lifetime ago, she'd fallen in love with a boy. Today, she stood before the gorgeous man he'd become.

And couldn't form words through the Sahara of her mouth.

"You ok, baby?" He scanned her face, hazel eyes assessing...and so warm. She noticed his pupils were blown. Honor might not be a sexual savant...yet...but she could recognize the signs of lust.

And that included the tenting of Brinder's shorts.

She swallowed reflexively, licking her lips, desperate for something to ease her parched mouth.

Brinder's lips quirked in a smirk, and he handed her a half-full glass from his nightstand. "It's not cold, but it should help."

If he could read her that easily, he could probably also sense the aching void of her...well, her *pussy*. Even though she'd been raised to think of that word as vulgar, it was actually perfect, given how it practically purred for his touch.

Honor took the glass, hyperaware of the sudden steadiness of her hand. She should have been nervous. But she wasn't. She trusted Brinder. And she wanted him, with a fierce desire that stunned her. That eclipsed anything she'd experienced as a horny teenager.

She downed the water and then placed the glass—which matched the one he'd given her the other night—back on his nightstand. Firm resolution partnered with the hum of arousal in her body, making her bold.

"Thank you, Brinder. That hit the spot." Her words were intentionally vague. She could have been referring to the water. Or to what had just happened on his *dining room table*. Before she could lose her bravado, she lowered the register of her voice, watching him from beneath her lashes. "But I need more."

He blinked once, then again and again in rapid succession. "Oh, I can get you more water—"

She palmed his hard cock, the warmth and size of it within his shorts stunning her. Honor swallowed down her nerves. "Not water, Brin."

She squeezed gently and he sucked in a breath while saying her name.

"I need you to fuck me, Brinder." Honor thought the word tasted almost as good as she knew his cock would.

"Baby," he breathed. And then...

One moment she was standing before him. The next, she was sprawled on the bed, Brinder caging her with his arms as her hips cradled him.

If she thought it was decadent before to be unclothed and held by Brinder Desai, that couldn't match the sheer eroticism of Brinder, fully dressed, propping himself over her, his hard cock nestled against the vee of her naked body.

"Take off your clothes, Brinder," she commanded on a steady whisper.

His eyes flared. Then he shifted off her and stood, facing her, indecision and lust playing out on his handsome features. "Are you sure?"

She nodded.

"Words, baby." His voice was strained, but she watched his hands shift to the hem of his black T-shirt.

"Yes, Brinder. I'm sure." She propped herself up on her elbows, preparing for the Brinder Show. She'd already seen his sexy, chiseled chest. But the rest? Well, now she felt like a kid on her birthday, waiting for her present. "Take them off," she repeated with a steadiness that belied the rapid beat of her pulse.

He reached for the back of his shirt with one hand and tugged it over his head, as his other hand gave a firm squeeze to his cock.

Honor's mouth watered. "Now the shorts, Brinder," she rasped. "All of it."

In one smooth move, his shorts and boxers were down at his ankles, where he kicked them off.

"*Shiitake.*" It barely even registered as a whisper, her shock at the size of him stealing most of the air in her lungs. His cock...had it always been that big? It rose from between his legs, hard, proud, and so very large, a hint of precum glistening at the tip of the engorged head. And was that? Holy wow...he was *pierced*.

The balls of a curved barbell shone in the soft light of the bedroom. When had he done *that*? And...more importantly, what would it feel like rubbing against all her most sensitive places?

Honor swallowed convulsively. She wanted that in her. Now.

"Please, Brinder," she whispered, holding out her hand.

For long moments, they stayed like that. Eyes eating each other up, taking it all in.

She loved that he had chest hair. Was fascinated by the swirl of his tattoo up his arm and across the head of his shoulder. His flat, brown nipples were as puckered as hers, and she followed her instinct, sitting up and placing her mouth there, flicking with her tongue.

Brinder's breathing increased, and his cock kicked between them. "Jesus, Honor," he murmured, laughing and easing away. Although not too fast, she noticed smugly. "I, uh"—he ran a hand through his hair— "I want to make this amazing for you, baby. And if you keep doing that, we're going to have a repeat of our first time."

He winced and blushed, clearly recalling their first frenzied coupling. Yes, it had been quick. Yes, it had been initially painful. No, she hadn't come. But also no, it wasn't terrible. In fact, she'd loved it. Loved the sensation of him inside of her. Filling her up. Thrusting above her.

Honor's hips shifted, seeking to recreate the memory. Only better. So much better.

"Brinder, show me." She held his gaze. He had to understand that she needed this. If he stopped now, she would collapse—in sexual want...and sorrow. She yearned for him, physically, in the way of couples across time immemorial. Beyond that...she wouldn't think. This was just sex, with Dr. Desiiigh. And nothing more. Well, maybe with a touch of freshly dusted off friendship. But that was it. "Please."

Brinder closed his eyes for a moment. When he opened them, Honor was shocked by the intensity, the hazel she'd always loved nearly swallowed by his enlarged pupils. "Lie back, Tish," he ordered. "Open those legs and show me what I've been missing all these years."

Instinct warred with timidity, and Honor's legs shook.

"Now, Tish." A chill raced down her spine at the command in his tone, and her nipples hardened to aching nubs that desperately needed his mouth. She opened her legs.

"That's my girl," he whispered, never taking his eyes from her as he reached for the drawer of his bedside table, scanning from her pulsing center to her eyes. And, catching those, his own gaze softened. "You look so beautiful in my bed, baby."

He dropped a condom next to them. The gold wrapper painted a sharp contrast against his slate blue comforter. And even as nerves raced through her, a small part of her thrilled that he was the kind of man who made his bed. It was so...domestic.

"We, uh, we should pull this down so it doesn't get ruined."

"Don't fucking move an inch." Brinder knelt between her legs, fisting and stroking his cock, almost absently, as his soft command ratcheted her arousal. "I want you to come on my duvet. I want your sweet cum mixed with mine. I want to see it."

Her eyes widened, core clenching at the explicit utterance. Dr. Desiiigh indeed. After a lifetime drought, he had her so primed she could practically burst just from the visual he painted.

He quirked a smile at her. "Good?"

"Good," she confirmed, somewhat shakily, remembering his mandate for her words.

"Roll over."

"What?"

"Honor," he replied in a strained but patient voice. "Don't make me repeat myself. In here, you are mine. You listen to me and you do. What. I. Say."

Honor met the heat of his gaze, then nodded, rolling over, trying not to think about his view of her fleshy bottom.

"Up on your knees."

Her sex clenched at his gravelly command. And now, she was officially desperate for him to slam into her from behind.

Honor braced for the welcome assault. Instead, she whimpered at the sensation of her cheeks being parted. *"Oh God,"* she whimpered again, uncaring that she took the Lord's name in vain. She had a feeling she'd be doing that a lot. "God," she cried again as he licked her from nub to her other opening. She squirmed.

"Hold still, baby," he cooed.

Then he flipped her over.

Chapter Thirty

Brinder

He quickly slid on the condom. Although he'd been tested regularly—and wanted nothing more than to feel her bare—he wasn't sure of her birth control status. That was a conversation for another time. In fact, the idea of her needing birth control with someone else almost made him lose his erection. Almost.

But then he watched her, arms thrown wide, panting and glistening from her orgasm, and knew no one had ever fucked her like he would. Not before and not ever again.

He reached down and eased between Honor's legs, his cock straining toward her.

Her sex-hazed eyes landed on his. "Do it," she commanded, soft but firm.

And he slid home.

"Honor," he breathed out, fighting not to lose himself in her glorious tight warmth and start rutting like an animal on the savanna. He held still, citing random animal mating facts in his head until he was sure he wasn't going to blow his load on the first thrust.

Eventually, Honor rocked her hips impatiently. "Brinder, please," she framed his face in her hands, and the tenderness of it almost completely undid him. "I need you." Her expressive eyes held his, confirming her desire.

He eased almost all the way out of her, luxuriating in the slide of his cock along her walls.

"No," she breathed, clearly thinking he was stopping, then cried, "Oooooh, fuck!" as he gave in and snapped his hips forward, burying himself all the way inside of her again.

Again and again, he pulled back and thrust in, bottoming out each glorious time. The sounds of moans and flesh slapping filled his bedroom.

"More more more," Honor chanted, meeting him thrust for thrust with the rise of her hips.

He shifted his hands under her sexy asscheeks, tilting her hips and changing the angle, knowing what would happen next. He pulled back and then slammed home, watching as her eyes rolled back in her head in ecstasy as he hit that special knot of nerves inside, the sensation made even more pronounced by his piercing.

"Brinder...God...*please*..." she moaned, head thrashing side to side. He could feel her walls clamping down on him and he gritted his teeth, determined not to go over until she did.

She reached around and grabbed his butt, pulling him harder into her and spurring him on. Brinder was tempted to flip her over again and finish her doggie style, knowing she'd combust at that angle. But *this* time—their first in two long decades apart—he wanted to watch her face. Watch her unravel and come apart in his arms.

He slowed to a gentler pace, grinding against her clit as he pulled out.

She groaned. "Don't stop."

"Never," he whispered, and then leaned over her, pressing his lips to hers.

She opened and he licked inside, tangling his tongue with hers as he slowly increased the tempo of his thrusts. Hooking his arms under her knees, he opened her wide, pulling her legs up and slamming home over and over.

Her moaning pants turned into sexy cries against his mouth as she rose to meet the pounding of his cock into her slick pussy. With singular attention, he chased the high—his and hers—lost in the clamp of her channel. As she tightened further, his teeth clenched. It was like being in a hot, pulsing vise. He thrust deeply, feeling his impending orgasm about to explode.

Brinder lifted her hips just a bit higher, widening her, and buried himself. Honor arched her back and detonated with a loud cry, taking him over with her.

"Honor!" he yelled, drowning out her own cries as he exploded into the condom, then collapsing to his side and pulling her against him.

In that moment, he knew. He never wanted to be separated from her again. Wherever she was, he was going to be. For the rest of his life. He just needed to earn her trust and his place by her side.

But for now? Rest. And then, he planned to have his mouth on her again.

CHAPTER THIRTY-ONE

HONOR

What alternate universe was she living in right now? Honor needed to know so she could visit anytime she wanted. It *had* to be an alternate existence. How else could she explain it all? Four days ago, she'd been at home in Pembrokeshire, polishing the script that had consumed her attention for months. Three days ago, she'd been rocked to the core by the grossest of violations and whisked to the U.S., where the man who'd stolen her heart nearly two decades earlier had somehow manifested back into her life.

And today? She'd been rocked to the core in an altogether different way.

Now, at least four orgasms (*four!*) later, she lay boneless against Brinder's chest, thoroughly...well...*fucked,* and beyond sated.

Honor shifted, wincing slightly at the twinge of faint pain in her gloriously abused flesh. No, she hadn't been a virgin, with teenage Brinder and two other partners notched on her unimpressive bedpost, but she surely felt *awakened.* That was the only way to describe it.

She'd been sexually asleep. Now? Her exhausted body hummed at the mere thought of what Brinder had just done to it. Everything ached, in the best possible way.

She was thirty-seven years old, and thanks to the boy who broke her heart, her body was *finally* wonderfully, gloriously awake.

Honor tensed—stunned, overwhelmed, and suddenly self-conscious that she lay naked, sweating, and musky in his arms.

Brinder tightened those sculpted arms around her and kissed the top of her head. After all they'd done, the places he'd had his mouth (she flushed at the memory)...*that* kiss felt far more intimate.

"You ok?" He murmured into her hair, softly stroking it and lulling her back into boneless complacency.

She rested her cheek against his chest, soothed by the beating of his heart. "I'm good," she confirmed. And she was. She was also... sticky.

And...he was still inside her. Her eyes flew up to his, her cheeks heating. The room smelled of sex. "Uh, maybe I should clean up?"

Brinder's heavy-lidded gaze scorched her insides as it shifted around her face. He cocked his head. "Are you uncomfortable?"

"I just..." She swallowed. "I just feel"—she motioned with her hand —"sticky," she finished in an embarrassed whisper.

He smiled and dropped another kiss on her head, then groaned as he gripped the base of the condom and slid out of her. A fresh wave of their tang assaulted her senses, and Honor battled between embarrassment and an ache at the loss of him inside her.

He slid off the bed and kissed her shoulder. "Be right back."

Honor listened to the sound of the faucet running, absently surveying the room. She was sideways on his very rumpled bed. With a mixture of mortification and satisfaction, she noticed the evidence of their pleasure on his comforter. As he'd predicted.

Honor wasn't sure whether to get up, or maybe to get under the covers? This was uncharted territory.

Before she could stress-ruminate further, Brinder appeared in the doorway, a cloth in his hand. His half-hard cock hung heavy between his legs, the piercing visible past the foreskin.

She looked up and realized he'd caught her staring. At *him*. Her cheeks burned. She knew she was likely bright pink.

"You can look, you know," he offered casually. "It's been inside you, after all."

Honor flung her arm over her eyes, groaning in embarrassment. Then she gasped, jackknifing into a seated position as a warm cloth touched her tender places.

"Easy, baby," Brinder murmured from between her legs. "I'm just cleaning you up."

He looked up and...*fudge*...winked so sexily, Honor wanted to grab him and pull him back inside her. What had possessed her? She'd never been such an insatiable horndog. Brinder dabbed the soft cloth over her skin, the tickle of the fabric igniting her nerve endings.

She instinctively rocked her hips. He hooked another grin. "That feel good?"

Honor nodded and bit her lip. "I'm sure it smells better down there now," she managed past her shame at what she suspected was a musky mess.

A frown appeared on Brinder's handsome face. "What do you mean?" His hand stilled, halting the dance of arousal building at his gentle touch.

Good. Maybe she could finally think straight.

"You know." She briefly closed her eyes against the mortification, swallowing against her dry mouth.

Brinder noticed and handed her a fresh glass of water. He must have grabbed it and refilled it when he retrieved the washcloth.

Taking her time with the water, if only to collect her erratic thoughts, Honor explained, "Well, it's just...it just um"—she motioned toward the vee of her body—"it has an odor," she finished on a waver, finally succumbing to the embarrassment.

"Of course it does." Brinder's voice was both soothing and matter-of-fact. "Scent is a powerful aphrodisiac in the animal kingdom."

Her eyes widened. "Oh, well, I mean, I guess with animals..."

"Humans are animals, Honor," Brinder remarked placidly, head cocked, and then tossed the cloth to the floor.

He got back into bed, this time with his back against the ebony woven-cane headboard, and eased her into his arms so she rested between his legs, her back against his chest. "Are you...ashamed...of how you smell? Of how *we* smell?" His low words, tinged with that sexy posh accent, tickled against her ears.

Honor shivered and then winced, glad he couldn't see her face. "I mean..." she trailed off, unsure how to continue.

"Did someone tell you that you don't smell good?"

Now her cheeks really burned. And, yet, this was *Brinder*. He had a way of lowering her defenses. Always had. "Yes," she whispered.

"Who?" His voice was hard, with an edge she'd never heard before. Honor started to pull away, but Brinder simply anchored his arm more tightly around her. "Who, Honor?" he demanded again, although Honor knew his ire wasn't directed at her.

"Crispin." It was something less than a whisper. She may have even just mouthed the name. It almost felt like an admission of guilt. Though, perhaps...*yes*...not her own.

"Your twat of an ex told you that you smelled bad?"

She nodded.

He muttered something incomprehensible under his breath and then relaxed his hold, gently turning her to face him.

"That assbasket had the most perfect woman in his arms and he let her get away." Brinder frowned and shook his head before bringing his full focus back to her. "You smell like heaven, Honor. And you taste like..." He exhaled hard, dragging a hand through his hair. "Honor, I want to bury my face between your legs and spend the rest of my life there." He pointed to his cock, which was now standing at attention. "Do you see what the mere *hint* of the scent of your arousal does to me?"

Her eyes flared as her heart beat a ferocious tattoo.

Fast as a panther, he grasped her around the waist and flipped her so she was under him. "Honor..." He held her face between his hands as he rested his weight on his elbows. "Never ever feel you need to clean up for me. I only brought a flannel because I wanted to alleviate your discomfort. But make no mistake about this"—he pinned her with his smoldering hazel gaze—"I am obsessed with your scent. Your taste. I could *gorge* on you. I want to wring so many orgasms out of you that the scent of your cum never leaves my nose. I'm addicted." He shifted off her, propping himself up on an elbow. "And if I didn't know you were as sore as you are, I would be feasting on you and pounding you into this mattress until they could hear your screams in Wales."

"Brinder," she rasped, desire thudding as she reached for him. "Please...touch me." She ached for him like they hadn't just screwed each other senseless.

"Do you believe me?" he pressed, his intense gaze practically boring into her very soul. "Honor, answer me."

"Y-yes," she sighed on a stutter, suddenly very tired.

"Good girl," he smiled. "Now, have some more water and let me hold you."

Honor dutifully drank from the proffered glass, and then watched in fascination as he downed the rest of his, his Adam's apple bobbing. How was that so freaking sexy? And what alchemy did he practice that one moment he was a sex god, making her cry out in ecstasy, and the next he was a caretaker, cleaning her up and ensuring she was hydrated?

Brinder wiped a stray trickle of water from his chin then dropped his arm so it rested casually against her, his knuckles intentionally grazing her side. The glint of his piercing and the tattoos on his arm competed for her overstimulated attention.

Her conscience screamed at her, joining the party. "Brin, I," she began awkwardly. Why was this so difficult? "I just wanted you to know...before, when I, you know..." she attempted, too shy to say the actual words. "Those were real..." she trailed in a shaky whisper. "I wasn't acting."

Brinder's gorgeous hazel eyes, so mesmerizing against his lightly tanned skin, crinkled at the corners, the side of his lips tilting up. "I know, baby."

Chapter Thirty-Two

Honor

Why was his voice so darn sexy? Seriously? Brinder Desai was a walking, talking aphrodisiac.

"Tish?" he asked, a touch of vulnerability on his handsome face. "Were those really your first orgasms? Nothing before then?"

She nodded. "First ones"—she swallowed nervously—"not self-given."

Now a satisfied gleam replaced the vulnerability. "I'm glad it was with me."

"Me too," she whispered.

"I own your firsts, Tish." He pierced her with a steady hazel gaze, lips quirked in a devastating smile.

Holy wow. Who was this self-assured, hot, dominant, gentle lover? Never in her dreams had she even hoped to experience sex like this with someone like him. Perhaps it was for the best their exploratory teenage sex hadn't held a candle to what had just happened. If he'd been capable of all this back then? She probably would have allowed him to tie her to his bed permanently, and she'd have eagerly thrown away her career just to be his sex slave.

Honor giggled a little at the thought.

"Care to share with the class, Miss Wheatley?" He grinned at her.

"I was just contemplating what it would be like to be tied up in your bed as your sex slave."

Now his gaze darkened, his smile fading into what could only be called a smolder as his eyes devoured her.

"Shift over." The low grumble of his tone was almost too much. She was tempted to push him on his back and impale herself on his enticing length.

He raised a brow and Honor recalled his enjoyment of being in charge in the bedroom.

She complied, wondering what he had in store for her as she moved toward the middle of the bed.

Then he surprised her by lying on his side, tugging her down and against him so her bottom was nestled against his cock, which was still semi-hard.

"You have no idea how much that fantasy of you tied up in my bed will live rent-free in my brain until I can replace it with the real thing." Honor shuddered at the implication of his words. "But, right now, we need to rest that pretty pussy."

He wrapped his arm around her, resting it between her breasts. Her nipples wanted to restart the party. But the rest of her body? Pleasantly exhausted.

Still, her hand twitched, longing to feel the slide of him within her grip. And she wanted a closer look at that piercing.

Curiosity nagged at her as they rested in contented silence. Eventually—as almost always happened—she gave in.

"Your, uh," she paused, trying to summon an air of casual interest, but completely unable to turn over and actually look him in the eye. "Your piercing—how long have you had it?" Her voice actually broke on the last word, like a prepubescent boy. *Mortifying.*

She felt more than heard the chuckle from Brinder. "A long time. I was getting a tattoo in Vegas and just...decided to do it. We were definitely a bit tipsy."

"Did it hurt?" She idly played with his fingers, a wave of arousal coursing through her at the mere thought of his dick.

"It did." Brinder was blunt, and Honor couldn't help a sympathetic shiver. Noting her reaction, he added, "Not horrible, but certainly a fleeting pain."

"Did a male or female do it?" Yep, those were her cheeks, burning in embarrassment.

This time he laughed louder, squeezing her hand. "It was a male. Same guy who did the tattoo."

"Why is that so hot to me?" *Oh, shi...itake.* "That was my outside voice, wasn't it?"

Honor closed her eyes and relished the decadent rumble of his amusement.

"Not sure 'hot' is how I'd describe it. More like...businesslike. This is his livelihood. He wouldn't jeopardize it by inappropriately fondling a client's junk. Besides, his wife also works in the shop, and she was tiny but scary." He tugged her closer. "Like you," he added, pressing a kiss to the sensitive area under her ear, causing her to squirm against him.

"Unless you want me to pound you into this mattress again, I'd hold still." He canted his hips against her backside, reinforcing his meaning as he stroked along her arm with the backs of his knuckles.

"Then don't nuzzle me in places you know are going to turn me on," she replied primly on a giggle.

Suddenly something he'd said about his piercing sunk in. "You said 'we.' You were with someone?"

"Yes," he replied, voice so soft but firm. "My ex."

"Ah," she managed, wrestling with the empress of jealousy monsters clawing at her guts. "You got the piercing for her." Not a question.

"I got the piercing for *me*." He kissed her temple. "Honor, baby, the piercing wasn't about Kira or for her. I'd always been intrigued by them. Had a college buddy with one and he said the pleasure for him and his partners was off the charts. So I did it. And, yes, I was tipsy."

Another kiss on her temple, this one lingering. Empress eviscerated. The jealousy knot unraveled. In its place was the bizarre shock that Brinder truly had built an entire adult life in their absence from each other. Rationally, it made sense. Of course he would. So had she.

But being confronted with evidence of all the things she didn't know about him? It bothered her—even more than the thought of him with Kira. Or Ross. Or Laurel. Or anyone, for that matter.

Determined to relearn him, Honor trailed her fingers along his tattoo, tracing the pattern of his inked sleeve.

"And when did you get this?"

"I started it in college with some symbols that reminded me of... home." His breath hitched on the word 'home.' "Then I added to it over the years, always with personally meaningful images."

"Like what?" She pulled his arm out a bit to examine the intricate black ink artwork.

"Around my wrist is the profile of a lion, which, as you know, is the symbol of England, along with this stylized St. George's Cross." He pointed to the ink on the inside of his wrist. "After med school I added the caduceus." Honor traced the medical symbol with her forefinger, noticing the rise of chills on his arm as she did so. "The G is the Georgetown University logo, with its signature Hoya Saxa cheer inked around it."

He stopped suddenly and sat up, eyes serious, forcing her to rotate to her other side so she could see him fully. "Everything I have on my arm is intensely meaningful, Honor."

She smiled back softly, loving that Brinder, who was such a deeply ingrained part of her heart, was so new to her in other ways. "Tell me about more of them, Brin."

He swallowed, pointing to the crest on his outer biceps. "The Cheltenham College crest." He smiled at her. The town where they'd met, as Year Nine students. He kept going. "Some connecting artwork just for continuity." He turned his body toward her, motioning to the design on the ball of his shoulder that stretched front to back—three lions back-to-back on a circular abacus. "The state emblem of India for my father's family," he explained, voice cracking—along with her heart —as he mentioned Dr. Desai. Honor knew from her parents that Brinder and Rahul had been estranged for almost as long as she'd been apart from him. "The lotus flower, also for India, but also because the lotus is a symbol of strength, resilience, and rebirth."

"Beautiful," she murmured, fighting the urge to run her tongue along it, and settling for her fingertips instead. "This ox?"

He paused with a sharp inhale, as if pained, then continued, softly. Carefully. "It's for Luke. It's the symbol traditionally associated with the disciple Luke in the Bible."

"Why is it wearing a stethoscope?"

Brinder chuckled. "Well, because Bible Luke was believed to be a physician, just like my friend. And I loved the idea of my stubborn ox of a friend immortalized this way. It's whimsical...but accurate." Brinder's eyes were sad again. "He was a great man. I got it a few months after he passed."

Attempting to change what was clearly a painful subject, she pointed to another—a dove holding a gem with JS in its facets. "That's for Tiercy's daughter, my goddaughter, Jemma. Her name means 'precious stone,' but in some cultures it also means dove."

"That's so beautiful, Brinder. Your arm is a canvas of meaning."

"It is." He nodded, then reached over and tucked a loose strand of her hair behind her ear. Chills danced across her body at the tender touch.

"And this one?" She ran her fingers across the simple arrow that took up most of his inside forearm.

"It's uh..." He reached his other hand over to hold hers momentarily, briefly stroking the skin on the back of her hand, and then dropping it back to his side. He licked his lips, staring at the tattoo, slowly lifting his eyes until they affixed to hers—intent, serious...sad. "It's a Tiwaz rune. The first tattoo I ever got."

"What is it? What does it mean?" she asked, and then waited patiently as he seemed to struggle for an answer.

"The Tiwaz rune is a powerful Viking symbol of bravery," he paused, "and honor."

CHAPTER THIRTY-THREE

BRINDER

Her eyes filled with tears and then spilled over.

"You—you have a symbol for me?" Her voice was barely a whisper, her lower lip trembling.

Brinder gathered her into his arms, pulling her onto his lap and slowly rocking her. "Yes, baby. So I would always have you with me. Every time I'm writing or typing, or doing a procedure, I look down and I see the symbol for the bravest person I've ever met." He took a deep breath. "And the only woman I've ever loved."

She gasped, and her hand flew to her mouth to muffle the sobs that now wracked her body. "Brinder, I'm so sorry. So sorry," she wept. "I should have taken your calls. Answered your emails. L-let you explain."

"Sssh, baby. It's ok." He gently shushed into her soft hair, now messy from their lovemaking. Because that's what it was for him. Not just meaningless sex, which is what all his other encounters had been.

"It's *not* ok."

He shifted her back so he could look into her eyes. "It *is* ok, Honor. Because here you are, back in my arms." *Where you belong*. But it was too soon to say that last part aloud.

Before they could say anything else, a loud growl filled the air and he grinned at her sheepish smile. "Hungry?"

Honor tucked her head down, and for a moment, the shake of her shoulders led him to believe she was crying again. Until he realized...she was laughing. Hard. Silently. Her body vibrating from it.

And as was the way of a laughing jag, it was contagious, and he started laughing too. For long minutes they belly-laughed, her nestled in his arms. And he recognized...the moment was as emotionally cathartic and powerful as their earlier orgasms. Because both were the release of pent-up feelings, just in different ways.

When they eventually collected themselves, she sat back, gathering her hair in her hand and draping it over her shoulder. The curled ends rested against the top of her teardrop breasts. "I guess I worked up a bit of an appetite." She giggled, smiling at him so broadly he was absolutely sure she was made of pure stardust.

CHAPTER THIRTY-FOUR

HONOR

It was after midnight, and they sat in Brinder's kitchen eating grilled cheese on sourdough. He wore nothing but his boxer briefs, while she practically swam inside his T-shirt. What was it about wearing a man's clothes—particularly those of someone you were crushing on? Honor grinned at the mental note that this T-shirt would likely join his hoodie in her private collection.

She polished off her last bite and took a sip of the sparkling water he'd poured. "It's quite late, and you have to get up early for work," she declared, beginning to clear their plates. Brinder had long since inhaled his own sandwich.

"How do you know that?" he asked, handsome head tilted in curiosity.

"Because"—she waved a finger at him—"you're a creature of habit. You've always been an early bird, and the few mornings I've spent here have confirmed this is still the case."

"Really?" he grinned.

"Truly," she rejoined. "Tell me I'm wrong."

He threw his head back and laughed. "No, you're right, Honor. I like to get up early, work out, and then head to the hospital."

"So," she pronounced, bumping the dishwasher door closed with her hip, "it's bedtime for Brinder."

"And what about you?"

"I'm still adjusting to east coast time. It feels like early morning to me right now, even if I haven't slept. My internal clock is so freaking confused."

"Well, then, it's bedtime for Tish now too. Although anymore beauty rest for you and you'll be so devastating it'll hurt to look at you. In the best possible way," he teased, grabbing her hand and leading her to the hallway.

Honor's heart did a little tap dance. Lord, he was so freaking swoony.

Outside the guest room door, he paused. Honor could practically see his wheels spinning. Feeling bold, and deciding to put him—and herself—out of misery, she tugged him further along the hall to his own room. "You coming?" She motioned to the primary bedroom door. Where she planned to sleep. With him. In his bed.

"I think I did earlier." Brinder winked and gave her what could only be described as a salacious grin. Then his eyes turned serious. "You're sure, Honor?"

"Very."

Chapter Thirty-Five

He woke just before the chime of his alarm, his body conditioned to go from sound asleep to fully awake in moments. And, yet, for the first time in his adult life, Brinder didn't want to get out of bed. He was tempted to call in sick, but his work ethic would never permit it. Instead, he allowed himself ten extra minutes to luxuriate in the moment. Honor, peacefully asleep, on her side. Him...curled around her like they'd never been apart for thousands of days.

He stroked her hair, smiling as she mumbled in her sleep, smacking her lips and burrowing deeper against him. She was so petite, his frame engulfed hers. It stirred something primal in him, his delicate—but feisty—Honor lying serene and trusting within his arms. She wiggled again, pressing against him in her sleep, one hand fisted under her cheek.

He took the opportunity to catalog her, every touch of his eyes a lover's embrace. Her tousled light brown hair with its golden streaks. Her aquiline nose. The long lashes rested on cheeks that were less round than in their youth. The rise and fall of her breathing, powered by a heart made strong and sure from two different delicate surgeries performed by his own father.

And...that was enough to deflate the hard-on he'd awakened with.

Reluctantly, he peeled himself out of bed, careful not to jostle Honor as he slid his arm out from where it rested under her pillow. Carefully, he shook away the pins and needles resulting from the long-held position. Then, because he could, he pressed a soft kiss to her cheek.

"Have a wonderful day, Stardust."

Her lashes fluttered, but her eyes never opened. Brinder smiled at her curled up in bed—*his* bed—practically disappearing inside his T-shirt, sheets rumpled around her legs. She'd always been an acrobatic sleeper. He wasn't the only one whose basic habits hadn't changed.

He crept into the bathroom and began his day, his smile as big as the hope in his heart.

The hope—and his good mood—continued as he strolled into the administration suite, whistling. He was going to triumph over this mess. Prove his worth and his...well, his *honor*...to Agnes and the rest of the team.

"Someone's in good spirits today," a voice called from across the suite.

Still smiling, he stepped into Agnes's corner office. In his time at St. John the Evangelist Hospital, he'd only managed to beat her into the office once. And that was only because she'd had a flat tire. Which she'd changed in the pouring rain and still managed to only be ten minutes behind him.

"Good morning, Agnes."

One pale eyebrow went up. "I'll say it again. You're in a good mood today." She scanned him in a manner comparable to a medical assessment.

"I am," he replied, feeling full of beans and optimism.

"Any specific reason?"

He paused, then decided it was now or never. Last night, as he'd grilled the cheese sandwiches, he and Honor had discussed the rudiments of a plan for their fake dating. Well, it might be fake to Honor, but it was totally real to him. And by the time they were through with that ruse, he was confident it would be real to her too. He couldn't help but grin. Then there was also his "other" assignment. The one where he got to be her guide on her sex-plorations.

He quickly stifled that thought. All things considered, it would be beyond bad form to pop a boner in Agnes's office.

"As a matter of fact," he cleared his throat, "I've recently reconnected with someone special in my life. And I'm feeling really good about it." There. Not a lie at all.

He hated having to 'fake' something he truly was feeling, including lying (ish) to his new boss. That extended to not being fully upfront with Honor about his feelings. But he also didn't want to scare Honor away. Even though he suspected she was falling back in love with him the way he was with her.

Now, both pale eyebrows lifted in her unlined forehead. Once again, Brinder was impressed that she had accomplished so much at such a young age. And Agnes was barely getting started. He wanted to be a part of that journey. To make a difference, the way he and Luke had always hoped.

"And you're dating?"

"Yes. And before you jump to any conclusions, we didn't begin anything until after I, uh, ended my, uh...thing, with Laurel." He fought the wince at any reference to that psycho, and forced himself to stand still. "We'd been emailing and texting, talking on the phone, but no flirting. Just old friends who reconnected." Brinder really did loathe having to lie to Agnes, but there was no other way to do this and shield Honor's reputation. "She's..." He paused, thinking of how to frame it in a way that supported Honor's dignity. "She's had something shoddy happen to her, and needed some time away as things settled." That was an understatement, but also the truth. "I offered for her to stay with me."

Agnes just watched him, her poker face giving him absolutely nothing to gauge her thoughts.

"And, um—" He halted, hating that his palms were now sweating.

"I really care for her." He let out what he hoped wasn't a visible shaking exhalation.

"Your friend is staying with you and now you're dating?" Agnes probed in her medical diagnostician voice. Brinder could see how she'd been a shrewd ER doc prior to earning her master's in healthcare administration.

"Yes." Christ, his mouth was bone dry. This was it. She either went for it...or the whole thing would be bodged.

Agnes was quiet for long moments as she studied him. Eventually, she nodded and gave him a small smile. "Good. I'm glad you have this support. I know it's been a rough week, and I'm sorry for that."

His head dropped briefly, in sheer relief that she'd believed him. And also that he had her support. Once again, he had the sense she knew more about Laurel than she was saying.

"Thank you, Agnes," he said, and meant it, grateful his boss was a class act.

"My pleasure. I like you, Brinder, and I like your work. I believe, as I said when I offered you the position, you have the potential to do great things here."

"Thank you," he repeated, realizing that if he didn't get out of there quickly, he might cry tears of relief. "I'm just going to grab my tea and then head to the surgeons' lounge."

Agnes nodded and then started to turn back to her monitors. "Oh," she called over her shoulder, "make sure you bring your friend to the fundraising dinner this Saturday."

Chapter Thirty-Six

Honor

Honor was ensconced on Couchie, working on her screenplay. This had been her passion project for more than a year—something she'd pursued quietly, not telling her parents, her agent, her friends...anyone, really. Except for Crispin. And that was only because he'd read the words on her screen over her shoulder before she even realized he was there.

Unfortunately, it then became an obsession for him. He wanted to know her vision for it. Was constantly lobbying to read more. And it was all part of an exhausting push from him to eventually direct it.

Honor rolled her neck and stretched. She'd awoken not long after Brinder had left, her body still fighting the time change, her blood humming with the need to write. To create. In fact, sex with Brinder had proved a powerful muse.

She scanned her laptop. It was the most she'd written since before her ugly breakup with Crispin, which had drained her energy and dried up her normally insatiable desire to write.

The hours had flown by, and before Honor knew it, it was close to four o'clock. She'd barely moved except to make herself a salad for lunch from Brinder's fully stocked fridge. He hadn't gotten a food delivery or gone shopping since she'd been there, so Honor determined that Brinder was not only a gym rat, but a serial healthy eater as well.

Detouring through the kitchen on one of her trips to the bathroom, she'd scanned his cupboards for something salty to eat. Shark week was coming, according to the calendar and her body. Honor couldn't help but smile at the contents. The man didn't have anything remotely junk-foody at all. This must have been part of Brinder's evolution as an adult, because the teenage version of him adored all manner of sweets. And he'd been such a beanpole, he could consume whatever he wanted in whatever amount he wanted, and not gain an ounce. Unlike her. At just a smidge over five feet, there were only so many places for calories to land.

Honor's stomach gave a ferocious growl. The lack of tasty treats for someone about to bravely surf the crimson wave was definitely something they'd have to remedy if she was going to stay.

No, not *if* she was going to stay. She was absolutely staying. At least for a while. But only for the fake dating slash reputation rehab for both slash sex tutelage deal they had forged.

Right?

Putting her laptop aside, Honor leaned back and closed her eyes, picturing Brinder over her, the bliss on his face as he slid into her. The cords of his neck straining as he exploded with his release. The rumble of his laughter. The way he took care of her.

And then there was this morning. She'd been barely awake when she'd heard—and felt—him stir behind her. His dick was awake before Brinder was, she suspected, recalling how it felt when she'd pushed her rump against him to entice him into continuing what they'd started the night before.

Crispin had never liked morning sex, grumbling about bad breath, so they never did it then, especially given the likelihood of missionary sex. And if she got up to brush, he'd say the mood was broken.

Whatever.

Because this morning, all she could think of was kissing Brinder, any thoughts of sour breath—his or hers—rendered moot. She wanted to fuse her mouth to his, just as they'd done yesterday.

But Brinder, clearly not wanting to 'wake' her—she was, after all, a good actress—merely held her. She could feel his gaze on her, and she'd been about to open her eyes and act on the lust building in her body, when he'd eased out of bed. Then... he'd gently kissed her, calling her 'Stardust.'

That needed some explanation.

After allowing herself a few pouts about her unsuccessful seduction—she'd have to work on that...for the *role* obviously, not for herself—she was inspired to write a new love scene in her screenplay.

Sometime later, she stretched again and glanced at the clock. It was just before six and her stomach growled angrily. Since she hadn't changed out of Brinder's T-shirt, nor done anything beyond brush her teeth and wash her face, Honor hopped in the shower, shaved everything that needed shaving, and then threw on her favorite pale pink sundress. It had a high halter neck—which she preferred since it flattered her bustline—a fitted waist, and a skirt that flared out slightly just above her knees. She dusted on some foundation and bronzer, lined her lips, and put on a coat of mascara. She was just clasping her favorite silver loop earrings when she heard the door.

"Honey, I'm hooooome!" Brinder called out, causing her to giggle.

"In the bedroom, dear," she called back.

Brinder appeared in the doorway of the guest room, causing her breath to stutter. *Cheese and crackers*, that man was truly a Hottie McHot Pants. No other way to describe it.

"Woman," he continued with the playacting, "what are you doing in this room? I told you that you sleep where I sleep. Except for when we *don't* sleep." He waggled his eyebrows, then took a couple steps into the room toward her, suddenly serious. "You look beautiful, Honor."

Her pink cheeks didn't need any blush, Mother Nature handling it for her. "Thank you," she smiled shyly.

"You, uh, you could move your things into my room," Brinder offered, and Honor swore she saw a matching blush rise up his neck.

"I didn't want to presume," she replied, suddenly overcome with an inconvenient case of nerves. It wasn't like she hadn't considered moving her things, but it just felt...big...to shift her things into his space.

Brinder gave her a wide smile she was sure was responsible for panties disintegrating from Baltimore to Charlottesville…and beyond. "Honor, I've had my mouth on your pussy. Presume away."

Now her cheeks really flamed. Then a laugh burst from her, and she held a hand to her chest. "Oh my gosh, I can't believe you just said that out loud."

He grinned. "You can believe I did it, just not that I said it out loud?" His smile softened and he held out a hand. "C'mere, Honor. Please."

As if pulled by a magnetic field, she crossed the room, stepping into his outspread arms, which he promptly wrapped around her. She rested her head against his chest, breathing him in.

That feels good.

She sunk into the embrace, where they stayed for wordless minutes. Eventually he leaned back, peering into her eyes. "What do you say we take advantage of your pretty dress and make your first big appearance? I made reservations for seven o'clock at a tiny Italian bistro I love."

Honor's stomach bottomed out. The idea of facing the general public was nothing less than overwhelming. In fact, it was terrifying. It wouldn't take long after she was spotted for the vultures to be alerted and begin gathering, especially with the proximity to DC and its large media market reporters. They'd circle, diving in to peck at her, harassing her relentlessly.

And Brinder? He had no idea just how ugly it could be. Sure, he was exposed to her parents' fame. But in their teen years, they were both largely buffered from it by school and by the privacy of her parents' extensive Cotswolds property.

But to go out in public and have a meal? Even with her private security detail—who'd had very little to do in the last several days other than ensure no one got to her at the condo or the Graces'—they'd be besieged.

Honor knew she had to do it. Part of this PR campaign was to be seen in public, smiling and thriving, not hiding away. What worked for a few days would now only add fuel to the fire. In absentia of her presence, the story would morph ugly tentacles, none of which would be true or flattering in any way.

She dropped her head, resting it against Brinder's broad chest. Their height difference was so pronounced that, in her bare feet, she barely reached the middle of his chest. It was tempting, oh so tempting, to just stay there in the sanctuary of his strong arms. And maybe tempt him to bring her to ecstasy again with his own special sex magic.

"Baby, are you alright?"

Her tummy did a flipflop at the endearment, one he'd always used back when they were a couple and had slid seamlessly into usage again.

"Yes," she managed. "I know I need to do this. But it doesn't mean I'm not dreading it."

He shifted back, scanning her face. "We can delay it."

Honor shook her head. "No. It's time. It's already been a few days. Benny was texting me today to ask about my plans. I told her we'd probably go out tonight."

"And she didn't ask for specifics?"

"She will." Honor looked at her watch, a delicate vintage platinum Hamilton—a gift from her parents when she won her Best Supporting Actress Oscar. "It's midnight there, but I'll text her. She'll have it vetted within twenty minutes."

Brinder gave her the name of the restaurant. Within fifteen minutes (Benny was nothing if not efficient), they had the ok to go. Her longtime detail—two retired Army Rangers who'd been alternating shifts—would tail them. One would stay outside of the restaurant, the other stationed inside at the bar. For the duration of her time at the condo, they'd been taking turns staying in an empty condo one floor down, on Honor's dime of course, which Benny had swiftly arranged once Ross's cottage flooded. This had turned out better than the initial plan, which had one of the guys sleeping on the cottage couch while the other was on duty staking the perimeter.

Now, it was all set. They'd be leaving within minutes.

Honor released a deep sigh that she felt to her toes.

Showtime.

CHAPTER THIRTY-SEVEN

BRINDER

Waves of nervous energy radiated off Honor. He glanced over at her periodically during the ten-minute drive. Her jaw was set, eyes straight ahead, her hands clasped in her lap. Only the bounce of her leg from the tap of her high-heeled sandal gave her away. Well, that and the periodic unclasping of her hands so she could rub her scar between the pink fabric neckline of her dress.

Soon, too soon, he pulled into the lot adjacent to the bistro. It was a quiet but delicious eatery. There were fancier restaurants in the area, but he'd intentionally selected this one because he knew the owner, who served on the hospital's Board. He'd hosted Brinder there for an after-interview meal on his first trip to visit Evangelist, and it was one of the most savory meals Brinder had ever consumed.

The restaurant, La Capaninna, was like its name implied—a cozy bistro with only about ten tables, as well as an adjacent wine bar. It would be intimate and manageable, versus a large restaurant with dozens of tables. As another plus, the security review confirmed easy egress from the back of the kitchen, which also led to the parking lot.

Scanning the area, he made eye contact with her detail. In his head, he referred to the built men as "Hans and Franz," from the old SNL routine Luke had made him watch on YouTube. While he knew their names were really Bauer and Grayton, he hadn't yet determined if those were first or last names. He just knew they oozed badassery and confidence. He was pretty sure they could drop someone with their bare hands. And that was good enough for him.

Bauer (or maybe it was Grayton) nodded at him, and then proceeded into the restaurant. Grayton (or Bauer) stayed in the other car—the town car that had transported Honor from the private airport to Ross's—presumably to manage the exterior of the restaurant should the need arise. Or maybe to assist in a quick getaway.

Brinder turned off the engine and walked around to open Honor's door. As she placed her slightly shaking hand in his, he gave it a gentle pump of encouragement.

Honor rose from his G-wagon, practically having to hop down given her stature. He kept a firm grip. When she looked at him with sad, vulnerable eyes, he fought the urge to deposit her back in the car and floor it out of there. Every instinct in him screamed to protect her.

Then he watched the most incredible transformation he'd ever seen. One minute she was small and practically trembling. The next? She rose to her full height—which wasn't much, but still—and raised her chin in the air. Shoulders back, she arranged her features into a mask he recognized from obsessively seeking out her pictures.

This wasn't his Tish. His Stardust.

This was a product. It was a performance. It was Honor, but not *his* Honor.

No, this was something altogether different.

Carefully, he tucked her hand under his arm and guided them to the front door, where Enzo himself was waiting.

"Welcome, Brinder and his signorina, to my little hut. I am Enzo, and it's my honor to host you tonight." Enzo, only a few inches taller than Honor, bowed over her hand with his signature Italian flair. Brinder bristled, growling softly, even though he knew Enzo was gay and happily married.

The restaurateur looked up and grinned, bringing Brinder in for a hug and a robust back slap. Given their height difference, Enzo, like

Honor, barely reached Brinder's chest. He couldn't help but chuckle at the man's enthusiastic greeting. Releasing Brinder after a few more back pats, Enzo turned back to Honor, and Brinder saw the moment recognition dawned.

Honor, looking like the girl next door rather than a world-famous actress, couldn't help but exude the star material that made her stand out from so many others. It may have been her family name that got her in the door, but it was her charisma and talent that kept her in the spotlight.

"Bella signorina, le mie scuse. Mi dispiace," he prattled in Italian, clearly flummoxed. "My apologies. I'm sorry. My friend told me he was bringing a guest for dinner. But he didn't indicate *who* his friend is." Enzo cast a baleful look at Brinder. "I hope you find my little hut acceptable."

Honor's polished smile slid into something more authentic. He could see her striving to maintain her poise, but the little Italian man was clearly vexed. And his thoughtful Honor would never want anyone to feel uncomfortable. She reached for his hands, clasping them in hers. "Grazie, Enzo. Il vostro ristorante è incantevole. Grazie per averci ospitato. Non vedo l'ora di cenare qui. Brinder dice che il cibo qui è eccezionale."

Brinder's eyes could not have been any wider. *She spoke Italian?* The only words he caught were 'thank you' and his own name. Once again, he was struck with the realization that there were many new facets to Honor for him to explore. He was nothing short of enchanted.

Honor turned and smiled at him. "I thanked Enzo for hosting us at his charming restaurant, and let him know you've already told me how outstanding the food is."

At his unspoken question, she continued, "I learned Italian when I stayed in Lake Como for eight months for a role. I loved it so much, I hired a private tutor after the filming. I'm not fluent, but consider myself conversational."

Enzo beamed like a proud papa. "Now, let me escort you to your table. I had planned to offer you a window seat, but perhaps you'd prefer our table in the alcove. It provides the most privacy," he offered with a sympathetic smile.

That's when Brinder realized not only did Enzo recognize Honor, he knew about the video scandal. A wave of ferocious protectiveness coursed through his veins. Brinder hated that Honor had been exposed, literally, to millions. He forced a calm breath to ease the blend of powerlessness and rage thrumming within.

For her part, Honor's smile stayed, but the natural sparkle in her eyes dimmed. *Fucking bollocks. If he ever found out who did this to her, he'd flatten them.*

"Thank you, Enzo," she replied. "I appreciate your discretion."

"Certo, bella regazza. Da questa parte. This way."

Within moments, they were seated. Thankfully, on a Wednesday night at seven, the restaurant wasn't full. There were a few tables of diners, with others seated at the bar. Including Bauer. Or Grayton.

I really need to figure out who's who.

So far, no one had realized they had a celebrity in their midst. Hopefully, it would stay that way for a while. It was unrealistic, however —as well as counter to the publicity plan—to assume Honor could remain unnoticed for too long.

Sipping a bold red wine, with her back to the room, Honor looked beautiful. And tense. She'd told Brinder before she rarely drank—the other day notwithstanding—but when the waiter offered a complimentary glass, Honor politely accepted.

"You don't have to drink it." Brinder kept his voice quiet, the low light and candles adding to the feeling they were alone.

"I know that. I'll have a few sips and then switch to water." Honor's small smile wavered.

"How are you feeling?"

"Honestly? Terrified that I'll see paparazzi flashes any minute. Or that someone is going to accost us and call me a slut."

"Honor," he sighed, heart breaking for her. "You're not a slut. And if anyone dared to call you that, Grayton and I"—he motioned to the man at the bar—"and probably also Enzo, would ensure they never did anything like that again. Enzo may be small, but he's feisty. Like someone else I know. In fact, you two may be scarier than Grayton and Bauer."

He smiled at her and heaved a small sigh of relief when she giggled.

She leaned in conspiratorially. "That's Bauer at the bar, by the way. Grayton is taller. He has a bit more hair than Bauer, and it's more gray. But don't tell him I told you that."

"Good to note." He winked at her and tucked those helpful differentiators away. It was difficult, generally only seeing them one at a time, but he'd do his best. He figured it would get easier the more he saw them anyway. Keeping that promising thought in mind, he relaxed further into the natural companionship he and Honor had always enjoyed.

CHAPTER THIRTY-EIGHT

BRINDER

Some other time, perhaps, they'd linger over a meal. But tonight they ordered quickly. For him, the Florentine steak. She ordered agnolotti piedmontese di magro. They both selected the caprese salad as a starter.

Of course, the waiter was starstruck, but Enzo had clearly coached him, as he refrained from acknowledging who Honor was. That didn't stop him from casting surreptitious glances at her, though.

As they waited for their entrees, his heart sank at the squaring of her shoulders. She was bracing herself.

Then inspiration struck.

"Did you know male pufferfish swim along the floor of the sea and flap their fins to create intricate circular shapes in the sand, then decorate those with shells and sediment to attract a mate?"

Honor paused with her water glass at her mouth. "What?" she whispered, confusion evident in her wide brown eyes.

He grinned at her. "Pufferfish with mating on their minds make those mystery circles, often taking them more than a week, to attract females. Once a female is fertilized, she lays her eggs in a nest at the center."

Honor placed her glass at the table. "And why are you telling me this now?"

Brinder shrugged his shoulders. "Just thought it was interesting."

"Ooookay," she drew out. "Um...that is *interesting*." She shook her head a little and picked her water goblet back up.

"It gets better. Dolphins get high off of pufferfishes." He grinned at the drop of her jaw. "Yep. Pufferfish release a type of toxin as a defense mechanism. Turns out, in small doses, it acts as a narcotic. Researchers have observed dolphins very gently handling pufferfish, causing them to release small amounts of toxin. Then, the dolphins pass the pufferfish around."

Honor's brown eyes were huge as she took in his fun fact—*thank you, Sir David and the BBC*—but now sparkling. The tilt of her head and the press of her lips were clear signs she was holding back laughter. He mentally patted himself on the back for pulling that much-needed giggle from her.

"After they take their puffer-hit, the dolphins then float near the surface, displaying unusual behavior and appearing to be...well...high." He lifted his shoulders, winking at her.

Honor snorted out a laugh and shook her head, finally taking a sip from her glass, which had been paused between the table and her mouth during his pufferfish trivia regaling.

Why stop now?

"Now octopuses, they're fascinating. Did you know they're petty and hold grudges?"

She dropped her head and shook it, a smile lighting up her face. When she looked back up at him from under those long lashes, his heart skipped about six beats.

Bloody hell. She was stunning. The girl he'd loved was now a beautiful woman. And essentially a stranger to him. He wanted to relearn her—all the new facets, habits, likes, dislikes. He wanted to explore every millimeter of her body with his mouth, his hands. Everything. Not to prep her for a film role. To make her his.

But first...she needed levity and distraction.

"Yep, I saw a documentary on it. Wild octopuses will launch shells, silt, even algae at nearby creatures, including fellow octopuses. I mean, this isn't an accidental toss. Oh no. These wily critters are clearly being aggressive, and likely territorial. Researchers observed them adjusting the direction and force of the throws.

"Also, female octopus have a unique habit. If a male tries to mate, and she's not in the mood, she'll let him insert his mating arm. She allows him to begin, but inches closer to him." Brinder took a leisurely sip of his water, appreciating Honor's riveted attention. Having learned a bit about dramatic pacing from her years ago, he was enjoying putting that particular skill in action now. "Then she'll strangle the unsuspecting, sex-addled male, killing him and feasting on him in her den for days after."

Honor placed the glass down on the table, a smirk playing at her lips. "Well, I'm glad we didn't get calamari."

Brinder chuckled and waggled his brows at her. "Oh, and back to animal mating rituals, since it's a fine dinner topic." She laughed softly and shook her head, and he fully delighted in watching her unwind and relax. "Adelie penguins are particularly romantic. The males will present pebbles to their desired mates as part of nest-building. It demonstrates their suitability as a partner."

Honor threw her head back and laughed, seemingly uncaring if anyone noticed. She was finally letting go and just...enjoying herself.

And there it is! Mission accomplished.

For now.

"How do you know all that?"

"You don't remember my love of BBC wildlife documentaries?" Brinder's tone was teasing, but inside he sank a bit. He used to bring over his favorite videos to watch with her as she recovered from her valve surgery.

Honor's answering smile transformed her face. She was radiant. And he? Well, he was breathless.

And falling beyond in love with her all over again.

"I do remember. You used to share your favorites with me. I especially remember the one on baby orangutans." Her eyes grew misty.

"I always wanted to go to Borneo or Sumatra to see them in their natural setting, but never had an opportunity."

"You still could," he offered, instantly imagining taking her there.

"I could," she mused, a soft smile on her face. "I love that you're still a Sir David devotee."

"I'm still a nerd."

"A handsome, thoughtful nerd." Honor reached for his hand, squeezing it gently. "I know what you were doing. Distracting me with random animal facts."

"Did it work?" He caressed the soft skin of her hand with his thumb.

She dropped her head and chuckled. "It did."

Their meals arrived, and as they ate, he regaled her with more facts. How male black widow spiders signal their arrival to females by shaking what are essentially their bums. Male mice, he shared, sing special songs in the ultrasonic range to impress the lady mice. He avoided bringing up how male giraffes taste the urine of potential mates to determine if the cows are fertile. He thought that might be crossing the dinner conversation line.

At her laughing encouragement to keep going, he had just finished telling her about how dairy cows can have best friends and started in on how the unique nose prints of dogs are like human fingerprints, when Enzo scurried over to the table, concern etched on his features.

"Brinder and bella ragazza, I have unfortunate news."

Honor's eyes darted to Bauer at the bar, who was making his way to them also.

"It seems the paparazzi have discovered your presence here. Mi dispiace profondamente."

Honor, to her credit, took the news like the class act she was. Placing her napkin on the table, she rose, kissing Enzo on each cheek. "Thank you for dinner, Enzo. It was delicious." She turned to Brinder. "We should get the check."

"No, bella. This is on the house. My pleasure to host you here. I am only sorry you have been disturbed."

Honor inclined her head and then nodded at Bauer—yep, now he could see the difference—who took the lead escorting her to the front door.

"Honor," Brinder reached for her. "Let's go out the back."

"No," she shook her head. "The point was to be seen. So let's be seen." Her brow wrinkled. "Unless it's too much, which I'd understand. I can go with Bauer and Grayton, and you can leave separately."

"Absolutely not. We are in this together."

Honor blew out a breath. "Then let's do this. Keep your head down or the flashes will blind you."

Brinder nodded, placing his hand against the warmth of her lower back—for her sake or his, he couldn't be sure—and guiding them to the door.

As soon as they crossed the threshold, flashes exploded around them. At least a dozen paps, plus a large crowd of bystanders, huddled outside the door and on the sidewalk nearby.

"Honor!" they clamored.

"Tell us about the video!"

"Who's your date?"

The crowd aggressively pressed into them. Fans and passersby held up their smartphones, taking photos and video. Brinder, having forgotten her advice in the deluge, blinked against the flashes. His need to protect Honor prevailed, and he tucked her under his arm, grateful for her diminutive stature so he could physically shield her from the onslaught.

Shocking him, Honor stopped and stepped a bit away from him, pasting on a magazine-worthy smile. Flashes exploded again. "I just had an amazing meal with a special, dear friend. Thank you." Then she nodded graciously and walked toward the curb, as if she didn't have a care in the world. As if a media mob weren't screaming her name and asking all sorts of unfortunate and inappropriate questions.

Grayton pulled up in the town car and hurried around to open the rear doors, muscling the paps out of the way and easing Honor and Brinder in before closing the door. The flashes continued to light up the night sky. The windows were tinted, but Brinder wondered if the burst of light from the cameras would still illuminate them.

"Fuck," he whispered on an exhale, shocked at the shaking of his hands.

"Just smile and try to act natural," Honor instructed from her seat, further from him than she'd been all evening. She clicked her seatbelt into the buckle.

"Hold on, ma'am," Grayton instructed. "As soon as we get away from this crowd, I'm going to pull some evasive moves, just to try to keep them from tailing us."

Brinder had the unique sensation of being in a Tom Cruise action film. Except...this was Honor's reality. And now his.

"They'll figure out who you are soon, if they haven't already." Honor spoke woodenly, eyes fixed straight ahead. "We'll probably lose them, but they'll be at your place within the hour."

Grayton made eye contact in the rearview mirror. "Bauer is taking your car back."

Brinder instinctively patted his pocket for his fob, finding the familiar lump. "How will he—" he started, confused.

Grayton smirked. "I noted where you keep your spare key when we did our initial recon Sunday. Bauer grabbed it before we left."

Huh. And he'd had no clue. These guys were *good*.

"But from now on, one of us will escort you to work, Dr. Desai," Grayton continued in a tone that brooked no argument. "At least until this is over."

Until this is over. Meaning the fake dating, of which both Bauer and Grayton had been apprised, being Honor's longtime detail and trusted friends.

Except this wasn't fake for Brinder, and he definitely didn't want his time with Honor to be 'over.'

He reached across the void between them and held her hand. She allowed it, but for the first time, she didn't return the grasp. Instead, she stared out the window, her face blanching—likely at the overwhelming phalanx of reporters and curious bystanders. She blinked a few times, then closed her eyes and breathed steadily through her nose as Grayton zipped and turned through the peaceful streets, eventually turning into his private garage.

Brinder scanned the garage as Grayton slid the town car into a spot. "Do you think they followed us here?"

"I lost the motorcycles, but it's hard to say for sure," the former Ranger responded noncommittally. "Let me bring you up the elevator and double check your condo. Once I clear it, I'll go back to the TOC condo. But Bauer and I will stay alert." He scanned Honor, only the flicker of concern in his eyes evincing any emotion. Then he added softly, "You're safe, ma'am."

"Thank you, Grayton," Honor replied with a tremulous smile. "I appreciate you."

"My pleasure, ma'am. Let's get you into the condo."

CHAPTER THIRTY-NINE

HONOR

Honor kicked her shoes off and sunk wearily onto Couchie. No matter how many times she faced the gauntlet of aggressive paparazzi—and it had been thousands upon thousands of occasions—it never got easier. Especially when others were caught in the crosshairs of the pandemonium of her celebrity.

"Here. I thought you might need some water." Brinder handed her a tall glass of ice water, which she gratefully accepted and immediately gulped down half. "I don't know about you, but I feel like I've just had an intense workout."

Honor rested the glass on one of the dark blue stone coasters. "It's a lot like a workout. Racing heart for an extended period and whatnot." She scanned his handsome face as he flopped down next to her, long legs stretched out. He looked exhausted. "I'm really sorry to drag you into this, Brin. It's the last thing you need right now."

Brinder shook his head. "You are everything I need right now, Honor."

The fake dating. The sex. That's all he meant. Probably. Likely.

She hoped not. But if that was the case, she was going to ride this

Brinder wave to wherever it took her, even if it broke her heart again. He was worth it.

Honor reached for his hand, placing hers over his and marveling—as she always used to—at the size differential. His darker masculine hand with its long fingers, juxtaposed with hers, so much smaller and paler, having inherited her mother's very fair skin.

Brinder's eyes tracked the movement.

She flashed to the vivid memory of his fingers on her—*in* her—and a hum of arousal built between her legs.

"I feel—" She halted and licked her dry lips, then drank a bit more water, trying to both ease her cotton mouth and collect her thoughts. "...Strangely horny."

His eyes crashed into hers. "It's just the adrenaline rush from earlier," Brinder scraped out, his voice like gravel.

"Maybe. But I don't think so," she whispered, building courage. "I've had many run-ins with the paparazzi. But never this particular reaction." Honor held his intense gaze. "There's only one difference this time."

"And what is that?" Brinder rasped, pupils blown wide, overtaking the intoxicating hazel.

"You."

Her bravado faltering, she added in a barely managed whisper, "I want you." A quick glance at the clock revealed it was just a bit after ten. "But I know it's late."

He gave her one of his swoony smiles, shifting to fully face her. "It's not too late, Honor."

Oh for that sentence to have two meanings. Not too late for them to have sex? Or not too late for *them*?

In her heart of hearts, Honor wanted both to be true. But for now, she'd settle for the former. As if having Brinder between her legs...*inside* her...required any settling. Far from it.

"Take me to bed, Brinder. Take my mind off all this. Please?" She heard her need in the huskiness of her voice. Felt it, a pleasant and hungry ache, in her core.

His teasing smile fell just a bit as he scanned her face. "You're sure,

Tish? That was stressful for you. How about I just hold you until the adrenaline fades."

"How about you hold me after you give me a different kind of adrenaline rush?"

Brinder chuckled softly and Honor reveled in the surge of sexual power as she noted the significant bulge in his trousers. He followed her gaze. "And here you were worried about being able to convincingly play a temptress."

In one smooth move, he grabbed her and tossed her over his shoulder. Honor shrieked, laughing and swatting at his back as he strode toward his bedroom with long, loping steps.

"Put me down, you goon!"

Blood rushed to her head, and she placed her hands on his bum and pushed away, trying to gain some equilibrium. *Great Gatsby,* his tush was firm, and so freaking sexy. She wanted to lick the cheeks, bite them, dig her nails into them as he thrust into her.

Desire jolted through her, settling at her core and making her even wetter. The devil on her shoulder incited her, and Honor gave in, squeezing those tempting sculpted cheeks and eliciting a hoarse bark of laughter from Brinder.

"Now you're in for it, Stardust." He strode to the upholstered bench at the bottom of his bed and carefully righted her, placing her just in front of it. Then he nudged it out with his foot so it faced at an angle.

Honor's breathing sped up, everything inside of her positively humming in anticipation.

"Clothes off. Now."

"I will if you will," Honor challenged, noting the rapid rise and fall of her own chest...and Brinder's, which seemed to be intensifying as well.

Not taking his eyes from her, Brinder undid the row of buttons on his dress shirt, then shrugged it off.

Mirroring him, Honor reached behind her neck and unhooked the straps of her dress, letting the front drop.

"No bra," Brinder practically wheezed, his eyes eating her up as her nipples pebbled in response.

Shiitake. All she wanted was the warm tug of his lips on them.

"Keep going," he commanded.

His hungry eyes swept over her as she found the hidden zipper and dragged it down. The dress pooled around her ankles, leaving her in just pink lacy boy shorts.

He made a ridiculously sexy growly sound and Honor swore his erection grew from its already impressive state. "I love those knickers. Saw them the other night in your suitcase, and they keep appearing in my fantasies of you. Now that I've seen you in them...fuck, Honor..." He dragged a hand through his hair, staring at her as if he had x-ray vision. Honor could have spontaneously combusted from the heat of his gaze.

"You now," she croaked, clenching her aching core.

With one hand, Brinder undid his belt, snapping it out from the loops. Dampness flooded between her legs. She wasn't sure she'd ever been wetter, and given the sexual pleasure he'd already given her, that was astonishing.

He slid off his trousers and kicked them away, then pushed down his briefs, his beautiful cock springing up, the head an angry red, the moonlight shining through the windows glinting off his piercing.

She started to push down her panties.

"No. Keep them on." His voice was barely a whisper, but held the command of a king as he lowered himself to the bench. "Come here, Stardust."

Honor was so far under his seductive spell, she barely caught the repeat usage of that nickname. She filed away a mental note to ask about it. *If* she even had any brain cells left after he scrambled her completely.

He adjusted the bench slightly so it was cantilevered diagonal to the bed. Brinder motioned her to him, and Honor licked her lips at the play of muscles under his tattooed skin. "Sit."

Wordlessly, Honor complied, facing him and starting to straddle him.

"Uh uh, Stardust." He made a turning motion with his forefinger. "Other way."

Beyond aroused, Honor complied, sinking onto his firm thighs, her legs shaking under the weight of her pulsing need. He tugged her back and she gasped as his erection pressed along the cleft of her bottom.

Brinder bent his legs, then widened them, causing her own legs to open indecently wide. "Beautiful," he growled, resting his hands on her shoulders. "Now look."

He nudged her chin up and she gasped at the image before her. Brinder had positioned the bench so it faced his wall mirror. Honor had admired it that morning. A gray, rustic wood frame mounted on black wrought iron that resembled the track of a barn door. Now? It was a mirror canvas, reflecting their embrace.

"Look," he rasped. "Watch how amazing we look together. You're going to see how beautiful you are when you unravel for me."

Honor moaned. Whether from anticipation, the image he painted, or her own ratcheting desire, she couldn't discern. Perhaps all of the above.

He reached around her and caressed her bare breasts with both hands, fondling her nipples and tugging oh so gently. Honor couldn't help but moan again, this time deeper and breathier. Her own arousal sounds were amping her up as much as his. It was glorious agony and she needed his mouth so badly.

One hand stayed, rolling and tugging, and when he shifted the other hand off of her other breast, she almost cried out at the loss.

Brinder watched her in the mirror, the passion etched on his face softening into something so tender, tears filled her eyes. Slowly, tenderly, he dragged the tips of his fingers along her scar. One, two, three times. Chills erupted across her skin.

"Honor," he whispered, "I am so sorry you had to go through this. Part of me hates that your pain is what brought us together all those years ago. But I'm also a selfish bastard. And I will forever be grateful for any force of the universe that brings you to me."

Heart pounding, her throat thick with unshed tears, Honor placed her hand along the back of his. "Sometimes, what's on the flip side of pain is more than worth the pain itself."

"Sometimes?" His hold on her tightened infinitesimally.

"Sometimes," she whispered. "Definitely in my case," she added, running her fingers over the graceful terrain of his hand.

She felt, rather than saw, his hard swallow. "Keep your hand on mine. Don't move it."

Mirroring his slow, soft benediction of her scar, he dragged his hand from the center of her chest, down her abdomen—which jumped at the touch—and then to the top of her boyshorts. Honor ignored the urge to suck in her tummy, to reposition so the softness below her bellybutton wasn't so poochy. It was frightening and freeing how easy it was to ignore that urge, giving in to the feelings and emotions swirling about her instead.

The cadence of her breathing kicked up again. It was unbearably sexy to watch him explore her, her own hand following his. *Touch me there. Please*, she willed internally, desperate for his fingers on her where she needed them.

He skated his fingers down, dragging them to the top of her mound...then stopped.

"Please touch me," she begged, aloud this time, pressing down with her hand to signal her needs.

"Sssh, baby," he murmured. "I'll take care of you. I know exactly what you need."

Then, with sultry, glacial movements, he slid his hand where she needed it, pressing on her clit through the lace.

"Yessss," she breathed, her hips canting forward to chase the almost hedonistic feeling.

He sketched his fingers lightly along her seam, still on top of the lace.

Take them off! she screamed inside. "More. More," she begged aloud.

His chuckle tickled her ear as his lips brushed the sensitive skin below, but she felt the kick of his hard cock against her and knew his arousal matched hers.

His left hand deserted her breast and Honor whimpered again at the loss.

"Patience, Stardust."

He dragged the lace between her legs to the side, then slid his fingers so they were resting just outside her pulsing opening. Returning to his ministrations on her breast, this time a bit rougher, he pulled a moan from her so intense, it would have been embarrassing if what he was doing didn't feel so freaking mind-blowingly amazing. Then he slipped two fingers inside of her.

"Watch," he commanded again, his voice soft, almost reverent, as her eyes fluttered shut.

Honor's head lolled against him as she fought to obey his sexy order. It was almost too much. His hand inside her lacy shorts, hers on top, shifting in sync with his motions, his other arm loosely banded about her as he tortured her nipple.

"Brinder," she cried out as he gathered her wetness on his fingers and then circled her clit. She was so close. More pressure. She needed more pressure. It was...right there.

But he kept the pressure steady, a slight smirk dancing on his face.

"Relax, baby. Trust me." Then he...

Removed.

His.

Hand.

"Noooo," she cried out, grabbing his hand and trying to force it back beneath the lace.

This time he did laugh, dropping a kiss on her shoulder.

"Why?" she begged, still grasping him.

"Have you never been edged, Stardust?"

"Nooo." She wasn't even embarrassed at her whining. She was too frustrated at her elusive orgasm. Her entire adult life, they'd been too hard to come by—ha...pun intended—and for him to tease her like that...it felt...cruel. "I don't like it," Honor added petulantly.

She saw the rise of his eyebrows in their reflection.

"Oh, I think you like it. And then you'll *love* it. You'll beg me for it."

Her eyes clashed with his in the mirror, and he had the nerve to chuckle again.

"Sadist," she muttered, and he laughed even harder.

"Take your knickers off, baby. I'll help." He lifted her slightly off his lap, releasing a groan as she inadvertently pressed harder into his cock.

Good. Let him be in agony too.

It was tempting to ignore his order, but something deep inside told her the best was yet to come.

She almost laughed again at her second internal pun, but then he grabbed the edge of the lace and tugged down hard, ripping the fabric as he dragged her boyshorts off her with one hand.

"I liked those," she lamented.

"I *loved* those," he growled. "And I'm buying you a dozen more in all different colors."

She started to reply, but only a gasp emerged as he slid two fingers inside her, scissoring them.

"Brinder!" she cried, clenching against the glorious intrusion.

"Work your hips over my hand, Honor," he gritted as he slid another finger in and tugged on alternating nipples. "You are so fucking wet. Let me hear my pussy squelch."

Honor ground against his hand, pressing back against the pressure he was creating as he glided his fingers in and out of her. Within moments, her arousal accelerated even higher than earlier, and she panted, chasing her release.

"I need...I need," she chanted, barely able to think against the glorious assault of his fingers.

"I know. I know, baby," he whispered, tracing the shell of her ear with his tongue and tugging gently on the lobe.

"Brinder, I need to come," she moaned.

"Soon, baby. You're doing so good. Look how pretty you are with my fingers in your pussy."

Honor dragged her focus back to the mirror and groaned. The sight of Brinder's fingers disappearing inside her, her legs stretched out and her nipples straining for attention, was filthy and decadent...and she never wanted it to stop.

She thrust her hips against his hand. If she could just...tip her hips a bit more...she could graze her clit against the heel of his hand. That was all it would take.

"So close, Brinder. Please let me come."

Then, realizing she wasn't powerless in this, Honor leaned forward and reached behind her, grasping his cock. She gasped at the new angle, grinding down on his hand.

"Fuck," he gritted out as she marveled at the silky hardness of him. She clenched against his fingers inside her as she teased his piercing.

"Fuck!" he cried, throwing his head back. Still working her over, he removed himself from her grasp. "Ok, baby. You win."

Carefully, he eased his fingers out, the sucking sound so dirty and arousing Honor almost asked to hear it again. Almost, but didn't. Because before she could utter a single sound, he bracketed her hips with his hands and lifted her. Then with delicious, agonizing slowness, he impaled her on his cock.

They both groaned as he fully seated himself inside her.

"So full," she moaned.

"Christ," he managed. "You are choking my dick, Honor."

Honor squeezed her internal muscles.

"Ah, baby...wait...not yet. Just...watch us."

The image reflected in the mirror burned itself into her core memories. Wrapped in his strong arms, her hands grasping them, his cock buried deeply in her. Stretching her. It was indecent and exhilarating. Sexy and salacious.

She loved it.

"Do you see how your pussy loves my cock, Honor? Look at it, so stretched. So wet. I can feel you fluttering. You're so close, baby." Brinder's voice was low, entrancing, sexy...an embrace in and of itself.

"I need you, Brinder," Honor choked out, rocking against him. "Fuck me. Now. Please!" she begged.

Her agonized cursing must have done something, because then he was thrusting.

"Help me, baby," he bit out and she rocked against his thrusts. "Yes, that's it."

And then she lost herself in their frenetic passion. The only thing she was aware of was the press of his hands on her hips as he lifted her repeatedly so she could come down hard on his cock. He slammed up into her, again and again, pounding deep inside.

The orgasm that he'd been keeping intentionally at bay built higher and higher. She clenched as hard as she could, everything in her centering on her pleasure.

"Yes, Brinder! Yes, yes, yes," she panted, as his thrusts grew harder and more erratic. "Please. So close," she rambled, desperate for release.

"Watch," he commanded again, a gritted breathless order.

Honor fought to comply, forcing her eyes to focus on the mirror.

Meeting her gaze in their reflection, he slammed her down, slapping her pussy at the same time.

"Fuuuuuuuck!" she screamed, everything inside of her exploding. "Yes!"

Everything pulsed as she felt a rush of liquid.

"Honor...fuck!" Brinder thrust hard...once, twice...then again... crying out her name at his apex. And then collapsed around her.

For long moments, the only sound was their erratic breathing. Brinder stroked her hair, her arms, her thighs, her belly. Then wrapped her in a reverse hug so tight and so tender, tears trickled from the corner of her eyes.

"I missed you," she whispered. His only response, the tightening of his arms around her.

Chapter Forty

Brinder

After they both caught their breaths, he'd gathered Honor in his arms and carried her to his bed, where they now lay, bathed in moonlight, her head tucked into his shoulder, one shapely leg draped across his, a pale pink fingernail tracing lazy patterns on his chest.

Happy.

This is what happy felt like.

It was late, but a contented buzz hummed under Brinder's skin. He wasn't even close to tired. He never wanted to close his eyes...because he never wanted this moment to end.

Honor Wheatley. The girl who ran away and broke his teenage heart.

Now she was a woman, and back in his arms. Where, as far as he was concerned, she belonged. Forever.

He frowned. Did she share the depth of his feelings, or was this simply a temporary sanctuary for her? An inflection point—albeit a sexy, meaningful one—in her life. And then she'd move on.

Brinder's breath caught, heart pinching in his chest at the thought. In just a few short days, Honor had managed to retake possession of his very soul. And he needed her to know that. Needed her to know she was his everything. As she was all those years ago, almost from the moment he met her. And now, she'd reclaimed her rightful place as the sole owner of his heart.

He was just about to confess all this when she spoke.

"You hurt me." It was barely a whisper, her soft breath dancing on his skin.

He startled, turning on his side so he could see her better. His heart bottomed out deep in his belly at the thought of causing her pain. "Honor... I'm so sorry. I know I wasn't"—he swallowed past the massive knot in his throat—"gentle earlier, but I didn't mean—"

She reached out and put a staying hand on his arm. "No, not when you—when we"—she blushed—"did that earlier."

Dizzying relief whooshed through his veins.

"Then what—"

"When you never reached out. After. It gutted me."

"Honor," he started, searching for the right words. "I had no idea why you disappeared. Just a note—which I didn't even receive until your parents collected your things from Cheltenham." Brinder's voice shook from years of accumulated sadness. "You hurt me too."

She rested a hand on his face. "I know that now. I'm so sorry, Brinder."

They stayed like that for long moments, just staring into each other's eyes, regret for the lost years pulsing around them.

"So stupid," she muttered, a small frown appearing between her brows.

"Sorry?"

"It's all so stupid. I should've just found you. Confronted you. Then you would've explained. I would've believed you. And we wouldn't have lost almost twenty years."

He pulled her off the pillow and back on his chest, kissing her forehead.

"Don't do that, Stardust. The past can't hurt us anymore. Not unless we allow it. Besides, we each had a journey to be on. If we'd have stayed together, maybe you wouldn't be the award-winning actress you are. You definitely wouldn't have taken a role that had you in Indonesia for almost a year. The role that won you a Best Supporting Actress Oscar and launched your career. And I wouldn't have met Luke or Tiercy and Jemma. Wouldn't have built my career the way I have." He paused, reflecting on the life he had, then whispered, "Wouldn't be who I am today."

"I wouldn't be embroiled in a sex video scandal, though," she added.

"And I wouldn't have a Board chair crawling up my ass," he replied matter-of-factly. "But we can't regret the things that make us who we are, that make us stronger. We can grieve the life we thought we'd have. But then we move on and celebrate the one we earned."

She shifted, resting her chin on his chest. "We hurt each other so much, Brinder."

"Ancient history, Honor. It's time to let that go." He pressed another kiss to her forehead. "Don't think about our time apart as anything other than the intermission between the first and second acts of our relationship."

"There is so much I want to ask you about," she whispered. "It's strange, how you can be so familiar to me and yet so new."

"Then get to know me again. Ask away." He laced their fingers together, resting them on his chest.

"Tell me about Luke."

Brinder closed his eyes against the wash of pain at the mention of his late friend.

"I'm sorry," she blurted. "I shouldn't have asked."

"No, please don't apologize. I just...needed a moment." Brinder took a deep inhale. "It was the first day of med school at Georgetown and I was wound tighter than a spring. My father had just found out about my marriage...though not my divorce. Rahul had some, well, let's just say some *strong* words for me.

"That evening, I ended up on a basketball court, just shooting the ball over and over again. A guy I recognized from my university apartment complex jogged onto the court with his own ball. We started playing one-on-one. He had me laughing within five minutes. I think he could tell I was stewing about something, but he never pressed. Just helped me work out my frustrations on the court." Brinder blinked back tears. "That was the start of it. Instant friendship.

"We ended up rooming together the rest of med school. And when we both matched at Georgetown for our residencies, we shared a town house. By then, he and Tiercy had long been an item, and I'm pretty sure I dated all her friends at one time or another." He cracked a sheepish grin.

"Like Ross," Honor prompted, something unreadable on her face.

"Yes, I dated Ross for a hot second. But we definitely didn't click as a couple."

He paused. Even though he'd done his fair share of therapy, it never got any easier talking about this. "Luke and I ended up at the same hospital in Baltimore. It's so odd to think about that, but I got an offer first in the radiology department. Tiercy was from the area and wanted to stay, so Luke ended up taking a job in their ER. I was," he paused, swallowing down the tears, "with him when he died."

"I'm so sorry," she murmured, eyes filling with her own tears.

"And not long after, Tiercy found out she was pregnant. I was there for them."

"For Tiercy and Jemma." Honor scanned his face, reading him and clearly seeing what he was too cowardly to tell her. "You fell in love with Tiercy."

It wasn't a question.

"Yes," he confirmed. "At least, I thought so at the time." At Honor's confused frown, he clarified. "With hindsight, it was really just infatuation, mixed with what I thought I was meant to do. Take care of my best friend's widow and daughter."

"Did she—did she love you, too?" Honor's eyes darted back and forth between his, like a truth detector.

"As a friend, yes. Nothing more. And when Cole came barreling into her life, she fell head over heels in love with him, even though she fought it."

"And that hurt you?"

"Not really. Maybe for the briefest bit. But you can't be around Tiercy and Cole and not see that what they have is, well, it's something really special." He stroked up and down her arms, not sure if the calming motion was for her or him.

"And you never told Luke about us?"

"No," he confirmed. "It hurt too much at first." He saw her wince in sorrow and caressed her arm with soothing circles. "I did my best to bury it. Apparently, I was never fully successful. It became my own private grief. So stupid."

Brinder huffed an ironic laugh at a memory. "Once, he asked me if I knew you. He noticed the way I froze in the grocery store checkout line when I saw you on a magazine cover. It was far from a normal reaction. I just said you reminded me of someone, and left it at that. Luke wasn't the kind of guy to press. He'd meet you where you were and let you get there on your own.

"Except...I never got there. And I will always regret that he never knew a fundamental piece of who I am."

Honor tilted her head, sympathy emanating from her expressive eyes.

She was quiet for a minute, but he knew better than to think she was finished. He remembered this about her—her relentless curiosity, the byproduct of her smart and inquisitive mind.

"And you and your dad are still estranged."

Again, not a question. But Brinder knew a leading statement when he heard one. "Yes," he replied, the weathered edges of his anger long worn down.

"What happened? I mean..." She paused, shifting so both arms rested on his chest, her chin resting on her clasped hands. "I pretty much know your dad's side of the story."

Brinder's eyes flared at the thought of whatever vitriol his father had unleashed. And the fact that Honor had been there to hear it.

"Just from overhearing my parents," she added. "My dad has a theater actor voice. He doesn't know how to speak softly." She smiled sadly. "I know your dad wasn't happy about your choice of college. Or med school. Or your marriage."

"Or my divorce. Or my choice of specialty. Or where I chose to live. Basically, I'm a walking disappointment to him."

"Oh, Brinder, I don't think that's the case."

"Honor," he replied, rubbing the soft strands of her hair between his fingers, "I *know* so." He grimaced, recalling the many shouting matches over the years, until he'd finally cut off contact shortly before completing his residency. "He was so angry when I didn't go to his choice of university or medical school. I only went home a few times during med school, and each time, we fought. After I eloped with Kira, I told Mum. Who told my father. Who went ballistic."

"What happened with Kira?"

"I met her in undergrad at Georgetown. She got into med school at Hopkins. She's fucking brilliant." Brinder watched as Honor's eyes darkened. In jealousy? "We actually got married on a spontaneous trip to Vegas. Everyone around us was taking graduation trips. Neither of us had family nearby, with no one coming to our ceremony. So Kira and I took off for Vegas. And, yes, we were on our way to drunk when it happened. Such a cliché." He shook his head at the memory. "Within a couple months, we knew it was a mistake. Her med school was in Baltimore. I was staying in DC. We wanted different things." He gave a rueful smile. "It was over almost before it began. And we parted amicably, thank God."

"Where is she now?"

He grinned. "She's one of the top pediatric neurosurgeons in the country. And she's remarried. Last I heard, she had two children."

"Wow, impressive." And, yes, that was definitely jealous snark in Honor's voice.

He tugged her up higher on his chest, pressing a kiss to her pursed lips until she softened and let him in. Christ, she tasted delicious. He wanted to kiss her for hours.

She sighed against his lips and he smiled, ending the embrace and kissing the tip of her nose.

"Ask it, Honor."

She pinned him with a glare, then sighed again, vulnerability rolling off her in waves. "Did you—did you love her?"

"No, not really. Not like I should have to marry her."

"Oh," she replied, biting her lower lip.

"My heart belonged to someone else. It wasn't mine to give her. And she knew it."

Honor's eyes flared and then twin tracks of tears spilled down her cheeks. He gently thumbed them away, then kissed along the pathway.

"Sorry," she whispered, gathering herself.

"Don't apologize. I think we're both experiencing twenty years of emotions in a very short timeframe."

Suddenly she stilled, eyes widened.

"Wait, you told me you got your piercing in Vegas." She frowned. "Was that the trip where you," she bit her upper lip then continued, "married Kira?"

He cradled her face in his palm, unable and unwilling to stop touching her. "Yes. All part of the same trip."

"I see," she whispered.

"I'm not sure that you do. Honor, what I did with Kira—our ill-advised marriage—was not about any feelings of love we had for each other."

"Just lust." Her frown deepened.

"Lust, yes, but not love. Not really. More…convenience. Hell, other than the first night of our marriage, we didn't even have sex again because my piercing had to heal. But," he paused, tracing a finger along her check, "we liked each other. We were friends. There was just no…no '*there*' there, if that makes sense."

He moved his hand to her hip, giving a comforting pat. "As much as it makes me look like an insensitive ass, I promise what I felt for Kira wasn't even close to what I know love should feel like."

"I'm sorry to pry."

"Pry away. There's nothing I want to hide from you."

She smiled softly, watching him with sad eyes. "Will you finish your story about your dad?"

He snorted a small laugh. She truly was relentless. And he loved that about her.

"Not much more to say. When I went home for the last time—during my first year of residency—and announced that I was studying interventional radiology, not cardiac surgery like he'd assumed," Brinder halted, a flash of the scene bursting behind his eyes, "he exploded. Screamed at me."

"I can't imagine your dad screaming." Honor shook her head slowly, clearly shocked.

"Sadly, I don't need to imagine it. It happened way too often from when I was eighteen until I finally cut things off with him about six years ago."

"I'm so sorry," she whispered.

"I'm not. Not anymore." He kissed her softly. "Subject change? Is it my turn to play Spanish Inquisitor yet?"

She laughed and rolled off him, propping herself up against the headboard. "Turnabout is fair play. But, it's definitely past both our bedtimes now. How about we pick this back up tomorrow?"

He glanced at his clock. Twelve-thirty. He was going to be hurting tomorrow.

But rediscovering each other was beyond worth it.

CHAPTER FORTY-ONE

HONOR

The insistent chirp of her phone startled Honor from a sexy dream. She and Brinder were walking along the rugged Welsh coastline near her home. He'd just picked her up, wrapping her legs around his waist, to carry her back to her home. He was kissing and touching her, strumming within her the powerful ache of desire.

Her phone chirped again and Honor groaned, stretching, then freezing in place as she realized one hand was between her legs. Honor bit her lip, recognizing she'd been touching herself in her sleep. She was soaked. And so freaking horny.

She rolled onto her back. There was no way she could function. She needed to do something to assuage the ache between her legs.

She'd rarely been successful bringing herself to orgasm this way, with just her own fingers and no toy. But something told her this time would be different. Honor gathered up some of her arousal, then rubbed firm, tight circles on her clit, moaning softly in the quiet of the condo. Before long, her orgasm was building. Remembering the previous night, she gave herself an experimental swat, groaning aloud at the increase in sensitivity and intensity.

Holy wow…

She increased her tempo and the pressure, sliding a couple fingers inside herself. Within moments, she was crying out as her orgasm crested, her heart thudding.

"Now that," she sighed, giggling, "is one way to start the day." She rolled sideways and swung her legs over the side of the bed, remembering the missed call. The display on her phone told her it was just after nine. *Shidoobie.* She'd slept right through Brinder getting ready for work and leaving.

And no wonder. After what he did to her body last night…

Honor shivered in recollection.

Her phone chimed again, startling her. She yelped and the phone slipped from her fingers onto the plush gray rug.

Chuckling at her own silliness, Honor slid off the bed. The mattress was pretty high off the ground. Befitting a giant like Brinder, it was not as easy for wee people like her to navigate.

Dropping to her knees, she retrieved the phone. "*Shiitake.* This man knows how to select comfy rugs." Honor sighed, squinching her toes in the plush fibers as she stood.

She woke up the display. Two missed calls from Ross. Instinct had her insides twisting with worry. "Please don't be bad news," she whispered, throwing on her robe before hitting Ross's name on the display to return the call.

"Well, good morning to you," Ross drawled. "And how is my favorite Oscar-winning actress-slash-bestselling author friend?"

Honor snickered, the sound of Ross's carefree voice always bringing a smile to her face. "Aren't I your only friend who matches that description?"

"Eh," Ross snorted, "details. Anyhooooo, Benny and I have already talked. We poured over the coverage of your date last night. It looked like you two were really an item."

Honor's mind, its thoughts thoroughly heading only one way, tracked immediately to a flash of her legs splayed wide across Brinder's lap, his cock slamming into her.

"Uh…I—yes," she stammered.

"Hang on a sec," Ross chirped. "Methinks I need to switch to ye olde FaceTime."

"Why are you talking like you're at a RenFest?" Honor giggled.

The call connected over to FaceTime and Ross's tired but always stunning face filled the screen. Reflexively, Honor returned her grin.

"Who knows." Ross sighed, rubbing her eyes. "Random shit keeps pouring out of my mouth. My precious miracle has decided sleep is for weaklings, at least at night. And I am clearly a weary, rambling weakling, because I am desperate for six solid hours of nocturnal slumber."

"I'm so sorry. That stinks."

"It does," Ross affirmed with a wink, "but it's so worth it."

Once again, as often seemed to happen with Ross, Honor pushed down a surge of envy. In the last year, Ross had transformed from a man-eating commitment-phobe to a happily married mother of two. It was mind-blowing the difference one trip around the sun could make.

Honor had honestly never reconciled her life with marriage or a child. But holding little Leah in her arms the other day...well, it must have sent some sort of primal, biological morse code to her aging ovaries.

"And now back to the reason for this call." Ross's teasing tone pulled Honor from her thoughts. "As I was saying, you certainly looked happy tucked under the muscular arm porn of Dr. Desiiigh."

Why, yes, Ross. And I also looked happy with his cock filling me up. Honor's cheeks burned bright at the sexy memory.

"Aha!" Ross shouted. "And this is why I needed to see your face. What was that? Spill it, Wheats." Ross waggled a finger at Honor, her phone bouncing at her boisterous movements, causing a slight vertigo sensation.

"Simmer down, Ross. Nothing to tell. And hold your phone still or I'm going to puke."

"Don't distract me, Wheats. I've said it before...you are a lying liar who lies. And you should never, *ever* lie to your Fairy Rossmother, Honor," Ross chided, a sly smirk on her face. "Did your date with the deliciously dreamy Dr. Desiiigh have a happy ending?"

Honor, who'd relocated to the kitchen in search of sustenance and, more importantly, coffee, froze with her hand perched over a thermos. A note from Brinder read: "*Enjoy.*" Three x's and o's were scrawled beneath the single word.

She sighed in swoony appreciation...and then Ross's words sunk in.

Honor snorted. There was no use hiding it. After working for months on her memoir with Ross, Honor was well-accustomed to her bulldozing ways. "You are as subtle as a jackhammer."

"Methinks someone got jackhammered last night. Did my MiniWheats get *frosted*?" Ross's smile was huge. She was clearly enjoying herself.

"Aaaand I'm back to FaceTiming with Henry the Eighth," Honor giggled, uncapping the thermos and breathing in the heavenly aroma of her coffee.

"I prefer Anne of Cleves. She was a badass. At least in *Six* she was." Ross pinned her with a look—well, as much as one could on FaceTime. "Spill it, Cupcake, before I drive over there and yank it out of you. It's the vast, empty time between coffee and cocktails—also known as the shoulder season of libation joy. I'm tired, I'm cranky, and I need to do something other than be a human cow with a precious but voracious parasite sucking at my once lovely boobs around the clock."

Even that image didn't manage to unravel the baby fantasy currently being embroidered in Honor's active imagination.

"Ok," she relented, both to put Ross out of her misery, but also because she wanted to share this bonkers situation with her friend. "Yes, Brinder and I, we've, uh, been intimate."

"You don't say," Ross drawled. "I figured that out as soon as I saw his love bites along your neck."

Honor slapped a hand to the column of her throat, rushing to the hall mirror and peering at her reflection. Yep. All along her neck were the aforementioned love bites...and the classic contusions of hickeys.

"Oh, shiiit-ake," she gasped, getting a better look at herself. Her hair could rival Medusa's. Her lips were puffy. And hickeys. *Everywhere...*

"You have the undeniable look of a woman well-fucked," Ross pronounced. "And I say, 'well done, you.'" She offered a dramatic slow clap.

With one last passing glance in the mirror, then remembering his *other* mirror, Honor blushed and retreated to the sanctuary of Couchie, her coffee safe in one hand as she cradled her phone in the other.

"Well, how was it?" Ross prodded.

Honor allowed a smile to bloom across her face. "It was...amazing," she whispered.

"OK. That settles it," Ross announced. "I was already planning to see if you wanted a girls' day out with Tiercy and me. If I don't get out of this house, I'm going to lose what little mind I have remaining. So this is a win-win. Benny said you need to be seen again"—Honor couldn't help but wince at the thought of facing the swarm of paps—"and I want full details, in all their salacious glory, told in person so I can truly live vicariously through your sexual depravity."

Honor huffed out an incredulous laugh at her friend's teasing tone. "What makes you think what we did was"—she licked her suddenly dry lips—"depraved?"

"Uh, because I know Brinder. And I've heard way too much about his sexploits over the years. Duh." Ross waggled her brows lasciviously. "I'd be thoroughly *devastated* if it were otherwise."

Honor bit down a knowing smile. Maybe what they did wasn't depraved. But images of his pierced cock sliding in and out of her, him smacking her pussy to a gushing orgasm as he made her watch in a mirror...well, that was fabulously hot.

"Now you're thinking about it," Ross pointed an accusing finger at her. "Ok. Tide me over and just tell me this: he rocked your world, didn't he?"

Honor nodded, a sly smile on her face. Yep, Mona Lisa had nothing on her this morning.

"Mah girrrrl!" Ross cheered. "Alright, Wheats, way to tap that!" Ross's vibrant green eyes danced as she lowered her voice and looked around, probably checking to make sure Petey wasn't in earshot. "Just tell me one more thing until I drag the details out of you in person—is it true that he's pierced?"

Honor knew her cheeks were bright pink. She tucked her chin to her chest...and nodded.

"Shiitake," Ross breathed. "Dayum. I know he's my friend...but that's just hawt." Ross fanned her face with her hand. "OK,

MiniWheats, Tiercy and I will see you at ten-thirty...ish. Wear something cute. Cover Brinder's handiwork with some makeup. Or a turtleneck. And prepare to spill. The. Tea."

Honor laughed, ignoring the roil of unease in her belly about another appearance. "Noted."

"And meanwhile, I may jump Xan's bones for a quickie. Assuming we can get a minute of privacy."

"You do that." Honor laughed again, shaking her head at her irrepressible frienditor.

"Oh, I intend to, my friend," Ross murmured. "I intend to."

CHAPTER FORTY-TWO

BRINDER

Brinder sighed quietly. He'd been compartmentalizing all morning, forcing any thoughts but the work in front of him out of his brain.

He'd just finished a needle biopsy of a breast mass on a young woman. Brinder had reviewed her chart as part of the safety check prior to surgery. Just twenty-four. Too young, although there was never a good age for this type of diagnosis. No, the results wouldn't be back for a bit, but his well-trained instincts told him she would be facing a battle —a winnable one, but a challenging one nonetheless.

For whatever reason, this young lady tugged at his heart. She was younger than Honor, but her brown eyes and petite build reminded him of her. And he knew it would wreck him to see Honor suffer in any way.

He remembered her recovery from valve surgery, as vivid as if it had been last week and not twenty years ago. He wondered if she'd ever had a mammogram. She was a bit young for it. But then again, so was the woman on his treatment table.

Brinder eased onto the rolling stool behind him, reaching for her shaking hand.

"Am I ok?" she whispered, tears forming on her lashes.

He made sure to use his most calming tone. Brinder was known for his bedside manner, which he drew from the weeks when he'd helped care for Honor post-surgery. "Yes, Lina," he soothed. "The uncomfortable part is over. Now we wait for your results. I put in a stat order for you." He rubbed the back of her hand.

"It's cancer, isn't it?" Her voice wavered and the cluster of tears fell onto her cheeks.

"We don't know that. But it may be."

She took a shuddering breath.

He guided her into a sitting position, still holding her hand as his favored nurse, a wizened Filipino woman named Magda, passed her a tissue. "And it may not. But, as you know, it looks suspicious. And if it turns out to be positive for malignancy, I will personally make sure you are connected with our top oncologist and the best breast surgeon." He stood, feeling a thousand years old. "Right now, my prescription is to head home with your dad and relax as best you can. We'll be in touch as soon as possible with your results, and then we can talk through any necessary plan of action with your GYN."

He patted her hand and then squeezed, knowing that simple action couldn't ease her worries, but hoping it conveyed his emotional support. He marveled, as he had many times over the years, at how some patients just inched their way into your heart. He knew he'd be following her case, for his own sake if not hers.

Plus, he'd become casual friends with her father, Gideon, via Ross, who dated him before she was with Xander. Ross and Gid were still friendly. Even Xan had reluctantly come around. Hard not to. Gideon was a stand-up guy.

"Get dressed. Magda will help you. And I'll go see your dad."

Brinder exited the procedural suite and headed to the small waiting room, immediately spying Lina's father.

Even after having met him last year at Ross's birthday bash, the men bonding over good Scotch and shared appreciation of travel to unique places, it still surprised him that he was friendly with Gideon O'Grady, the retired Gold Glove winning third baseman. Word in sports media was that he would be a shoo-in for Cooperstown on his first ballot. Gid had to be in his late forties, but didn't retire until he was forty-three, sharing with Brinder that he'd been unwilling to part from the lure of the game he loved so much until his knees screamed at him to stop playing.

Brinder had visited Gid in New York last fall when he attended a medical conference in Manhattan. That led to an invitation to watch a World Series game in Gid's private box. They'd stayed connected since then, sending occasional texts about sports or life.

When Brinder took the job in Charlottesville, he'd messaged Gid, sending a picture of his celebratory Scotch—a Laphroaig Limited Edition twenty-eight-year-old single malt he'd picked up for a cool eight hundred dollars to toast his new position. The same bottle Honor had consumed half of the other day.

Brinder chuckled, remembering her drunken ramblings, then refocused his mind away from the delectable and devastating Honor Wheatley.

Gid's younger daughter attended law school at UVA. When her GYN found a lump and sent her for a mammogram, Gid had called Brinder, asking for his help. Within two days, Brinder had Lina in his procedure room.

And now it was time to update Gid.

The former major leaguer had been staring out the window from his perch on the requisite vinyl and laminate chair, so ubiquitous in waiting rooms.

"Gid." Just one word and Gideon's head whipped in his direction.

"How is she?" Gideon's almost-black eyes searched Brinder's face, worry etched in his expression.

"Getting dressed. She'll be out shortly and you can take her back to her apartment."

"What"—Gid swallowed, his Adam's apple bobbing—"what did you see in there?"

Brinder sighed, rubbing the back of his neck. "It does look suspicious, Gid."

His friend's shoulders slumped and Brinder dropped into the chair next to him. It was a small waiting room, one of two they had in this area of the hospital, and he'd ensured no one else would be placed there. Gid had enough to worry about without having to deal with overzealous, if well-meaning fans. Brinder spared a quick thought for Honor, who would probably really like Gideon. They could bond over the painful glare of an unforgiving spotlight.

"But," Brinder added, "we can't know for sure until the labs are back. Which should be this afternoon at the latest." Usually, preliminary results were available in one to three days, sometimes taking up to a week. Brinder wasn't going to allow that to happen here.

Gideon sighed deeply, staring back out the window. "What if it's cancer?"

"If it is, then we treat it. She's young and strong."

"She still has a year of law school left. Can she take classes if she's in treatment?"

Brinder put a hand on his friend's shoulder, ignoring Gid's subtle swipe under his eyes. "Let's not get ahead of ourselves. But, if it comes down to it, she should absolutely be able to manage treatment and school. However, Gid, truly…let's slow your roll. I know it's hard not to scramble for immediate answers, but we'll get her taken care of, and we'll do it quickly. Right now, you need to breathe. Lina's going to need her dad."

Brinder rose, preparing to head back to the administration suite. Gideon also stood, and Brinder caught the wince on his face. "Knees still bothering you?"

"Getting worse," Gid gritted, bending to massage his right knee. "And I don't have time to deal with it."

"It may not give you a choice, brother. Those are two pissed off knees."

"Tell me about it," Gid sighed. "One thing at a time. Let's take care of Evangelina, and then I'll deal with my old man knees."

Movement in the corner of his eye caught Brinder's attention. "Here she is," he murmured, squeezing Gid's shoulder in solidarity and then turning to greet Lina, who fell sobbing into her dad's arms.

"Come on, princess. Let's get you home." The deep rumble of Gideon's voice, so rich with a father's love, caused a pang of sadness to radiate deep in Brinder's gut. Not even at Brinder's lowest moments had his own father ever shown even a third of the compassion and love Gid was displaying for his daughter.

As he had many times over the years, Brinder neatly compartmentalized the messy feelings about his father, focusing on the here and now. Which meant heading back to his office, catching up on paperwork...and maybe checking in with his sexy houseguest. He wondered what she was up to today. Hopefully it wasn't emptying the rest of his scotch after her run-in with the paps.

Shaking Gid's hand and giving Lina a hug, he guided them to a little-used employee exit the hospital used for VIP patients. Within minutes, Brinder was at his desk. Instead of finishing his charts, he gave in to temptation and tapped on Honor's name on his phone.

"Helloooo, you've reached the voicemail of that tart and sexy slut known as Honor Wheatley. Wheats is busy trying on half of a boutique right now. How may I assist you?"

Brinder released a much-needed laugh. "Hello, Ross. Does Honor know you have her phone?"

"Of course," Ross replied, and he could practically see the smirk in her voice. "She gave it to me for safekeeping after she left it in the last dressing room, leading to a robust game of Where in the Everloving Fuck is Honor's Phone?"

Brinder snorted. "I thought you were giving up cussing?"

Ross snorted right back at him. "I can't go cold turkey, Brin," she chided. "It's bad for my chakras."

Brinder shook his head, grinning at her saucy impudence. Ross Beaufort-Grace was a piece of work. But she was also a fierce and protective friend, something that eased his heart when he realized Honor clearly had braved another appearance in her PR battle.

"I take it you all are out and about?" He shook his mouse, waking his computer.

"Affirmative," Ross confirmed, and his stomach twisted a bit on Honor's behalf.

"How much of a shitshow has it been?"

"At first, it was a right royal mess," she replied, taking on an English accent. "Tiercy and I drove to your place after pumping so our hubbies can enjoy baby-milk-puke while we gallivant about town." Ross snort-laughed. "One of Honor's Hottie McHot Pants security duo drove us in the fancy town car."

It must have been Bauer. Grayton had accompanied Brinder to work, driving his G-wagon and leaving Brinder feeling like an emasculated passenger princess next to the buff former Ranger. Dude was jacked. And taciturn. Brinder didn't often worry about comparing himself to others, but Grayton was a specimen. After the drive, Brinder resolved to spend a bit more time lifting in the gym.

"What happened?" Unease trickled down his spine. He hated not being there for Honor.

"Oh, the usual malarky. A lot of yelling and camera flashes." Ross paused. "Some of the yelling was from me, until Tiercy clamped her hand on my mouth. Sorry, not sorry. That ass-pap was a total twatwaffle. Benny said Tiercy and I are already a meme. And we've gone *viral*." Ross positively chortled with glee. "They don't even know or care who we are. Apparently, some celebrity blogger saw it, set it to an edit, and now it's trending. A friend slapping a hand over a bestie's mouth is apparently entirely relatable." She giggled.

Brinder opened his web browser, keying in the terms he hoped would lead to the meme. "How do you know all this?"

"Oh, Benny's been texting Honor and me nonstop. The media are apparently loving the 'gal pals' spending time together, laughing and shopping. We even gave them great footage as ladies who lunch."

Bingo. On his monitor, the image of Tiercy's hand over Ross's mouth, both sets of eyes wide with laughter, brought a smile to his face. Ross was right. It was viral. Of course, the sordid underbelly of the web also was speculating on who these women were with the famous Honor Wheatley...and coming up with some nasty theories that centered on women, threesomes, and porn.

Out of caution for his blood pressure, which skyrocketed at some of the comments he'd scanned, Brinder closed the browser.

"Would you ask her to call me?" Brinder realized he probably sounded pathetic. But...it was true. He was whipped. And if anyone would figure it out quickly, it would be Ross. The woman seemed to have a personal—and unfiltered—radar when it came to sex and relationships.

"I can do you one better." Brinder heard rustling and the sound of voices, although he couldn't make anything out. "Oh, Honor," came Ross's trilling voice, "I have a caller for you on line one."

Good Christ, she was a hoot.

More rustling. The sound of a door. And then...

"Brin?"

Her classically trained voice, clear but low and husky, filled the phone. Brinder closed his eyes, gripping his armrest with his free hand to keep from launching himself from his desk chair and into his car so he could find her and gather her in his arms.

Where she belonged.

Once again, he'd struggled to get out of bed in the morning. It was so tempting to call in sick just so he could hold her. All damn day.

"Hey, Stardust. I was just checking in on you. This has been my first chance to catch my breath." His stomach chose that moment to announce its ravenous state in a ferocious growl. He glanced at his Tag. It was past two and he hadn't eaten a bite since the yogurt he'd hoovered in the physician's lounge that morning.

Her laugh, low and happy, carried across the line. "Was that your stomach I just heard?"

"Yes," he confirmed, the sound of her happiness causing both his mouth and his heart to smile.

"Well, never let it be said that I have the loud tummy."

"Oh, yours is even louder, which is all the more impressive given your wee stature. That makes it, like, twenty times as loud as mine when adjusted for body volume."

A cascading peal of laughter erupted from Honor, like singing church bells.

Brinder knew he had a goofy smile on his face. And he didn't fucking care.

"So you, Ross, and Tiercy are out gallivanting?"

"If you count shopping and lunch as gallivanting...then, yes!"

Brinder could practically hear the smile in her voice.

"That sounds dangerous," he teased.

How had he gone this long without her in his life? She'd slid effortlessly back into his world with an ease that should have frightened him—but didn't.

In fact, it exhilarated him.

"Tell me about it. Did you know Ross and Tiercy are a viral meme now?"

He heard movement, like she was shifting around.

"I heard. And just saw." More noise, and then a clatter.

"Sorry!" Honor called into the phone. "I'm still in the private dressing room—this thing is nicer than my bedroom—and I was putting clothes back on hangers. Then I dropped my phone."

Brinder chuckled. "I just wanted to hear your voice. I'm glad you're having a good day."

"Thanks, Brin. I am." She paused...and then he heard it in her voice. The same neediness he was experiencing. "What time will you be home?"

He glanced at the color-coded schedule his gift-from-God assistant, Amani, printed out every morning and placed on his desk. "No later than six."

"I can try to make us some dinner," she offered.

Now Brinder really laughed. "Has something changed dramatically with your kitchen skills in the last two decades?" Honor had been a menace in the kitchen, once burning a pot of three-minute ramen so badly her dorm kitchen stunk for hours.

"Hey!" she laughed. "I was just trying to be helpful."

"How about I order for us. You in the mood for Indian?"

"Always. Curry is my love language."

"I'll pick it up on my way."

"Sounds good. See you when you get home."

"Bye, Stardust. Oh, and when I get home, it's *my* turn to grill *you*."

"Oh...shidoobie," she laughed. "I'll gird myself."

"See that you do."

It wasn't until they disconnected the call that he realized...she referred to his condo as 'home.'

In spite of the eggshells he walked on at work, Brinder couldn't wipe the smile from his face the rest of the day.

Chapter Forty-Three

Honor

Even with the paps popping up out of thin air for almost the entire day—her only reprieve the dressing rooms of the handful of boutiques they'd visited—it had been a good day. A very good day.

She, Tiercy, and Ross flopped on Brinder's heavenly furniture.

"Omigod," Ross moaned dramatically. "This couch is ridiculously comfortable. I may love it more than I love Xander. Or at least close to as much."

"I know, right?" Honor grinned. "Don't love it too much. I don't want to have to throw hands for my Couchie."

Tiercy tucked her long legs under her as she nestled into one of the chairs. Good lord that woman was tall—a good nine inches taller than Honor. Ross's willowy bestie had worn adorable kitten heels and Honor had slid her feet into her favorite black wedge platform sandals...and still the height difference was enough to make Honor feel like a troll. She was starting to wonder if she should give up acting and find a nice bridge somewhere to hide under, where she could dispense riddles to unsuspecting travelers. "Couchie?"

"My pet name for this perfect beauty." She patted the buttery leather from her corner of Couchie.

"My dogs are barking," Ross announced, kicking off her strappy sandals. "Given the prospect of being ambushed by those stupid paps, my vanity wouldn't let me wear anything other than adorable shoes. But boy am I paying the price." She groaned and rubbed the lines marking her feet.

"Poor widdle sausage toes all cramped up," Tiercy teased, blue eyes sparkling with laughter.

Ross threw a pillow at Tiercy, stabbing a finger in her direction. "Not nice to bring up my sausage toes, Tierce." Then she snort-laughed. "I think they're even sausagy-er since I had Leah," Ross lamented, lifting a foot and waving it at Tiercy. "What do you think?"

"Get those things away." Tiercy swatted at Ross's feet, laughing.

"Also, I'm pretty sure I just made up a new word. Just call me Merriam. Or Webster." Ross waggled her brows, then grimaced. "My pre-lunch pumping session is wearing off." She reached for her full breasts. "Mind if I relieve a little pressure here?"

"Me too," Tiercy chimed. "My nursing pads are getting wet."

"Of course," Honor replied, suddenly feeling oddly left out of the nursing mommies group. "Can I get you anything?"

"I still have water in my bottle," Ross replied, reaching for the discreet black bag that held her pump.

"Ditto." Tiercy was already pulling her top up.

"Girl, you haven't been in town a week yet, and you've already seen our boobs way too much," Ross teased, then held up a finger. "Now, given that you are the only one of us in the room who isn't a dairy cow at the moment, would you please entertain us while we drain our milky sacrifices for our babies."

"Ross...gross," Tiercy snickered. "It's not a sacrifice."

"Have you seen my boobs these days? Droop city. That, my dear, is a sacrifice. But worth it."

Deciding it was probably better to change the subject before Ross got going on vaginal rejuvenation again—which she'd muttered about under her breath at one of the boutiques as she tried on a sexy number

—Honor jumped in. "What? Do you want me to sing? Dance? Perform a Shakespearean soliloquy? I'm at your service, ladies."

"The fact you can do all that is so unfair," Tiercy pouted.

Ross snorted. "Oh, Honor can*not* sing."

"Really?" Tiercy turned big blue eyes on her, shifting the pump. Honor couldn't believe how fast the bottle was filling.

"Truly," Honor replied, deciding that, as incredibly curious as she was, it was probably tacky to ask more about the pumping. "As my dad would say, my singing voice is best appreciated by the shower walls."

"Nope," Ross chimed in. "We aren't talking about that right now. Change of subject. I've been practically dying all day to ask you about," she motioned to her crotch, "the peen piercing."

Tiercy started coughing, hard enough that Honor jumped up and patted her on the back, handing Tiercy her water bottle.

Tiercy took long swallows, then wiped tears from the corners of her eyes. "Give a girl some warning, Ross."

"What?" Ross replied, eyes wide in innocence. "Honor and Brinder *got it on* last night...and she confirmed what I've always speculated." Ross dramatically stage-whispered, "Brinder's peen is pierced!"

"We got it on the night before, too. But yesterday was in front of his mirror," Honor added shyly...but also slyly. She knew how to pull a reaction from Ross.

"Well, yassss! I'll be hornswoggled!" Ross made a scene of fanning her face. "In front of a mirror. Daaaayum!" Ross smirked at her, teasing dancing in her eyes. "Sooooo, don't keep us in suspense. For all the bedsport I've enjoyed over the years, I've never been with a pierced peen. Was it as good as I've heard?"

A blush crept up Honor's neck at a particularly vivid memory of his pierced cock sliding into her, the sensation of it rubbing against her walls unlike anything she could properly explain. She opened her mouth, struggling to find the words. "Well," she eventually said, "suffice it to say...it felt freaking fabulous." *Holy wow* was that an understatement.

"Lawd...is it me or is it hot in here?" Suddenly, Ross turned to Tiercy, one eyebrow raised high. "Why don't you seem as shocked by the firsthand confirmation of the Pierced Desiiigh Peen?"

"I, uh," Tiercy coughed again, shifting in the chair. "I knew about it."

"Why didn't you confirm for me?" Ross shrieked, throwing her hands in the air. "Some bestie. I always want to know about the peen. You *know* this about me, Tierce." Her eyes widened. "Wait just a hot-damn second, missy. Do *you* have firsthand experience with it?"

"No!" Tiercy yelped. "I swear." She held up her hands in surrender. "Luke told me."

"And you kept it between you in the marital bed. Savage, Tierce. That's just cold savage."

"Sorry, Ross Ellen."

To Honor's eyes, Tiercy didn't look sorry at all. In fact, that was definitely a smirk on her face, accompanied by an equally 'not-sorry' shrug.

Tiercy held out her hand, which Ross grabbed with a fake pout and then grumbled, "It's a good thing you're cute, Tiercy Colburn," before leaning over to place a smacking kiss on the back of Tiercy's hand.

Tiercy giggled while simultaneously turning off her pump, then turned her attention to Honor. "So...you and Brinder, for realz, huh?"

While Honor would consider Ross a close friend, she'd only known Tiercy a few days. And, yet, she could see why Ross adored her. There was something so...kind...about Tiercy. Not only was she beautiful, she just exuded warmth. And her hubby? *Sheweeee*...Honor had only seen him once, but that man was devastatingly gorgeous. He was better looking than many of her leading men over the years.

But, in her humble opinion, still not as handsome as Brinder.

"I mean...yes?"

"You sound uncertain for a woman who's had his pierced peen in her. Repeatedly," Ross interjected, a knowing smile on her face.

"No, I mean...I know we're hooking up. I just..." *Don't know what it all means*, she finished in her head, unwilling to share the mental and emotional gymnastics she'd been torturing herself with since she first agreed to stay with Brinder.

"I get it. Relationships, especially where you have any kind of baggage coming in, can be tricky." Tiercy offered her an understanding smile.

See? She was so freaking kind. Honor got the sense Tiercy was referring to her own late husband and her struggle to let herself fully love Cole. Ross had shared some of it shortly after Tiercy got engaged, as they were just beginning work on her memoir. Then, as now, Honor was blown away by Tiercy's strength. Losing Brinder all those years ago gutted Honor, and that wasn't even the permanence of death. Honor couldn't fathom—didn't *want* to fathom—a world without Brinder Desai in it.

Ross stretched, rolling her ankles. "Ok, bitches. This has been an amazing day. But your girl here needs a little nap before Princess Never Sleeps begins another night in her reign of terror."

"You really should sleep train her Ross," Tiercy replied, her concern so obvious Honor was a bit jealous of their deep friendship. "I can help you. I did it with Jemma and again with Augie. It's a lifesaver."

"We'll see," Ross shrugged. "If she doesn't figure out her nights versus her days soon, I'll take you up on it."

Tiercy glanced at her phone. "Oh gosh! I didn't even realize it was close to four. We've been at this since before lunch! Cole probably thinks I've fled the country."

"Cole knows better than that. He knows you love his big D and would never leave it." Ross snarfed at her own joke.

"Nice, Ross." Tiercy shook her head, a smile playing at her lips. "But you aren't wrong," she added, an impish gleam in her eyes.

"Oooohooo...look who's got jokes," Ross rejoined.

"Not a joke," Tiercy giggled.

Honor stood, helping her friends collect their various bags. She stacked a few on her arms, knowing Bauer would help get the bags into Ross's car.

"And with that little seed planted in your fertile imagination, Honor, we shall commence to remove ourselves from your Brinder-and-the-Pierced-Peen Love Shack." Ross held out her arms. "Bring it in for a hug." Honor put her bag-laden arms around Ross, bumping her in the tush accidentally. "Sadly, that's the most action I've gotten in days." Ross laughed. "Group hug!" she called out, and then tugged Tiercy into the hug with them.

Wrapped in the arms of her friends, after a fun and healing day—

paps nothwithstanding—Honor had the distinct sensation of being very short...and very happy.

CHAPTER FORTY-FOUR

BRINDER

"Ok, general, I'm girded as instructed. Fire at will," Honor pronounced from her favorite spot on his couch. "But be gentle, as I'm not sure the last time I've eaten so much. Helllloooo, food baby," she murmured, patting the sexy softness of her belly and then smiling at him from under her lashes.

He grinned and shook his head as she released a throaty chuckle. He loved that particular laugh of hers. Carefree, but sexy. His cock liked it too, giving a kick in the shorts he'd changed into after work.

He'd been home for a half hour. They'd quickly devoured their meals—chicken biryani for him and a paneer tikka for Honor, plus some veggie samosas to split. Brinder poured himself a small nightcap. But Honor, still scarred from her bout with his expensive 'Brown Acid,' demurred, opting for a Nimbu Pani.

Brinder swirled his drink, watching the dance of colors and enjoying the smoky fragrance of his Old Fashioned. Meeting her gaze with a wink, he jumped right in with what had been on his mind all day. "I have to start with an apology."

Brinder hated to kill the mood before it really began, but he needed to get this off his chest, dread and embarrassment commingling in discomfort he hadn't felt in a long time. If ever.

"I am so sorry, Honor."

"About what?" Confusion filled her eyes.

"Last night, when we were together, I got carried away. I forgot to use protection. I was just so caught up—"

Honor held up a hand. "It's ok."

Her smile was relaxed, unraveling the knot in his belly that had been there since this morning when he realized what he'd done...or, more accurately, what he'd *not* done.

He hurried on, desperately needing to clear the air. "Are you sure? You know I'd never put you at risk. I test regularly, and definitely did after—" he didn't even want to say the name of his new nemesis "—her."

"Brin," Honor soothed, "I promise. It's ok. I was tested recently too. After...Crispin."

Brinder had to work not to scowl at that wanker's name. But there was one more part of this to clear up. "And birth control?"

Now Honor rolled her eyes. "I'd never put myself or my career in a position like that with an unwanted pregnancy."

His stomach roiled. Of course a pregnancy from this...whatever it was...would be a concern for her. *Unwanted*. As much as he wanted otherwise, he knew this arrangement was temporary, until the worst of the scandal for both of them passed, and his belly cramped at her words. But why did his heart soar when he thought about her pregnant with his baby?

And she clearly saw it, leaning forward to catch his attention, which had drifted into a thousand-yard stare out his windows.

"Brin, look at me." She waited until he could manage eye contact. "I'm on birth control. And I...I didn't mean to hurt your feelings. I just...I have this role coming up, and it's far outside of my comfort zone. I've worked too hard and too long to do anything to jeopardize it."

"I understand," he managed. And he did. But that didn't make it not hurt. And, yet, she was here with him now. He'd be damned if he wasn't going to take advantage of every precious moment with her.

Shaking himself out of any blues, he smiled at her. "You're

incredible." She opened her mouth to reply, but before she could form the words, he continued, "And you aren't getting out of the rest of this inquisition, Tish. Not after the grilling you gave me."

"Well then," she smiled, relief evident, "do crack on."

Brinder flashed a reflexive grin at the British cadence to her speech. Her decades abroad had definitely tampered with her American accent. And he loved it.

"You cursed," he blurted. Oh, he was absolutely failing on the smooth factor tonight.

"Pardon?" She tilted her head, as if she wasn't quite getting a translation.

"The other night. And also last night. When we"—he motioned between them—"had sex." *Made love.*

"Oh." Honor's cheeks pinked, something he'd always loved about her, but knew she detested.

"Oh?" he teased, beyond curious about her situational potty mouth.

"Well," Honor took a long draw of her Indian lemonade, clearly stalling.

"Out with it, Tish," he prodded, reaching out to tap her foot with his, and then giving into temptation and sliding it along her bare leg to her knee.

Her eyes flew to his, her cheeks even pinker. He watched her breathing escalate. Yep. She was getting as turned on as he was, and this didn't even count as foreplay. Not in his book.

"Ok, Gomez." She rolled her eyes like she was exasperated, but he saw the tilt of a smile on her pouty lips. "You know I've just never been someone who cusses. It has to be, or...well *I* have to be," she took a deep inhale, "worked up."

"Worked up." He took a sip of his cocktail to cover his smirk.

"Yes, you pain in the butt. Worked up. Either really angry..." she began, biting her plush lower lip.

"Or..." he led.

She met his gaze, brown eyes intense. "Or, apparently, really turned on."

"What does that mean? *Apparently*?"

"I, uh, I never had a reason to, um, let it fly like that. In bed. Before," she finished, cheeks so red he considered getting her a cold cloth.

Instead, Brinder moved from the chair to the couch, lifting her legs onto his lap. They were petite, like the rest of her, but toned and shapely. And smooth. So fucking smooth. She was still wearing a navy-blue sundress from her outing with the girls. It cinched at her tiny waist and the sexy rise of her breasts peeked out. He wanted to peel the thin straps from her shoulders with his teeth. And then make her curse. Again and again.

"So it's a passion thing."

She nodded.

"When you really get revved," he added, enjoying this.

"Yes," she groaned, clearly embarrassed.

"When you're just so turned on, when that pussy is so wet and aching and ready to—"

"Yes!" she yelped, swatting at him and laughing. "Stop! You made your point. Your amazing tongue—"

"And my big thick cock," he interjected, grinning.

"Yes, Brin, and that, too. You just..."

"Get you revved," he finished for her.

She rolled her eyes for the millionth time since he'd walked in the door. Fuck, he loved needling her. She was an easy and easygoing target for his gentle teasing.

"Now that we've settled that you have—"

"A certain set of curseworthy skills?" he prompted.

"—let's move on with the inquisition," she continued, brushing off her hands theatrically, as if he'd never spoken. But the sexy blush of her chest, neck, and cheeks told him everything he needed to know.

"Tell me about Wanker Crispin."

"That's not a question, Sir."

Sir...

Suddenly, the idea of her lightly bound and calling him that had his cock turning to steel in his shorts. He subtly (he hoped) pressed the heel of his hand to his crotch, hoping to calm the fucker down. *Not yet, buddy.*

"Would you please tell me about Crispin?" he revised, now rolling *his* eyes in fake frustration.

"There's not much to say," she began, nibbling again on her lips.

"There must be, given that you were together for five years."

Her eyes grew even wider. "How do you know that?"

"How do you think, Tish? You are a public figure. And I've been, shall we say, an interested party."

"An interested party," she murmured, a small frown between her brows.

"Ok. I devoured every and anything I could read about you," he blurted. Somehow she brought out the unsure and awkward teenager he'd long left behind. Such was the odd time warp he was in with her.

She startled him by bursting into laughter. "I don't know why, but that makes me feel rather...satisfied."

"Cruel, baby. That's just cruel," he teased. "Suffice it to say, I've tracked you and your career. Since," he paused, waving his hand in dismissal, "well...*since*. But that doesn't mean I don't want to hear about it from you directly. I have a slight suspicion the entertainment media and social platforms may get some things very wrong."

"Ya think?" One more epic eyeroll from Honor. She sighed. "I'll summarize, since I really don't want to give him any more of my time."

"That's fair," Brinder nodded.

"We met when my parents hired him to be a manager at their summer playhouse. During spring, they prep the performances. Summers are packed with shows on the main stage and our side venues. Fall is prep for next year. They take winters off for film roles, but still needed someone to manage the business. He has a business degree from Cambridge. And did a directing internship with the Royal Shakespeare Company at the Barbican in London, which is where my dad met him and later offered the position."

"Right place, right time."

Honor snorted. "More like right family connections and family money to grease the skids."

"So he worked for your parents?" Brinder prodded, insanely curious about—and jealous of—the twat who'd shared her life for many years.

"Still does. Even with the break up," she confirmed, but her eyes were troubled. "My parents were willing to cut him, but that didn't seem fair. He does a good job in the role."

"Why'd you break up?"

"He started pushing to direct. He had designs to do so for both the stage and the silver screen." She sighed, pinching the bridge of her nose. "Mom and Dad gave him a shot. And it was...pedestrian at best."

Honor rolled her shoulders, as if the mere discussion was knotting her muscles. "I felt bad for him, but instead of being in any way dissuaded by the lackluster reviews, he just kept going. He wanted to take my script and be the director. And I could act in it. He also wanted me to fund a production company. Big plans for Crispin."

"You have a script?" Another facet of adult Honor was revealed, like a surprise gift at the bottom of a Christmas stocking.

"Yes. I've been playing around with it for a while, but have really only gotten serious about it over the past year."

"For screen or stage?"

"I'm thinking screen. Only because I know my dad would salivate to put it on his stage if it was even decent."

"And everyone would cry 'nepo baby,' right?" Brinder knew the answer even before asking.

"Absolutely," Honor replied. "Hence the name of my memoir. I've worked hard to carve my own path, far from my parents and their prodigious influence."

"It couldn't have been easy," he murmured, stroking small circles on the inside of her tiny ankle.

"Don't get me wrong. I know I'm fortunate, and I'm always grateful for the launch my last name gave me into a career I love. But if I had no talent, I never would have gotten this far. For all the successful nepo babies out there, there are many, many, *many* more who either didn't inherit the family talent, or ran far, far from this bonkers lifestyle."

"Good point," Brinder mused. "I never thought of it that way. You really only hear about the ones who make it."

"Right, and proportionally, the ones who don't are a much higher number. But, as always, it comes down to media spin."

"So tell me more about your screenplay."

Honor took a deep inhale. "I don't want to act forever. I'm tired of that grind. I love writing. Designing a scene in my head, and telling a story with words and actions. I'm pondering a transition to more writing when this role is finished. And maybe some producing, but we'll see."

"Wow, now that definitely wasn't on TMZ."

Honor threw her head back and laughed. "No, I've kept this pretty close."

"In case...?" he probed.

"In case I stink at it, of course. The media would flay me alive. They love nothing more than lifting you up, only to spitefully tear you down. It's disgusting." Honor shook her head, her hands clasped so hard in her lap, Brinder was pretty sure she was leaving nail imprints in her palms.

He reached for her, gently unclasping them and weaving the fingers of one hand into hers, still stroking her with his other.

"So, the media are twats. That's settled. Now, speaking of twats, back to Crispin."

Honor released a soft chuckle. "Not much more to say. Crispin has family money, but beyond a modest trust fund, won't really have access to it until his parents pass. And they're only in their sixties and in good health."

"Aw, poor Crispy has to make his own money?" Brinder drawled.

"Exactly. In addition to his other asks, he'd been after me to fund a production for him. It was at a small theater in Soho. Actually pretty shabby. And the play? Uh..." Honor cringed. "Truly terrible. Although Crispin insisted it was award-worthy. He was sure it would spotlight his talent as a director."

"So you refused to fund it?"

"Repeatedly."

"Smart."

"And, along with my refusal to allow him to direct my screenplay, the cause of many arguments with Crispin. When we were in London, meeting with Benny and reviewing my book sales, Crispin begged me to visit the theater. All it did was reinforce my decision not to back the project. I thought he'd be livid. Instead...that was the night..."

"Of the video," Brinder finished for her, his blood pressure rising in anger.

Honor nodded, her eyes filling with tears.

Brinder took a calming breath. "And you're sure it wasn't Crispin behind this?"

She gave a small headshake, letting out a shaky exhale. "No, I don't think so. There wouldn't have been time for him to set up the cameras. Besides, he was as incensed as I was. I—I haven't talked to him since we broke up in March, the week after that trip to London.

"That was an ugly fight. We'd been off and on for the previous few months, but that fight was the final straw. At least for me. I've been avoiding all his calls and leaving his texts on read. He must have gotten the message, because when the video came out, instead of calling me right away, he immediately called Benny, demanding to file a lawsuit against the hotel for breach of privacy. He could be a myopic jerk at times, but there was a lot of good there too."

Brinder frowned. Somehow it wasn't all adding up in his head. And Crispin, the wanker, was an obvious choice as culprit.

"Honor, have you heard of Occam's Razor?"

"I've heard of it, but I'd probably need to phone a friend to actually tell you what it is."

"I learned about it when I got my MBA a few years ago. It's a principle of problem-solving that operates on the notion that the simplest explanation...is usually the right one."

Honor watched him carefully, the slow blink of her pretty lashes her only movement as she processed his words.

"Well," she eventually said on a rough exhale. "That's not the first time this theory has been floated. I can't," she began, shaking her head, "I can't even begin to process that. But it would be awful if it were true."

He gave her a small smile. "No more than having a private moment filmed without your consent and then blasted all over the internet."

Honor flared her eyes, puffing out her pink cheeks on a robust exhale. "You're not wrong."

Chapter Forty-Five

Brinder

They were quiet for long moments, Honor staring at the floor. He wanted to break the silence, but wasn't sure how to read her. Did she want a change of subject? To keep talking? He sensed kissing her, which he'd been aching to do since he got home, would be an absolute wrong move right now.

In the end, she answered it for him. Grinning, she wriggled onto her back on the couch, pulling him on top. Christ, it felt like heaven.

"Ok. No more of that. I'll send Benny a message about your theory, although she's already all over it. No stone unturned and all that. But how about we continue this grilling. My girded self is back to ready state, so don't blow this opportunity." She smiled up at him, and he could sense her willing him to pick up her needy cue for a mood change.

"Well, Ms. Wheatley, I do have a very important question for you."

"I'm waiting...." She tapped her foot dramatically against his leg.

"You mentioned the other day that you earned a...red belt?" He lifted his brows in question and she nodded her confirmation.

"Yes, in Taekwondo. I started studying it for the film *Junbi*."

"You were amazing in that. I saw it three times," he admitted.

One sandy brow rose. "I thought you told me the other night you saw it twice. Once with Tiercy and once on a date."

Now it was his turn to blush. "Busted." Bloody hell, her mind was like a steel trap! "I also saw it by myself, on release day."

Her mouth dropped open as she processed that little morsel. "Wow," she eventually said, shaking her head as if to clear it. "I think you could knock me over with a feather right about now."

"Why?" He was the one feeling unsteady, and a feather could probably do a number on him too.

"I just always thought..." she briefly closed her eyes "...that you forgot about me."

"Never!" he whispered fervently. "Try the opposite."

"Wow," she breathed. "I, uh, I don't even know how to take that in. Or what to say. It's so contrary to what I've always believed to be true."

"And you and I both know, all too well, that the alternate realities we weave—or those around us weave—can be far from the truth."

"Indeed," she murmured.

"And," he continued, tilting her chin up with his thumb and forefinger, "in the spirit of transparency, I have to tell you I don't believe your claim that you could flip me."

Now Honor's eyes flared impossibly wider, a huge smile breaking out on her lovely face. "Oh, now you've asked for it."

She shimmied out from under him and quickly moved his table to the side—impressive, given that sucker weighed a good fifty pounds. "Stand up, Desai," she ordered, and a small chill went down his spine at her commanding tone. He was accustomed to being the dominant one, but he definitely could get used to his little dictator. That was *hot*.

He stood, chuckling a bit at their significant height—and weight— differential. "Ok. This should be interesting."

Honor merely smiled serenely.

And then...

...One minute he was standing there, smirking, confident in his own athleticism.

The next?

He was flat on his back, staring up at his ceiling in shock. Huh...he'd never noticed how attractive it was.

Honor's grinning face popped into his field of vision, huge brown eyes sparkling with glee. "You were saying?" she teased, scratching her chin. "What was it? Oh, yes, you said it *should be interesting*." Her grin grew wider, gloating. "And indeed it was."

Brinder huffed out a laugh. "What the hell was that? How did you do it?"

"Easy." Honor sat back on her heels, dusting off her hands with exaggerated theatrics. "I caught you off guard and used a sudden sweeping motion to disrupt your balance. Then, I employed a basic hip-toss technique to get you on the ground. The element of surprise is the key."

"Easy," he teasingly mimicked in a high voice, causing her to giggle. "Not from my vantage point." He ran his hands through his hair, still stunned at how fast she'd taken him down. "That was fucking impressive, baby." He grinned up at her. "And also...you were right. This rug really *is* fucking comfortable."

"Right?" Honor's peal of laughter, the slight flush of triumph on her neck—*Christ*...just her...*every damn thing* about her—sent blood rushing south.

He cocked a brow, dragging his gaze along her body. "As long as I'm down here..." He reached over and tugged her onto him—making sure she felt the hard ridge of his desire along the way—as she gasped in surprise. "Might as well take advantage of it."

Honor adjusted herself so she was straddling his waist, cheeks now blazing red, her chest rising and falling rapidly. Oh yeah, he had definitely telegraphed his intentions with that move. He was no martial arts red belt, but he did know how to seduce a woman. He was a master at that shit.

"Come up here," he commanded, anchoring his hands on her hips and pulling her forward.

"P—pardon?" Honor breathed, one hand rubbing her scar.

"Has anyone ever eaten you out while you sat on his face?"

The look of shock blended with arousal on her face was intensely satisfying. But not as satisfying as things were about to get.

"Come on, Stardust. Climb on my face and let me get you all

'worked up,'"—he intentionally used her words—"so I can hear that sexy mouth swear like a sailor."

Honor was frozen, her eyes blinking rapidly.

Then he saw it—the shift into a wicked smirk. And then she was lifting her skirt and climbing over him.

Boom!

Chapter Forty-Six

Honor

He pulled her panties to the side, and Honor was glad she'd worn a simple cotton thong with some stretch to it. She barely had time to process that when he yanked her up against his mouth and began to... feast. There was no other word for it.

His tongue lashed at her, again and again, her clit hardening beneath it, her arousal blending with his saliva, dampening her legs in such sexual decadence that Honor could only wonder at why she'd never tried this before.

He certainly hadn't had this weapon in his arsenal back when they were teenagers. Honor stifled a giggle amidst the rapidly growing ache between her legs.

Brinder shifted his mouth off her and she practically whimpered at the loss. "What was that little giggle for, baby?" he murmured, rubbing the stubble on his face across her electrified ladyparts.

Holy wow...that feels good.

"Tish," he urged, lightly blowing on her clit, causing chills to erupt across her body as arousal sizzled down her spine. "Tell me."

She rested her hand on the seat of the chair behind his head, needing some kind of stability or she'd collapse from the intensity of what he was doing with his mouth.

"I just...ohhhhh," she moaned as he sucked hard. "I..." she trailed, momentarily unable to verbalize her thoughts given the intense ministrations of his tongue between her legs. After one particularly spectacular swirl of his tongue, she couldn't help but whuff a shocked laugh.

"Why the giggle, baby?" He purred into her soaked center.

"I was," she paused and gasped as a thick, long finger slid inside her. "I was just recalling that you didn't have this particular set of skills back at Cheltenham," she managed, panting at the sexy onslaught of his lips and tongue and finger—*holy wow*—*fingers* now between her legs. Honor instinctively ground down on his hand, pressing herself further onto his face.

She briefly worried she was suffocating him, but then quickly abandoned the thought, giving in to the mindless thrill of his mouth on her as she rode his face.

She was *riding Brinder Desai's face.*

Talk about things she didn't have on her bingo card.

He lashed at her clit with his tongue, flicking and sucking until she was a writhing, panting, ball of arousal, every nerve focused on the orgasm that was rapidly building.

In tune with her, Brinder added a third finger, pressing so deep she was sure he could feel whatever organ was on top of her uterus. She'd ask later. When her brain wasn't so scrambled.

He picked up his pace, sucking, sucking, sucking...then a hard flick...working her nub with his tongue. Then...he curled his fingers, expertly finding the knot of nerves inside, which she'd never believed existed. Until this week.

She gasped when he teased her *other* hole...not breaching it, but pressing as he worked his other fingers inside her...and gently bit her clit.

"Aaaah!!!! Fuck!" she screamed, her release seizing her. "Yes!" she cried, panting and rocking against his mouth, chasing the glorious tail end of her orgasm while battling the sensitivity of her clit.

Honor slumped over, resting her head on the chair cushion as she caught her breath. That's when she realized she was still sitting high on Brinder's chest.

Her cheeks flamed and she hurried to move off him, but he clamped down on her thighs.

"Uh uh, baby," he chided, his chin and lips glistening with her arousal and release. She wanted to be mortified...but that was one of the hottest things she'd ever seen. "Stay here. You smell incredible." He took a deep inhale. "My favorite perfume. Parfum de Honor." Then he nuzzled her, causing little shocks in her lady garden. "Mmmmm," he hummed against her, the vibration almost enough to get her going again. "And you taste like the most decadent dessert. I'm never eating anything but your pussy ever again."

She put a hand over her mouth, half in shock. "Holy freaking wow, Brin," she said through her shaking fingers.

He grinned up at her. "Did you like that, Stardust?"

She exhaled a tremulous laugh. "I'm not sure 'like' covers it, Brin." She giggled, still in shock at what just happened. And how fast it happened.

After never experiencing a man-made O, Brinder certainly had altered her reality by positively owning her body and playing it like a virtuoso.

Honor glanced behind her. Brinder was so hard, his shorts were aggressively tented. She bit her lip, mortified at her own embarrassment —if that was a thing—at the question she was about to ask. She was thirty-seven, not the teenager who cautiously explored her burgeoning sexuality with the teenage version of the man who'd just *let her ride his face*.

Sadly, she wasn't all that more experienced than those early days. Rather pathetic. But the last several days had demonstrated she was far from the prude Crispin had called her whenever he wasn't particularly happy with her performance in bed during their infrequent couplings.

Maybe the embers of her desire had been smoldering for decades, and it just took Brinder to deftly coax it into a conflagration. She wanted to explore her sexuality with him. Oh, boy, did she ever. And a fresh wave of shock....and desire...built within her.

She struggled with eye contact for a moment, looking off to the side from her unique vantage point atop his chest. *Shidoobie*. She was on. Brinder's. Chest. Honor forced herself to woman up and look him in the eyes.

It was time to own her sexual confidence. Not for her upcoming role, but for *her*.

Honor cleared her throat. "Brin?"

"Mmmm?" He regarded her with a heavy-lidded gaze that had her ladyparts thrumming.

"What about"—she motioned behind her—"you?"

Her cheeks blazed. This sexual confidence thing wasn't easy. Maybe she could talk to Ross? She wouldn't pull any punches, that was for sure.

In a feat of impressive ab strength that had Honor lamenting that he hadn't removed his shirt so she could see the dance of his six-pack, Brinder shifted into a seated position, maneuvering her so she straddled him.

"This time was all about you, Stardust." She noticed his now-faded British accent intensified during their encounters.

"Don't you need to...you know? Won't you get blue balls or something?"

He chuckled. "Contrary to male sexual lore, we can actually function and survive if we don't nut. And, often, the delay makes the eventuality even better. Remember when I edged you last night?"

"Oh." That was all she could manage. Because the *eventuality* was guaranteed to leave her in a sweaty, sated state of glorious oblivion. In reality, just Brinder's lips on her ignited that long-latent desire.

As if reading her mind, Brinder cupped her face in his hands and kissed her deeply.

She could taste her own tang...which was ridiculously sexy. Not at all the turnoff she'd always assumed. Honor kissed him back, trying to infuse in it all the really big, really intense feelings that were roiling inside of her—Arousal. Satiation. Wonder.

Love?

Love.

And wasn't that a plot twist.

Chapter Forty-Seven

Brinder

If you'd asked him a week ago what he thought he might be doing today, he probably would have answered 'work, gym, and maybe some drinks with friends.'

But Honor—*his* Honor—reappearing in his life, staying with him, sharing her delectable body, weaving her special kind of magic? Well, that would have been the furthest thing from his mind, as unattainable as a joyride on Haley's Comet.

Speaking of rides...Honor on his face? They were definitely repeating that experience—many times—for her sake, but especially for his. Something told him she had no idea that giving your partner pleasure was itself a form of sexual fulfillment. Yet another reason to loathe her exes.

He loved that she'd shyly expressed concern about him achieving his own pleasure. He *had* achieved pleasure, simply from hearing the cries he'd wrung from her. And as much as he loved burying himself inside her tight pussy, the delayed gratification would be epic for him. That didn't mean he wasn't drowning in the sheer surreal carnality of her naked pussy against him.

He rocked his hips gently as their tongues tangled, Honor gripping his head with both hands as if she were holding on for dear life. Eventually, they came up for air, their long, sexy kisses blurring into soft brushes of their lips.

Honor rested her forehead against him, breathing heavily. "I really like what happens when we eat Indian food, Brin."

He leaned back, reveling in the laughter in those beautiful brown eyes. "You don't say?" he teased, not sure when he had ever experienced such deep satisfaction. It went beyond sexual satiety.

So. Far. Beyond.

He tamped down the deep thoughts, not wanting to scare her and lose the vibe. Another time. *Definitely* another time...soon.

Instead, he trailed the tip of his tongue up her neck to the hollow below her ear, tasting salt as he skimmed his fingers along the baby-soft skin on the other side. His cock kicked, hard, and goosebumps danced across her arms as she let out a soft moan.

"I didn't realize it was such an aphrodisiac."

"If it wasn't before, it certainly is now," she replied with a breathless laugh.

They stayed entwined for long moments. Brinder was so content, even the ache of his cock couldn't stir him. He just wanted to savor the glorious sensation of Honor sexy, relaxed, and sated in his arms.

"I have one more question," she whispered, then shifted to press her lips gently to his. "Please?"

"Of course, Stardust. What is it?" He was intensely curious, especially given what appeared to be a re-emergence of her shyness with him.

"That," she said, motioning to him with a hesitant smile. "Why do you do that?"

"Do what?"

"Call me Stardust." Her eyes darted between his, as if she could read the answer on his face.

He broke into a wide grin. "Ah...well...it started with something I learned one weekend during college, shortly before seeing you in your first film role."

Honor's smile faded a bit.

"No, don't be sad, baby," he soothed, dropping a kiss on her nose as he tucked an errant piece of hair behind her ear. "Forget the circumstances and just listen, ok?" He ran his thumb along her cheekbone and she leaned into the caress, nodding.

"I was watching a documentary—"

"Of course you were," she teased, her eyes and smile so soft, so loving, he wondered if his heart could explode from the power of sheer happiness.

"It was about how most of the elements in our bodies were created in stars, over billions and billions of years. Oxygen, carbon, nitrogen, iron." Brinder punctuated each word with a soft kiss. To her palm. Nose. A satiny smooth cheek. Forehead.

He used to apply the much-loved forehead kiss as a tool of seduction. Now? He realized it could be more emotionally intimate than going down on a woman. Or perhaps not just any woman. *Honor*. She had always been...exceptional.

Collecting his scattered thoughts, he continued, "The scientists and astronomers interviewed theorized that when the Big Bang happened, all those elements danced off into space, eventually forming the planets. And life." Honor's eyes shifted between his, her nose scrunching adorably as she clearly tried to process. "Nearly all of the elements in every human body originated from a star."

Honor cocked her head. "Really?"

"Really." He smiled and kissed her forehead again. Yep—intimate times a million. "So, it could be said that we're all...made of stardust."

"Oh," she whispered, a tiny frown line appearing between her brows.

"And," he continued, knowing he was about to reveal a long-hidden corner of his heart, "it occurred to me as I was watching you light up the screen, that I believe you are made of more stardust than most. There is something...cosmic and elemental about you. Something ageless and timeless. Like stardust."

Tears filled her eyes. "Brinder," she sobbed out, dropping her head onto his shoulder and lacing her arms around him in a fierce hug. "I think that's the most beautiful thing anyone's ever said to me."

"You're the most beautiful person I've ever known. In every way,

Honor," he whispered into her ear, nuzzling the soft shell with his nose. "I'm in awe of you. You're magnificent."

She shifted, grabbing the sides of his face and crashing her lips against his, her tears and her smile blending into the sweetest, most intense kiss of his life.

Eventually Honor exhaled against his lips. "Wow...we are definitely ordering Indian again."

Chapter Forty-Eight

Honor

Brinder's rumbling laugh did amazing things to her. Mostly it helped soothe all the hurting, wounded places from the past week...and the past eighteen years. Just the sound of his laugh, as decadent and rich as his sexy voice, could bring a smile to her face.

He nuzzled her nose with his. "I do have a request of my Stardust."

"Anything," she promised, realizing that if he asked her for the world—for the sun, the moon, and the stars—she'd do everything in her power to give it to him.

He shifted her so she was cradled across his lap. "I have a work event this Saturday."

Honor's heart dropped a bit. She hadn't even been there a week and she was already internally pouting about losing part of the weekend with him.

"And," he continued, "I was hoping you'd attend with me?"

The lump in her throat felt like a boulder. "As your fake date?" she whispered, proud that her voice didn't shake at all.

"No, Stardust. As my real date. As my girl." He smiled gently at her, understanding in his eyes. "There's nothing fake about this for me."

Honor's heart did a crazy little jig. The moment she'd realized she was falling back in love, that emotion became tangled in pervasive worries. That this was just an act for him to get through his own scandal as he helped her through hers—as friends and nothing more. That for Brinder, their toe-curling, passionate couplings held nothing more than lust and desire. Doing her another favor with those lessons that, for her, had quickly morphed into lovemaking, but for Dr. Desiiigh was just scratching a convenient itch.

And none of that worry spiral...was true.

There's nothing fake about this for me. She would likely hear this on treasured autorepeat in her head for the rest of her life.

The ravaged look emerging on Brinder's face smacked her into awareness that she hadn't replied. And if he was going to bare his heart? She was brave enough to do so as well.

"Me either," she admitted on a quick exhale, and then tasted the salt of a lone tear of both relief and pure joy that had tracked down her face to her lips.

His face cleared into the sweetest smile—one that reminded her so much of that teenage boy she'd fallen for all those years ago. It was like that beautiful, kind face was a perfect match, unlocking feelings that were bigger and deeper than any other in her life.

With aching tenderness, Brinder kissed her, touching the tear with the tip of his tongue. "I'm still trying to wrap my brain around all of this —and my heart, to be honest—but all I know is that I'd love for you to be by my side this Saturday."

"Will Clark be there?" she bit out, half hoping he wouldn't be. She didn't trust herself to be civil. But she found another half of herself wishing he would be, so she could ice him out. Summon the full force and haughtiness of her inner Hollywood princess.

She didn't deploy that move often. It wasn't her M.O. to be unkind. There was too much of that already in her industry. But she'd happily weaponize her years of award ceremony skills on Brinder's behalf. She could cold shoulder with the best of them. But only when the person deserved it. And Clark most definitely did.

"I'm impressed you remember his name."

"I always remember the names of my mortal enemies," she replied, a hint of evil queen in her tone. As hoped, it elicited that sexy laugh from Brinder.

"I think you've been hanging around Ross too much."

"Or," she parried, "perhaps it's Ross who's been hanging around me too much."

"Either way, you two are a potent combination. Add Tierce to the mix, who looks all sweet but can hold her own with the best of them… and I'm actually a little afraid. And amazed you all didn't get into trouble today."

"Who's to say we didn't?" Honor shimmied her shoulders, sucking in her cheeks.

"The media. We'd have heard about it long before now. And Benny would have already sent out a strike force."

"Ooooh…Bauer and Grayton, doing their thang," she drawled. "Ross would *loooove* that. She's all about the military romances these days."

Brinder threw his head back and laughed. "OK, that's enough. I'm exhausted. Haven't slept much lately," he added with a salacious wink. "How about we hop in bed and cuddle?"

"Cuddle?" Honor parroted theatrically. "Is that Brinderese for *fucking*?" She raised a brow.

His eyes flared, Adam's apple bobbing. She could feel him stiffening again beneath her, well aware he hadn't yet had his release. Honor loved that she could get a…rise…out of him just by the power of a well-placed curse word.

"Well," he announced, standing with her still in his arms—another impressive feat of his physicality—and striding in the direction of the bedroom, "it wasn't before…but it sure is now."

Chapter Forty-Nine

Brinder

One week. It had been one week since his life was shaken up in ways he could barely wrap his mind around. First, the beyond twisted lies of Laurel, leading to the unwarranted 'Clarkfrontation,' as Honor had also started referring to it. Then Honor's stunning reappearance in his life. Her devastating scandal, which made the Clark situation as insignificant as a tiny seashell in the ocean. Their cohabitation of convenience. Fake dating that quickly ended up not being fake...for either of them.

And now...falling in love with Honor.

Or maybe it wasn't so much falling in love as blasting through the carefully constructed walls around a long-buried love. Walls he'd painstakingly built to protect the heart that had belonged to Honor from the moment he met her.

Brinder sighed, rocking back in his office chair and dragging his hand through his hair, which was likely sticking up all over the place given the path his hand had traveled over and over as he ruminated.

He was supposed to be reviewing OR block time reports and provider appointment availability analytics, but had been reduced to fruitlessly toggling between the two Tableau reports in a so-far frustratingly unsuccessful attempt to actually do his damn job.

Brinder looked at his watch, rolling his eyes when he saw the time. Four o'clock. He'd wasted the last ninety minutes, with absolutely nothing to show for it. One week post-Clarkfrontation, and Agnes would be justified in exercising the termination clause in his employment contract simply because he couldn't get his mental act together. Oh, when he was in a procedure, he was laser-focused. But as soon as he got in front of his double monitors, his mind wandered.

"Focus, asshole. Do your fucking job," he muttered.

"I see we are using positive words of affirmation this afternoon."

Startled, Brinder's gaze darted to the door, where Agnes leaned against the frame, arms crossed, the corner of her mouth tilted up. "Rough day?" the hospital president asked, not unkindly.

Brinder pinched the bridge of his nose. "Honestly? Rough week."

Agnes eased into his office, closing the door behind her as she motioned to one of the two upholstered guest chairs in front of his desk. "May I?"

"Please," he nodded, turning his chair to face her.

Agnes heaved a deep sigh. "It has been a long week."

"I'll say." He took a deep swallow from his aluminum Evangelist-branded water bottle and returned it to the Georgetown University slate coaster as he worked to collect his thoughts. Why was she here? Was she going to drop the hammer? These things often happened on Fridays.

Agnes scanned his face, a sympathetic frown creasing her otherwise unlined forehead. Once again, Brinder was reminded of how impressive she was, running a hospital with calm precision, with timely compassion, and always with a backbone of steel.

"I just got the updated financials. Our OR throughput has almost doubled in the last four weeks. The year over year numbers are even more impressive."

A surge of pride coursed through him, superseding the ever-present worry that had gnawed at his gut for days. One of the first opportunities for change he'd uncovered was a poorly run OR. They had been losing money unnecessarily, and causing frustrating delays for surgeons and their patients. He'd worked with the chief of surgery and the surgical director of nursing to implement some immediate changes. That was the report he'd been—unsuccessfully—trying to analyze this afternoon. The data indicated things had improved notably, with many happy surgeons stopping by his office to share their positive feedback over the last month, but he wanted more time to dig in by surgeon and by shift. Brinder knew there was even more to optimize. If only he could fucking focus.

"The team's working hard," he acknowledged.

Up went an eyebrow. "*You're* working hard."

He wasn't quite sure how to respond to that.

"Look, Brinder, I'm not one to dance around things. You've had a shit week, and quite frankly, it's not your fault."

Something that felt a lot like hope rushed into his troubled heart.

He opened his mouth to say something. Anything. To put into words how much he loved this job, Clark notwithstanding. But before he could form a thought, much less expel it from his mouth, Agnes continued briskly.

"You're one of the best damn chief medical officers I've worked with, and that includes a superstar at Stanford. I can already see the difference you're making at Evangelist. And I refuse," her voice took on an iron edge, "to let a rogue Board chair and some questionable actions by his daughter take that away. We just got rid of a terrible leader, and I'd be a fool to let an outstanding one slip through my fingers."

Holy shit. Brinder's heart was thudding in his chest, his lips going a bit numb in relief.

"Agnes, I—" he began, but she continued smoothly as if he hadn't spoken.

"I am sharing this with you within professional confidentiality. I haven't been happy with Clark. Not with his cronyism, his pompous attitude, his utter lack of care for the importance of his role in helping guide this hospital—not to mention his fucking noxious cologne that he douses on his body—since my own first week here. I will not allow him to drive you away."

Brinder let out an exhale, just realizing he'd been holding his breath.

"That..." He shook his head to clear it, running his hand through his hair for the gazillionth time that afternoon. "...is not what I expected to hear this afternoon."

"But it's what you *needed* to hear this afternoon, Brinder. You work hard. You care. You're a talented physician and a thoughtful leader. All the things that made Ben Lopez at Fellowship-Unity recommend you for this position and came shining through in your interviews are one thousand percent true."

"Agnes, I—" he started again, praying for eloquence.

Again she continued, ignoring his pathetic attempts to reply. "I could hear you sighing and muttering all the way in my office down the hall."

Now he raised an eyebrow. That wasn't possible.

"Ok," she conceded. "*I* didn't hear you. But Amani did. She's worried about you. As am I. For the last week, you've had this ridiculous probation over your head. You haven't let it impact your work"—she nodded toward his monitors with a sly smile—"much. But one of my responsibilities as the president is to manage every member of the team, either directly or indirectly. I allowed Clark to bully me, using threats of pulling key donor contacts of his in our fundraising pipeline and my own worry about another damn scandal to sway a decision I shouldn't have made."

Brinder was pretty sure Amani, his diminutive well-meaning traitor, could hear his heart beating from her desk outside his office through the closed door.

"Before I came in here, I informed the Board—including Clark— I'm ending your probation as well as your interim status, and enacting your formal contract as Vice President of Medical Affairs, effectively immediately. You are officially our chief medical officer. Congratulations."

An uncharacteristic wide smile broke across her face as she stood and walked to his desk, holding out her right hand and placing papers he'd just noticed in the other on his desk.

Brinder stood on shaking legs and took her hand, smiling so wide his cheeks actually hurt.

"Thank—" he started, and realized he was getting choked up, relief surging through his veins. He took a moment to compose himself.

"Thank you, Agnes. For believing in me. For *believing me*." He put extra emphasis on the last words, the confirmation that Agnes recognized Laurel's lies almost buckling his knees. "This is my dream job, and I've been heartsick the last week."

"I know." Agnes nodded her head, then removed her hand from his grasp. Christ, he hoped his palms weren't sweating. He did a quick check. *Whew.* Dry. "Your permanent contract." She waved toward the document. "Take a moment, review it—it's identical to what you signed before, minus your interim status—then sign it and give it to Amani to process with HR."

"Of course. Yes. Thank you," he rambled, rolling his eyes internally at his bumbling. His father would be horrified at his lack of poise. He inhaled a calming breath and began again, this time feeling more like himself. "Thank you, Agnes. I'll review it right away."

"Good. Let's put this all behind us and move forward." Her tone was brisk as she headed to the door, stopping with her hand on the knob. "I will say," she added, an eyebrow raised once again, "I didn't see your relationship with Honor Wheatley coming." She smiled again, warmth in her eyes. "I can tell she's good for you. The buzz in the hospital is that Dr. Desiiigh," Agnes gave him a knowing smile, "is officially off the Evangelist meat market."

Brinder rolled his eyes for real this time at that unfortunate moniker, one that seemed to follow him from residency, to his job at Fellowship, to Evangelist.

"And when you aren't huffing and sighing at Tableau reports,"— now Brinder barked out a laugh—"you've seemed different. Happier. More at peace. Even given the Clark situation."

"Clarkfrontation," Brinder murmured.

This time both of her eyebrows went up. For a moment she just stood there, and then burst into laughter. "Now *that* is damn funny." She put a hand over her mouth for a moment. "I shouldn't be laughing at that. But I find that I can't help it, and I don't mind." She chuckled again and he released his own laugh, amazed at the emotional whiplash of the last week. "I'm looking forward to meeting Honor tomorrow."

"It may be a bit of a media shitshow," he warned, not for the first time. "Honor and I are both concerned it will overshadow the event."

"And as I said before, I'm not worried about that. The PR team has a plan in place, and we've hired additional private security for the venue."

Brinder was impressed. Agnes was always a step ahead.

"I can put Juan in touch with her agent," he offered, referencing their VP of Public Affairs. "Honor also has two dedicated guards, and I'm sure her agent would like to coordinate security. In fact, I probably should have thought of this sooner."

"You've had just a bit on your mind, Brinder."

"Indeed," he sighed, a wave of appreciation for his boss tightening his throat. "Juan is going to hate me for doing this to him on a Friday afternoon."

"Nah." Agnes waved a dismissive hand. "He and the philanthropy team have already been putting in the hours. It's always chaos leading up to these events. I'll make sure they get time off next week. Besides, Juan thinks Honor's attendance will be good for us. The video is clearly BS. Her strong reputation precedes her. And the donors will salivate over meeting her." Agnes shrugged her shoulders. "Not to monetize your girlfriend, but I'd be a damn fool not to lean into this opportunity. And I"—she leveled a look at him—"am not a fool."

No. She most definitely wasn't. "Understood. I'll work with Honor, Juan, and her agent to finalize security, any PR needs, media management, et cetera."

"Thank you, Brinder. I appreciate it."

A worrisome thought popped into his head. "What about Clark?"

"I'm taking care of him," she offered enigmatically. "You just focus on your job...and your girlfriend. Seems like she's a keeper."

His girlfriend. That sounded so damn good. And, yes, she was a keeper.

Chapter Fifty

Honor

The phrase 'walking on air' was a common throw-away idiom. But when Brinder walked into the condo early that evening, Honor saw it in sharp and honest action. As he practically danced toward her into the kitchen, wearing one of the widest smiles she'd ever seen on him, it was as if Brinder's feet barely touched the hardwoods.

"Honey, I'm hooooome," he called out—in what was becoming a truly endearing habit—as he made a beeline in her direction. Wrapping his arms around her, sweeping her off her feet and spinning her around, he peppering her face and neck with smacking kisses.

Honor squealed, laughing at the ebullient welcome. "Brinder," she shrieked, giggling at the assault, "what did Amani put in your water bottle this afternoon?"

"Loooove potion and redemption," he sang, lifting her onto the island. Framing her face in his large, strong hands, he planted a deep, filthy kiss on her that went on forever.

She was *not* complaining.

When he finally pulled back, leaving both panting and Honor more than a little turned on, he wrapped his arms back around her waist, forcing her to reciprocate with her legs around his. She had Velvet Smoke playing on his surround sound, and he twirled with her over to the couch, once even dipping her backwards, eliciting another shriek from her. Honor's belly flip-flopped with the movement, and her once-faulty heart soared with his infectious happiness.

"Brinder," she laughed breathlessly, "stop! You're making me dizzy."

"Good. That makes two of us. I'm dizzy with joy." He spun her once more and pressed his lips to hers again. No tongue this time, but somehow it felt even more intense. Brinder peppered kisses all over her face. "I. Love. This. Face."

Honor threw her head back and laughed. "What's gotten into you today?"

His hazel eyes sparkled. "Agnes came into my office this afternoon and proceeded to tell me I was one of the best chief medical officers she's worked with in her career. That I'm having a demonstrable positive impact on Evangelist's operations. Aaaand," he drew out, "she rescinded my probation, indicating her dislike and distrust of both Clark and Laurel."

"Yes!" Honor shouted, throwing her hands in the air.

Brinder gripped her more tightly and she clamped her legs against him so she didn't fall out of his arms. Not that he'd ever let that happen. He was a protector at heart.

"And," he continued, "she concluded the interim period and handed me my official permanent contract to sign!"

"Brinder!" Honor cried out. "That's amazing! Congratulations! We have to celebrate!"

"My thoughts exactly," he purred, moving them toward their bedroom.

Just when in the last week had she begun thinking of it as hers? *Theirs*? Given the large male who was jouncing her as he hustled down the hall, that was a thought to unpack at a later time.

"No!" she laughed, and then laughed harder at his theatrical pout as he froze comically. "I mean, yes we can celebrate that way—" Brinder grinned and started moving again, "—*later*." He stopped again, with drama that would have made her parents proud. She snickered. "But first we need to celebrate with friends."

"I'm not into that." Brinder winked at her and Honor thought she would pull a muscle in her abdomen with her convulsive giggles.

She smacked at his arm. "You know what I mean. Dork."

His hazel eyes softened, the gold coming out. "You haven't called me that in a long time."

"You haven't earned it in a long time," she parried.

"Touché." He smacked another kiss on her lips. "What do you have in mind?"

"First, Dr. Desai, I want the full version of this amazing turn of events. And, then, I thought we'd see if the crew wanted to go out somewhere."

The crew. It was how she'd started thinking of Ross, Xander, Tiercy, and Cole. She'd had good friends all her life, including some close friends. But somehow, this crew of four, plus Brinder, had emerged as, well, her people.

Brinder pouted again. "I wanted to celebrate another way." He thrust his hips to underscore his meaning.

"And we will. We most definitely will." The parts of her that had heated up earlier with his devastating kiss began tingling and aching again. "I've never had sex with an official chief medical officer before," she teased.

"And he is going to fuck his happiness straight into you and make it so you walk bow-legged for a week."

"Oooo...promises, promises," she taunted.

He gave a low growl. "Now you're in for it later."

Honor couldn't help but shudder in sheer anticipation. In the last week, courtesy of this man, her body had done and experienced things she never could've imagined.

And she was there for it.

"I take it the thought of that appeals to you?" The pupils of Brinder's eyes had dilated so only a thin ring of hazel was visible.

"Mmmmhmmmmm." She channeled her inner seductress with her moaning assent.

It worked.

Several minutes later, after he'd thoroughly ravaged her mouth, leaving his hands frustratingly anchored around her so she wouldn't slip from her perch—instead of where she wanted them, the freaking tease —he rested his forehead against hers.

She caught her breath, hyperaware of her soaked panties resting against his abdomen. "I'm so proud of you," she whispered.

"Thank you, baby," he replied, nuzzling her nose with his in a gesture that flooded her system with a satisfying dopamine rush. "What did you do today?"

"Mmmm. I did some yoga. I wrote. Then I tried on some dresses for tomorrow that Benny had delivered."

"Any winner in there?"

"You'll see tomorrow," she teased. "And no peeking in the guest room closet."

"Never. I want the big reveal. Then what did you do?"

"FaceTimed with Bash. Then my parents. Then Benny. Molly too. Took a little nap because someone," she cleared her throat, "has been keeping me up late."

"Sorry, not sorry."

Honor snickered. "Ditto. When you came in, I was in a standoff with the refrigerator, hoping it would cough up some dinner ideas."

"Any luck?"

She reflexively smiled at the teasing lilt of his sexy voice. Brinder was well aware of her lack of culinary prowess.

"What do you think, Dr. Desai?"

"I think we are going out to dinner."

"Ding ding ding. You are correct, sir!"

His eyes darkened again. "I like that."

Honor raised a brow. "Like what?" she asked, even though she had a strong inkling.

"When you call me 'sir,'" he practically growled, and she could feel the rumble of his response in her own chest, only inches from him. And in her drenched core. Definitely there.

"Maybe, if you're very good tonight, I'll say it while you ravage me bow-legged."

"Deal." His sexy voice dropped an octave and Honor shivered again. Suddenly, she realized he'd been holding her since he'd walked in the door nearly thirty minutes earlier. Her cheeks heated. "Um, do you want to put me down?"

"No."

"Oh."

He pressed her back into the wall. "Honor?"

"Yes?" It came out a strangled whisper.

"I'm going to fuck you against this wall now."

"Ok," she managed.

"And I'm not going to be gentle."

CHAPTER FIFTY-ONE

BRINDER

MacGillivray's was a popular bar-restaurant with a small stage where local performers graced the stage most nights and on weekends—except Fridays, which was karaoke night. Mac's (as it was nicknamed) was owned by a retired surgeon who'd quickly grown bored and wanted a new challenge. It was a hospital hangout, but also brought in a diverse array of patrons, many of them music lovers who enjoyed hearing local talent. The food was tasty, the drinks were strong, and the vibes pristine.

Surprisingly, it wasn't a hospital colleague who'd introduced him to Mac's, but Xander. He'd discovered it his first year living in the area, and now it was a reliable, fun go-to when they all wanted to go out.

It was an ideal setting for Honor's next public appearance—a relaxed environment and friendly territory with an accommodating owner. More than that, hanging with 'the crew' was always a good time and exactly what Honor deserved given all the stress she was under.

After alerting Benny, and then a recon by Grayton—which included a courtesy heads-up to Tom, the eponymous owner of Mac's, given the paparazzi spectacle plus crowd buzz that would definitely swell as soon as they spotted Honor—Brinder and Honor finally drifted in. It was close to eight-thirty at that point. Truth be told, Brinder was gassed after a long-ass week, followed by the adrenaline rush of his good news, and then not one, but two fast, sexy, fierce fucks with his girl. He wanted to just curl up with her and cuddle (translation: *fuck*), but she had been crawling the walls and it didn't seem fair to isolate her beyond what she self-imposed.

Grayton walked through the doors first, followed by Honor, Brinder, and then Bauer. Brinder gripped her hand in his, although so far no paps had found them and the patrons hadn't yet realized who was there.

"This is so fantastic!" Honor looked around, taking it in. "I love the exposed brick walls and these high ceilings and the wood beams." She pointed to the floor, which was a patterned taupe and cream slate tile. "Oooo, I love this floor more than a person should love a floor."

Brinder chuckled at her enthusiasm.

Seating was a mixture of booths with rust suede cushions, reclaimed wood tables and chairs, and high-backed stools at the bar. In the winter, Tom or the on-duty manager would ensure the large stone fireplace had a roaring fire, and in warmer weather, he filled it with low, wide vases of thistle and other wild blooms.

Brinder could see why the architect in Xander loved it here. It was cozy and charming, with touches of Irish pub commingled with a hip flair.

He caught the eye of Tom, who was standing behind the bar mixing a drink. They gave each other a chin nod, and Tom finished his pour. Wiping his hands, he came around.

"Brinder, good to see you." Tom turned to Honor and smiled, offering her his hand. "Tom MacGillivray, Ms. Wheatley, it's an honor to have you here." The cheeks of the normally unflappable former surgeon flushed. "Sorry about that."

Honor laughed. "Happens more than you'd think with a name like mine. And, please, call me Honor."

"Well, Honor, thank you. And it really is an honor"—Tom winked and she laughed again—"to host you in my establishment. Whatever you need tonight, just say the word, and I'll do whatever I can."

"I appreciate that. Brinder tells me you were a highly regarded surgeon and now you run the most popular bar and restaurant in town."

Tom chuckled, but Brinder could see his chest puff a bit in well-deserved pride at her praise. Good lord, she was incredible.

"Well, I don't know about either of those statements. I was a bartender during college, which helped fund med school. I usually like to have some time behind the bar when I'm here. Feels like coming home."

Brinder marveled at Honor's composed but warm graciousness as she eagerly hung on every word Tom said. She was clearly practiced at these scenarios, creating a comfortable level of connection relevant to the situation.

"I sure have been fortunate to do things I love," Tom offered. "Which is really the trick to a satisfying life. That and"—he pointed to his wedding ring and winked at Brinder—"the love of a good life partner. Well, I best get back. Tonight's one of our busy nights." Tom tipped his head deeper into the room. "Your friends are waiting for you in the large corner booth. I gave you the one with the most privacy but still a view of the stage."

As their host wished them both a good evening, Brinder tucked Honor under his arm and headed in the direction Tom indicated. He looked down at his petite date, nestled against him. Her hair was up in a high ponytail with soft curls. She wore very little makeup. He'd watched in fascination as she slid a mascara wand along her lashes. She'd brushed a little foundation powder on her face and then slicked a pale pink gloss on her lips. That was it. She wore white, distressed (and temptingly short) jeans shorts, a navy one-shoulder knit top that hugged her gorgeous breasts, and sandals with straps that wound around her ankles and lower calves—which he couldn't wait to untie with his teeth back at home. All around him, women wore gobs of makeup and short dresses. But his girl didn't need all that. She was a natural beauty. Of course, when she got all dolled up, she was stunning. But he liked this version of her best of all.

Ross waved them in. "Hey, lovebirds. I'm surprised Brinder let you out of your not-so-secret mortification lair slash love shack." Honor's 'frienditor' snickered, and he watched Honor's cheeks flush, loving that she still could be flustered by innuendo. For all her poise and polish, plus her success on an international acting stage, his Honor was still the sweet, sometimes shy girl he crushed on all those years ago.

"Jeez, Ross Ellen, ease up. They just got here." Tiercy swatted at her teasingly. "There has to be a grace period. Oh!" Her eyes widened in surprise at the unintentional use of Ross and Xander's last name, and she giggled as she said, "Pun not intended."

"And yet, well played, Tierce." Ross nodded her head once in recognition. "And you're right. Usually I wait at least thirty minutes so I don't cramp. It's like eating and swimming."

Xander grinned at his wife like the lovestruck husband he was.

Brinder guided Honor into the booth next to Ross, and then scooted in next to her. This way, she could see the stage, but her back was to the room, and Brinder's much larger body mostly blocked her. He laced his fingers through hers and rested their entwined hands on his leg. Honor squeezed his hand and smiled up at him.

His heart leapt at that simple gesture. Yep. He was as lovestruck as Gracie.

"Who's got the kids?" Brinder knew nights out for this foursome were rare and treasured.

A radiant smile broke across Tiercy's face. "My parents. They're moving down here!"

"Woot!" Ross chimed, adding an Arsenio Hall arm pump.

Tiercy shared a smile with her lifelong bestie. "They sold their real estate business and put their house on the market. They came down to house hunt this weekend. Mom said she couldn't stand to be away from Jemma and Augie any longer, and Petey and Leah are like grandchildren to her too. She insists Petey call her Lovie, just like Jem. They hope to officially move by midsummer." Tiercy and Ross grinned at each other again.

Brinder had always appreciated their siblings-of-the-heart bond and the devoted love of Neal and Cathleen for both women. Now, as often, he lamented the lack of that from his own parents. His mom loved him —he knew that—but she was also a very traditional woman who deferred to her husband for the most part.

He turned his attention back to Tiercy as she explained, "Lovie and Pop are getting their fix. All four kids are at our place, and then Ross and Xan will pick up their progeny on their way home tonight." The friends shared knowing glances. "Ross and I can't be out too long."

"Or two sets of boobs will leak like a screen door on a submarine." Ross snickered.

"Nice, Ross," Tiercy replied with an affectionate eye roll.

"I just speak the truth, friends."

"That's so fantastic that your parents are moving closer. You must be thrilled, and I know they are." Honor smiled at the women, and Brinder was deeply relieved by her smooth change in subject. He supported breastfeeding, but he certainly didn't want to think about his friends' leaking boobs.

Now, Honor's luscious breasts leaking with breast milk? His cock started to fill at that image, as his mind leapt to getting her pregnant, her body growing and nursing their child...

He forced himself to return his attention to the conversation, recognizing he'd likely revisit that fantasy. And the many positions he could use to fulfil it. Honor took a long draw from her glass of water, and Brinder tried not to preen at the realization she was probably still parched from their earlier *pregaming*.

"My mom has been haranguing my brother and me to have kids for years," Honor said as she set the nearly empty glass back on the table. "She keeps saying they aren't getting any younger and she wants grandbabies before she's too old to enjoy them." She turned to Xander and Cole. "I was a bonus baby and my brother, Bash, is an inveterate bachelor, à la Clooney before Amal. So Mom's getting antsy."

Xander tut-tutted in a teasing tone. "Ms. Wheatley, you act as if your family aren't all public figures and we all didn't consume your autobiography. You dedicated half a chapter to your mom's granny lust."

Now it was Ross's turn to smack Xander. "Be nice. We still have"—she checked her watch—"twenty-five more minutes until we can officially tease Honor."

As they all laughed at the gentle joshing, Brinder was filled with an incredible sensation. Of belonging. Of puzzle pieces slowly snapping into place. The only missing piece, one that troubled his heart when he allowed himself to ruminate in that direction, was....what happens next?

Honor wasn't based out of the States. She was a U.S. citizen by birth and through her mother, who was born and raised in the Bible belt, and her father, a Hollywood scion who still owned the home his own father bought in Hollywood Hills in the 1950s. But now, her folks largely lived in England, taking advantage of the Indefinite Leave to Remain status they'd been granted in the nineties when they'd started their summer play festival in the Cotswolds. He knew from long hours talking during their teen years that Honor'd grown up bouncing between southern California, Tennessee, and London until her parents finally permitted her to attend Cheltenham Ladies College.

She'd shared with him earlier in the week how she also now held Indefinite Leave to Remain status. Her primary home was in Pembrokeshire, Wales, and apparently she owned a beachfront place in Malibu. In that same conversation, he'd learned she was slated to head to Boston in under a month to begin filming her new role—the one he had to thank, at least in part, for the toe-curling sex they'd been sharing.

His life, his career, were here in Virginia. Various visas had carried him through his schooling and first years of practicing, but when Luke died, he'd applied for U.S. citizenship. Although he hadn't been speaking to his father by that point, he'd learned through his mother that Rahul Desai had been livid with his decision—which was ironic given that his father had become a UK citizen not long after marrying his mother. Hypocrite.

He shook that thought away, refusing to let Rahul, as he often thought of him, ruin his good mood.

He turned his attention to the server, who was taking drink and food orders from the other couples, working her way to Honor and him.

"You good?" She kept her voice low and private, scanning his face with concerned eyes. She could still read his moods like a book.

He shifted and dropped a kiss on the top of her head. "With you by my side? I'm fantastic."

The server, to her credit, played it cool and classy when it came time for Honor's order. He suspected Tom had prepped her for their VIP guest.

Brinder scanned the room. No one had a clue she was here, and he wondered how long they could manage it. Anyone on the stage would be able to see her, and it was karaoke night, so any minute now, there would be a revolving door of patrons on the stage.

As it turned out, she was almost immediately spotted. Honor, a practiced hand at navigating similar scenarios, suggested Tom go on stage and confirm her attendance, requesting that patrons respect her evening out. He told the crowd Honor would be happy to sign autographs later, a perfectly vague firewall of sorts. In the meantime, Bauer served as a bouncer and carefully checked entry to exclude paps as well as manage the size of the crowd.

"I heard a rumorrrr," Honor drew out, and Brinder quickly clocked her drink status, given her track record of not being able to hold her liquor. She appeared to be halfway into her glass of hard cider.

Not wanting her to get anything more than tipsy—both to avoid a potential scene of patrons taking unflattering videos, and to ensure he could fuck her senseless tonight—he passed her a glass of water and eased the cider away.

Honor smiled at him. "Thank you, Gomez, for looking out for me."

"Anytime, Tish."

"Oh, I think I just threw up in my mouth," Ross announced with a fond smile. Then she turned to her husband with a frown. "Hey, why don't we have pet names for each other?"

Xander's eyebrows flew up and he turned to his wife, murmuring, "Don't we, Principessa?"

"Oh, yeah." Ross snort-laughed. "I forgot about that."

Xander shook his head, his lips tilting up in the corners.

"But we don't have matching ones like Honor and Brinder," Ross insisted. "What goes with Principessa?" She frowned.

"How about a spanking?" Xander offered, and Brinder wasn't sure his friend was joking.

Ross's lips parted, but before she could get a word out, Cole smacked the table. "I have matching nicknames for you. Prince and Princess Overshare." The glower he aimed at them was rendered ineffective by the smirk that emerged on his lips and the laughter that coursed around the table.

"What rumor did you hear?" Brinder asked Honor loudly, cutting through the chuckles and ribbing that kept going.

"I heard," Honor began, pinning Xander with a stare, "you have a really incredible singing voice."

"I should show you the video from my birthday party last summer," Ross offered.

"Another time," Honor demurred, and, recognizing her tone, Brinder girded himself for her ask. He'd bet his retirement account on his hunch. "I would like to hear you live and in person. Along with Cole and Brinder."

Yep. Called it.

A chorus of no from all three guys met her suggestion.

Honor pouted prettily. "Why not? We want to watch our hot men sing on stage, don't we, ladies?"

Ross and Tiercy chimed in loudly with their approval as their husbands shook their heads.

"Pretty please?" Honor batted her eyes at him.

Brinder broke into a grin. He was quite familiar with this side of her. She could be relentless, and he knew she wasn't giving up on this. "Ok. We'll do it."

"What?" Xan and Cole responded in unison, as all their ladies cheered.

"What my Stardust wants, my Stardust gets. As long as it's in my power." And he meant it.

Chapter Fifty-Two

Honor

She was laughing so hard she couldn't catch her breath.

After Brinder browbeat Cole and Xander into agreement, hustling them onto the stage before they could weasel their way out, the men spent a few minutes scanning the song list. Brinder pointed to a song. There were some animated hand gestures, some snickers, and an eye roll from Xander. But they went with Brinder's selection.

Now? The three men were up on the stage belting out "It's Raining Men" by The Weather Girls. Xander's deep, sexy voice carried the song, with Cole joining in gamely. But it was Brinder's theatrics that had them all in stitches. He was practically performing interpretive dance up there, and not only were she, Ross, and Tiercy howling with laughter, the crowd was screaming its approval. There were loud claps, catcalls, whistles, and swells of rising laughter as Brin danced around the stage, preening and shaking his incredibly toned tush, pulling Cole into a spin and dip, sharing a mic with Xan, and then at the conclusion, yanking them both into a spirited, sloppy kickline. The Rockettes' jobs were certainly safe.

Honor pressed a hand against her aching stomach. She was quite sure she'd never laughed so hard in her life. And with Brinder's arm porn revealed via his rolled-up sleeves, a familiar and welcome urgency was building between her legs.

Honor dragged her eyes down his sexy body. *Shiitake.* He was turning her into a sex maniac.

And she was most definitely here for it.

Ross released a piercing whistle as the guys jumped off the stage to the crowd's standing ovation, inclusive of Honor and her friends. Brinder stalked toward her, eyes somehow smoldering and sparkling at the same time. One moment, she was standing there admiring him. The next, he was swinging her into his arms bridal-style, and planting a sweaty and sweet kiss on her lips. His lips were soft, but the fleeting tease of his tongue on her lips was a clear rain check for later. Smirking, all sorts of sexy promises dancing secretly between them, Brinder set her down, stepped back, and offered a flourishing bow that would do a Renaissance courtier proud.

Honor was aware of cameras trained on them. How could she not be? It was sixth sense at this point for her. And, yet, she found she didn't care. *To heck with it.* Honor reached for his face, stood on her tippiest toes, and planted a wallop of a kiss on him that left them both breathless.

"That may have been the single greatest performance I've ever seen in my life!" Honor kept his face cradled in her hands, beaming at him.

"Anything for you, Stardust." Brinder winked at her. "It was either that or 'Pink Pony Club.'"

"Next time," Xander chimed in with a grin.

"Thank you for indulging me, Gomez."

Given that Brinder had to bend practically in half to kiss her, he groaned theatrically as he straightened and held his back, all while scanning the room. "Getting busy in here, Tish. And before we went onstage, Grayton messaged me that we have paps out front."

Ross motioned to the door. "We should all head out. Tiercy and I need to pump, and I think the crowd outside is about to overrun poor Bauer."

Brinder assessed the room. "Good idea. Besides, no one's topping that exquisite performance." He grinned cockily.

Honor shook her head and chuckled. "Stop bloviating, you incorrigible brat."

"Ooooh, double SAT word bonus points," Ross cooed, sharing high-fives with Honor and then Tiercy. "Well done you." She snapped her fingers on both hands in appreciation. "I doth believe the student may become the teacher."

Xander tugged his wife to his side. "Time to get our kids and head home, Principessa."

Honor couldn't hear what Ross said to him in response—it was loud in there and Ross was whispering in her husband's ear—but she definitely picked up the word 'spank.'

She gave a quick side eye to Brinder, wondering if he was into that. If *she* would be.

"Want to head out the back, Tish?"

"Nope." She popped the p. "I want to sign autographs for Tom and our server, and any guests who want one. I'll take some pictures with them. Then we can head out front. We'll just ask Grayton to have the car ready."

"You sure, babe?"

"Absolutely," Honor nodded. "Everyone has been so courteous and respectful tonight. I adore my fans, and I am fully aware that it's only because of their support that I can do the thing I love. I want to thank them."

For the next forty-five minutes, she took selfies and signed autographs until her wrist cramped. She turned to the final patron waiting, an elderly man with wild wispy hair and rheumy eyes who had wowed them all with his rendition of "Desperado." Apparently he was a regular and a fan favorite. He also had the kind of charisma that made stars. Honor wondered what his story was.

As she signed a napkin for him, he put a spotted, wrinkled hand gently on her arm. "Chin up, girlie. Don't let that video mess with your mind. You know your character." He turned to Brinder. "Take good care of her. I can see the love here. Don't take it for granted."

With a wink and a smile, he returned to his perch at the bar, where Tom had a club soda at the ready for him.

"You sure you want to go out front?" He scanned her face, concern clearly etched between his brows.

"Absolutely," she affirmed, her confidence in that decision part real, part bravado. "The whole point is to be seen. Just like the other night, I'm going to stop in front of them, smile, pose for some pictures, and pretend not to hear their obnoxious questions." She took a deep breath. "And, I'll say it again, you do *not* need to put yourself through that gauntlet, Brin. It's a lot. If you want to wait and go out the back, we'll swing by and get you."

Brinder pinned her with his eyes, everything on his face showing he was affronted by her offer. "And I will say it again—I will absolutely not be going out the back. I'll be by your side, where I belong. I'm not letting you face any of this alone."

Where he belonged. Her repaired heart fluttered. How random was life? One minute you're an actor mired in scandal. And the next?

You're hurtling back in love with the only person capable of shredding you to pieces.

Chapter Fifty-Three

Brinder

She was damn impressive. Honor held up like a champ. Smiling like the paps' flashes weren't blinding her. Like their revolting questions weren't skewering her spirit. Like the glorious goddess she was and always had been.

Even at her most frail and vulnerable, Honor had a dignity about her. He supposed it partly came from years of being in the spotlight. Perhaps her Hollywood DNA. But there was more to it. She just had a reservoir of graciousness and class, an innate goodness and kindness most people—except maybe the paps and her twat of an ex—couldn't help but appreciate.

Sure, she had charisma. His Stardust had star quality in spades. But she was so much more than that.

He figured after celebrating his good news, and then a fun night out with friends—not to mention his over-the-top karaoke performance that he'd summoned just because he craved her laughter—that she'd be in a good place mentally and emotionally.

According to Benny, and everything he'd also obsessively read, public support was very much in her favor. Benny's team hadn't captured the perpetrators, but the scandal was waning.

So why was she perched on the edge of his bed, tension lining her posture and the beautiful planes of her face as she disappeared into a thousand-yard stare?

He knelt in front of her, breaking her reverie.

She blinked a few times and then offered a half-hearted smile.

"Sorry, baby. I didn't mean to startle you."

"Don't apologize. I was lost in thought."

He rested his hand along her smooth cheek, which had finally lost its flush from the intensity of the pap deluge. "Doesn't seem like they were good thoughts. Want to talk about it?"

Honor closed her eyes and then inhaled a shaky breath. "It's nothing."

He stood, wincing at the pops of his knees, and settled in next to her, wrapping his arm around her. She was stiff for a moment, and then sighed and sank into him.

"I'm pretty sure I saw Crispin."

Brinder clenched his jaw as every muscle in his body went rigid. "You what? Are you sure?" Adrenaline kicked in and he had to force himself not to rush out of the room and call for Grayton. What the hell was that wanker doing here?

She stood and walked to the dresser, where she removed the small silver hoop earrings she wore along with the thin sapphire band on her right hand. He remembered that was her favorite stone.

"Yes. I'm sure."

"Where? Here?"

He watched her haltingly peel away her shorts and top, leaving her in a thong and simple strapless bra, which she robotically removed. His reptilian brain homed in on her luscious naked body, egging him to reach for her. To touch her until she screamed her pleasure, and then he could sink into her. But, thankfully, his rational brain had command. For the moment.

"No. Outside Mac's. He was across the street. As we were getting in the car, movement caught my eye. He stood in the street for a moment. And—and he glared at me."

She reached into one of the drawers he'd emptied for her and pulled out a navy, thigh-length nightgown. Cotton with lace on the edges. Slipping it over her head, she adjusted the twisted spaghetti straps, fiddling with one side with shaking hands. It was relatively modest, but with her hourglass shape, nothing was ever completely demure.

He forced himself to focus. "Christ, Tish. Why didn't you say anything? I can't believe Grayton or Bauer didn't notice."

"Grayton was busy behind the wheel and Bauer was clearing paps out of the way."

"If he had been a lunatic with a gun, you could have been shot!" Brinder's heart raced like he'd just finished an intense workout.

"It didn't sink in until we pulled away. I was...disoriented. I didn't expect to see him and, for a moment, I thought my eyes were playing tricks on me. But I've been sitting here replaying it over and over. And I'm sure it was Crispin. And that he looked...angry." She finished the last word on a shaky whisper.

"What the fuck excuse does he have to be angry? And never mind that, what reason does he have to even be here? None." Brinder stood and began pacing. "That tiny twatty bloke was behind the video, Honor. I know it!" He reached into his pocket for his phone. "I'm texting Benny, Grayton, and Bauer."

"Wait." She held out a staying hand. "Please. I just—I need a minute to process this. As soon as we alert the cavalry, it's going to set off a whole chain reaction. I just need some time to get my head on straight." Her chin wobbled.

"Baby. Come here." He pulled her into his arms, kissing the top of her head and gently rocking her side to side. "I'm sorry. I didn't mean to overreact. It's just—I know your exit from Mac's was under control. But it felt so out of *my* control. And it scared me. You did so beautifully, Tish. But all those sweaty, smarmy paps pressing toward you and screaming at you." He shuddered. "I don't know how you handle that. And then when you said your ex appeared... Well, it all came flooding back. And I realized I'm doing a shit job protecting you."

She hiccupped a sob, nuzzling into his chest. "You don't have to protect me. I'm a big girl," she mumbled against him.

"But I want to. I want to take care of you. Keep you safe. Make you laugh."

Love you.

Honor rubbed her hand on her face, wiping tears that had tracked down her cheeks. Then she wrapped her arms around him, practically burrowing into him.

He held her like that until he sensed her breathing settling. When she released a huge sigh, Brinder leaned back so he could see her face, and tipped up her chin. Her skin was blotchy, but her eyes were now tearless, albeit a bit red-rimmed.

"I think we need to let your team know. Sooner rather than later."

She nodded. "I'll get my phone. I left it in the kitchen when I grabbed my bedtime water."

He loved that she always needed that water at her bedside. It was one small thing from *before* that hadn't changed. "I'll get it, Stardust. You climb into bed. And I'll meet you back here in a minute."

He was going to use the trip to retrieve her phone to send his own message to Benny and the guys.

"I need to wipe off my makeup and brush my teeth."

"Take your time. Need anything while I'm in the kitchen?"

"No. I have my water. And we need to get to sleep soon or I'm going to have bags under my eyes for your event that no makeup artist will be able to conceal."

"Ok, Stardust. I'll grab your phone, get some water for myself, and I'll be back in. I need to scan work emails briefly just in case anything at the hospital needs my attention." A lie. He'd done that in the car on the twenty-minute drive back from Mac's. All was well at Evangelist.

Listening for the water in the bathroom, he strode into the kitchen while typing out an SOS to Benny, Grayton, and Bauer. A quick scan around and he immediately spied her phone where she'd left it on the counter under the cabinet of glassware. As he picked it up, his attention fastened on a home screen alert. From Crispin.

He knew her passcode. It was the six-digit date of her second valve surgery. She'd told him once when she was in the shower and wanted him to read a text from her mom that came in. He'd meant to have a conversation with her about easy-to-crack passcodes. But now wasn't the time. Fortunately, her lax password security played to his advantage, as he was now able to access her phone to read the messages.

As he unlocked the device and read her message, the blood drained from his head.

Brinder reached for the counter behind him to steady himself. That nasty wanker. He'd sent a particularly graphic screenshot of the video, following it up with a screenshot from an email that looked to be from Honor to Crispin, suggesting they film a sex video and then release it to generate more publicity for her memoir and upcoming film.

Fuck.

In his next text the asshole threatened to release that email unless she agreed to his demands—directing her new screenplay *and* funding a new production company that he would lead.

That fucking shitstain. He was *blackmailing* her.

Brinder never considered himself a violent man. But right now? Rage coursed through his body as he imagined pummeling Crispin to a bloody pulp.

Fucker. From the start, Brinder suspected that smarmy, short shite, with his Ken-doll shellacked hair and his arrogant bearing, was behind this whole sordid saga. Honor had the kindest, most accepting heart of anyone he'd met, including Luke...and that was saying something. Instead of being jaded, as one would expect from an international star, it was clear Honor had retained her trusting and down-to-earth personality, seeing the good in people versus their flaws.

Despite Crispy's faults—and Brinder suspected there were many she'd excused over the years in the name of *love* (and he wanted to vomit at the thought of her in love with that assbasket)—Honor believed her ex to be a good person. Definitely not someone capable of this heinous betrayal.

Brinder's shaking fingers flew across the keys of his phone as he forwarded the images, which he'd first sent to himself, to Benny. Within moments his phone rang.

"That disgusting piece of shit." Benny didn't even bother with the niceties of a greeting. Her strident voice carried across the transatlantic connection and he could sense her anger. "I will eviscerate him. And then I'll hack off his balls and his pathetic useless willie with a rusty knife and stuff them in his lying mouth until he suffocates."

Brinder choked down a chuckle. Benny was fierce. And he was grateful. "Other than torture, what are you thinking as a next step?"

"Does Honor know?"

"Not yet."

"Are you at your place?"

"Yes."

"Anyone else around?"

"No."

"Good. I'm sending Grayton and Bauer over. In the meantime, I need you to hang up and gently break the news to Honor that her ex is even more of a dirtbag than we thought." He heard Benny take a deep breath. "Then we go after this son of a bitch."

CHAPTER FIFTY-FOUR

HONOR

It was like last Sunday all over again. Only much worse. Because it was clear now that Crispin was behind a disgusting blackmail scenario, which only amplified the horrific violation of the video. She'd spent years and years with him. Laughing with him. Traveling with him. Loving him. And he'd betrayed her in the very worst possible way.

Honor cradled her head in her hand, all the pieces coming together in a bleak picture. He'd gone into her email and sent a message suggesting the video from "her" to him. Then he arranged to set up the hidden cameras, film them, and release the video to the sordid online gossip site owned by an unethical mogul who didn't give a whit about the truth—and probably paid Crispin a small fortune for the video. As if that humiliation weren't enough, now he was going to lie to the world, presenting his "evidence" as proof that the video was all a highly planned publicity ploy orchestrated by her.

Tears poured down her face that she didn't even bother wiping away. The hand not holding up her head was clenched into such a tight fist, she knew there were crescent-shaped divots forming on her palm, possibly even breaking the skin. Even her beloved Couchie was cold comfort.

Brinder and Grayton hurried in from the bedroom, the latter with her laptop firmly in his grasp. Bauer was outside with another three members of their security company who'd arrived an hour ago. They were setting up a perimeter in case Crispin tried to breach the renovated factory.

Brinder hurried to her, gathering her in his arms. "Ssssh, baby. Please don't cry. We're going to fix this. Benny's on her way here. She's got the top digital forensic team on this."

"Which is useless." Honor hiccupped a sob.

"Where's a damn box of tissues when you need one?" Brinder muttered, lifting the hem of his shirt to wipe her face.

After carefully breaking the news, and then picking her up from the floor—where she'd collapsed in a wail of shock and horror—he'd slid her arms through a robe and guided her to the couch, placing a still-untouched glass of water on the table in front of her.

Her stomach roiled. If she even had a sip, Honor knew she'd throw up.

"Why is it useless, baby?" He took the tissues offered by Grayton, mopping her face and her snotty nose with aching tenderness.

"Because they won't be able to prove it wasn't me who sent it."

"But he hacked into your computer."

"No," she moaned, unable to believe this amazing night with Brinder had devolved into such a nightmare. "I gave him access. He—he said his laptop was broken and he really needed to work on something for my parents' theater. He was going to log in to his work email from my laptop until he could replace his. I—I remembered him having trouble with it. It was shutting down randomly and not saving his work. That's what he said."

"That sonofabitch," Grayton snarled. "Always detested that puny weasel."

"So I gave him my password to log in to the computer."

"Fuck," Brinder breathed, closing his eyes.

Honor shook her head, a fresh wave of tears spilling. "There's no way to prove he wrote that email. It came from my laptop, not his, from my email account." She put a hand over her mouth to try—fruitlessly—to hold back her sobs.

Brinder pulled her onto his lap and rocked her, which only made her cry harder.

"Oh God, Brin," she gasped, realization slamming into her. "This is going to blow back on you. You'll look complicit. That Clark jerk will try to invoke your morality clause again. I need...I need..."—she could barely get her thoughts together—"to get away from here. From you."

She watched his face lose color and tried to get up from his lap, needing to physically remove herself from him. If only to think straight for a moment—something she'd clearly failed to do over the past days. She'd dragged him into this mess, and now it was going to hurt him too. What a prized idiot she was! Brinder was in the midst of his own vulnerable situation. As a friend—nevermind someone who loved him in such a soul-shaking, fathomless way—she never should've let them get in so deep before her own sordid scandal was resolved. She'd allowed her own yearning, *burning* need for him to eclipse her rational brain. *Putting. Him. At. Risk.*

"No." He tightened his arms around her. "That is not going to happen. We're going to prove he set you up."

"I should just do what he wants," she whispered, her fingers finding the scar on her chest out of long stress-induced habit.

"You damn well won't," Grayton barked. "Ma'am," he added with an apologetic smile.

"I don't see any other way."

"Listen, Ms. Wheatley, this guy is a snake, and not particularly smart." He raised his brows as if to say 'Go ahead and argue that point. You know you can't.'

"That doesn't mean he doesn't have me over a barrel and at his mercy."

"No, it means there's a snag in this scheme of his somewhere. And our team, plus the digital forensics team, will find it, pull on it, and the whole ridiculous blackmail plan will unravel. Even the smartest criminals get tripped up and leave a trail. This guy...is not that."

She should have known it was Crispin behind all this. They'd had that massive fight the week before her London trip—the same old argument around her refusal to fund his ambitions carte blanche. After days of icing her out, suddenly he'd warmed up. He'd apologized, sincerity shining in his eyes, and offered to accompany her to London.

Honor inhaled a shuddering breath, focusing on the soothing stroke of Brinder's thumb on the back of her hand. He lifted and rotated her hand to kiss her palm—which she'd always loved him doing—and then winced when he saw the broken skin.

"Jesus, Tish. You hurt yourself."

Grayton looked over the back of the couch at the damage she'd done. "First aid kit?"

"Under my bathroom sink. Left side. Big royal blue nylon bag."

"Copy that. Be right back." Grayton strode out of the room, commanding the space along the way like the retired Ranger SpecOp he was.

"It's fine." She tried pulling her hand away, but Brinder held on, firmly but gently.

"I'm going to pummel that wanker when this is over. He's hurt and threatened my girl. He won't get away with this."

My girl. His possessive terminology, and tone, shouldn't have thrilled her. But it did. In the midst of the horror of the moment, Honor realized she might be developing a bit of an alpha kink. But even that wasn't enough to cut through her misery.

Grayton appeared before her, and she was stunned, as always, at how light on his feet he was. It wasn't the first time her trusted security seemed to emerge out of thin air. Benny told her he was a decorated Ranger, who once saved his squad in Jalalabad by hanging out of a Black Hawk with a team of Night Stalkers—members of the 160th Airborne —and taking out an enemy convoy.

"Let's get this disinfected, ma'am."

"I've got it." Brinder's voice brooked no argument. Honor rolled her lips to prevent a smile as the alphas assessed each other.

After a brief staredown, Grayton nodded. "Yes, sir. I'm going to check in with the digital forensics team. And, ma'am?"

"Yes, Grayton?"

His deep blue eyes softened. He was like the world's coolest big brother—although she'd never tell her own big brother that. "It's almost two in the morning. You should get some rest, ma'am. We'll fix this for you. We won't let you down."

"Thank you, Grayton." She blinked back tears of relief. And for the first time in the three hours since her world had turned upside down—again—a sliver of hope emerged.

CHAPTER FIFTY-FIVE

BRINDER

After examining the prescription Benny had tucked into Honor's purse last Sunday, which had so far remained untouched, Brinder tried to coax Honor into taking a mild sedative. His stubborn girl had insisted she didn't need it and had mulishly lain in bed curled on her side, squeezing her eyes closed, stubbornly insisting she needed to be alone.

Quite sure his current wired state would be more disruptive to her than helpful, he left the room with a deep reluctance that screamed at him to do otherwise. Only his concern for fueling her distress with his own propelled him out of the bedroom door and into the living room. He stalked to his liquor cart and poured a hefty glass of whiskey while Grayton articulated the work happening on Honor's behalf to find further evidence of Crispin's entire blackmail scheme and exonerate his girl.

He'd watched Honor withdraw the moment she decided she was a risk to him. Bullshit. The only risk was losing her again. And he'd never let that happen. He would be bloody-well damned if he let this shitstain's attempt at blackmail rip Honor from his arms. He'd only just gotten her back. No fucking way was he losing her again.

The sounds of stifled sobs filtered through the condo, and Brinder rushed into the bedroom, only to find Honor weeping into her pillow. He wanted to howl in rage at that fuckwit for hurting her so much.

After kissing her tears away, again, he convinced her the low dosage of the sedative was safe and appropriate, considering the situation. Shaking out a pill, he watched while she reluctantly swallowed it with her ever-present 'nighttime water.'

He settled in behind her, curling around her and nestling her hands within his until he felt her limbs slacken and her breathing even out as she drifted off. And then he followed her into sleep.

His eyes flew open. Momentarily disoriented, he took a moment to catalog the situation—a grounding trick he'd learned in his residency.

Shit.

The hellscape of last night crashed into him. He looked at Honor, still sound asleep, but now rotated so her head lay on his chest. Christ, if circumstances were different, he'd love to slowly wake her with his mouth on the nirvana between her legs. Another time. That was a certainty.

Brinder shifted to reach for his phone, making his movements small so he didn't disturb her sleep. Almost ten in the morning. Well, at least they'd both slept for a solid eight hours.

He examined the faint blue stress smudges under her eyes. The glam squad Benny was sending wouldn't arrive until two in the afternoon. With any luck, Honor would sleep another couple hours.

He inched his body to the side, holding his breath as he eased her head from his chest onto a pillow. Other than a few nonsensical grumblings, she didn't stir. Good.

Not wanting to risk the sound of dresser drawers, Brinder pulled on the flat-front khaki shorts and button down he'd worn the day before. He'd shower and change later. First, he needed to check in with the team. And Benny should be arriving by noon. The private jet Honor had used wasn't available, so Benny had grabbed the first commercial flight out of Heathrow.

Grayton looked up at him from his post at the table and nodded. A legal pad filled with notes rested next to a military-style laptop. Brinder wondered if the guy had even slept at all. He suspected the former Ranger, like every medical resident, learned to function on little-to-no sleep for extended periods. Still, the guy had to be late forties or early fifties, even though he looked younger than that and was in better shape than Brinder. Regardless, loss of sleep got harder and harder to manage as one aged.

"She still sleeping?"

"Yes, thank God. The glass of cider she drank plus that mild sedative several hours later really knocked her out."

A small frown marred Grayton's brow and Brinder was instantly defensive. "In normal circumstances, I'd never let anyone mix alcohol and a sedative. But she only had one drink with a low alcohol content, and it was five hours prior. And the sedative is one of the mildest. She's fine." Physically maybe. But he knew she was emotionally wrecked by Crispin's treachery.

The Ranger nodded. "I know. Neither of us would ever put her in harm's way. I trust you with her." He shook his head. "I should've been more vigilant with that rat bastard."

"You didn't know. And I imagine, even if he was a bit of a weasel, Honor trusted him. She loved him." A thought that rankled. "He works for her parents."

"Not anymore."

Brinder was shocked. "Is that a good idea? Won't that just incite him to pull the trigger on the email?"

"No. We alerted the Wheatleys last night. Jock was so livid, Clementine thought he would have a heart attack. After he calmed down, a team of us, including her parents, decided to pretend to play his game. Jock sent the dirtbag a message that he understood from Honor that Crispin would be taking on a new professional role with her. He played it cool, saying big things were in Crispin's future." Grayton snorted in derision. "Big things. Like prison for revenge pornography. It's a priority offense in England under the Online Safety Act. He's looking at two-to-four years."

"Once we catch him."

"Oh, we'll catch him. The digital forensics team is already compiling what they need."

Brinder's hand stalled as he reached for his tin of Earl Grey tea leaves. "You're that close?"

"Oh yeah. That fucker is going down. Soon."

Brinder was almost dizzy with relief. If it weren't so important for Honor to get some restorative sleep, he'd wake her immediately with the good news.

Reading his mind, Grayton offered a rare smile. "Let her sleep. Hopefully by the time she wakes, we'll have a more solid update for her."

"So there's a chance we won't nab him."

Grayton narrowed his eyes. "We've already got him, Sir. He just doesn't know it. Yet."

CHAPTER FIFTY-SIX

HONOR

Hubbub outside their bedroom had pulled Honor from sleep shortly before noon. It was Benny, arriving like the tour de force she was. Within minutes, after a fierce hug from her agent, Brinder sat her down in front of his large screen TV for a video conference call with the digital forensic lead, a sixty-ish Black man named Andre whose thin, wire-framed glasses surrounded a set of the kindest eyes Honor had ever seen. He was a fascinating blend of friendly favorite uncle and all-business former CIA—the latter of which she knew to be the case from Grayton's brief introduction.

"Are you ready for your update, Miss Wheatley?" Andre's voice was as pleasant and kind as his eyes. She'd bet her britches he'd been wildly successful as a CIA operative, his natural warmth likely lowering many raised guards to extract what he needed from an asset.

"Call me Honor. Please." She wiped the sleep from her eyes and took a restorative swallow of the latte Brinder had handed her before dropping onto Couchie next to her. The worry and exhaustion bracketing his mouth nearly unraveled her. Had they failed to get the evidence they needed? Honor reached blindly for Brinder's hand, unable to tear her eyes from the screen. He laced his fingers with hers and gave a little squeeze. She inhaled a bracing lungful of oxygen and slowly released it. "Where are we with this?"

Andre nodded briskly. "As predicted, Crispin Lascelles left a messy digital footprint. Overnight, Ms. Tambeaux and your parents reported the hate crime to the police. Mrs. Wheatley called in a favor with a well-placed judge to accelerate the procurement of a warrant to investigate Crispin's personal email on probable cause."

Honor absorbed that statement. She would need to call her parents after this meeting. They were probably beside themselves with worry for her.

"After that, it all moved quickly," Andre continued. "According to the evidence, after Mr. Lascelles logged into your laptop, Honor, he used your email account to create and send the fake email from you to him. It appears he sent some decoy emails to your parents from his work email as cover. Your parents' shared work email corroborates this."

Bloody hell. At some point—but definitely no time soon—she was going to have to revisit years of interactions with Crispin to examine them for hidden signs of his treachery. How had she been so blind to his true character?

Honor did a quick grounding exercise, focusing on the soothing sensation of Brinder's hand connected with hers. That simple skin-to-skin contact was as intimate as any sexual act they'd performed this week. Perhaps even more so. She turned her head and caught him gazing at her. They hadn't said the words yet, but she could read the love in his captivating hazel eyes.

She may have badly, and dangerously, misjudged Crispin, but at least the innate goodness of Brinder's character remained clear and true. No matter what she'd convinced herself for so many long, lonely years.

Realizing Andre had stopped talking, Honor tore her gaze from Brinder.

The investigator smiled softly and raised his brows in an unspoken 'OK to continue?'

Honor nodded.

"Mr. Lascelles—" he began, before Brinder cut him off.

"I wish you wouldn't give him the courtesy of an honorific," he practically snarled. "I propose we refer to him as Vile Shitbucket."

Honor couldn't help it. She burst into much-needed laughter. At the sound, Brinder blinked away the glower he'd been sporting, a sly grin replacing it. With that simple look, the sharp edges of her terror and worry...evaporated. It was going to be ok. *It had to be ok.*

With Brinder back in her life, there was no other outcome that mattered.

"The *perpetrator,*" Andre continued with a smothered smile, "was either lazy or stupid enough to log in to his own personal email."

"Meaning, anyone with decent hacking skills could recreate the digital pathway and connect to his account. Which is exactly what happened. Fucking moron." Benny chimed in, arms folded and a satisfied smirk on a face that was way too polished and put together for a person who'd flown across the Atlantic and likely been up all night. Honor wanted to be like Benoite Tambeaux when she grew up.

Andre adjusted his glasses, consulting a paper in his hand. "From there, detectives found emails from the perpetrator to an email belonging to a twenty-two-year-old aspiring actress named Portia Evans. In their exchanges, they developed a plan to extort Miss Wheat—" he caught himself. "*Honor.* Their plan hinged on a sex tape and a planted email. Miss Evans—"

"Who shall forthwith be known as Dirty Cuntwaffle." Brinder wore his own satisfied smirk.

"—secured a job in housekeeping at the boutique hotel Honor frequented in London," Andre continued without losing a beat, only the upward tilt of his lips giving away his amusement at Brinder's interjection, "and switched shifts with a colleague, ensuring she'd be working the penthouse suites the night Honor and the perpetrator came into town. Under the guise of prepping their suite, the *co-conspirator* planted two hidden cameras."

Andre paused, pulling off his glasses. "I'm afraid this next part may be rather upsetting, Honor."

Now what? How could it get much worse?

Famous last questions, apparently.

Andre watched her cautiously, his caring somehow emanating through the screen.

"While Honor continued her meeting with Ms. Tambeaux, the perpetrator checked into the hotel. He, uh—" Andre swallowed and cleared his throat. "He 'practiced' the set up with Miss Evans to ensure the most graphic angles."

"Dirty Cuntwaffle!" Brinder roared, his free hand fisting on his lap.

Nausea slammed into her gut, forcing a wave of bile up Honor's throat. She slapped a hand over her mouth and leapt off the couch, running to the bathroom where she forcefully threw up at yet another horrifying facet to her ex's betrayal. The idea that he'd had sex with someone else, and then not five hours later had sex with her—unprotected—made her retch over and over until her latte was long purged from her stomach. It would be a while, if ever, before she could overcome the horror of that scenario. Thankfully, in a small consolation, she'd been tested as a precaution after their breakup and her tests were all negative.

At some point, Brinder had knelt behind her, draping a cold washcloth on the back of her neck, which helped ease her overheated skin. Eventually, with a hand from Brinder, she stood on shaky legs. Tears pricked her eyes. She knew at some point the rage would hit. But for now? The deep hurt held center stage solo.

"I just can't get over the depth of his—of his…I can't even think of a word that conveys what I want."

"Revolting assholery?" Brinder offered.

"Not strong enough," she muttered as Brinder pulled her into his arms, pressing a kiss on the top of her head before gently releasing her. "How ironic," she continued, "that the best directing I've seen from Crispin was in this hideous video."

Brinder's lips twitched at her pathetic attempt at a joke, but his eyes were serious and sad. "I'm so sorry, Stardust. So very sorry."

This man. This beautiful man and his tender concern—so opposite of Crispin's duplicity and faithlessness—almost undid her all over again.

Instead, drawing on some very necessary inner reserve of resilience, Honor sniffled and wiped her nose with a tissue from the box on the bathroom counter, slowly pulling her shattered pieces together. "I need to hear the rest."

She reached for Brinder's hand, guiding them to the living room where everyone was clearly waiting for her to re-emerge from her vomiting session. She ignored the currents of concern vibrating in the paradoxically sunny room, and listened numbly to the rest of Andre's report.

A series of emails between her ex and his accomplice laid out Crispin's assurance that he would cast Portia Evans in a beefy supporting role in the filming of Honor's screenplay, and that he'd set up his lover in a place in Belgravia in West London.

By ten in the morning London time, a pair of detectives had descended on that woman's tiny flat in Camden.

"Thankfully," Andre added, "It didn't take much for her to crack and admit the entire plot. She also provided access to her emails in a plea deal to avoid prison time as an accessory to a crime."

"So what's next?" Honor was proud of herself for the calm in her voice, which was probably a result of her emotional numbness versus any inner peace. *But whatever.* At this point, she'd take what grace she could get from the universe.

Now Grayton spoke up. He hadn't moved from the dining room table, only turning the chair to face the large-screen TV. "Under mutual aid, a team of officers is on its way to a hotel down the street from here to arrest Crispin and extradite him to London. Where he will face a series of charges," he added, a hard glint in his eye. "Bauer is with them. We wanted our own eyes on this."

It was probably highly intentional to select Bauer for this duty. He was definitely the most even-tempered and unflappable of them all. Honor wasn't sure who would be the most vicious if facing her ex in person—Grayton, Benny, or Brinder. If pressed, her money was on Benny, who could rival a mama grizzly protecting her cubs. But Grayton was a veritable human lethal weapon and loyal to her to the core. And Brinder? He had sheer rage on her behalf to fuel a commensurate response.

Wait...*down the street?*

Honor's eyes flew back to Grayton. "Was he—" she halted, and composed herself as she tried to calm her racing heart. "Do you think he was planning to come here?"

Grayton caught Benny's eye. Her agent gave one brief nod, then quickly looked away and back to Honor, two spots of color emerging on her cut-glass cheekbones.

"Appears likely, given the proximity of his hotel to Dr. Desai's home. There's more, ma'am." Grayton watched her with worried eyes. "When Bauer surveilled his hotel room last night, he saw something as Crispin stood by the window. He had a gun with him. We don't know if he intended to use it. But it's been my experience that when bad guys find themselves in desperate straights...they do desperate things."

Blood drained from Honor's head and she swayed a bit on the couch before Brinder put a steadying arm around her.

"He's been texting me this week," she admitted in a soft whisper, wringing her hands to try to regain lost feeling in her appendages.

"What?" Brinder and Benny exclaimed in shocked unison. Grayton and Andre wore matching faces of deep concern.

"I thought he just wanted to commiserate on the video. He kept texting me that 'we needed to talk.'" She made air quotes with shaking fingers. "I just didn't have the emotional bandwidth to deal with him."

"Why didn't you tell me?" Shock. Frustration. Worry. All of it laced Brinder's stunned question.

"Or me?" Benny added, a frown creasing her smooth forehead.

"I just," Honor began, and then closed her eyes, trying to corral the thoughts and feelings hurtling through her. "I just thought he was being *Crispin*. Benny told me he'd contacted her and was making noises about lawsuits. I couldn't deal with him. I've been on utter emotional overload. Then his texts got more and more belligerent, insisting on seeing me. Another part of me was worried he planned to accuse me of setting the whole thing up. For publicity. Just like the nasty rumors. I— I just deleted his texts. Out of self-preservation."

"You should have told us." Grayton's reprimand was softened by his warm tone, but it was still clearly a reprimand.

"I didn't think he'd be capable of this. So I didn't give much weight to his texts."

"We, however, *did* think he was capable. Which is why he was suspect number one from the beginning. His lawsuit blatherings were nothing more than a pathetic red herring." Benny's voice was laced with disdain. She'd never liked Crispin.

Suddenly it was all too much. Honor exploded. "Why didn't you tell me you were that sure it was him? I know you mentioned you were looking into it, but I didn't give it much credence. Dammit, Benny! I'm not a naive child. I'm a grown woman, successful in my own right, and more than capable of handling bad news. It's *my* life—my crisis," she practically shrieked. "And you owed me the full story!"

Ah...*here* came the rage. It was bound to make an appearance.

Benny came over and sat on the arm of Couchie, laying a hand on Honor's arm, which was rigid with her anger. "We know that, Honor. When it was just a strong hunch, we didn't want to alarm or concern you with theories. Andre had a sense early on that this would resolve quickly, so we wanted to present you with the full story." Benny rubbed soothing circles on Honor's arm. "We all know how strong you are, Honor. It was my decision to keep our conjecture quiet until it coalesced into fact. I'm so, so sorry if I hurt you by trying to present you with the full picture. Hindsight twenty-twenty, I'd do it differently. I swear to you."

"Fuck," Honor breathed, dropping her head. "Such a nightmare."

"The worst part's over, Honor." Benny shifted to kneel in front of her. "I feel horrible that my decision hurt you." Benny's striking ice-blue eyes filled with tears, effectively dissolving Honor's pique.

She shifted forward to hug her friend, who was so much taller that Honor ended up tucked under Benny's head, breathing in her signature exotic perfume. That familiar scent was as healing as the hug itself. "It's ok. I'm not mad at you, Benny. I understand why you did what you did."

Benny eased out of the hug, whispering a soft thank you, then gracefully lifted herself back onto the arm of the couch as they resumed the rest of the meeting.

By the time they disconnected the video conference, the whole thing felt like an out-of-body experience. It had been barely thirteen hours since Crispin tried to blackmail her, causing her world to spin and then crash around her.

Now it was over.

Well, almost. There would certainly be a media feeding frenzy. Her profile, plus her parents' and her brother's, would ensure that. But Benny and her PR team would be all over it—in the same way they'd worked double time to scrub the video from the internet as best they could. They'd release appropriate statements, while guaranteeing every reputable news and entertainment outlet—plus some of the disreputable ones—knew of Crispin's deceit and her innocence in the entire matter. She'd likely have to testify at a trial, although Benny said a sworn statement might suffice and, if she did have to testify, she may be able to do it via teleconference since she'd likely be filming in Boston.

She couldn't think about that, though. It meant she'd be leaving Brinder again. It was a heart-wrenching parallel to the forces that pulled them apart so long ago. Every time she permitted her mind to wander to this upcoming cleaving, her heart ached fiercely. And it was becoming distressingly clear that their lives were incompatible, just as they were all those years ago.

No, she most definitely wouldn't think about it. Not today. Not tomorrow.

She didn't have to go on location for four more weeks. And she intended to make the most of that time. To wring enough joy and happiness from this Brinder cocoon to sustain her forever.

Starting with the event that night.

CHAPTER FIFTY-SEVEN

BRINDER

Honor, Benny, Ross, and a glam squad consisting of a stylist, a hairdresser, and a makeup artist, had ensconced themselves in the primary bedroom beginning at two. Brinder was relegated to the guest room to get ready, which would take him a fraction of the time and effort being devoted to his beautiful date.

Grayton, who was still anchored to his spot at the dining room table while he reviewed last-minute logistics for the night, snorted a laugh into his sparkling water as he brought the glass to his lips. "Why do I feel like a dad watching his son get ready to pick his date up for prom?"

Brinder had grown fond of the former Ranger and rolled his eyes with a smile. "They teach you that in the Rangers or you pick it up at home?" He remembered, with an internal cringe, Honor had shared Grayton was divorced, with no children she knew of. He'd always told her the life of a Ranger was incompatible with a happy family life. Which had to be BS, but who was he to judge?

Grayton's smile faded a bit. "No, they didn't. But I imagine it would be pretty similar to this. You want me to run out and get a corsage?"

They shared a chuckle—Brinder deeply relieved that Grayton

hadn't seemed to take offense at his foot-in-mouth moment. Brinder looked at his watch. It was just after six, and Honor's team promised she'd be ready to leave by six-thirty. The event started at seven with cocktails and a silent auction, followed by dinner and a live auction. They'd be lucky to make it home by eleven, at which time, he planned to make up for last night's missed opportunity to fuck her bow-legged. He had ideas. Yes, he did.

"You know I can read your intentions right on your face, don't you?" Grayton's sardonic tone cut into the fantasy Brinder planned to make reality.

"Pardon?" He swiveled his head back toward Grayton from his vantage point in front of the floor-to-ceiling windows by the liquor cart. He remembered scooping a drunk Honor off the floor right by there. How was that only six days ago?

"You telegraph your intentions. Never play poker."

Brinder snorted. He was decent at poker. Ok, he wasn't *terrible*. But he also didn't usually win. Maybe Grayton was onto something.

He decided to call him on it. "So in addition to badass Ranger skills, you're apparently a mindreader. Ok, what am I thinking?"

Grayton pushed back the chair and stalked over to him with the grace and physicality of a man whose body was a finely honed weapon, stopping a couple feet in front of him. "You're imagining how this evening is going to end. What you're going to do with her. What you didn't get to do last night. You're thinking of how you're going to savor every moment with her, knowing that time is slipping away."

Brinder's jaw dropped. "Fuck," he breathed. "Am I that transparent?"

"Yes," Grayton smirked. "And I'm that good. Besides, I know you two have been, shall we say, very much enjoying all aspects of each other's company." He paused a beat. "And I know you're deeply in love with her."

He shook his head, amazed at the uncanny accuracy of Grayton's assessment. "So I'm that obvious."

"Not a bad thing in this case, Brinder."

That was the first time Grayton had referred to him by his first name. Usually it was 'Sir' or 'Dr. Desai.'

"And, yes, I intentionally called you by your first name."

Now Brinder laughed, shaking his head again. "I bet you were unstoppable in the Army."

"Not so much," the older man replied enigmatically, his face neutrally blank. "I used your first name because this isn't an official conversation. This"—he waved his hand between them—"is two people who both care deeply for Honor. I need you to know I think you've been really good for her. You *are* really good for her. Even with the fucked up circumstances, there's a lightness to her I've never seen. She's discovered her own happiness with you, Brinder. And that, from any person, is a remarkable gift. One not to be wasted."

"What are you saying?"

Grayton shook his head. "I've said enough. You need to find your own way with this. You're smart. And despite your previous manwhore tendencies"—Grayton's eyes gleamed with humor, but there was steel behind it—"your loyalty to Honor, your fidelity, is clear. Now you need to decide if you're man enough to do the right thing."

Before Brinder could even begin to process his words, much less formulate a cogent response, the door to his bedroom opened, a wave of excited chatter flowing through it.

Benny stepped into the room, positively beaming. "Are you ready? She'll be out in one minute."

Even in his heightened state of anticipation for the big reveal of his date, Brinder didn't miss the way Grayton took in Benny, his shoulders squaring as his Adam's apple bobbed. Benny's eyes darted quickly to the former Ranger and then away again. But a curious flush rose across her chest.

"All this anticipation is giving me a power surge," she quipped, laughing awkwardly as she fanned herself with her hand.

Brinder was fascinated. He'd never seen Benny flummoxed. She was always cool and in command. Well, except that one moment the prior night when she'd colorfully threatened Crispin's evisceration.

Benny, a former model of Swedish descent, was stunning. Honor told him she was forty-eight, though he'd be hard-pressed to believe that. She looked easily a decade younger. Benny was married—although how happily was a question, as Honor had hinted at past infidelity by her husband—with a teenage son who played hockey.

Brinder wasn't the only one who was easy to read at the moment. The energy snapping between Grayton and Benny was palpable. *Interesting*.

"I, Ross Beaufort-Grace, otherwise known as the Fairy Rossmother, do hereby present Academy Award-winning actor...Honor Wheatley!" She, Benny, and the glam squad erupted into cheers, forming a 'saber arch' with their arms for Honor to walk beneath.

Brinder's breath caught in his throat. In fact, he was pretty sure his heart fully stopped for a moment as she glided gracefully into the room, affectionately patting 'Couchie' on her way to him.

She stopped halfway between him and the couch, a shy smile on her face.

"Damn, Stardust. You're a vision. I've never seen anyone so stunning."

She wore a dark red couture cocktail dress and strappy nude sandals whose heels elevated her stature to maybe five feet four—still thirteen inches shorter than he. Her dress was one shoulder and asymmetrical, with fancy draping. What was the word she'd taught him while flipping through a *Vogue* one night after dinner? Shirred. He could add that to his complement of animal facts. The fabric conformed to her hourglass shape, highlighting her legs and her supple curves.

He loved that she never attempted to hide her scar. It was as much a part of her as her striking brown eyes and the tiny freckles dotting her shoulders, which he'd traced with his tongue so many times, creating an Honor constellation. In many interviews over the years, she'd shared how she wanted to normalize surgical scars, particularly for children and young adults who faced scar-inducing procedures. There was nothing ugly about scars, she insisted. Instead, it was a badge of courage. Of survivorship.

The glam squad had blown out her hair into long, soft waves, and he suspected put in some fresh blonde highlights. Whatever they did with her eye makeup, it made them pop—even bigger than usual. Her lips were a bold red.

Ah, fuck. Now all he could imagine was that lipstick smearing on his cock as she took him in her mouth. He closed his eyes and commanded his dick to stand down.

When he opened them, Grayton was smirking at him again.

Yep, he *was* that transparent.

Honor frowned a bit, uncertainty flickering in her eyes. "You like it?"

"*Like* isn't the word, Stardust. You are glorious. I'm awestruck. I actually don't think a word has been invented to describe how beautiful you are."

She let out a little exhale of relief, and her lips curved into the sweetest smile. "Oh, good. You were quiet for so long, I thought maybe it was too much for tonight. I tried to pick a look that was appropriate."

Brinder crossed the space separating them in three long strides, unable to be separated from her any longer and despising any physical distance. Once he touched her, he wasn't letting go. He'd ensure she was glued to his side the entire night. Anything other than that would be unbearable.

"You knocked it out of the park, baby." He dropped a gentle kiss on her lips, not trusting himself to do more lest he completely ravage her mouth, earning the ire of the glam squad, who'd have to put her back to rights.

"You clean up nicely too, *Dr. Desiiigh*." She grinned at him.

How was he ever going to allow her to leave? It was like God or the universe designed the perfect person for him, the one elemental combination that completed him. Pure chemistry. A balanced equation.

And if she left?

He'd be forever out of balance and incomplete.

Chapter Fifty-Eight

Honor

No one wants to be vain, but she had to admit to a thrill of happiness that she'd caused Brinder to be initially speechless when he saw her.

She felt much the same.

Brinder was delicious in his three-piece, charcoal gray, pinstripe suit, a crisp white dress shirt, and a tie that matched her dress. And...*wowza.* That man could wear the heck out of a three-piece suit. Something about that vest. He was a walking, talking thirst trap.

He'd run out for a haircut. It was still medium length, just short of the top of his collar, and longer on top, reminding her of Tom Cruise in *The Last Samurai*—only way taller and hotter. He was freshly shaved, and his spicy cologne filled her nostrils. That, plus his natural pheromones, had immediately triggered her desire. She instinctively clenched her legs, trying not to bounce them in sexual anticipation.

"All the ladies will hate me tonight for being your date. I'll probably choke on the accumulated jealousy of the masses."

Brinder laughed, the lovely posh sound she adored. If she were wearing panties—which she wasn't, because panty lines—they'd have melted right off her.

"Nah, everyone will be looking at you, mesmerized by that special charisma you have."

Honor tucked her head and smiled, secretly delighted he was so taken with her. Everyone deserved to feel cherished. Wanted. Desired.

Brinder certainly did that for her.

As the glam team had worked their magic, leaving her with little to do but contemplate all-things Brinder for multiple hours, Honor couldn't help but wonder if he'd fallen as deeply in love with her as she had with him. The rediscovery of her feelings for Brinder came on slowly...until they landed with force. Last night, as he'd cradled her protectively in his embrace, she'd realized a pure truth: She loved him, and she wanted more than anything to figure out how to reconcile all the challenges around living the rest of her life with him.

That is, assuming he felt the same.

Honor was pretty certain he did, although neither of them had admitted it. He'd come pretty darn close, though, several times. She knew it, instinctively sensing the unsaid words.

Honor looked down at their clasped hands between them—how right it was—and knew, before the weekend was out, she'd profess the deepest desires of her heart and hope the power of her love was enough to overcome their separation.

"It'll be nice to be in public without the weight of our respective burdens."

"Freeing." Honor smiled at her guy. This was the happiest she'd been in a long time. Maybe all her life.

The news hadn't broken yet about Crispin and the blackmail—the detectives had a tight lid on the release of information until Crispin was safely on English soil and in their custody. Benny estimated some time Sunday afternoon the frenzy would start anew, triggered by a very necessary press release from her team.

Only this time, there was a clear end in sight, along with the promise of new beginnings.

Chapter Fifty-Nine

Brinder

Aside from the ever-present paps alongside the screaming fans who'd caught wind of Honor's attendance, their entrance at the restaurant that was the setting for Evangelist's fundraiser was as low-key as they could manage in the situation. Honor had merely smiled and waved at the crowd, Grayton and Bauer artfully boxing out any interlopers. When she made meaningful eye contact with him, Brinder gently tucked her arm into his and guided her to the door.

Far from Enzo's intimate bistro, the steakhouse was a large, opulent space, with multiple rooms upstairs and down, as well as a covered patio. Evangelist's philanthropy team had worked hard to create a cozy yet sophisticated environment. This was one of the hospital's core fundraisers, going back more than a decade. A young female pianist was at a baby grand. Brushed bronze sconces and candles on many of the surfaces created subtle ambient lighting. Fresh flower displays in gold and green—the hospital's brand colors—dotted surfaces.

The cocktail hour had just begun, but the room was already crowded. It was impossible to miss the not-so-understated glances darting in Honor's direction. Thank heavens part two of the scandal hadn't broken. It would have been a complete shambles, and they likely wouldn't have been able to attend.

His girl was gracious and composed, nodding politely and smiling whenever someone caught her eye, and focusing her attention on each person to whom he had to introduce her. Some of the more overt Board members and donors had already put themselves in their path, clearly angling for an introduction to his famous girlfriend. He kept an eye peeled for Clark, but so far, no sightings of the balding, pot-bellied assbasket.

After about twenty minutes of the annoying faffle, he'd had enough.

Brinder knew the side dining room was dedicated to a silent auction, featuring weekends away, boat trips, timeshares in the Caribbean, pricey bottles of wine, art, and more. The live auction was slated to be even more extravagant, featuring a week in Napa with private tours; two TBD World Series tickets, compliments of Gideon O'Grady in gratitude of the care his daughter was receiving; a safari in Tanzania; and a week on a catamaran in the British Virgin Islands. There was more, according to the list he'd reviewed with Agnes earlier in the week, but that was all his brain had retained.

After finding and greeting Agnes and her wife, then introducing them to Honor, he carefully steered his date to the silent auction. It was a bit quieter than the main dining room and Brinder needed a moment to catch his breath.

Honor handed him one of two crystal glasses of water she must have snagged from the bar on the way in. One eyebrow lifted. "You good?"

Brinder scrubbed a hand down his face. "Yes, just...I forgot how exhausting these things are." He downed the water and set it on a nearby tray.

Honor broke into a wide grin, her eyes knowing. "I forgot what an extroverted introvert you are. You can play the game, and people always think you're having a blast, but in larger groups, your battery drains quickly."

He huffed a laugh of acquiescence, dropping a kiss on her forehead and tugging her just a bit closer. "You do know me."

"I love how that part of you hasn't changed," she added softly, gazing up at him.

"Do you find that a lot's changed?" He cocked his head, examining her lovely face. Those eyes...Damn...They got him every time, from the very first time.

"Some," she offered. "And some is the same. It's like revisiting a childhood neighborhood, cataloging all the things that have changed and savoring the things that are still the same."

"I get it," he whispered, keeping his voice down. No one was near them, but no one needed to overhear this conversation. "I feel like I've been on a voyage of discovery this past week—what's new and what is so familiar. It's like a warm hug when I experience it."

Now her head tilted. "So what's new with me that you've noticed?"

"Hmmmm..." He pretended to think, rubbing his chin between the thumb and index finger of the hand that wasn't holding hers. "Where to begin?"

"Stop teasing." She swatted playfully at him. "Tell me."

"How about...you speak Italian. You know Taekwondo. Your face" —he traced along her cheek—"is more angular, your cheekbones more pronounced. Like you grew into your adult face. But," he continued, gazing into her eyes, "your laugh is the same. Your humor. Your poise, that you had even at fifteen. Your stunning eyes. Your sexy body. The way you fit perfectly under my arm."

"Stop," Honor whispered, eyes shining.

"Why?"

"Because you're about to make me cry. And I don't want to ruin the glam squad's good work...or create a scene. There's been enough of that lately."

Brinder chuckled. "Ok, Stardust. Suffice it to say, the past six days have been a beautiful montage of discovery and rediscovery."

"Oh, aren't you the king of pretty words." The sarcastic comment sliced through the cocoon he'd been in with Honor. *Bugger*. He knew that voice.

He turned, and, as expected, met the hateful glare of his Board chair's daughter. *Bloody cunt*.

She was done up in full Laurel mode. Her blonde hair, which he knew was augmented with artful extensions, was sleek and smooth, hanging halfway down her back. Her injected lips were pouty and full, painted some taupe-ish color. Her dress, a vibrant coral color, dipped low in the front. In her heels, he'd bet she was almost six feet. She towered over Honor, which she attempted to use against his girl.

"Honor Wheatley. Rumor had it you went running from your sex video scandal to hide with the delectable Dr. Desai." Laurel shifted to loom closer over Honor, who, in a show of true class, merely lifted her chin, a neutral look on her face. To anyone watching, they may as well be speaking of the weather. Until you looked at Laurel's left hand, which was balled in a tight fist. "Has he been dazzling you with flowery words of seduction and empty promises of the future? That seems to be his forte, among other....skills," she added, every word dripping with venom.

Honor merely smiled, resting her hand on his arm. It was a subtle move, but Laurel immediately clocked it and practically snarled. How the fuck had he not seen her crazy sooner? It was as if she'd been able to put on the mask of a carefree hookup...until she couldn't manage the masquerade any longer. No one could sustain something they truly weren't. Not over an extended time. Eventually the façade shattered.

As he knew all too well.

"I'm sorry. Have we met?" Honor smiled sweetly at her, as if Laurel hadn't just spewed her word rot.

"I'm *Laurel*," the tall blonde replied haughtily.

Nothing from Honor but an infinitesimal wrinkling of her perfect nose. "Again, you have me at a disadvantage. I'm afraid I don't know who you are."

Laurel's face drained pale before it turned bright red—either with embarrassment or rage, or perhaps a mixture. Brinder couldn't be sure.

Brinder worked to swallow a laugh. Laurel's reaction, and Honor's cool poise—it was priceless. He was tempted to chime in, but Honor clearly had this situation under control. Instead, hearing the echo of Grayton in his head, he worked on a neutral poker face.

"I am Brinder's former girlfriend. The one he dated and cared for. And then dumped. And clearly for a sex video slut."

"You will not speak to my girlfriend like that," Brinder growled, his voice low and threatening. That was a bridge too far.

But Honor merely smiled again, widening it just a touch more, and leaned into Brinder, softly patting his arm as she cut him off. And likely preventing him from screaming at the unhinged woman in front of him.

"Again, never heard of you." She turned a perplexed face to him, clearly (to him) faking confusion, but probably effective for someone who didn't know her. "Baby, when we were sharing about our previous significant relationships, I don't recall you talking about a Laurel."

Christ, she was a glorious, hilarious liar. And he loved her so much. It was all he could do not to slam his lips into hers and then carry her out of this ridiculous command performance.

"That's because we were talking about significant and long-term relationships, *baby*." He enjoyed tossing the diminutive back to her. "And what Laurel and I had was merely a mutual fling."

Now Laurel sputtered, her eyes bulging.

"Tone it down, Laurie." Honor's voice was satin over steel. "People are starting to watch. And it's not a good look for you."

Laurel's heavily mascaraed eyes darted around. "It's *Laurel*," she sneered, but with much less force.

"Now," Honor continued, blatantly not acknowledging the name correction, "I suggest you take your skanky ass and quietly walk away. If you don't, and if you continue to verbally harass my *boyfriend* and me with your pathetic lies, I will be forced to have my agent share with your father about your relationship with the former chief medical officer at Evangelist. You know, the one where you and that *married* physician executive engaged in a salacious affair. And how you threatened his wife at their marital home with a butcher knife when she wouldn't divorce him. And how you lied and told him you were pregnant with his child."

Brinder's jaw came unhinged, dropping open in shock.

Laurel wasn't in better condition. Her mouth opened and closed, like a koi fish seeking food, no sound emerging. Eventually, she snapped her mouth shut, her head whipping around as she scanned the room— likely for her father. "How," she wheezed, "how do you know all that?"

"Laurel—that's your name, right? It wasn't hard to find out. You see, when my boyfriend told me a stage five clingy psycho was engaging in damaging behaviors and spreading lies that threatened his livelihood, I immediately had a vested interest in finding out the truth."

"How?" Brinder made sure to keep his voice low, trying to block this exchange with as much of his body as possible. The gossips would have a field day with this if they overheard.

Honor shrugged. "Benny has contacts. She called in a favor for me."

"So that was the scandal that forced out the former chief medical officer?"

"Precisely. It seems *Laurel*," Honor hit her name hard, "has a nasty habit of preying on the physician executives of Evangelist."

"I didn't prey!" Laurel screeched, causing more than a few heads to turn. Thankfully, she had the presence of mind to lower her voice. "Barry loved me."

"I'm sure," Brinder murmured. "Just like you thought I did."

"What do we have here?" Clark boomed, all jovial and 'hail-fellow-well-met' for the benefit of the handful of guests in the room. "My daughter cozied up to her dirtbag former beau and his little sex video harlot," he added more quietly between clenched teeth.

Terror etched Laurel's face, her eyes wide and beseeching to Honor. It was clear Daddy Dearest had no idea of her past indiscretions with the former leader, and even more clear Laurel didn't want him to know.

Agnes, appearing by Clark's side, cut in smoothly, "Let's not call names or throw mud, Clark. It's behavior unbecoming of a leader of my hospital." She pinned him with a cold smile.

"But this—this—" he sputtered, waving at Brinder.

"This what? This talented physician? This dedicated executive who is vastly improving our medical operations? Who has been nothing but classy and respectful in the wake of an unfair and unsettling accusation and its fallout?"

"It wasn't unfair," Clark snarled. "He led her on, then dumped her and broke her heart. Clearly his little porn star was waiting in the wings."

"Clark," Agnes calmly replied, "in my life, I've discovered there are two sides to everything, and the truth lies somewhere in the middle. And in this case, I think the truth is much closer to Brinder than you could ever imagine." Agnes leveled a glare at Laurel that, had it been aimed at him, would have shriveled his balls. "Now, Ms. Kenrick, I ask that you please leave Dr. Desai and Ms. Wheatley alone. And, if you cannot behave like a polite and rational adult, I expect your father to remove you immediately and quietly from my fundraiser."

"Bugger," Brinder breathed after Clark took his daughter by the elbow and led her from the room. Gone was Laurel's snotty, cruel melodrama. In its place was sheer terror as she tottered out. Clearly Daddy finding out her role in the last CMO's exit would be terrible for her.

Agnes watched Honor and Brinder wordlessly, a small, satisfied smile dancing on her lips.

Then it hit him. "You knew about Laurel and Barry Babcock."

"I did," Agnes confirmed, shifting them away from where a couple of nosy guests had tuned into the drama. "Barry came to me and confessed everything, trying to salvage the tattered remains of his job. He admitted to the affair, to Laurel's fake pregnancy, and to Laurel's appearance in his family home with a knife. His wife called the police. They ended up not pressing charges and enacted a restraining order on Miss Kenrick."

Brinder turned to his boss, incredulous. "Why didn't you say anything to Clark?"

"It wasn't my place." Her face was a mask of neutrality.

"Ok. But why didn't you at least say something to me?"

"Again, it wasn't my place. Trust me, I wanted to. When Clark came barreling into my office, accusing you of unethical and immoral behavior with his daughter, I almost spilled the whole story. As it was, Barry's departure was cloaked in a confidentiality clause. I wasn't at liberty to reveal any of the details—to Clark or to you."

"There was no way to defend me without sharing what you weren't permitted."

"Exactly." Agnes nodded, rubbing a finger over her brow. "Here I had one of the best physician leaders of my career gracing my admin suite, and Clark was screaming for your termination. He threatened to pull donors from tonight if I didn't take action. The probation was all I could think of. I trusted you'd be able to ride it out until I could resolve this situation."

Brinder grabbed the back of his neck, exhaling slowly. "And now it's resolved?"

"Mostly," Agnes murmured. "Clark's term as Board chair is up in a month. However, I'm assembling the rest of the Board on Monday. We'll be voting him out based on evidence that's recently been shared anonymously with me. Seems there have been some shady business arrangements led by Clark within Kenrick Enterprises."

She let that sit for a moment.

Brinder's gaze swung to Honor and back to Agnes as he took in the turn of events. Eventually he released a long exhale, shaking his head. "How did someone like him even end up as Board chair?"

A flash of sadness—blink and you'd miss it—passed across Agnes's otherwise inscrutable face. "From what I'm told," Agnes began slowly, as if parsing her words carefully, "Clark was quite respected in the early days of his Board tenure. But," she glanced in the direction of the doorway through which Clark had hightailed it, "unfortunately, sometimes good people get a taste of power, get too big for their britches, and become unrecognizable. I won't tolerate that. I'm grateful to the person who called our compliance line. She identified herself as Benoite Tambeaux." She arched a knowing brow.

Brinder knew he should put on a poker face—but he couldn't help but grin from ear to ear. This was Honor's doing. His girl had metaphorically thrown down powerful hands to protect him, leveraging her agent's considerable influence to save his reputation. And she did it without a word to him. Honor didn't need or want the recognition. She did it quietly, privately...no fanfare. For *him*.

The force of his love erupted in an almost dizzying wave.

He loved her. She was his forever. The rest? Just details to be ironed out. It might seem as if their lives were pulling them in opposite directions—again—but he'd blast through any barrier to be with Honor Wheatley.

The Crispin situation was managed, and now Clark and Laurel were done and dusted. Everything was falling into place.

And when they got home? He'd show her exactly how much he

appreciated her intervention on his behalf. One screaming orgasm at a time.

Honor looked up at him, a beautiful smile spreading across her face. If she only knew what he was thinking, a riotous blush would join it.

A subtle cough interrupted his musings.

He met Agnes's gaze, both eyebrows raised high on her forehead.

Bloody hell. It would be mortifying if his boss suspected the direction of his thoughts.

Then something occurred to him. Brinder looked around, ensuring no one had maneuvered into earshot. "Why didn't you do this before tonight?"

Agnes smiled like the cat who ate the canary. "Like I said yesterday, Dr. Desai, I'm not a fool. I'll take the money of Clark's cronies for my hospital *before* I oust him."

Chapter Sixty

Brinder

"Now that's what I call a *Clarkfrontation*," he whispered in Honor's ear as Agnes sashayed away—shoulders back and head held high—to greet more guests.

From then on, Honor would break into periodic giggles. First, as they perused the silent auction, with him eventually bidding on a particularly appealing Napa cabernet. Then, repeatedly during dinner, seated at a round table with some of his service line chiefs and their significant others. Instead of explaining to their curious tablemates, he merely tugged her chair closer, kissing the palm of her hand and reveling in the fact that she was his.

As the live auction started, he saw her biting her lip, clearly trying to hold it all in.

"Why are you so giggly, Stardust?" he murmured into her ear.

She dipped her head, pinching the bridge of her nose for a moment, as if to contain her mirth. When she got herself back under control, she leveled him with a heart-stopping, beatific smile. Honestly, she outshone the brightest stars in the sky, practically shimmering with her special magic.

"I'm just really happy." Her eyes shone with unshed tears.

"And that makes you giggly and weepy?" Brinder raised his brows theatrically at her.

She pinched him playfully on the underside of his arm.

"Ow, Stardust," he gasped, all fake drama. "You have strong fingers for such a wee thing."

"I guess both sets of our fingers are...noteworthy for what they can do," she drawled, dragging her gaze down his body.

Brinder let out a sharp exhale, his cock rising to semi status—and not too far from a full-fledged hard-on. "Tish," he murmured. "Stop. You're killing me. These docs already think I'm an unrepentant horndog."

Now Honor released another giggle. "I'm sorry, Brinder." She coughed as she worked to contain herself. "I really am so happy. And I just keep picturing Clark's florid face and that little bit of spittle on his lower lip when Agnes schooled him. And then Laurel"—she shook her head—"she just looked like a fish flopping around on deck. I just keep... *seeing* it. And I'm so darn relieved, I just can't stop giggling."

"Probably just the release of pent-up emotion," he nodded, understanding. "You've been carrying a lot for the past week. Sometimes that release comes out in unexpected ways." He kissed her forehead. "Like giggles." They grinned at each other.

Later, he was going to absolutely devour her. Brinder's mind was already spinning with plans of how to...*release*...some of his own pent-up emotion.

"And now for a very special entry in our live auction." The voice of their auctioneer—a local television broadcaster who'd delivered her twins at Evangelist—cut through their private-in-public moment. "As you may be aware, we have a VIP attendee tonight, Oscar winner Honor Wheatley."

The room erupted into applause, with some whistles too. When he looked over, Brinder realized those came from Agnes and her wife, who smiled unabashedly at him. He shook his head and laughed.

"Ms. Wheatley contacted Evangelist's philanthropy team and offered a surprise item. She is offering a signed copy of her memoir...and a dinner with her at La Capaninna, the charming bistro owned by

Evangelist's own Board member, Enzo Rossi. Enzo couldn't make it tonight. He had a pressing family matter out of town." The auctioneer paused and smiled in Honor's direction. "I think I speak for all of us when I say, wow. You are even more stunning in person. You're an incredible actress and your memoir was fascinating. The Evangelist family and I look forward to your next role. And," she drew out, "in addition to dinner and the signed book, Ms. Wheatley is offering a personally guided behind-the-scenes tour of the set of her new film, set in Boston."

Brinder whipped his head to face her, surprise and love filling his heart. His generous girl. He squeezed Honor's hand as a blush stole up her cheeks. She started to reach for her chest—he suspected to touch her scar, as was her nervous habit—and then stopped, instead planting a quick, chaste kiss on his lips that still had his heart thudding.

"I'll start the bidding at one thousand dollars."

Within minutes, the bid was up to five thousand. Honor's cheeks were bright pink, but she laughed along with the auctioneer, encouraging the audience to increase their bids.

It hit Brinder, mid-bidding frenzy, that he'd have to give up a precious evening with Honor to whomever the winning bidder was. Nope. Not gonna happen. Not when their time was dwindling.

He raised his paddle to add his bid, but Honor put a staying hand on him before the auctioneer could acknowledge him.

"No, Gomez. Don't do it. I know what you're thinking."

"That I don't want to share you with anyone? Not even for a few hours? And that I'd love to visit you on set?"

She giggled again. "It's one dinner, Brinder. You and I can have dinner together all the other nights." She nuzzled into him. "And you don't need to bid on seeing me in Boston. I would be devastated if you didn't come visit me on set."

Visit her. The words stung. You *visited* a friend. But she was so much more to him. Was she already mentally moving on?

"I don't want to share you, Tish." He drank her in, uncaring if eyes were on them. "Every minute you aren't with me shreds my heart. That's how much you own it."

Honor's eyes filled, and she caressed his cheek with her delicate hand. "You own my heart too." Her voice trembled, just slightly. Honor inhaled and let it out slowly. "But you'll survive without me for one dinner. I'll make sure Cole and Xan take you out for a bromance night."

"Not an acceptable substitute," he muttered. "They'll just shove baby pictures under my nose and moon over missing their wives."

"And you won't moon over me?"

"I moon over you the second you leave my sight, Stardust." He pressed a tender kiss to her lips. "That's not going to change."

"Sold!" the auctioneer boomed, jarring them apart and setting Honor off into another fit of giggles. "For twelve thousand dollars to Agnes and Letitia Greco-Martin."

Brinder turned to face his boss at the table next to them, who was high-fiving her wife and the others at their table. His brows shot up and he grinned at Honor.

"You're going to have dinner with my boss and her wife?"

"Apparently," Honor replied, sounding smug. "And we're going to talk about you behind your back all night." Then she broke into giggles again.

He hauled her against him and laid a not-work-appropriate kiss on her, silencing her laughter...and showing everyone present—including the curvy dream girl by his side—that he belonged to her, and she to him.

Chapter Sixty-One

Honor

The morning sun poured into the condo, patterns from the sun dancing across the floor. After it became clear her night's sleep was over, Honor had grabbed 'her' hoodie and slid on a pair of boyshorts, relocating to the living room so as not to disturb Brinder's much-needed sleep.

From her cozy perch on Couchie, a restorative latte in hand, Honor couldn't help but catalog the difference one week could make in a life.

A week ago, she was in her home office, looking out a wall of windows with the expectation of enjoying a Welsh sunrise and getting some words in on her screenplay. Today was a remarkably similar tableau on the surface, but once you scratched it, a very different, very mind-blowing set of circumstances.

Last Sunday began with the one-two punch of the video shock and being whisked from her home to hide in a different country. It ended with the uppercut of seeing Brinder and the jab and cross of hiding in this very condo as her temporary sanctuary.

At the time, her emotions were a roiling cauldron of shock, anger, fear—and not all of it attributed to the video and its fallout.

Honor snorted into her mug. If she were honest with herself—and what better time for a personal come-to-Jesus than during the soft light of dawn, on the world's most comfortable and otherworldly couch, quietly savoring the nectar of the java gods?—within just a couple days, the boy-turned-man who broke her teenage heart had quickly become her primary focus, eclipsing the video with a speed that should have been shocking. But wasn't.

Nope. Nothing about Brinder and this situation surprised her. It tracked. Such was his magnetism. Such had always been their unique chemical reaction. It was the inexorable draw to each other that had almost led her to throw away the role that launched her career. It was that same draw that had seen Brinder struggling with a critical education decision, almost tossing over his dream college to stay in England with her.

Honor shook her head and glanced at his clock. Just after six in the morning. She'd risen with the sun today, somehow wide awake after barely six hours of sleep. It was amazing what a night of revelations and the resulting uninhibited joy could do for the soul, along with a few hours of much-needed restorative slumber.

She and Brinder had shuffled through the doors of the condo just after eleven last night. They'd started their nighttime ablutions domestically side-by-side in the bathroom. Not surprisingly, he'd finished well before her, dropping a sweet kiss on her lips and sliding into bed.

After removing all her makeup and brushing her teeth, Honor had removed her dress. She'd initially kept it on thinking he'd want to peel it off her, discovering what she was—or more precisely *wasn't*—wearing underneath. But she'd changed her mind, the urge to get out of the couture and return to her real self too strong to resist.

She'd debated about sliding into a nightie, but then discarded the thought as casually as she'd discarded her dress. Given their almost-insatiable need for each other, they'd likely end up naked in moments anyway.

Private foreplay only they understood had been woven throughout the evening. Meaningful eye contact with entire wordless conversations. Small touches. The tender brush of their lips. Subtle scans, as if mentally undressing the other. Honor could happily admit to being distracted all night, imagining what new passions he'd unlock within her when they returned to the condo.

Some sixth sense had cautioned her to enter the bedroom quietly, where she'd found Brinder, curled on his side. Fast asleep.

Honor's heart had squeezed and flipped over about five times in her chest, a tiny sob escaping as she worried her scar with the tips of her fingers.

He was so beautiful.

And she loved him. She loved him with a life-changing ferocity. No, not a turn-her-life-upside-down-ignore-her-own-needs ferocity. Rather, a move-heaven-and-earth-to-figure-this-out ferocity.

Perhaps that was the difference between teenage love and adult love with the same person. Both were tethered in powerful feelings. But only one of those came with a necessary additional anchor—knowledge of oneself, and an inherent respect for that self-awareness that can only be gained from life experience. Without that, a relationship could easily come unmoored.

Just as theirs had eighteen years earlier.

Honor drained the last of her coffee, yawned, and snuggled into Couchie's cozy embrace.

Her upcoming role. His blossoming career. Her writing. His life in Virginia. Hers in Wales.

Honor's last thought before drifting off into a mid-morning nap was...*figure it out*.

"Heeey, sleepy head."

A sexy, gravelly voice roused her from a decadent dream. They'd been in her sunroom-slash-office in Wales, and he was taking her from behind up against the one-way glass.

"Mmmmmm."

"Sleeping beauty, open those stunning brown eyes."

A tender kiss.

She knew those lips. Intimately.

The last misty tendrils of sleep evaporated, taking the lovely dream with it. As Honor's eyes fought the pull to open, a wicked idea curled around her mind. She almost smiled, but...she *was* an award-winning actor, so she feigned sleep.

Another brush of his lips on hers. *Shiitake.* He smelled good. Like spicy bodywash mixed with his own intoxicating scent.

"Mmmm..." she moaned softly, smiling inside. "Idris," she whispered, silently giggling at the use of her celebrity crush. "Morrrre please."

"Hey!"

Brinder's shocked response had her eyes flying open. She slapped a hand over her mouth, erupting into a gale of laughter. He was standing over her, hair wet and tousled, shirtless in only athletic shorts. His hands were on his hips, fingers just below that unreal Adonis belt of ab muscle.

"I'm so—sorry," she yelped out between fits of laughter. "I could—couldn't help it."

He dropped his head and shook it, a smile dancing on his lips. "You better have been acting, Stardust." His warning held no bite, impossible with the laughter in his eyes.

She untangled herself from Blankie and stood high on her toes to wrap her arms around his neck, smacking kisses all over his face. Then, she stopped, remembering her sleep-plus-coffee breath.

"Don't stop, baby." He grinned, tugging her closer.

Dayyyyuuuuuum. That was some impressive morning wood.

"I need to brush my teeth," she muttered through a mostly closed mouth, hoping to spare him the olfactory assault.

Instead of letting her scurry to the bathroom to address said self-care, Brinder only held on tighter, a sexy smirk doing all sorts of squishy things to her insides. Truly, his sex appeal was potent.

"Tell me," he rasped, "you were faking that dream, Tish."

"No, I was dreaming." Before he could form a reply, she took him out of his misery. "About *you*. I was dreaming about you. Us." And here came the blushes, right on cue.

"What were we doing?" His lids were heavy. Swoony.

"You were," Honor took a deep breath and licked her suddenly very dry lips, "you were taking me. Against the bank of windows in my sunroom back in Wales."

The sexy smirk spread.

Lordie. Her seafoam green boyshorts were already wet.

"Is that something you want, baby?"

Her heart thudded, mouth dry. She nodded.

"Words."

"Yes, Brinder. I'd like you to take me up against the windows."

Her mind whirred as he started to tug her in that direction. There was something else she wanted first.

"Wait. I—there's something I-I want to do. To you."

Now her heart was really racing. She didn't have much experience in this, so she said a quick prayer to the oral gods for inspiration as she dropped to her knees.

Brinder sucked in his breath. "You sure, baby?"

She answered him by dragging his shorts down. *Holy shit*. He was commando. His thick, long cock sprung up, already hard.

Honor took a fortifying breath. *Just do what seems right and pay attention to how he reacts. Just like he does with you.*

"You really can't get this wrong, Honor." Brinder's smile was soft and gentle, but she could tell he was holding himself back, a study in coiled energy. "Just don't bite it. Although feel free to use your teeth—agh! Fuck!" Brinder threw his head back, clenching his fists, as Honor took him into her mouth and sucked. Hard.

"Christ, Honor," he groaned. "If you keep going like that, I won't even last thirty seconds."

Good start. A very good start, Honor. She tried not to smile. And she definitely didn't talk.

It was rude to talk with your mouth full, after all.

While she was proud of herself, she wanted more than half-a-minute of this. When they dated as teens, Honor hadn't worked out the courage to do this for Brinder, and he'd never pressured her. Hand jobs became her go-to. With her other boyfriend, and later with Crispin, she did it sometimes, but hated it.

With Brinder? She didn't want it to end. She loved the sensation of him in her mouth. Loved that she could bring him pleasure this way... reciprocate for the wonders of his own mouth that he'd so generously bestowed on her this week.

Honor eased back, licking along the rigid length and then swirling her tongue around the swollen head.

"Honoorrrr," he moaned. "More." His muscular thighs contracted.

She reached between his legs to fondle the sack that was already tightening in impending release. At the same time, she flicked her tongue along the slit of his cock, teasing the barbells.

"Yes!" Brinder cried out, now grasping the sides of her head with both hands. He held her gently, not making any effort to move her face or his hips. But Honor knew he was actively stopping himself from thrusting in her mouth.

She removed her mouth, eliciting a small groan from him. "Patience, Brinder," she whispered. "What would it feel like for you if I did this?" she wondered aloud. Before he could react, she drew her tongue along the seam of his sack, which tightened even more.

"Christ, baby, your mouth..."

Remembering the articles she'd consumed this week for tips and tricks, she began working him with her hand as she bobbed and sucked on his cock.

Unable to hold still any longer, his hips began moving in subtle thrusts. Honor continued her ministrations, moving her other hand between his legs and softly pressing on the skin behind his balls.

"Honor," he groaned, increasing the intensity of his thrusts. Not hard. But enough that Honor's own arousal surged to urgent levels.

She brought the barbell at the tip between her teeth and tugged oh-so-gently. And when Brinder sucked air through his own clenched teeth, she went to town. Sucking, licking, tugging. Taking him back as far as she could, past her gag reflex, and swallowing the tip of him.

"Ungh..."

Honor looked up to find his head thrown back, chest heaving.

"Honor, you better stop or I'm going to come down your throat."

Oh, hell no. She wasn't stopping. Instead, she redoubled her efforts, snaking a hand between her legs to work her clit.

"That's it, baby. Touch yourself."

Honor squirmed, her orgasm building, building, building as she took Brinder into her mouth over and over.

Just as she was about to crest, and based on the salt on her tongue she thought he was too, he pulled his hips back, removing himself from her mouth.

"Nooo," she whined.

"Honor. Get up. Over to the window. Now." He gritted out the commands, giving his cock long, hard strokes from root to tip.

How. Was. That. So. Freaking. Hot?

"Honor," he barked. "Now."

She scurried up and over to the windows.

"Take off your clothes."

Within seconds, her boyshorts and his-slash-her hoodie were tossed on the table.

"Good girl."

He took in every bare inch of her, eyes dark and hot, lighting her up everywhere his gaze touched. All the while, Brinder's hand maintained a hard, steady pump of his cock, the tip glistening.

Honor's mouth watered. She'd wanted him to come. Wanted to feel and taste his release in her mouth, her throat.

"Hands against the glass. Bend over."

Ok. This had *literally* been her dream. But she'd just gotten past one naked scandal. The idea of anyone seeing them...

"It's privacy glass. No one can see in."

How is he so good at reading me?

Brinder swatted her on the ass. "I'm not saying it again."

A shiver of anticipation slid down her spine, her thighs already damp with her own arousal as she followed his commands.

"Brace your hands on the glass."

That was all the warning she got before he drove into her.

"Christ, Honor, you feel so good. So tight."

All she could do was moan in response, lost to the rhythm of his thrusts. The grip of his hands on her hips.

Smack!

"Ungh!" she cried out as his hand connected with the swell of her right butt cheek. For a moment, she was stunned, unsure if she liked it. And then...

Smack!

He did it again, this time on the other side, smoothing his hand over the area.

"You look so pretty like this, Honor," he purred, still thrusting. "I love when you blush, when the pink of your cheeks frames your beautiful eyes." *Smack!* "But I may love *these* pink cheeks just as much."

Honor moaned, pressing her bottom toward him. Seeking.

More. She needed more.

"You like that, baby. You're drenching me and choking me at the same time."

Smack. Smack. Two more, in quick succession at the crease of her bottom.

Honor's sex clenched around him, straining and aching as she took him in. She felt ridiculously, breathtakingly full. From this angle, bent over with her sweaty palms sliding on the glass, he was hitting her g-spot over and over with the pierced tip of his cock.

Brinder was practically doubled over her at this point, his left arm locked against the window to absorb some of the power of his thrusts. His right arm wrapped around her torso, except for when—

Smack. Smooth. *Smack.* Thrust. Thrust.

They were panting and sweating. Grunting. It was filthy and sexy. Animalistic and amazing.

She never wanted it to end.

"Keep your hands on the window, Honor," he gritted when she shifted her hands to reach for that glorious bundle of nerves she'd never truly appreciated until this week. "Hands on the window. Or I stop."

She whimpered at the fullness of him. At her ache to just...shatter.

"Don't worry, baby. I'll take care of you." His voice rumbled, setting alight even more decadent nerve endings.

Brinder pulled back, almost completely out of her, then slammed into her again, both of them groaning when she canted the angle of her hips a bit, taking him even deeper.

She was going to explode. This...this was transcendent. Mystical.

She was there, and she was not there, hovering above her body as

Brinder destroyed and rebuilt her, over and over, while the ache between her legs sharpened almost to pain. She rode that line, building and building. Seeking. Straining.

Begging aloud for release.

"That's right, baby. Good girl. You ready to come?"

All she could manage was a moan. Every part of her body was alight. Tensed. Clenched. Ready. So so so so ready—

Brinder pulled back, then, as he thrust, he reached around and pinched her clit.

Honor screamed. And flew. He followed her over with a deep bellow, sliding to the floor with her in his arms.

It was minutes or hours when Honor finally regained her breath, nuzzling into her boyfriend's sweaty, sated body.

"Mmmmm," she sighed. "Much better than Idris."

The sound of Brinder's laugh tickled the edges of her consciousness as she slid into boneless sleep.

Chapter Sixty-Two

Brinder

"It's time, Honor. You can't weasel out of it."

Brinder raised his brows. Waiting.

Honor frowned, looked at the box in front of her on the dining room table, and rolled her eyes.

"You chicken?" He bawked like a chicken, goading her.

"It's not about being chicken. It's about this being the world's most annoying board game."

"Heathen!" he called out, clutching his chest. "How can you say this about Scrabble? Why, it's America's board game. It's as wholesome as apple pie and July Fourth fireworks."

"Aren't you a British citizen by birth?"

"Ha! I became an U.S. citizen solely based on my deep love and appreciation of this game."

Honor snorted at his drama. "Simmer down there, Desai. It's just a game, it's not your life."

"A good game of Scrabble makes life beautiful, Tish."

Honor sighed, shaking her head and giving in to laughter. "Eighteen years, and I have not played this game once. I can't say I've missed it."

"You wound me, woman. I have so many treasured memories of playing this with you."

Theatrics aside, that part was true. When she was recovering from her pulmonary valve replacement surgery, he'd spent many afternoons playing various board games with her. She hated Scrabble even then, which made him want to play it even more. The competitive side of her would get dramatic and feisty, and Brinder loved every moment of it—particularly knowing her body was healing. That the scary fatigue, the palpitations, the terrifying-to-witness shortness of breath were all in the rearview mirror.

He reached for her hand and kissed the palm. "Ready to play?"

Honor snorted and began setting up, muttering about fake words and the stupidity of spelling letters.

"Oh, I should have mentioned that we're playing this a bit differently."

She frowned. *God, even her frowns were beautiful.*

"We're playing Strip Scrabble." He grinned as her eyes grew impossibly wide. "For every fifty-points one of us scores, the other person must remove an article of clothing. And," he added, watching her process his words, "if you score fifty or more points from one word, the other person has to take off two articles of clothing."

"Brinder," she sputtered, her competitive flag flying, "that is so unfair. You know all the sneaky tricks to this game. It puts you at an unfair advantage."

He sat back. "So, if I'm hearing you correctly, you're worried about losing and having to remove all your clothes."

He watched her swallow, eyes darting around his face, and laughed internally at her busy mind going a mile a minute.

"Honor," he continued, hearing the want in his voice. "I promise you, this is one game where the loser is actually the winner. Because there is no way I'm going to sit here and watch you uncover that delectable body and not want to put my mouth on you and have you screaming my name in minutes."

She looked at him, blinked, looked at her tiles, and then proceeded to play the word 'damn,' a tiny smirk on her face.

Game on!

"That is so ridiculous!" Honor was incensed. "Wiz is not a word! It's an abbreviation. It makes zero sense that you can use that abbreviation but I can't use m-g-m-t as an abbreviation for management."

"Them's the rules, Tish. I don't make 'em up." He smirked, holding up his hands, palms-out, in the universal sign of 'it's not me.'

Her skin had a lovely pinky flush going on, reminding him of the vibrant color he'd smacked on her ass cheeks earlier. His cock gave a little kick of gratitude. *Soon, buddy, we'll have part two.*

Honor rolled her eyes. Hard. Then removed a sock. And flung it at him.

He caught it out of the air, brought it to his nose, and sniffed deeply.

"Gross, Brin." She snorted, giggling at him and waggling her now-bare toes.

Oh, yes, at one point—right after she realized she was only wearing two articles of clothing and he only had three, including his boxer briefs —she'd called a temporary pause and escaped to their bedroom. Within minutes, she'd pranced back in wearing pants, shorts under the pants, socks, a shirt, his-slash-her hoodie, and a baseball cap she'd found on his dresser. He'd barked out a laugh and continued the game, giving her the clothing handicap. It wouldn't matter, she'd still end up nude.

And so it came to pass, he was so far ahead of her in the game, Honor was now in just a lacy bra—which did nothing to hide the tempting buds of her nipples—and the fresh pair of boyshorts she'd changed into after ruining her last pair with her arousal.

She'd finally hit fifty points, so he took off his shirt. But he could tell she was frustrated by her letters.

Grumbling, she put down 'ass' and he snickered. She glared at him, making him laugh harder. So far, most of her words were two and three letters. The game would be over soon. But first, he was going to toy with his meal.

He laid down 'dee.' It was just a stalling word, but it worked.

"Arrrgh!" Honor threw her hands in the air in disgust. "I forgot how much I hate that."

He was all placid concern. "Hate what, baby?"

"The way you 'spell a letter.' It's the dumbest thing I've ever heard. Why would the letter d be spelled d-e-e. It should just be spelled 'd.' It's Scrabble's stupid way of trying to sucker people."

"I don't think that's what happens—"

"Just like how you can use Greek words, but I can't use Italian or French. Double standard!" she bellowed, waving her hands. "It's like the psychotic gamesmakers were like, 'Oh, I have five ways to make this game nonsensical. We'll let them spell letters, use Greek words but *only* Greek and no other language but English, and we'll also allow only some random abbreviations.' Oh, and don't forget to use the word 'za' as slang for pizza. But I can't use 'chos' as my slang for nachos." She punctuated her outrage with a dramatic bite from the plate of nachos sitting between them.

He opened his mouth to say something and she barreled on.

"And don't you say, 'It's in the dictionary, Honor.'" She mimicked his voice with freakish accuracy. "This entire game is a load of hooey." She harrumphed, folding her arms, then unfolding them to grab another nacho, waving it at him like a warning finger, and then shoving it in her mouth. "Stupid game," she muttered through the mouthful.

He waited a beat. "You good? Feeling better now you've gotten that off your chest? I know this is...nacho favorite game." Brinder couldn't help it, and he broke into a wide, teasing smile.

Honor groaned and burst into laughter at his pun. "You're worse than Bash with the terrible dad jokes. You truly suck," she groused.

"If you're lucky," he murmured, enjoying her gasp for just a moment before she flicked him in the forehead.

"Ow, Tish!" he whined dramatically. "What did I tell you about those freakishly strong fingers?"

"If you don't zip it, I'll shove them where the sun doesn't shine, Desai."

"Don't tempt me with a good time, baby," he purred, grinning at the flare of her eyes.

If he had to pick his favorite version of Honor, this would be a contender. Her hair was up in a sloppy bun. She'd inhaled half a plate of nachos, periodically licking her fingers and moaning in appreciation for what she kept calling 'manna from heaven.' And he'd lost count of the amount of times she'd broken into delighted laughter at the old stories they shared between playing words.

He loved 'dolled up Honor,' like she was the night before—date-night Honor was breathtaking. Her naked and sprawled across him, sated from their lovemaking was also a favorite.

But this? The whole moment was so blessedly ordinary. And in that ordinary, the extraordinary. Today, he would finally say the words he'd been holding in his heart. Just...not quite yet.

Honor played another simple word, the five points enough to push her over one hundred. She missed an easy opportunity for a triple word score, and he almost pointed it out. But, at this stage, he just wanted to get her naked. It was that simple.

"Ha! Strip, Desai!"

He smirked, tugging off his shorts, then tossing them on her head.

Honor stared at his crotch with an exaggerated, lascivious gaze. "Mmmm....delicious, Dr. *Desiiigh*. Rawrrrr," she purred.

He said nothing, merely placed his next word on the board. It was just two letters, worth nine points by itself, but he took advantage of the double word score, bringing him up to three hundred eighteen points.

"JO! What the fuck kind of word is that?" Honor smacked a hand over her mouth.

"Ok, potty mouth. I guess it's not just during sex when you get worked up enough to cuss."

"Apparently." He could barely make out the muffled word through her hand and her shocked laughter. "Well, what does this fake Scrabble word mean?"

"It's a Scots word for sweetheart."

"But I can't use 'luv.' Dumb game."

He sat back in his chair, eyeing her. "So, whatcha gonna take off?"

She sucked in her cheeks, glaring at him from her brows. Oh, she was a fine little actor, but he could tell by the uptick in her breathing and the telltale flush spreading up her neck that his girl was getting as worked up as he was.

Leisurely, she stood, and then sloooooowly unhooked her bra. She let her hands fall to her sides and the straps dropped to hang on her upper arms. Then, with a little shimmy, her bra fell to the floor, revealing her glorious, succulent breasts.

His mouth went dry.

She leaned over the board and played one letter, turning jo into joy. "Your play, Dr. Desai," she drawled, toying with one nipple.

Ok. It was time to end this torture.

He touched the three letters he'd been holding onto. The last letter she'd played worked perfectly with his planned word, although it wasn't truly necessary for his turn as he had the only other 'y' tile. Hands slightly shaking, he placed two more letters on the board. And waited.

At first, he was greeted with silence. Honor stared at the board, a small frown creasing her brow.

"What the heckety heck word is that? And don't tell me it's some crusty old English word or I may rip off your arms and beat you with them."

"My, my," he teased, past his own racing heart. "It's not an old English word."

"Then what is it? Put me out of my misery."

"I'm surprised you don't recognize it. It's a pretty modern initialism."

She studied it in silence. Then her eyes filled with tears, which spilled over her cheeks and splashed onto her tile rack. "Oh my gosh oh my gosh," she chanted. "Are you sure? Say you mean it." Her words were barely a whisper.

He trailed the tip of his finger across the letters, bringing it to his lips and then hers.

ILY.

"I do mean it. I love you, Stardust. A long time ago, I fell in love with the kindest, most beautiful girl. But I lost her. Then I lost myself along the way, for a long time. Too long, and somehow just long enough. Because last week, you appeared before me, an angel in my hoodie. In that moment, I knew. I just knew. It's always been you. It will always be you. I love you, Honor Wheatley."

"I love you, Brinder Desai." Her radiant smile lit the room.

Core memory made.

They gazed at each other, soaking in the moment. Eventually, she cleared her throat, a small smile playing at her lips, bringing out the tiny dimple in the corner next to her lower lip. "I have something else really important to say, Brinder."

"You have the floor." He held his breath.

She motioned to the board. "ILY isn't a word."

After a stunned beat, Brinder barked out a laugh, pushing those tiles to the side and playing the real word he'd been plotting—Qi.

Her jaw dropped.

"It's a circulating life force that's the basis for Chinese medicine. Oh, and I got a triple word score on it, so that's thirty-three points. Putting me over three hundred and fifty." He stood and walked over to the rug, pushing the table out of the way. "Drop those knickers and crawl to me."

And she did.

God, he loved Scrabble.

Chapter Sixty-Three

Honor

If there was truth to a natural balance in the universe, Honor was experiencing an indisputable example. The drama, hurt, and fear that had exploded in her life exactly one week earlier had faded, balanced by sheer contentment of a lazy Sunday with Brinder.

After Scrabble, and some enthusiastic doggie-style sex on Ruggie—she was definitely a fan of that position—they'd relaxed on Couchie and read, Miles Davis softly playing in the background. Now they were sitting at the table enjoying Thai, Honor not even trying to ignore the flashes of memory of her stretched out like a meal herself on this very table.

Her core did a happy little dance, tightening.

Who was this sexually insatiable woman? In the early days with Crispin, they'd had sex fairly regularly. It was nothing to write home about, but she'd always thought it was decent, albeit never ending the way she now knew it could. In more recent years, with her filming schedule and his work at the Playhouse, the frequency had diminished to maybe once a month. Sometimes less if she was filming somewhere and he didn't visit. Which wasn't uncommon.

But now? Honor was pretty sure she'd had more sex this past week than over the last five years. Maybe longer. That is, if you could even compare the unsatisfying act she'd experienced before with this sexual utopia Brinder had revealed.

"A quid for your thoughts?" Brinder's teasing eyes danced between hers.

Her eyebrows shot up. "A quid?"

"The price of your thoughts are more valuable than one pence."

"Way to blend British money with an American idiom." Honor smiled, but there was a sadness in Brinder's eyes that pinched her heart.

Brinder carefully spun his wine glass, the crisp rosé swirling gently. "We seem to have done the same."

"Pardon?"

He took a slow sip of the rosé then placed it back on the table, eyes fastened there. He was struggling with something.

"Talk to me, Brinder. What has you so pensive?"

"I asked you first," he demurred, his teasing smile failing to distract her from the unease etched on his handsome face.

She was tempted to argue, since her sexy musings seemed frivolous in comparison to what was clearly troubling him.

"Please?" Those hazel eyes, which could make her ladyparts molten at a glance, now beseeched her. It wouldn't work to push him. He'd share his thoughts when he was ready.

Honor nodded. "Ok, but...*quid* pro quo."

It worked! Brinder rolled his eyes and smirked at her bad pun.

Honor swallowed, feeling oddly emotional. "I was just thinking... how you've opened my eyes. I had no idea sex could be like"—Honor motioned between them—"this."

Now a bigger smile formed on his lips. "And we've barely scratched the surface, Tish."

Her skin heated at the mention of more. *Yep...you're officially a Desiiigh-obsessed nympho.*

Yet, as tempting as it was—and Honor was pretty sure he was trying to distract her with his panty-melting ways—Brinder had something on his mind.

"Why the sad eyes, Gomez?" She was prodding, but Brinder wasn't the type to hold back what he was feeling—at least not with her. All those years ago, anyway.

Brinder leaned back in his chair, dropping his head back and releasing a long sigh. "Just like we alternated currencies earlier, you and I have done the same." When she cocked her head, confused, he continued. "*We* flip-flopped, Tish. I just keep thinking about how our lives have played out. You, the American, who has now lived most of her adult life in Great Britain."

Honor nodded, knowing where this was headed. The same thoughts had tormented her the past few days.

"And I, a Brit, living the same amount of time in the U.S. And now a citizen."

"It is strange, isn't it?" Now it was her turn to toy with her own mostly full wineglass. She'd only permitted herself one drink tonight, still internally cringing at her spectacular inebriation of last Monday.

"Our lives don't seem to want to align," he sighed out, his years-faded accent a bit sharper with tamped-down emotion.

"Have you ever thought about returning to the UK?"

Brinder closed his eyes and shook his head, a sad smile playing on his full lips. "No. I mean, I think my mom would love it. I talk with her once a week. Sometimes while I'm driving to work, and sometimes we'll FaceTime on a weekend when—" he halted, rubbing circles on his temples, "when Rahul isn't around."

"I can't tell you how sad I am things have been challenging between you and your dad." Because she knew he wouldn't appreciate it, Honor managed to keep the pity out of her voice, and mostly tempered the sadness. She didn't see her parents frequently, but when they reunited, it was a dramatic scene befitting a household of actors with large personalities who adore each other.

"I take it my dad and yours have stayed close." It wasn't a question, his voice wooden—almost stripped of emotion.

"They still get together a couple times a year. It's difficult with my parents' schedules and your," she hesitated, "and your dad's."

He winced at her use of the term, then locked his gaze on hers. "Have you seen him?"

"Your father?"

He nodded.

"Only a few times over the years."

"When was—" he croaked, and cleared his throat before beginning again. "When was the last time?"

Her heart ached. Brinder's face was a study in barely concealed emotion. Not anger, as she might have expected. No, this was pure sadness. "I saw him about eight months ago. I still get regular checkups with my cardiologist." She rolled her eyes. "My parents would lose their minds if I didn't."

"They love you very much, Honor." He smiled. "There are worse things than protective parents."

She nodded, her love and affection for her parents a much-needed balm to soothe the lifelong irritation of their over-protectiveness. "It's just how they're hardwired at this point. Once a deathly sick child, always a deathly sick child." Honor shrugged. "Anyway, it gives them peace of mind when I see a cardiologist."

He raised his brows and motioned for her to continue.

"At my last appointment, your dad happened to be at the hospital. We ran into each other on the way in and ended up having lunch."

Brinder's face was a mask. Anything could be happening under there.

Honor continued, sensing he wanted to hear more, even if he'd never admit to it. "He looked good. Older. Grayer. Seeing you now after having seen him fairly recently, you do favor him in some ways."

Brinder snorted.

Honor ignored him. "We kept the conversation pretty surface level. It was good to see him, Brinder." She reached for his hand, rubbing it with her thumb. "Do you—do you miss him?"

He huffed a laugh. "I don't miss being told I'm a failure. A disappointment. I don't miss him yelling at me. Looking at me like I'm a walking, talking parenting letdown."

Honor couldn't picture words like that coming out of Dr. Desai's mouth. The times she'd seen him with Brinder, during Cheltenham visits, he seemed to be a proud father. The smiles he regarded his son with were real and, dare she say it, sometimes tender.

"I never saw that side of him." It was barely a whisper.

Brinder smirked and shook his head. "Me either. Until I defied him about Georgetown, and did it again with my specialty selection, and then really did it again when I quote-unquote 'threw away my citizenship like a toddler insisting on his own way.'" The edge in his voice was sharp and serrated. "Although, *technically*," he hit that word hard, "I have dual citizenship. Not that Rahul cares."

Honor closed her eyes against the tears filling them, swallowing a few times to gain her composure. "I am so sorry."

"Nothing to be sorry for."

"I hate how he treated you." She cradled her palm against his cheek. He hadn't shaved since yesterday and his delicious stubble rasped against her skin. A shiver of arousal skipped down her spine, such was his primal effect on her. "But I also owe him my life, Brinder."

He said nothing, just reached for her hand and laced his fingers with hers.

Honor took a deep breath, filling her lungs with air and stiffening her spine with resolve. "I was born with a broken heart, Brinder. Your dad fixed it. Twice." She swallowed and licked her suddenly parched lips. "And then you shattered it."

His eyes shot to hers.

Brinder took a shuddering breath. "I want to heal it. For good."

CHAPTER SIXTY-FOUR

BRINDER

Brinder hit save on the report, never quite trusting AutoSave with his work. It had been a productive morning. He'd managed to tear himself from their tangled embrace—the lure of Honor's tiny, curvy body a glorious temptation—in time to hit the gym. And he was at his desk by seven-thirty, successfully cranking away on several projects.

He recognized, and was grateful for, the fresh start Agnes had provided. And her trust. Her belief in him meant more than he could articulate. Motivated by redemption and sheer passion for his job, Brinder dove into work, successful in keeping a sexy little minx from creeping into his thoughts.

Well, mostly successful. It was *Honor*, after all.

Brinder had come to accept over the past week that this woman had always owned every ounce of him—mind, body, and spirit—and always would. After professing his feelings with the help of a Scrabble board, albeit not asking her the question that had been dancing on his tonuge —not yet anyway, but *soon*—she'd given him a tender, almost wistful kiss. They'd curled up on his couch, and it wasn't long before he'd tugged off her clothes, pulled her on top of him, and buried himself where he belonged again and again until she cried out her release and slumped over him, pressing kisses into his neck.

He'd carried her to bed—he loved tucking her against him and the way she molded to him—and she'd dropped quickly into a deep slumber.

It had taken a couple more hours to quiet his mind enough to sleep. Instead, he'd worked their situation over and over in his head, trying to solve it and getting increasingly frustrated. And sad.

Their lives had flipflopped, with her largely an ocean away and lifestyles that didn't naturally mesh. Should he give up this dream job and follow her to Wales—and wherever her roles took her? Would she want to base herself out of Virginia? Would he be happy with her gone for weeks and months at a time? He couldn't exactly drop everything at work and fly off to see her in whatever corner of the world she was filming.

Would she want to get married? Have children? Other than that period of time when he thought he might be Jemma's stepfather, Brinder hadn't thought about kids as a reality in his life. He assumed he'd stay unmarried, content to be married to his work and engaging in healthy encounters with consenting women.

In one week, that plan—soulless and largely empty as it seemed now —was blown to smithereens. Instead of seeing himself growing in his C-suite role—his previous preoccupation—he imagined returning home after a long day to find Honor tucked into Couchie. He could see himself visiting her on set, or even walking the red carpet, beaming with pride at her side.

And, with healthy but welcome shock, he pictured Honor sharing a positive pregnancy test, then doting on her as her belly rounded with their child. That visualization was a new favorite.

What he couldn't fathom was how to actually manifest these scenarios into reality. Every time he tried to work it out, his head simply ached.

Added to that, while he knew Honor loved him, he wasn't sure of her endgame. What did she imagine in the wee hours? What preoccupied her mind? Work? Him? The same ruminations that pinged around his head like a bouncing logo on a screen? Or—and it pained him to face it—maybe she wasn't struggling at all the way he was. After all, when he all but revealed his long-term intentions, she didn't reply. At least not verbally.

But the effortless, magnetic, explosive, tender way they came together after perhaps conveyed what words couldn't.

They were meant to be. He just needed to figure out how.

Four quick raps on his door—one-two, one-two—snapped him from his musings. It was Amani's signal to him that he had an unplanned visitor. One knock was just her needing something. Two was for Agnes. Three was a scheduled meeting. Four was...joker's wild. Who knew what would be revealed behind the door.

"Be right there," he called out, infusing warmth into his voice. Usually this ended up being a staff physician taking advantage of his open-door policy to talk with him.

Brinder stood and stretched, smiling at the sunshine beaming through the window. After resolving whatever his visitor needed, maybe he'd take a quick walk while he downed a sandwich—assuming it wasn't too muggy. June in Virginia was often swampish, but some days were pleasant surprises.

The door opened.

Fuck. So much for pleasant surprises.

They stood frozen, staring at each other.

For a moment, Brinder thought he was seeing things, even blinking his eyes to clear them.

"Son. May I come in?"

Brinder caught Amani's eye over his surprise guest's shoulder and gave her a small, mechanical nod in response to her unasked 'ok to leave?', which she returned. Expertly easing his father into his office, Amani closed them into the space that suddenly seemed way too small and far too warm.

"Baba." He could barely manage the word past the tightening of his throat. He loosened his tie, which he'd worn because of an earlier meeting with Agnes and the president of a sister hospital, hoping it would help.

His father was silent for a moment, eyes traveling over him, as if cataloging, his face otherwise expressionless. Brinder took the opportunity to reciprocate.

And was shocked.

He hadn't seen his father in person since he was twenty-six. Eleven years. And they hadn't talked at all since their raging blow-up, via FaceTime, over Brinder's naturalization as a U.S. citizen.

Brinder did the math quickly in his head. His father had left India for medical school, trained in the UK, and stayed, having met the rebellious youngest daughter of a marquess. Brinder had a hard time picturing his very proper, very English mother as rebellious, but she'd defied family to be with Rahul. And his father? He'd created pandemonium.

His grandfather, also a surgeon, had planned for Rahul to join him in practice back in Mumbai and marry a woman his grandfather had selected as an optimal bride for his only son. Instead, his father chose his mother, meeting and marrying her during his first year of residency. She'd been pregnant within the year, with a baby she'd miscarried.

Brinder was born eighteen months later on his father's twenty-ninth birthday. A fact he chose to ignore by ignoring his own birthday. At nineteen, coinciding with his first year in Washington, DC, it became just another date on the calendar. Mostly.

Sixty-six. His father was now fully gray. Baba's skin, a few shades darker than his own, had weathered with lines that weren't unattractive. Rahul Desai still stood tall, topping out a few inches shorter than Brinder's own six-six, but now seeming a bit smaller than that. He was still trim and Brinder knew from Mum that he still enjoyed a running habit he'd picked up in medical school—albeit much slower these days. His mother always said his father was the most handsome man she'd ever met—the dashing young resident who'd assisted on her father's heart surgery.

Brinder saw physical evidence in himself of the blend of both his parents, with his mom's hazel eyes and his dad's tall, lean build and dark hair. Many had told him he resembled his father, a sentiment he'd never agreed with in his youth.

Now, however, with the passage of time and distance, he could see threads of himself on his father's face, which now held an uncertain—and atypical—look for the strong-willed patriarch.

His father took a visible, deep breath. "I know this is an unexpected visit."

Brinder said nothing in response—too conflicted as he fought the urge to either scream at his father for the random drop-in, or rush past him out his door and take that walk he'd pondered.

"I, uh, I apologize. I'm in town to see a colleague and I took the opportunity to visit."

"And you didn't think perhaps a call or some kind of heads-up would have been appropriate, versus just appearing in my doorway at work?" Brinder struggled to keep his voice even, clenching his fists to stop the shaking of his hands.

"I knew you wouldn't accept the visit if I did that." His father lifted his chin with a well-recognized set of defiance.

"And you'd be correct." Brinder rolled his shoulders back, forcing eye contact with this stranger who was his father.

"I'd apologize for the intrusion but," he swallowed, "I'm not sorry."

Brinder's eyes flared. The absolute, unmitigated gall of this man. "Baba, the last time we spoke—and that is phrasing it gently—you screamed at me for my life decisions. Which was part of a long pattern of you doing the same." He took a step closer, though still maintaining several feet between them. "Why the fuck would you ever think I'd want to see you again, much less in my place of business?" Brinder gripped the back of his neck as he fought to lower his voice. The last thing he needed was more workplace drama. He'd *just* put one to rest.

His father winced at the expletive—one he'd forbidden use of in their family home—and yet, no reprimand came. Instead, Baba held out a shaking, placating hand.

He'd never seen evidence of nervousness with his father. A tiny piece of Brinder's hardened heart softened. Before his entire wall of painstakingly built defenses crumbled, leaving him vulnerable to a signature Rahul Desai attack, Brinder took a fortifying breath—

"I had to see you, son."

And released it on a frustrated whoosh. Brinder rolled his eyes. He knew he was acting petulant, but it didn't matter how old he was or what he'd accomplished—his father had always seemed to bring out the rebellious, snarky child in him.

Well, maybe not always. Brinder flashed to a memory from long ago —one he hadn't remembered, or perhaps more accurately *allowed* himself to remember, in years. He'd been about seven and school was closed for a holiday. His mom had been hit with a bad case of the flu. Baba was paged to the hospital to check on a patient and brought Brinder with him—something that would not happen in today's hospitals, but for Brinder, planted a critical life seed.

He'd walked the halls by his father's side, eyes wide and just taking in the surroundings. Lost in the memory, Brinder could almost hear the hum and chime of various machines. The low murmur of visitors with loved ones. The squawk of the overhead page for a code blue. The chatter of nurses who oohed and aahed over him. *Ok...perhaps that had been some foreshadowing.* He'd been entranced.

At that moment, he knew his future. Knew he wanted to be a physician—not because of paternal expectation, but rather because his soul recognized the rightness of it all. He was home.

He'd loved that day with Baba. They'd had lunch in the cafeteria, Baba allowing him to order whatever he wanted. Brinder could still picture the smile on his father's face as he draped his stethoscope around Brinder's scrawny neck, patting his shoulder and guiding him to the lot where he'd parked their Rover 200 series.

Later, after Baba had checked on Mummy, they'd watched cricket on TV and eaten takeout curry.

A special day.

And, sadly, a rarity. A small, hidden gem of happiness dwarfed by an increasingly impenetrable quarry of coldness.

The sound of a throat clearing yanked him from the abyss of memories—good and bad.

"Son?" Uncertainty was written on Baba's face.

Brinder knew he had to acknowledge him. What Brinder really wanted to do was howl and yell and perhaps have a proper tantrum akin to the child he felt like inside.

Instead, he managed to school his features and respond in a

surprisingly even tone. "You haven't called me 'son' in a very long time. Usually you were just spitting out my name."

Now his father fully flinched. "And for that, I am sorry. More than you could ever know."

"Spare me, Baba." He shook his head. "Listen, you may have never respected my chosen professional pathway, but I actually have work to do." A small lie, since he had a tiny break in his schedule before his afternoon revved up with a fresh round of meetings. "Why don't you just get to the point and then head back to wherever you came from."

His father hesitated, then motioned to the chairs across from his desk. "May I sit?"

Clearly not a quick drive-by visit. Fuck.

Brinder briefly closed his eyes, nodding in resignation. Normally when he had visitors, he either sat in the chair next to them or they sat at his table. He always thought it was pretentious to sit behind a desk when meeting with coworkers and guests. Very 1950s arrogant businessman. Not his style.

Therefore, it was with no small amount of intention that he rounded his desk and sat in the high-backed chair, placing a desk between himself and his estranged father. He leaned back in the chair, elbows rested on the cushioned arms, fingers steepled together.

Brinder almost laughed when he realized it was the exact stance his father used to take with him when he was called into his home office for some youthful transgression or other. The instances were fewer and farther between as he got older, but only because they eventually sent him to Cheltenham Prep, and later Cheltenham College.

Instead, he merely raised his brows and waited. It was a power move, and he was relishing it—even as he studiously ignored the clear and uncharacteristic discomfort of his father.

Eventually the elder Desai cleared his throat and began. "I have so much to say to you and I had it all worked out in my head. Now I can't seem to determine where to begin or what to say."

Brinder shifted in his seat. "I have limited time, so I encourage you to figure it out quickly so we can both get on with our days."

Baba nodded, a frown creasing between his brows. "I was at the hospital in Georgetown."

Brinder's eyebrows hit his hairline. "Why?" His father was recognized in the UK as a top cardiothoracic surgeon, often being invited to lecture to those in the field. But, as far as Brinder knew, his father had only presented in Boston, Manhattan, and LA—and he only knew that because of his mother.

"About a year ago, I started feeling...unwell. I had some balance issues."

Brinder bit his tongue, his internal diagnostician instantly wanting to pepper his father with questions.

"I ignored it, until it progressively worsened."

The thud of his heartbeat filled Brinder's ears. "And you didn't think to tell me any of this?"

Now his father's brows rose. "Would you have cared?"

Would he? *Yes.*

"We may be estranged, but you are still my father," he gritted out. The shock of his father facing a health crisis warred with hurt and anger that Mum hadn't told him about this.

"And you are still my son." They locked gazes, but unlike in the past, there was no heat. His father sighed. "During a faculty meeting, my colleague noticed something I'd been ignoring." Baba cleared his throat, now clasping his hands on his lap. "A tremor in my hands. And some stiffness to my gait."

"Parkinson's." Brinder breathed out unsteadily, flashing to the shake of Baba's hands he'd noticed earlier.

"Yes. I'm in the early stages. I came to the hospital in Georgetown for deep brain stimulation that is showing encouraging results."

Brinder's mind whirled, landing on the pragmatic. Which was safest. "Your practice?"

Now his father gave a sad smile. "I gave up surgery. I am still seeing patients, but have to leave the surgeries to my partners. It would be unethical to do otherwise." His father pointedly placed his hands on Brinder's desk, where a faint tremor was indeed evident.

"Baba, I'm sorry," Brinder managed. "Your practice has been everything to you."

His father laughed mirthlessly. And...were those tears in his eyes?

"Yes, that's part of the problem. I put my career before everything.

My parents in India. Your mother, who I don't deserve, though I'm working hard to make amends now. And you. I failed you as a father, Brinder. And I am so very sorry."

Brinder's hand was back at his nape, squeezing. What the *everloving fuck*, as Ross would say, was happening?

"So you thought you'd just pop in and apologize after twenty years of assholery," Brinder scraped out, voice raw and uncaring of his father's cringe at his immature vulgarity, "and I'm just supposed to hug you and tell you that I love you, Baapu?" His voice cracked on the last word. He hadn't referred to his father as Baapu since he was a young boy.

"I know it's not going to be that easy, though I wish it were." His father's eyes darted around Brinder's face, assessing, but also…warm. That in and of itself was as jarring as his father's diagnosis. "It's unconscionable to behave as I did. And I apologize, from the depths of my heart, that it took the diagnosis of a progressive neurodegenerative movement disorder to see the errors of my life."

"Not to mention twenty years," Brinder muttered.

Baba stood, but didn't move closer. "Twenty years is grossly unacceptable. And I know that. Life is relentless in its path forward. You blink and a year has passed. Then another. And another. Seasons come and go. Hair gets grayer. My face is craggy like my own grandfather's."

Baba's voice broke on the last word. He took a moment to compose himself before resuming, a sad smile on his face. "And suddenly it's many years since I've seen my son and many more since we've had a civilized word. And that, son, is entirely my fault. I have let you down."

Now Brinder stood, his back to his father as he faced the sunshine that had been so tempting earlier. "I don't know what you want from me."

"I want a chance."

Brinder turned and moved so he was right in front of his father. "A chance at what?" He was glad his voice didn't shake, because his insides were quaking.

"A chance to make it up. To be a good father to you."

"And you think there's a chance of that happening?"

"I don't know. But I hope so. That's up to you."

CHAPTER SIXTY-FIVE

BRINDER

Brinder hung his head and shook it, reeling from the shock. His father. In his office. Baba's surgical career over. A life-changing diagnosis. And now asking for...what?

For a second chance.

Before he could form a response, his father spoke again. "I don't want to keep repeating the mistakes of my life. I left my father and mother in India and never looked back because they didn't respect my life choices."

Brinder couldn't help but huff out a laugh.

His father ignored Brinder's reaction and continued. "I never saw my father again. Never tried to mend those fences. When he was dying," Baba's voice caught in a contained sob, "I stubbornly refused to see him, even though your aunts and uncle begged me. I regret that decision, along with so many others, and I refuse to ruin another relationship that can be saved. I'm just so tired of being stuck in this festering swamp of anger and estrangement."

His father watched him with sorrowful eyes. "Brinder, I don't want you to live with estrangement and remorse the way I have. It's no way to live."

Brinder snorted in derision, one eyebrow flying up as he pointedly ignored his father's accurate assessment of his emotions. "What makes you think I feel any remorse about our utter lack of a relationship?"

Now Baba's brow rose, mirroring him—clearly seeing through his bluster. "Don't you?"

Brinder shook his head and laughed mirthlessly. "I can't just flip a switch, Baba. You were cruel. Hurtful."

"And I will regret that to my dying day, Brinder. My own Baba— your grandfather—was very traditional. I tried to emulate the firm discipline of his household."

"The same household you left because you wanted to explore your own opportunities. And then berated me when I did the same."

"I wanted to spare you what I experienced." Baba hung his head for a moment before looking up, tears clearly shining now. "My father loved me, even if his ways of showing it were old-fashioned. I left and never saw him again. I learned of his death from my sister's husband."

Brinder knew some of this. He'd visited his aunt and his cousin, Sanjay, two summers earlier in an effort to explore his Indian heritage. The trip had been eye-opening and affirming, allowing him also to see clearly that his infatuation with Tiercy wasn't in her best interest. Or his.

Baba continued, "I don't want the same for us. I've been in therapy since the diagnosis. Your mother's influence," he added wryly by way of explanation. "It hasn't been easy, but I'm dealing with many of my own issues. I can't get back my time with my father. I can't apologize to him. But I can to you. I want us to build something new." His father reached out a tentative hand and gently placed it on his shoulder.

Brinder's knees almost gave out at the weight of the barely there touch. It was their first physical contact of any sort since the day before he announced his intentions to go to medical school in America. A lifetime ago.

The weight of it...all of it...it was too much. Too much.

Recognizing his own assholery as he did it, Brinder shrugged off his father's touch, ignoring the burn of contact from Baba. He resisted looking at his shoulder, half expecting to see a singe mark on his dress shirt. But he couldn't miss the grimace on his father's face as Brinder rebuffed the gesture.

"You want to build something new?" Brinder shook his head, completely unable to contain a smirk. "That takes balls, old man." Another wince from his father. Brinder leaned against his desk, arms folded, unwilling to be swayed by Baba's surreal, and clearly emotional, presence in his office.

What a couple of mind-fuck-filled weeks this had been.

Brinder dropped his head, suddenly exhausted to the bone. He couldn't do this. Couldn't have this conversation. Couldn't even be near his father. He glanced at his watch, half-amused and half-disgusted that he'd always insisted on wearing the one gift from his father. Brinder had told himself it was because he liked the look of it.

Right?

He took a fortifying breath and then met his father's expectant gaze.

"I'm sorry, Baba, but I'm not sure that's possible."

In that moment, Brinder understood the aphorism about someone's face falling as he watched Baba's expression slide from hope...to misery.

After a moment, Baba's chin set in familiar intransigence. Only this time, he wasn't locking horns over university, or medical school, or his specialty, or some other disappointment at Brinder's hands. No, Brinder got the sense that Baba was intent on reconciliation. And Baba was nothing if not tenacious. It was how he was able to win the heart of a marquess's daughter. To build a prestigious career. To fight for lives in the OR.

"I understand, Brinder. Believe me, I understand more than I could ever express." Baba's eyes were sad, but there was a resolve to him that told Brinder this wasn't over yet. "I'm in Charlottesville until tomorrow evening. Then I fly home to your mother, who has taken up a rather messy pottery hobby. Right now, it's all a bit of lopsided mess, with clay splatters all over our sunroom. Heaven knows what she'll have made in my absence." Baba quirked an indulgent smile. "She says it's all rubbish, but I personally love my misshapen coffee mug."

His father paused and held out a hand. Brinder wasn't sure if the tremble was from the Parkinson's or emotion. Or both.

Brinder wordlessly took his father's hand. The same one that had healed Honor not once, but twice. A lump in his throat made swallowing painful.

"Thank you for seeing me, son. I hope to hear from you. And maybe then, you can tell me what's going on with you and Honor Wheatley." Brinder's eyes flew to his father's from where they'd been fastened on their joined hands. "If the rumors are true about you both, I'd say it's about damned time you both got your heads and hearts straight."

The glint in Baba's eye matched the amused smile at the corner of those normally stern lips, but Brinder didn't miss Baba's eyes filling with tears. "I love you, Brinder. I truly do. And I am so very proud of you. Of the man you are. Of what you've accomplished in spite of my poor parenting. I love you far beyond what I could ever convey. I do hope to see you before I head home. Goodbye, son."

Brinder could barely manage a rational thought amidst the jumble of emotions coursing through his body. "Goodbye, Baba," he finally scraped out as his father turned to leave.

Brinder spent long moments staring at the empty doorway through which his father, *of all people*, had just exited his office.

Amani, deploying her executive assistant ESP, shifted into view, her eyebrows arched in a 'you ok?' look. He thought he nodded, but couldn't be sure. Regardless, Amani knew what he needed. She closed the door behind her, leaving him in the stifling silence of his office. Within a minute, he overheard her tell someone he couldn't be disturbed.

And, yet, that is exactly what he was. Utterly disturbed.

Honor's face flashed before him. His afternoon couldn't end soon enough. He needed his Stardust.

Chapter Sixty-Six

Honor

It was a gorgeous June day, bright sun in a robin's egg-blue sky with a dappling of feathery cloud whisps. The ever-stifling humidity had disappeared, probably snapped via the overnight thunderstorms so common in this area in the summer.

"I know it's technically Monday, but it just *feels* like a lovely and luxurious Saturday." Ross stretched out on the chaise lounge by the side of the pool, pointing and flexing her toes. "This has been one of the best parts of my maternity leave. Completely forgetting the day of the week."

Honor, Ross, and Tiercy were relaxing by the pool at Ross's farmhouse, the babies napping in pack-and-plays under umbrellas. Petey and Jemma, newly on summer break, were taking turns jumping off the dive, attempting trick maneuvers, which Ross said was a common game played by Xander and Petey.

"Nice 'Xan-bam,' Petey!" Ross cheered, then turned to Honor to explain. "Xander's signature pool dive from high school."

"Ah...gotcha." Honor was technically American, but sometimes she felt so British, missing many typical American teenage experiences while at boarding school. And, you know, recovering from heart surgery.

"Ross and Xan have had many good times by this pool," Tiercy teased in a singsong. "It may be that little Leah was conceived poolside."

"Way to overshare, Mrs. Colburn." Ross threw a piece of strawberry at her bestie, who deftly caught it and popped it in her mouth with a wink. "Let's not traumatize poor Honor."

Now Honor laughed. "You two realize you're having a moment of role reversal, don't you?"

Ross paused, a bite of spinach and strawberry salad halfway to her mouth, and then snorted. "It only took thirty-two years, Tiercy, and we finally turned into each other. It's like Freaky Friday, except it's Monday." She paused, tapping her chin. "Magic Monday?"

As the women laughed and threw out other possible titles, Honor's eyes drifted closed, content in the blended sensations of warm sun, splashing children, and good friendship.

"Did Dr. Desiiigh keep you up late, Mini-Wheats?"

Honor's eyes flew open at Ross's question, the pink of her cheeks the direct result of the steamy memory rather than the sun's rays.

Ross grinned. "Bullseye."

Honor couldn't help it, she grinned back, admitting with her smile what was hard to say aloud. In the past, her girlfriends would talk about their sexcapades, but Honor never had much to add. Now? How different things were.

"Spill it, Wheatley. We have babies and young children and need to live vicariously through you. Smeggsy times aren't what they used to be."

"Speak for yourself," Tiercy murmured, a sly smile tilting her lips.

"Strumpet!" Ross hollered, laughing.

"Trollop!" Tiercy rejoined on a giggle.

"Hussy!" they whisper-shouted at the same time, clearly remembering their young children were nearby.

Honor watched them, eyes wide. Sometimes best friends could be so strange.

She loved it.

"Sorry, Wheats," Ross offered once she pulled herself together. "Long-time shtick with us."

"I don't mind." She didn't. Honor was just happy to be there, enjoying the splendor of friendship. Another unexpected gift from an unexpected week.

"Things are good with you and Brin?" Tiercy's topaz blue eyes scanned her face, her gentle kindness making them even more beautiful.

"Things are really good," Honor replied, immediately deciding to ignore her natural reticence and unburden her heart. "And confusing."

"Well you've come to the right place. The relationship doctors are in session." Ross turned wide eyes at Tiercy's snarfing noise. "What? Just because I was relationship-averse for my entire adult life, until recently of course, doesn't mean I can't be an expert now. I was a star pupil at Xander Hottie Grace Romance and Relationship School," she drawled. "Now spit it out, Wheats. From the *beginning*. I'm still ticked you kept this from me when we were working on your memoir." Ross wagged a finger at her.

Honor gave her an apologetic smile, though she wasn't sorry at all for the intentional omission. "I didn't want to share it. It—what Brinder and I had—was special, and private...and it hurt so much. I couldn't share it." She took a sip of her sweet tea. *Holy moly*, that beverage was addictive. Probably diabetes in a glass, but she loved it. "But now I think it's better if I do. I could use some advice."

"It's Marvelous, Magical, Miraculous Monday. We have no plans. Take your time." Ross polished off the last bite of her salad and leaned back on the chaise.

"Ok," Honor breathed out. "Um, where to start?" She reached for her scar and began. "After my first Tetralogy of Fallot surgery, my father befriended Dr. Desai."

"Brinder's dad who also was your surgeon," Ross clarified.

"Correct. I didn't meet Brinder, though, until right after I started secondary school."

Tiercy—a high school English teacher who planned to go back to work at the end of summer—frowned, probably trying to figure out what that translated to in U.S. schooling.

"High school. Year nine."

"Ah," Tiercy nodded. "A tender age."

"Mmm," Honored agreed. "And quite hormonal. I knew Dr. Desai's son was nearby. He'd started at Cheltenham Prep at age eleven.

When I begged my parents for a chance to go to boarding school, it was really to get away from their incessant hovering. We all knew I'd need a second surgery at some point, and my mom especially wanted me nearby. Other than letting me do summer plays with them, and a few bit roles in various films of theirs, it was just...oppressive.

"I think Dad and Dr. Desai must have been discussing my wishes to live more independently and Brinder's father convinced him that Cheltenham Ladies College would be a good choice. Close enough to my parents in the Cotswolds, but also, his own son was right around the corner at Cheltenham College and could keep an eye on me."

Ross snickered. "And did he? Quote 'keep an eye' on you, dearest?"

Honor blushed hard. "Hold that thought."

"Oh, I will. I'm getting all the deets, Wheats." Ross threw finger-guns and winked.

"I didn't meet Brinder until my second week there. He was standing outside one of the classrooms, waiting for me."

"Was he surrounded by a gaggle of drooling teenage girls?" Tiercy rolled her eyes affectionately.

"No. He was chatting with a couple guys. He was..." she trailed, lost in a memory.

"Dreamy?" Ross supplied, leaning forward a bit in her chair as she peeked in the portacrib to check on Leah, who'd begun making small noises.

"Ha, no." Honor laughed. "Dreamy is not the word. Nerdy. Tall. Gawky. But cute in a lanky baby giraffe kind of way."

"Reeeaaally?" Ross's eyes were wide. "I always thought he just emerged from the womb a Hottie McHot Pants."

"No. He was definitely not that. At least, not then. He came up, introduced himself and his friends, and then offered to walk me to lunch. From then on, I saw him at least once a week. Just as friends. I'm pretty sure I was crushing on him long before he thought anything of me. He was just so...kind. Charming. Quirky. He loved nature documentaries and would often just randomly offer a fact from the animal kingdom."

"That is soooo Brinder," Tiercy added, smiling.

Honor knew she had no reason to be jealous of the pretty blonde, but knowing Brinder once fancied Tiercy enough to want to marry her and raise Jemma, natural insecurity pinched at her gut.

"He loves you, you know?" Tiercy interrupted her thoughts. "Has he told you yet?"

Honor choked on her tea. "That," she gasped as she caught her breath, "was unexpected."

"I just wanted to make sure you knew that any silly infatuations of the past are nothing compared to the deep love he has for you, Honor." Tiercy reached across and squeezed Honor's hand.

Honor sniffled, not sure if it was post-sweet-tea-choke or tears in the back of her throat. "Thank you, Tiercy. I appreciate you saying that."

Tiercy squeezed affectionately again and then patted her hand, sitting back. "You were saying?"

"What happened next?" Ross mimed eating popcorn.

"We were just friends for the first few years. When I was sixteen, the inevitable happened. I started having shortness of breath. I was fatigued. I'd always enjoyed hiking and being outside, but I started not being able to keep up with my friends."

"I'm surprised you could do all that to begin with," Tiercy remarked. "I would have thought you'd have had more restrictions."

Honor rolled her eyes. "Only what my parents put in place. Dr. Desai and my cardiologist both said I could do most 'normal' things." She was quick to air quote that word. *Normal.* It was such a relative word it was laughable. "I mean, I couldn't run a marathon, and physical team sports wouldn't have been wise. But I biked. Hiked. Swam. Messed around on the netball court in intramurals."

"Until…" Ross prompted.

"Until I was getting more winded and short of breath with less and less exertion. I had palpitations. I knew it was time for my valve replacement. Dr. Desai had been clear with me about the signs. Over winter break, a week or so before Christmas, I had my surgery."

Instinctively, her fingers found her scar again, tracing a familiar path up and down the raised skin that was as much a part of her as her brown eyes and her tiny stature. "I was in the hospital for four days or so. I got home Christmas Eve. On Boxing Day, Brinder came to see me." Honor smiled at the memory. "He had this big box of DVDs and games. I think my parents knew I'd be climbing the walls. By that point, Brinder was my best friend, so they asked the Desais if he could stay at our place for a week, to keep me company while I recuperated. We watched movies and documentaries, and played Scrabble."

"Hate that game," Ross grumbled. "Stupid made-up words and dumb double standards on what you can and can't use."

"Exactly!" Honor cried out in solidarity, apparently too loud, because Leah erupted into a wail.

"I woke Leah. I'm so sorry!" Honor slapped her hand over her mouth, horrified.

Ross waved her hand dismissively. "Nah, she'd been making her warning noises. I know when she starts whimpering and grunting, she's either fixing to destroy her diaper or scream for my boob. Or both."

Ross reached into the crib and pulled out the crying baby, who immediately rooted around her chest. "She rarely even gives me time to change her. When Leah's ready to eat, she's ready. I'll deal with her diaper after."

Unselfconsciously, Ross tugged her bikini top to the side and Leah latched, her squalls miraculously silenced. Ross rolled her eyes and smiled. "Parasite," she whispered, kissing Leah's pudgy fist.

Honor's nipples tightened reflexively, her breasts aching for the tug of a child. That was new. Never before—at least as an adult—had she envisioned herself as a mother. Now? Her body physically yearned for it.

She'd have to process that plot twist later, because Ross was once again prompting her to finish her story.

"Anyway," Honor continued with a smile, grateful to return to the story instead of getting broody about babies—Brinder's babies specifically. "That week is when I officially fell in love with Brinder Desai. He was so solicitous. So funny. So smart. And he'd gotten so handsome. It was like," Honor gazed into the distance, remembering, "the planes of his face shifted. He went from my nerdy friend—"

"—to a Hottie McHot Pants." Ross finished for her.

"Exactly." Honor grinned. "He was so cute. Thank God my heart was newly fixed, because if it wasn't, it probably would have beat right out of my chest."

"What is it about a hot nerd?" Ross tapped her lip. "It's like...nectar for the lady garden." She sighed dramatically and shivered.

Honor nodded. "There was definitely always something so...yummy...about him. Like you could sort of see the hotness emerging, and it was amazing. But surrounding it, or maybe under it, was the same sweet, kind, thoughtful geek. All lanky. *Gads.* Those arms and legs before he grew into them." Honor chuckled, appreciating the opportunity to bask in memories she hadn't permitted herself to face for fear of ravaging an already-broken heart.

Tiercy's eyes softened, Augie now also nestled at her breast. They weren't kidding the other day when they remarked how the babies managed to be on the same schedule—at least during the day. Augie slept all night, something Leah apparently had yet to accomplish. "I would love to see the photographic trail of this transformation."

Honor broke into a wide smile. "I'm pretty sure my parents have pictures of us from their various visits to Cheltenham, and even Brinder's short stay with us in the Cotswolds while I recuperated. I can see about getting Mom to text some."

"Nice," Tiercy replied, laughing.

"So you fell in love," Ross prompted again, clearly itching to get the deets, as she'd phrased it.

"We did. We started dating that term. By that fall, our year thirteen, or what would be senior year here in the U.S.—" Honor paused while Ross mouthed thanks for the translation. Schooling terms were so different in the U.S. and the UK. "—we were inseparable. We were studying for our A-Levels, getting ready for university. We'd both talked about Cambridge." Her heart gave a familiar, reflexive pang of hurt as she remembered her shock when she learned he went to America. Of course, she'd left first. But, he'd already secretly committed to Georgetown, so their dreams of Cambridge were moot regardless.

"Then what happened?" Tiercy cocked her head, compassion written in every ounce of her bearing.

"That February of our last year of Sixth Form, we, uh..." Honor stalled, shyness closing her throat.

"You popped each others' cherries!" Ross declared.

"Rossss," Tiercy admonished, with a meaningful look in the direction of the kids playing in the pool. "Library voices, please."

"Eh," Ross waved a dismissive hand. "They're caught up in their game. I could call out that we have ice cream and they'd be oblivious. Watch this." She shifted and raised her voice to about the level she'd used a moment ago. "Ice cream..."

Suddenly, Jemma and Petey launched out of the pool, cheering and laughing as they scurried to the promise of a sweet treat.

"Uh oh," Ross whispered. "Ok. Point made." She turned to the excited kids. "I have ice cream bars in the house. Dry off with your towels and you can each have one." She leveled a look at her son. "*One* means one, Petey, you dig?"

"Yep, Mom. I dig." Petey gave her a gap-toothed grin. Both his top teeth had fallen out in the last week. He kissed Ross on the cheek and leaned down to do the same to his baby sister, clearly not embarrassed by his sibling's breastfeeding.

For the umpteenth time, Honor wished she could be like Ross, self-confident and mostly unfiltered. But so authentic and funny.

The kids ran toward the house, turning it into a game of tag. When the sounds died off, Ross turned back to the women. "I thought they'd never leave." She waggled her brows. "So you did the dirty with Desai. Was he good even then? I bet he came out knowing how to find the clit. Like a homing beacon." She nodded sagely, then burst into snickers at her own joke.

"Good lord, Ross." Tiercy shook her head and laughed. "You do *not* need to answer that, Honor."

"Yes, you do," Ross retorted. "So...he rocked your teenage world."

"Not quite." Honor ignored Ross's dropped jaw. "It was good. It was...new for both of us. We were figuring it out."

"Nothing like first orgasms," Ross sighed. "Best bodily discovery ever."

"Well," Honor continued, "our first orgasms with each other happened...um...actually a couple decades apart."

"What?" Ross startled, accidentally releasing Leah's latch. Before the baby could summon a wailing grievance, Ross deftly switched her to the other side.

"I never had one, you know, with someone else. Until this week."

Honor was pretty sure Ross's eyes were going to bulge out of her head. Oh well, in for a penny...or pence as it were...in for a pound.

"I didn't have an orgasm with Brinder when we dated in high school. Or with my boyfriend before Crispin. Or Crispin." She cringed at the bad taste his name left in her mouth. "I didn't have one that wasn't, uh, self-administered, until this week."

"I am d-e-d dead. Deceased. Flabbergasted. Gobsmacked. Blutterbunged. Brinder didn't take care of you all those years ago?"

"He didn't know," Honor offered weakly, now regretting—as she had many times in the past—that she hadn't been truthful with Brinder. "I just made it seem like I did."

"You faked it with Brinder Desiiigh?" Ross laughed in amazement. "I'll have 'sentences I never thought I'd say for a thousand, Alex.'"

The women cracked up.

"But he's made up for missed opportunities?" A single brow arched on Ross's forehead.

Now Honor's blush was furious. "And then some. I, uh, asked for his assistance in experiencing sexual passion and ecstasy. As research. For my upcoming movie."

Shidoobie, that sounded awful saying it aloud like that. But, it was true. And Ross and Tiercy were not the type to judge. Gently tease maybe, but always supportive.

"I'm sure he, uh, *came* through with flying colors." Ross snort-laughed at her pun.

"You're such a reprobate, Ross," Tiercy scolded, giggling.

"Nice SAT word, Bestie."

"So it took a couple decades, but Brinder Desai finally brought the Big O for you, huh?" Ross adjusted the baby over her shoulder, patting Leah's tiny back in the adorable pink-striped, ruffled swimsuit she was wearing.

Was that one of her ovaries howling in jealousy?

Honor swallowed, shocked at what she was about to reveal. "That's an understatement. He makes me come so hard I cuss. I can't help it."

"The f-bomb?" Through working on Honor's memoir, Ross had become well-versed on the impact the Bible Belt ways of Honor's late maternal grandmother had had on her, and was endlessly amused by her replacements for certain curse words.

"Mmhmm." Honor slid down a bit in her seat, remembering the four orgasms he gave her before bed last night...each of them punctuated with *that* word.

"Lalochezia." Ross pointed at Honor, waving her finger around.

"God bless you?" Tiercy joked.

"Ha. No. Lalochezia. It's the use of indecent—or shall we say vulgar —language to relieve stress and in other, shall we say... *intense* situations. Basically, it's cathartic swearing."

"Bestie," Tiercy interjected, a wide smile of admiration on her face, "I do believe you've just officially won the SAT Word Wars."

Ross threw an arm up in the air. "Yes! Victory! And with a word connected to vulgarity. Double win!" Leah barely moved, milk drunk and head lolling on her mother's shoulder.

Ooof. There went the other ovary.

"So what's next? You live happily ever after in Orgasm Land?" Tiercy patted her son's back, and Augie let out a massive, rumbling burp.

"One...I love that kid. He's going to be epic in college. Two...*I* wanna live in Orgasm Land. It sounds lovely." Ross shifted Leah onto the chaise, deftly changing the wet diaper and then lifting her up. She motioned to Honor. "Wanna hold her?"

"I may steal her. Along with Brinder's couch, his rug, and his blanket."

"Tiercella, what did you put in the sweet tea? I want a glass of that."

Honor held the baby to her chest, patting her back and rocking side to side in an instinctive natural motion that felt primal in its simplicity. And so right.

"I'm just not sure where Brinder and I go from here. I mean, my life and his aren't exactly aligned."

She shifted Leah to cradle her in her arms, wanting to soak in her little rosebud mouth and the soft skin of her cheeks. She understood how Brinder quickly became so besotted with Jemma, lavishing his goddaughter with a love that caused all sorts of twinges and yearnings inside her.

"So work it out."

That was Ross. Always direct. Always to the point.

"I'm trying to figure out how to do that. It's easier said than done."

"The things that are most worthwhile in our lives are often the hardest gained." Tiercy sat a wide-awake Augie on her lap. No milk coma for him. His blue-gray eyes were fixed on Honor. Or maybe on Leah.

Honor had a momentary vision of grown-up Augie and Leah dating. She suspected Ross and Tiercy had expressed the same hope. Parents could be such matchmakers, especially when they found someone they thought would be good for their child.

Like her parents with Brinder. They'd been almost as devastated as she when they broke up. Honor had often suspected they'd been more upset with that than with her decision to defy them and take a film role halfway around the world.

"I don't know *how* to make it work. That's the problem. I've been working this over and over in my head. I'm leaving in a few weeks for Boston, and will be there for at least two months while we film. His work is here, and it's a busy job. My primary home is in Wales. His is in the Shenandoah Valley, closer to Charlottesville than DC or even New York."

"You know what I'm hearing? A lot of excuses." Ross's voice was soft but firm.

Honor tipped her head back, closing her eyes. Tears worked themselves free from the corner of her eyes, trickling down her cheeks. Soon, she was sobbing.

"Oh, Wheats, I'm so sorry." Ross sat next to her, pulling her into a side hug so as not to jostle her sleeping daughter. "I didn't mean to upset you."

"You didn't. It's just this...this *fucked up* situation." Honor laughed through her tears. "Lalochezia rocks, by the way."

Ross wiped away her tears with a napkin she'd magically produced, using mom skills they probably teach in the hospital before releasing you with a tiny baby. Or one could hope.

"If anyone can figure it out, you and Brinder can." Ross gave her another squeeze. "You know what life felt like without each other. And now you've found each other again. It's such a special connection you have. Do you really want to let that go? Lose it again?"

Honor inhaled a shaky breath. "No. No, I don't."

The perfect weight of Leah, the warmth of Ross's arm around her, the touch of the summer sun—they all grounded Honor in her truth. This wasn't a time for tears. It was a time for action.

She didn't know what that action was going to be, only that she wasn't letting go of Brinder a second time. The rest? They would absolutely figure it out. Together.

Chapter Sixty-Seven

Brinder

For once, he beat her home.

Home.

It may have been just a week, but in his heart, it was Honor's home now as much as his.

Brinder shrugged out of his suit as he turned on the shower, needing a psychological cleanse as much as a physical one.

Laurel's dramatic lies. Clark's aggressive buffoonery. Crispin's sick duplicity. Baba's diagnosis and life epiphany. And, most of all, his Stardust's reappearance in his life—firmly securing her place in his heart for the rest of eternity.

You never knew the curveballs life would throw you. You just needed to be patient, watch out for errant throws (cough-cough...Laurel and Clark), wait for your pitch, and then knock it out of the park.

His years in the States had fostered in him a love of baseball, which was vaguely similar to the cricket he'd enjoyed as a youth. That had him thinking about Gideon and his daughter. Her results were back, and it would be an uphill battle indeed for Lina. He made a mental note to reach out to Gideon this week.

Gideon's devoted fatherhood had him thinking of Baba again. Brinder pinched the bridge of his nose. He didn't need to process this right now. Honor would help him sort this bollocksed-up situation.

Just the thought of her was soothing. His mind traveled the inevitable, well-worn path to thoughts of Honor and their future.

Brinder had every intention of knocking it out of the park with Honor. Not just a euphemistic home run—although he'd definitely be pulling more screams and f-bombs out of her tonight before plunging inside her where he belonged. His cock kicked in anticipation, and Brinder was tempted to jerk off. Instead, he tapped some inner font of self-control, content with the knowledge he'd have the real deal soon. Losing himself inside Honor versus a solo shower wank? Easy choice.

Other choices weren't so easy. Such as...after they married—and he would marry her...tomorrow if she'd agree to it—where would they live? Would he give up this job? Find a new one near her? Would she consider relocating?

His mind whirred as he mentally tested potential scenarios. He was so lost in thought, he missed the sexy, curvy body disrobing in his bathroom and climbing into the massive shower.

Brinder startled as arms wrapped around his waist from behind, giving a small jump and almost slipping on the sudsy stone tile beneath his feet.

"Oh my gosh! I am so sorry. I didn't mean to give you a start." Honor shook with laughter, the soft globes of her breasts pressed into his back.

His cock immediately went to full mast.

Wordlessly—because mere words were worthless in some moments —Brinder turned in her arms, cradling Honor's lovely face between his hands, and tipped it up to receive his kiss. It was a slow, languorous tangling of their tongues. No urgency. Just a dreamy, sexy connection between them.

Of course, this was Honor...naked in his shower. And he did have a raging hard-on. Their kisses turned more frenetic. Hands groped, teased. Breaths panted.

Dropping kisses along her neck, especially that sensitive area under her earlobe that transformed her to shivering boneless bliss, he turned Honor to face away from him. Adjusting one of the dials, he turned on the lower jets, changing the direction of the spray to hit between her legs.

He knew he'd gotten the right angle when Honor gasped, flexing her hips.

"Ooohhhh," she moaned, rocking her hips and tilting them forward, clearly chasing the sensation. "I love your showers."

Brinder reached around and tugged her nipples in turn, rolling them and pinching softly. He snaked his other arm loosely around her waist, teasing the baby-soft skin with his fingertips. "This is what you did that morning earlier this week, isn't it?" He tugged one budded nipple, rolling it between his fingers again.

"Yes!" She gasped. He wasn't sure if that was in answer to his question or the ministrations on her sensitive nipples. Chances were... both.

"Good girl. Your orgasms are heavenly. You should have as many as you want."

She rocked her hips and he could feel the tension stringing her body taut as she climbed toward her release.

"That's it, Stardust. Chase it. Get it."

"Mmmmm," she moaned, throwing her head back against his chest. "Brinder...I'm—"

That was all she managed before she clenched hard and exploded on the deepest, sexiest groan of completion he'd ever heard. Her legs went limp and he hooked his arm tighter around her.

His cock throbbed.

"Hang on baby. You ready for me?"

"Mmmm," was all he got in response.

He ensured her feet were solid on the ground—albeit on tiptoes—and anchored his arm around her waist. Then he bent his knees and plunged up into her.

"Oh!" Honor cried out, immediately going even higher on her tippy toes to take him in.

It was not the most comfortable position he'd ever fucked in, but he had enough leg strength and momentum to keep thrusting up, hitting that spot inside of her over and over. He reached and tilted the jet again, immediately rewarded with a guttural moan from Honor.

Another twenty seconds of filling her up and hitting her g-spot while the pulsing water relentlessly assaulted her clit, which was probably hypersensitive and filled with blood, and she'd go off like a rocket.

Brinder's balls tightened in impending release as he slammed into her.

"Oh god oh god oh god," she chanted. "Don't stop don't stop don't stop."

He pulled back, leaving the clenching warmth of her pussy, and thrust hard.

"I'm clos—" she started and then screamed out her release.

Seconds later, he joined her, his own deep groan echoing off the tile. He pumped into her, painting her insides with his cum and wishing she wasn't on birth control.

Add that to the goals list to work out.

CHAPTER SIXTY-EIGHT

HONOR

They stood side-by-side outside the massive shower, each drying off with the fluffiest towels she'd ever used. Honor made a mental note to add that to the Comfort Tally of Couchie, Ruggie, and the pegasus-feathers duvet. "I need to know…are these made from molted angels' wings?" she teased.

Surprisingly, Brinder didn't return her laugh. She'd grown accustomed to his ready humor, particularly his utter amusement at her fascination with his comfy household accoutrements. She looked over her shoulder, where he stood utterly still, a thousand-yard stare on his handsome face. Her heart gave a worried stutter.

"Brin?"

He startled, eyes darting to her and then away before giving a sharp shake to his head, water droplets flying from the damp black waves of his hair. "Sorry, Tish. Just lost in thought."

He anchored the towel low on his waist. Even though she'd just had a mind-blowing orgasm, the ache to be with him again bloomed between her legs. But the misery etched on his face quickly muted her arousal, replaced with deep concern.

Wrapping her own towel around her, she reached up to his shoulder, trailing her fingers on the stray droplets he'd missed. "What's wrong?"

Brinder sighed and dropped his head, shifting to lean on the counter and then pulling her between his legs. He rested his cheek on the top of her head, holding her for long moments. She contented herself with breathing in the citrus-spice of his bodywash, nestled against the comforting damp warmth of his strong chest. Experience had taught her that when Brinder was stewing on something, he needed to unburden himself on his own time.

She felt his inhale, but what came out of his mouth after shocked her so much she jumped in his arms, nearly smashing her head into his jaw. Thankfully, his reflexes were quick.

"Did you say—?" She took a small step back to see his face.

"Yes." Brinder nodded, loosening the circle of his arms but still holding her. "I saw Baba today."

"Fuck," Honor breathed.

One corner of his lips tilted up, but his eyes were sad. It had been a long time since Honor had seen that look—the one that encapsulated his complicated feelings for his father—but she knew it well.

Honor dropped her head to his chest, needing to be closer. To give him the comfort of her body. His heart was beating a ferocious tattoo. She pressed a kiss over it and leaned back again. "Wow. Knock me over with a feather, why don't you.'"

His lip twitched in a small smile. "I felt much the same."

"I take it this was a surprise appearance."

"You take it correctly." Brinder's tone was wry, but Honor felt his grip tighten reflexively around her.

"Do you want to talk about it?"

He shook his head, a mirthless smile on his lips. "Not particularly. But I think I need to."

She scanned his beloved face. He was miserable. Clearly conflicted by whatever they'd discussed. Honor reached up and rested her palm against his face, enjoying the rasp of his stubble. Slowly, she brushed her thumb across his cheek, trying to soothe the abject misery she saw.

Eventually, he continued. "Just before lunch, Amani signaled I had a visitor." Brinder closed his eyes momentarily. "And there was dear ol' dad." When he opened them, the sheen of tears in the hazel she loved made her heart ache.

"What did he want?"

Brinder blew out an exhale. "He'd been in DC, getting treatment at Georgetown. For Parkinson's."

"What?!" Shock coursed through her system. "Dr. Desai has Parkison's? Since when? Did you know? Is he ok?" Question after question tumbled out of her mouth.

"Easy there, Tish. One at a time." This time, Brinder's smile, while still small, was real. "Apparently he is in the early stages, but he's given up surgery."

Honor flashed to Rahul Desai's face. She thought of the lifesaving gift of his hands. "Oh, poor Dr. Desai," she breathed, sorrow flooding her veins. "What a loss for him and for all the people who'll never get to have their lives saved by him. L-like me." The last part came out on a choked sob. Honor quickly pulled herself together. This was not about her.

Brinder pressed a kiss to the top of her head. "For all my complicated feelings about my dad, I'll always be grateful for his profession. Not only did he save your life, twice, he brought you into mine."

Honor cleared her throat, which was thick with emotion. "Doesn't seem like a spontaneous visit. DC and Charlottesville aren't exactly right around the corner from each other."

"He made a special trip here. He—he wanted to tell me about the diagnosis. But," Brinder inhaled a shaky breath, "he also wanted to apologize. To reconcile. He's been in therapy and wants to rebuild our relationship. Although I don't know how you rebuild something that was never properly built in the first place."

"Oh, Brinder." Honor cradled his face in her hands. "Wow. I don't know what to say. What do you need from me?"

Brinder dropped a tender kiss on her lips, the intimacy of which far exceeded the things he'd done to her body. "Just listen while I ramble? I need to process all this."

"Ramble away."

Brinder was quiet for a moment. He gripped the back of his neck before dropping his hand to rest behind him on the smooth granite countertop. "The parallel of my situation with you and mine with Baba just keeps running through my mind."

Honor stayed silent, trying to infuse peace and calm into him through the touch of her hands on his arms.

"It's been a lifetime since I've seen my father. But it also had been a lifetime since I'd seen you. And, yet, in one week, here you both are back in my world. Except one of you I welcomed with open arms. The other? I could barely shake his hand."

She reached for his hand and squeezed.

"I couldn't give him what he wanted. Not right then. Not out of the blue. But Honor"—his hazel eyes pierced into hers—"I can't help but recognize one plain truth. Isn't Baba hoping to receive from me exactly what we both have been seeking from each other this week? Understanding? Recognition of past failures? Faith in our relationship. Forgiveness. Trust in the future." He paused, rubbing his thumb on the back of her hand. "Love."

Before she could even process a response, he continued. "All afternoon at work, and as I drove home, all I could think was I'd be a hypocrite if I withheld from Baba the very things I want from you.

"I did a lot of therapy after Luke died, and one thing I had to face is the anger I have at Baba's rejection of every major decision I've made. I know the best way to do that is forgiveness. I know I need to forgive him —for my own sake, if not his. But I just haven't known how to even begin."

Tears trickled down Brinder's cheek. Honor pressed her lips to the tracks, absorbing the salt the way she wished she could absorb his pain.

"But this week has given me a crash course in second chances, Stardust. And I-I," he choked out, "I forgive him, Honor. I love my father, and I want...I want what he wants. A second chance." He collapsed into her arms, weeping.

Honor gently rocked her dearest love side to side, his body shaking with what she prayed was the healing release of his tears.

With an endearing snuffle, he eased away, his eyes darting between hers. "I love you, Stardust. I know this week has been exhausting and emotional. Mortifying and terrifying." He trailed his fingertips across her shoulders, leaving a trail of goosebumps. "But it's also been the best fucking week of my life. Because I got you back."

"And your dad," she whispered past her clogged throat.

"And my dad." With that utterance, his shoulders relaxed.

"What are you going to do?"

Brinder filled his lungs deeply and released it. Honor swore she could see the stress of his decision visibly leaving him on that cleansing exhale. "I'm going to call him later tonight and see if I can take him to breakfast tomorrow before his flight back to England." A wide grin spread across his face. "And I plan to answer his very pointed, and rather nosy question about us."

Honor's heart did a startled stutter in her chest. "Pardon?"

Brinder leveled her with one of his trademark panty-melting smiles. Thankfully, the only panties being melted now were hers. Well, if she were wearing any, that was. "He asked if we'd finally gotten our heads and hearts straight."

"What will you tell him?"

"I'm going to thank him for fixing the heart of my Stardust so that I can spend the rest of her very long, very healthy life taking good care of it."

Chapter Sixty-Nine

Honor

The bed shifted as he slipped in behind her, wrapping his tattooed arm around her waist. She traced the symbol for her name. The simple Viking arrow he'd inked on his skin as a tribute to her.

"How was it?"

"Amazing. Emotional. Surreal. I've never heard my dad cry. But it was happy tears, Honor. It was...God...I don't even have the right words to explain this."

She shifted to trace the lion that represented his heritage. "I think this is one of those times when words aren't really needed."

"I love you. So very much, Stardust." He pressed a kiss to her shoulder and they lay in peaceful contentment for long minutes.

"I love you, Brinder," she whispered, tears of happiness filling her eyes.

He nuzzled her hair. "I've been thinking."

"About what?" She could barely manage a murmur, such was her contentment.

"Great crested grebes."

Startled, she rotated to face him, propping her head on her hand. "I have no idea what you just said," she teased, flicking him gently on his shoulder.

"Ow!" Brinder faked agony. "I told you...you have freakishly strong tiny fingers."

"Which will never pump your thick, long cock again if you don't offer a translation to that random non sequitur."

He broke into a wide grin. "You think my cock is long and thick?"

She rolled her eyes and giggled, looking down the bed at said member now beginning to tent the sheets. "You know it is." She swatted him. "Now, tell me why the heck you referenced crusty geese."

"Great crested grebes." He tapped her nose. "They are a fascinating species of water bird. They do this synchronized dance on the water to strengthen their bond."

Now she propped herself on his chest. "Is this your way of saying you want to take water ballet classes with me?"

Brinder roared out a laugh, one she felt from her heart to her ladyparts...and back. After he composed himself, he began again.

"It's just a beautiful courtship ritual in nature. Each grebe is looking for a mate to start a family with. The males and females dive and then glide across the water together in stunning harmony. They do this for a few days, almost like dancing dates to ensure they are aligned and confirm a connection. Then, they mate, build a nest, and raise their little grebe chicks."

She dropped a kiss on his chest. "That's beautiful, Brin."

"That's what this week has been with you. And our first years of friendship. Our early love. It's been a ritual dance of courtship, seeing how well we glide in unison."

Honor swallowed, sadness grasping her heart. "We didn't do so well with that."

"Not all those years ago, no." Brinder reached under her arms and scooted her up so she lay sprawled on him. "But this past week, we've been gliding, doing an elaborate mating display, and courting each other. Honor, I want to build a nest with you. Have baby Stardusts. Make a life together the way we always planned, albeit with an unplanned delay."

Honor started to speak and paused, struggling to find the words. "I want that, too. So much. I just don't know how to make it all work."

Brinder smiled sadly. "I've been struggling with the details too. But I want to know we are at least in unison in this courtship dance."

"We are," she whispered, a single tear dripping down her cheek.

Brinder ran his thumb across her face, catching the tear with his thumb. "No more tears, Stardust. We *will* make a nest. We'll work it out."

"But the details of it, Brinder—that's where I get stuck. Will you move? Will I? Will you follow me around from set to set? Or wait for me for long months while I work? Or, worse, quit your dream job with your dream boss?"

"Honor, baby, every solution that's worth having is worth sweating the details. But I don't think it has to be all or nothing. What if we just take care of things a week or a month at a time? We just take it as it comes. The most important thing is, you are my mate. And I'm yours. The rest will work itself out."

Honor nodded. "I just want to know *how*."

"Relentless," he teased, chuckling. "Let's give it a bit of time. There is nothing to say we have to figure this out today or tomorrow or even next week. Can you get to a place of peace to be my mate and trust that we will find a way to be together?"

"I can," she managed. "I can do that."

"Good girl." He pressed a kiss to her forehead.

"I have three weeks until I have to report to set."

"That sounds like three glorious weeks of sex tutelage to me."

Honor laughed and pinched under his arm, which he'd propped behind his head.

"Ouch, Tish!" he yelped. "Fingers!"

She giggled, biting her lip as arousal flooded her core. "I love the second act of our relationship, Brinder." She lifted herself to straddle him. "Now, teach me something new."

CHAPTER SEVENTY

BRINDER

Three weeks passed in the blink of an eye. Brinder's days were filled with work—the satisfying clinical and administrative rhythm of hospital life. He may have rebelled against his father, but like Baba, and the paternal grandfather he'd never met, medicine was in his bones.

Honor became his number one cheerleader in the cautious efforts to rebuild a relationship with his family. Text messages with Baba. A FaceTime with him and Mummy—another term he'd not used in years. Plans for them to visit him properly after Honor reported to set.

Too soon.

There would never be enough time with her. Eternity felt too short, much less three fleeting weeks. The seconds and days slipped away in a blissful bubble of love, exploration, and friendship. Even with the busyness of work and the budding reconciliation with his parents, the heart of his time for those twenty-plus days was owned by Honor. They tacitly avoided any discussion of logistics for the future, instead choosing to bask in each other for the time they had.

Too fast, the weeks ticked away to days and the days had ticked away to mere hours. Honor had an evening flight to Boston, reporting to the set the following morning for a table read with her castmates. She'd pushed it as late as possible, her assistant Molly securing a first-class seat on the last flight from Reagan National to Logan airport. Grayton would be arriving by six for the ten p.m. flight. And then she'd be in the air, flying away from Brinder.

But that was temporary. He was working on a plan.

Because the truth that consistently emerged was that Honor was the most important part of his life. Everything else ranked far below.

Brinder had been tempted a few times to share the plan gelling in his mind—one that involved a fair amount of compromise on his part—but he knew Honor would fight him. Best to keep it close until he'd enacted the necessary steps.

He looked over at her and smiled, his heart doing the strange combination of soaring and aching that only came when separation from the person you loved was imminent. She was ensconced in her favorite spot on Couchie—which he'd never think of any other way. Her hands were curled around a mug of latte as she perused her script, memorizing her lines. Every now and then, she'd mouth the words, and Brinder loved watching the expressions on her face as she began to slide into her role. Pride filled his chest. She was so damn talented. Perhaps even another Oscar was in her future.

Brinder looked at his watch. Nine a.m.

He'd risen early, driven by a visceral need to grasp every moment of the day, waking her with his mouth between her legs—something he'd been remiss in doing. Oh, he'd been between her legs plenty, but on work days, he was awake before her and hadn't wanted to disrupt her sleep as he readied for work. Her sleepy, sexy gasp as he licked her awake would live rent-free in his wank bank for the rest of his life. And probably after. Yeah, he'd probably impatiently wank off in heaven while she put on plays with the angels, biding his time until he could take her to a private cloud and plunge into her.

"What's that face for?" Honor's smoky voice curled around his silly fantasy, luring his focus back to her like a siren's tempting song.

"You are so beautiful," Brinder replied, taking her in. The sun poured in from the windows, small dust motes dancing in the beams.

Perhaps even stardust, drawn to her energy. "You look like you have a halo."

Honor laughed, a tiny blush tinging her cheeks. "Thank you. But why do I feel like there's more to the story?"

"You want me to tell you what I was really thinking about?" It was almost as if his heart was grinning as much as he was.

"Why do I get the sense it was naughty?"

Now his grin spread even wider as his cock signaled its accord with his fantasy. "I was imagining us as angels, after we're old and dead, following a long life together."

"Hmmm...somehow I don't think that really explains the salacious look on your face. Or that action"—she motioned to his shorts—"happening right there."

He chuckled. "If you must know, I was imagining us fucking on a cloud."

Now the blush spread, her chest taking on the same rosy glow as her cheeks. Under her thin silk sleep tank, her nipples hardened. Brinder's mouth watered while his cock grew even harder.

"Don't look at me like that, Stardust. Well, not unless you want me to ravage you. Teach you another lasting sextasy lesson for your character."

Honor's smile dimmed. She bit the side of her lower lip, unconsciously rubbing her scar. "I don't want to think about my role anymore today," she announced, tossing her annotated script on the coffee table. "Today belongs to you. To us. And I want you to *make love* to me," she emphasized, cheeks burning brighter. "Not to give me fodder for my role, but for us. Just for us."

Heart leaping around in his chest, Brinder strode in front of her and tugged her up against him. She went on her tip-toes, locking her arms around his neck. He bent and lifted her so they were eye-to-eye, her legs wrapping around his waist.

"Is that so?" Brinder's voice was gravelly with need, his heart expanding almost to the point of beautiful pain.

"Yes," she whispered, peppering kisses along his jaw and neck. "Please."

Just like when he caved to her request for sex that first week together after eighteen years apart, it was the *please* that did him in.

In a handful of long strides, he had them back in their bedroom, the sheets still rumpled from when he'd taken her earlier that morning. The memory of her, sleep-warmed and sated from her orgasm—after she'd screamed his name and a few choice curse words—lingered as he gently laid her on those same sheets, which still smelled of their passion. Slowly, reverently, he peeled off her clothes—venerating her body along the way with a devotion that had settled deep within long ago. One that would never fade. Only grow in the miraculous way of stardust-blessed love. He placed a tender kiss on her scar, then at the corners of her eyes where quiet, salty tears leaked.

She cupped her hand along his face and smiled sweetly, shifting so she could lift his shirt over his head. Those doelike eyes scanned him, as if mapping him into deep memory, and he ached to bury himself inside her and never leave.

Honor leaned forward and, with breathtaking tenderness, brushed her lips on his chest, exactly over where the heart she owned beat for her and her alone. Then she lay back, her hair spilling around her, and held out her arms to him.

"Stardust?" His mouth went dry as his eyes skated with reverence across her luscious curves. "You wreck me. In all the best ways."

She gave him a heavy-lidded smile, widening her legs as he lowered into the cradle of her hips.

"Tell me what you want, Stardust. Do you want it slow and tender, or hard and fast?"

Her eyes flew to his from where they'd been fastened on the decadent visual of his cock nestling between her thighs, weeping for entry.

"I just want you to make love to me, Brinder," she whispered, arching into him enough that his cock found its way to her entrance.

"Every time I've been with you," he whispered, fighting against the tears clogging his throat, "I've been making love with you, Stardust. Every time."

"Me too," she choked out, burying her face in his neck.

He could feel the wet warmth of her tears, and pulled back so he could kiss them away again, brushing her soft cheeks with his lips until they were gone. He licked the salt from his lips and then shifted on his side next to her.

Reaching over, he caressed her face. "I love you, Stardust. With my body, I thee worship."

Brinder didn't even realize he knew the words to those timeless marital vows until they poured from his mouth—and his heart. "One day, I will say those words to you in front of our families, our friends, along with the rest of my vows."

"Brinder," Honor sobbed out, fresh tears leaking from her eyes.

"Ssshh, baby," he soothed. "No more tears."

She nodded, her eyes dancing between him. "I love you, too. And I want that, too."

"And we'll have it. All the people we care about will bear witness to this beautiful love we've found. But right now"—he pressed open-mouth kisses along her neck, eliciting a wave of goosebumps on her—"we're alone...and I like it that way."

Honor shifted, reaching to pull him past her entrance, where he'd notched himself, savoring the delayed gratification as he held them both at bay so they could dance even longer to the perfect tune of their passion.

"Patience, my Stardust," Brinder gently chided, hearing his British accent grow stronger, as always, as his ardor built. Brinder loved that she could make that happen to him. "We're taking our time. This time."

Honor shivered, her chest rapidly rising and falling as she mirrored his own anticipation. "Yes, my darling," she whispered, her voice as smoky as her eyes.

A wave of love-filled joy poured over him. Nothing had ever felt like this before.

Overcome, he shifted forward on shaking arms, brushing his lips over hers. She opened for him, and their tongues tangled languorously as he skated a hand along her body. "Never enough, Stardust. Never enough."

CHAPTER SEVENTY-ONE

HONOR

He pressed kisses on her upper lip, her lower one—sucking it gently between his teeth—and then her chin. He worked his way down the front of her neck, alternating between the lightest touch of his lips and the swirl of his tongue. Continuing on the path, he paid homage to each of her clavicles.

Who'd've guessed *that* was an erogenous zone? Of course, Brinder Desai could probably make any part of her body an erogenous zone, such was the way he played her like a maestro, her very being an instrument designed specifically for him. And that's what she was—meant for him. Like a benevolent, generous God had built them for each other, so they'd only be complete together.

Brinder paused his sexy ministrations at the hollow of her neck, peering at her with smoldering eyes that also danced with humor. "I can practically smell you thinking. Out with it, Tish," he teased on a low whisper.

Honor giggled. She couldn't help it. She was discovering it was one of the very best feelings to laugh in unfettered happiness with your lover in the midst of making the sweetest love. "What does my thinking smell like?"

He grinned at her. "Like jasmine in the sunshine." Brinder brushed a kiss on the notch, then nuzzled it with his nose. "And sometimes smoke when you're thinking really hard."

"Brat," she giggled breathlessly. "I'd pinch you, but apparently you're a delicate flower."

"No distracting me, Honor," he play-growled, humor joining the desire in his eyes. "What were you thinking?" He nuzzled her neck again.

Her mirth faded as powerful emotion coursed through her. Never could she have imagined a depth of love like this. A love so pure and so powerful, even its delays and messy complications couldn't defeat it. She cradled his handsome face between her hands, sighing with pleasure at the rasp of his whiskers on her palm as she breathed in their love like oxygen for her once-battered heart.

"It's not thinking. It's *knowing*. I know with a certainty that transcends all earthly knowing that we were made for each other. That some higher being, in a moment of pure grace, created us for each other."

"Honor," he choked out, clearly overcome. "No words anyone has ever said to me have meant more than what you just said." He paused, sniffing back tears, tracing the line of her scar and then brushing a series of tender kisses along the path. "I hate that you had to go through this, but I also know it's what brought you to me. So I love it. I see your scar, and I see the force that guided our lives together. Is that weird? Or selfish?" Brinder scanned her face uncertainly, eyes jumping between hers.

She lifted her head, kissing him tenderly in absolution. For him and for her and for all their decisions and pathways that kept them apart over the years, which now she could clearly see were necessary and right despite the pain. It made them who they were.

"It's not selfish or weird. I've always regarded my scar as a necessary part of me. Its presence means I'm alive. Healed. And I don't take that lightly. So many people in my industry have fought with me to hide it—

the same ones who don't hesitate to body shame me if I gain a couple pounds. But I know who I am and what matters most to me.

"This scar"—she ran her fingers across it—"has always been a badge of destiny. If I weren't born with Tetralogy of Fallot, my heart never would've been surgically repaired by your father. That surgery led to the greatest gift of my life—you. And even when circumstance and youthful stupidity yanked us apart, and stubbornness kept us separated, deep down, this scar has been my private homage to you and the love we share."

She touched her nose to his, nuzzling him and breathing in that unique scent that was pure Brinder. "I am so sorry for all the hurt we've caused each other, but I will never be sorry"—she lifted his fingers to her scar—"for this. How could I be?"

A small sob broke free from Brinder. Tears tracked down his cheeks, blending with hers, as they melted into an all-consuming kiss, tongues tangling amidst soft sighs and tender whispers of endearments.

With a brush of his lips on hers, Brinder eased back, eyes scanning her face with a smile so gentle, so filled with promise, she fell even deeper in love with this beautiful man. "Enough talking, Stardust. I need to make love to you. Now."

"Silly man," she whispered, chills erupting on her body. "We've been making our love all along."

Gazes locked, he plunged into her, burying himself to the hilt in one powerful thrust, releasing the sexiest growl she'd ever heard from him. She locked her legs around his waist, both of them groaning at the intensity of the connection. Then, as promised, he slid in and out of her slowly, pulling almost all the way out before sinking back into her, bottoming out. Over and over. Building her up slowly. Decadently. Tenderly.

His lips found one of her nipples. He lightly flicked his tongue, and then tugged.

"Brinder," she moaned, hooking her heels around him to pull him deeper into her and keep him against her.

He reached down and shifted one of her legs over one broad, muscular shoulder, widening her legs and changing the angle. Honor gave a half gasp-half groan, her orgasm hovering close by. Then Brinder did the same to her other leg, essentially bending her in half.

"Fuuuuuuck," she breathed, feeling his cock *everywhere*.

"This ok?" he asked, the cords of his neck standing out, his hair rumpled from where she'd been essentially tugging it since the moment she'd awoken in the morning with his head buried between her legs.

"Mmmm, better than ok," she panted, her heart racing as he began to move inside her. "I feel so full this way. So deep." The last word came out on a groan as he bottomed out again. When he pulled out and pushed in even deeper, she gasped, arousal pooling between her legs. "Brinder," she begged, no longer sure or caring what she wanted, as long as it was more. More of him. Forever.

Then he was pounding. Thrusting. Going deep, grinding, pulling out. Again and again. She clenched hard against him, every nerve of her body electrified and homed in on that center of bliss.

And then, as she splintered into millions of pieces...she finally felt whole again.

Chapter Seventy-Two

Honor

Too soon. It was too soon. Their final afternoon flew by in a happy haze of sex, laughter, and cuddling. Eventually, they scraped their sated, boneless bodies out of bed to shower. As if their souls knew separation was imminent, they came together in a rush of heat and need under the comforting spray, lips crashing into needy, passionate kisses that said more than words ever could.

It was another half hour before Honor finally finished her shower. She begrudgingly dried her hair and put on a touch of makeup, spending time she'd have preferred to hoard exclusively for Brinder. It was either that, or be trolled by paparazzi for looking haggard.

Not haggard. Sex-drenched.

Honor snickered as she absently ran her hand over the buttery soft leather of Couchie, gazing around the place that once was completely alien to her. A month later, it felt as much like home as her waterfront estate in Pembrokeshire.

Strong arms wrapped around her waist. She leaned back into the comfort of Brinder's embrace, inhaling his spicy cologne and committing the feel of this moment to memory—to ease her hurting heart once they were apart.

"What was the little laugh for?" he murmured against the top of her head, then shifted to tenderly kiss the shell of her ear.

Honor rotated in his arms, burrowing into the lean, comforting muscle of his chest. "I was thinking how, to those unaware of today's depravities, I am probably going to look exhausted. But the reality is, I'm just utterly sex drunk. And if the paps knew all the deliciously raunchy things you've done to my body, I'd probably land right smack into another nepo baby scandal."

She smiled at the rumble of Brinder's laughter in his chest.

"Deliciously raunchy?" Brinder laughed, tucking her in closer and dropping a kiss on the top of her head.

That was right up there with forehead kisses for sheer sexy yumminess, she decided.

"I mean...you've done things to me I never could have imagined." Her cheeks heated with one particular memory. "You...uh...at one point you did put a body part in an exit only area."

Now he bellowed out a laugh. "Oh, Stardust. Trust me—that is an amazing entry point. And we've barely scratched the surface."

Honor shuddered, a thrill of arousal whirling down her spine at the thought of that.

"Stop, Tish, or we'll be *in flagrante delicto* when Grayton arrives to collect you. And I'm still slightly afraid of that dude. He could jack me up and not break a sweat."

Honor laughed, pulling away from him. "Liar. You two are practically BFFs now."

"Yeah, well that BFF can still kick my ass. And he's particularly protective of you in a scary big brother way."

"Much scarier than Bash," Honor snickered, thinking of her older brother Sebastian, who was a suave Hollywood ladies man, not a ripped human weapon like her bodyguard.

Leaning against the back of the couch, she sighed, brushing her fingers back and forth along the sumptuous leather. "I'm going to miss you," she shared, adding a dreamy wistfulness to her voice.

"I'm going to miss you, too, Tish."

"I was talking to Couchie," she teased, a smile tipping the corners of her lips. "I want to hug you, dearest Couchie, but I don't know where to put my arms."

Brinder barked out a laugh. "Be careful, Tish. I never thought I'd say this, but I'm jealous of a couch."

She turned and dramatically stroked it, running her fingers along the leather and moaning theatrically.

Brinder released a low growl. "Careful, woman, or I'll bend you over that and take you hard—and I won't care if Grayton has to bleach his eyeballs."

"Promises promises," Honor trilled, giggling as Brinder dramatically began to shift her position. She held up a staying hand. "Brinder, seriously, we've been at it all last night and today. My ladyparts cannot take one more orgasm." Even with the departure looming before them, happiness flooded her veins. "That's a sentence I never thought I'd say."

She inhaled, rolling her lips to stave the tears that suddenly threatened to pour out. She knew once she started—ideally, once she was safely ensconced in her Boston hotel—her tears would be copious.

"Thank you, Brinder."

"For the orgasms? Anytime, Tish."

She swatted at him, warning him with pincer fingers as he playfully shuddered.

Sobering, Honor reached for him, holding his face in her hands as she absorbed every bit of this beautiful man, inside and out. "I love you, Brinder Desai," she whispered, choking on unshed tears. "Thank you for being my sanctuary."

Chapter Seventy-Three

BRINDER

He'd never been so nervous. Belly knotted. Palms sweating. This was either going to be amazing...

Or horrifyingly embarrassing.

That was the thing with surprises. They either land just right. Or they backfire.

Brinder watched the monitor from his secret spot in the green room, where Liam Blum's production assistant had hidden him before Honor's arrival.

For seven months, Brinder and Honor had conducted a long-distance relationship. For the first two weeks, she'd been immersed in prep and filming. But after that, he flew to her almost every Friday night, returning home late in the evening every Sunday.

Once, she'd surprised him while on a break from filming. Not having any scenes for a couple days, Honor had arrived midweek and turned up in his office, a grinning Amani beaming over her shoulder. Agnes bullied him into taking a couple vacation days (ok...it took exactly zero coaxing), which he and Honor spent at a private Virginia horse farm and resort Molly had booked for them—and where he taught her a few more moves for her film.

They'd squeezed in as many days and nights together as possible, trying not to go more than two weeks apart at a time.

And, yet, it wasn't enough. Never enough.

Three months for filming and four more for post-production was... a lot.

Now, Honor was on a brief publicity junket, working to build excitement for the release in five months. Benny, ever savvy and efficient for her client, also worked in promos for Honor's memoir. Honor would have to do another junket with her co-stars much closer to the release, but for some reason, she and Benny had insisted on this particular appearance.

And it had spurred him into taking action.

Prior to tonight, he'd warned Agnes of the likelihood he may need to leave his job to relocate to Wales. Agnes, ever calm and unflappable, told him she'd support him in any decision—even suggesting he could stay on board and work remotely. Not as the chief medical officer, but in some other advising capacity. Stunned by her generosity, he'd held off on accepting the offer—which should be a joint decision with Honor.

In the meantime? He had a grand gesture to perform.

The show's PA, Alexis, hurried back to him. "She'll be on right after the break."

He clasped his hands together, trying to control his nerves. "Is everything all set?"

"I just double checked. It's exactly as you set it up earlier. Liam won't let anyone near it. When the interview is almost finished, I'll come get you and bring you to the performance set. It's blocked from all views by curtains, and I personally looked at it from all angles to be sure."

"Thank you, Alexis." A smile broke across his face, sheer excitement superseding his nerves.

"She's on!" Alexis whispered excitedly, listening to her headset and motioning to the monitor.

Brinder's heart thumped. "Here we go!"

CHAPTER SEVENTY-FOUR

HONOR

Liam Blum introduced her to the studio audience, greeting her with a warm hug. They'd spent many hours over the years talking about her Tetralogy of Fallot journey and his own brother's path to healing with the same congenital heart condition. It was a deep bond.

Plus, he was just freaking funny. And so thoughtful.

Honor sat, smoothing the fitted navy scoop-neck dress that hugged her curves but gave her room to breathe. She would never again shoehorn herself into something uncomfortable just to appease obnoxious producers.

Movement from the wings caught her attention, and Honor burst out laughing as one of the production team walked out with a plate of nachos.

"I thought," the host chortled, nodding to the audience, "that we'd enjoy your favorite treat while we chatted."

"You know me too well, Liam," she laughed, taking a huge scoop of nachos and devouring it while she moaned dramatically. "Have I mentioned you're my favorite talk show host?" she professed with a wink once she'd chewed and swallowed.

Blum cracked up and dug in as well. For the next few minutes, in between bites, he asked her various questions about her role as Adele, the high-class sex worker who falls in love with her emotionally remote client.

"The buzz from pre-release screenings is pretty strong that you're going to get a bit more hardware for your awards shelf," the late-night host suggested.

Honor merely smiled. Hollywood was fickle. There definitely had been chatter, but she was months from release, and it would be almost another year until the Academy Awards that the film would be eligible for. Anything could happen. "I'm just excited to share this movie. The director, Trish Shane, is a force and a visionary. It's been an honor to work with her."

"Your brother is making headlines, too."

Honor rolled her eyes. "When isn't he?" Bash was a notorious Hollywood bachelor who'd recently—and very publicly—dumped the much-younger starlet he'd been dating. The man was forty-seven. It was time for him to figure his stuff out.

Like she had.

Honor's heart rate ticked up, pulse now racing, as she contemplated the announcement she was about to make.

"You made your own headlines last May," Blum led, a pre-approved topic. Honor wasn't going to hide from the truth.

"Not by my own doing." Honor's smile was grim. She wiped her hands, now shaking a bit, on the cloth napkin they'd thoughtfully provided with the nachos. "I was a victim of revenge porn, but the perpetrator is now in jail, paying for his revolting crime."

"I'm sorry you had to go through that. But you were a class act in how you handled it." Liam nodded to the audience, acknowledging their roar of supportive applause. "And if I remember correctly, I think something really wonderful happened right after."

He motioned to a monitor displaying a picture of Honor and Brinder taken a few weeks earlier over the Christmas holidays. They were bundled up, necessary for the walk they'd taken on the beach in front of her property. In the photo—which Benny herself had provided

—they were wrapped in each other's arms, gazing at each other and smiling so softly.

It gave Honor chills the first time the elder Dr. Desai showed it to her. Now that he wasn't in the OR, Brinder's dad had taken on a new hobby, happily embracing photography and impressing them all with his talent. Not surprising. Like Brinder, Rahul Desai seemed to excel at everything he tried.

"Something wonderful. Yes, that is one way to put it. And an understatement." Honor smiled at the host and cleared her throat. Now was not the time to get misty. She breathed out a quick exhale. "I'd like to tell you a brief story. It's about a young girl with a broken heart. Literally. A talented surgeon repaired it not once, but twice. Then his son stole that heart.

"Unfortunately, their paths diverged and they spent many years apart. Still, he owned the pieces of her shattered heart, even from thousands of miles away. Then, last May, one of life's unexpected twists brought them back together. And they fell in love all over again. It was easy and magical to love like that."

Liam beamed at her, encouraging her to continue with a squeeze of her hand.

"Brinder Desai was my first love. He's the only man I've ever loved. He is my heart."

The audience oohed and applauded.

Honor grinned, acknowledging their raucous cheers. Buoyed by their energy, she took a deep inhale. *Here we go.* "And that's why I'm making some important, very necessary, very happy changes in my life. Professionally and personally."

Liams's eyes widened. He wasn't expecting this part. But the showman in him clearly recognized this was a ratings win for him. "Do tell, Nacho."

She laughed at his nickname for her, a needed moment of levity before she bared her heart. Prior to the show, she'd made Ross promise she'd have Brinder in front of the TV that night. The show was being taped in front of a live audience, but wouldn't air until eleven-thirty that evening. By then, she'd be on a plane, flying on a studio jet from

California to a private airport just outside Charlottesville. Just like the previous May, a private car would whisk her away.

Only this time, she wasn't fleeing scandal, she was soaring to the man she loved.

"This is my final film role as an actor."

The gasps from the studio audience conveyed as much shock as Blum's stunned face. "Now you've really surprised us. This is not what I expected to hear."

"I did warn you I was making an announcement," Honor teased, winking at her old friend.

"Yeah, Nacho, but based on that photo and some other things I know, I thought you were going to tell us you were getting married, or maybe you're pregnant."

Honor's cheeks heated and she automatically reached for her belly before quickly removing her hand. No need to start that rumor.

"No, not engaged or pregnant." *Yet.*

A small thrill fizzed in her veins. If Brinder agreed, they could pull the goalie anytime soon. She would be thirty-eight in a month, but her GYN did tests and assured her all her parts were in prime working condition.

"But," she continued, "my priorities have shifted. I've been given an incredible gift—the love of the most wonderful, thoughtful man. And I intend to cherish every moment with him. An eternity with him isn't enough."

"So you're going into retirement?"

Honor laughed. "I'm going into partnership, with Trish Shane. We are starting a production company, with the goal to finance and produce movies that are written and directed by women. We want to lift up rising female professionals in the film community. And I'll also be producing the movie for the screenplay I wrote last year, as well as writing other screenplays."

Liam clapped and shook his head in wonder. "Nacho, I am speechless. Which is rare."

"I sort of feel the same way," she laughed. "I plan to be based out of Virginia, so I can be with the man of my heart and the career he loves. He makes a difference in people's lives, and I want to support him in that." She aimed a megawatt grin at him. "By the time this airs, I'll be on my way back to him. To stay."

More thunderous applause. "Have a mic drop, Nacho, why don't you?" Blum's huge smile mirrored hers. "Congratulations!" He turned to the audience. "Ladies and gentlemen, we're going to break, and when we come back, if Honor would indulge us for a bit longer, we have a special surprise."

CHAPTER SEVENTY-FIVE

BRINDER

"It's a big night for surprises. And we have another one for you!"

Alexis situated him in place. His legs were shaking. Sitting in the green room earlier, it was all he could do not to rush the stage and sweep Honor into his arms. She was retiring from acting?!

His mind was going a thousand miles a minute, and Brinder could barely hear Liam over the thudding of his heart. From his spot behind the curtain on the performance stage, he wiped his sweaty hands on his black slacks and adjusted his old hoodie, which he'd swiped after his last visit with Honor.

Alexis listened on her headset and then nodded at him.

Showtime.

The curtains around him lifted, revealing the scene he spent months planning in cahoots with Ross, Tiercy, Benny, and Molly—and both sets of parents, who were over-the-moon about all this. Surrounding him was an elaborate, geometric circular pattern of sand and stones. It took pufferfish about a week to create the ornate mating structure. Thankfully, Blum's crew had worked with him, so it only took a few hours to fashion it on the set.

The klieg lights were bright, but Brinder found Honor's gaze immediately.

Her hand was over her mouth, tears streaming down her face.

"Go!" Alexis whisper-shouted from the wings, motioning furiously with her hand.

Brinder dropped to one knee, his own eyes brimming with tears. "Honor Elizabeth Wheatley... A long time ago, a beautiful young woman, with the strongest, bravest, most loving heart I've ever experienced, stole my own heart. I cannot remember what it feels like not to love you, and I never want to know." Honor's hands were clasped under her chin, and Brinder could hear her soft sobs from across the set. "The love we share is fierce and profound. Though we both did our best to bury it, even decades apart couldn't diminish it. But we ended up with matching heart scars, didn't we? *Shiitake*, we were fools." He shook his head, a small smile playing on his lips. Honor's tearful laugh caused his own tears to trickle. "Wisdom is hard-earned, and I definitely learned the hard way that being without you is an empty existence. When you reappeared in my life last May, everything clicked into place —just as it was always meant to be."

He inhaled and reached into his pocket, pulling out the velvet case he'd been obsessively checking and protecting for weeks.

Honor stood, somewhat shakily, smiling and crying. "*Shidoobie*," she whispered, but Brinder heard her and smiled.

Liam put a steadying hand on her elbow. "Go get your man, Nacho."

Within moments, she was standing before him, her long hair in soft waves. "Now I know why the makeup artist insisted on waterproof mascara," she offered with a wobbly laugh.

He looked up at her. There were people all around them. And yet they were alone. Brinder reached for one of her hands, and found it was shaking as much as his.

"It's never enough with you, Stardust. I would be honored to have you in my arms for eternity, and I'll be grateful for every moment of it. You've already owned my heart since the first day I met you. Now, nothing would bring me more joy than if you'd do me the honor of becoming my wife. Stardust, will you marry me?"

She dropped to her knees in front of him and their lips crashed. Brinder tasted the salt of their happy tears and nuzzled against her. Leaning back, he cradled her face in one hand. "May I have the honor of standing by your side as your husband?"

"Yes!" she gasped, crying fresh tears of happiness. "Yes, Brinder Desai, I'll marry you." She peppered his face with small kisses and then pulled back to look at him, giggling at what she saw. "Are you wearing my hoodie?"

"You can have it back on our wedding day, Stardust."

Epilogue

Honor

"No. No no no. This *can't* be real."

"Oh, it's real indeed, Stardust."

Brinder smirked at her from his spot on the floor. They were curled on Ruggie, eating nachos, and, unfortunately, playing Scrabble. The nachos hit the spot. The Scrabble...not so much.

"How do you even play a thirty-five-point word?" This was ridiculous. He was destroying her.

"Talent, my darling. Sheer talent."

Honor rolled her eyes. Her film had released in early June to rave reviews. The press junket before and after was exhausting, but she was finally home. Well, home for now.

Brinder and she had purchased land near Ross and Tiercy, effectively bringing them even closer to 'the crew' who'd become the dearest of friends. It also gave them more land and much-need privacy. Construction crews began work on their new home in February and it would be ready soon. Thank God. Because things were changing quickly.

Honor nervously twisted her wedding ring set. After her

announcement on Blum and then Brinder's romantic proposal, they didn't want to wait to marry. They'd held an intimate ceremony at their home in Wales with just family and close friends. Ross, Tiercy, and Brinder's sister were her attendants, while Cole, Xander, and Bash stood up for Brinder. In addition to both sets of their parents, Molly, Bauer, Grayton, and a newly divorced Benny also attended. The latter two had circled each other warily the entire time—but not in a flirtatious way. In fact, Benny seemed intent on avoiding Gray. Honor tried to pry information out of Benny, but she was a vault.

She and Brinder planned to honeymoon in the Maldives later in the summer, once her work was wrapped on the film's promotion, and then visit Brinder's family in India with his parents.

Of course, that was now slightly up in the air.

"Are you going to play a word, Tish, or do you want to concede my Scrabble superiority before it gets any uglier?" Brinder's teasing question pulled her attention back to him and the game.

She'd only agreed to play this dumb game because she had an ulterior motive. *That's one way to put it.*

Honor looked at her tiles and smirked. When he got up to use the loo earlier, she'd made a couple...adjustments.

"Oh, something big planned, Tish?"

"You could say that, Gomez," she offered, fingering her tiles. She'd been staring at the board, waiting for a place to play the three letters, and Brinder had set her up perfectly on that last move.

Building off a 'B' on the board, she added three more tiles with shaking hands.

E.

B.

E.

Honor turned a nervous gaze to Brinder.

Brinder rolled his eyes and chuckled. "No matter how many times you try, Stardust, you can't play French words. It's not allowed."

Instead of arguing that ridiculous rule—although it was tempting—she merely smiled, grasping her hands in an attempt to halt their shaking.

"It's allowed today. And for the next thirty-six weeks."

She saw the moment her meaning registered with him.

"Stardust?" he asked, a tremor in his voice.

"Yes," she said, her voice thick with tears as she affirmed her news.

Brinder crawled around the board and pulled her into his arms. "You're pregnant?"

"Four weeks. I just found out yesterday."

"We're having a baby?"

"Next winter."

Brinder let out a loud whoop and then kissed her until she was breathless and laughing.

"It's important to note," Honor added with a grin when he finally released her, "that I will not be having this baby underwater in the center of an elaborate sand circle."

Brinder barked out a joyful laugh. "Solid thinking, Stardust. Best leave that to the pufferfish."

There was nothing quite like speaking someone's love language fluently. And, with an internal smug smile, she'd hit a double with her animal trivia and Scrabble hijinks. *Speaking of...*

She pointed to the abandoned Scrabble board. "Well, Dr. Desiiigh, how many points was that worth?"

"An eternity's worth"

THE END

ACKNOWLEDGMENTS

I released my first novel, *Heartstrings*, in May 2025 and *Arches* the month after. While working on all the "authory stuff" for those novels, Brinder and Honor's story came pouring out of me. When I wrote Tiercy's story in *Heartstrings*, I always loved Brinder's character. While he wasn't meant for Tiercy (because...Cole!), it became clear to me that Brinder needed his own HEA. Then, in the midst of *Arches*, a character you only hear about via Ross captured my fancy. Honor, acting scion, would have a backstory—one that included Brinder. It was fun to plant those seeds and then watch them bloom in *Stardust*.

There are so many people who have supported me and cheered me on as I live my dream of sharing my stories. Rhon House, who is sooooo much more than my "assistant" (that word truly doesn't capture the gifts she shares with me). She is a friend, a confidante, a voice of reason, a trusted counselor...and birthday twin! She does so much, and I'm grateful beyond measure. Thank you, Rhon!

Borrowing Honor's term for Ross, my "frienditor" Michelle Fewer is a treasure. She's editor, cheerleader, therapist...friend. She is devoted to making stories stronger...and shiitake (as Honor would say), she is very, *very* good at it. I live for your snort-laughs and your commentary in the margins. I appreciate you so much!

Julie Collier...your formatting is a thing of beauty! Thank you for making the pages so lovely and for your insights on (many) other questions from this newbie author (and talking me off the ledge a time or two). Thank you!

Maria from Steamy Designs, *Stardust* cover is breathtaking! Wander Aguiar did it again with his amazing image of Victor. Happy-dance thank yous to Romance and Rosemary for the glorious character art.

Just like with my first two novels, you beautifully captured my vision! Hugs also to Sydnie Camassar for expert (and speedy!) proofreading!

There are several individuals who read every word I write—often again and again. My bestie and Chief Reader, Rebecca, is far more than a friend. She's a sister of the heart—who also makes awesome observations and crisp edits. My friend Marlena, lovingly known as ChaCha, is wise and perceptive. I am so glad to have her in my corner. My sister, Cyndi, is my cheerleader and eager reader. She gets so excited for these stories and makes me feel amazing with her support of my books.

Given the medical condition at the <ahem> *heart* of this story, expert insight was mandatory. Thank you to Tom MacGillivray, MD, expert cardiothoracic surgeon with MedStar Heart & Vascular Institute, for answering all my questions. If I got anything wrong in this story, it's my error and not for lack of thorough explanation. Also—as you requested, Tom, I named a bartender after you! Thank you also to Ed Woo, MD, who suggested Tetralogy of Fallot as Honor's congenital heart condition. (Sorry I initially freaked you out when I asked for medical advice!)

Brinder's father is Indian, and I wanted to be sure any terminology and other references are correct. Thank you to Seena and George Chettiveettil for your review and insights.

With all the references to the UK, I needed experts there too. Thank you to amazing author friend Wren Charles—especially figuring out the Cheltenham nuances and for allowing me to reference Velvet Smoke and your amazing characters! Special thanks to super talented author Koko Heart for introducing me to Hannah—a new friend and whose help I greatly appreciate. (I still like the word 'trousered.' LOL!)

I also had some Italian dialogue in *Stardust*. Google Translate rocks, but Mary and Daniele Mannucci and their cousin Fabio Mannucci reviewed and edited my translations. Thank you!

My readers—wow! Thank you for reading my words and loving these novels. I write for pure creative enjoyment...but knowing you are out there and I can provide some spicy, funny, swoony escapism? Well, that's special indeed. Big, virtual hugs for all your wonderful support!

My family means everything to me. My dad in heaven—I can sense him and I know he'd say, as he did anytime I accomplished something large or small, "This is my daughter in whom I'm well pleased." My mom, who is my role model for unconditional love. My sons, to whom this story is dedicated, are definitely made of stardust. They shine bright, and I'm so proud of them. My love for them is boundless, and they fill my heart with joy. And Robert—the man who captured my heart more than twenty years ago—how has it been two decades and our love continues to grow? Thank you for supporting me, for feeding me while I disappear in the writing cave (otherwise I'd forget to eat), and for making each day with you magical—the extraordinary in the ordinary.

A note about names. I often come across names I love and make a note for future stories. If I use a name for one of my characters, it doesn't mean the character is inspired by that real-life person or shares any attributes. In fact, that is **never** the case. It just means I like the name. Now, sometimes I throw in a minor character name as a nod to people who helped with a story or who are special to me. It's my own little Easter egg for them. Just needed to clear that up!

It has been a joy to write Honor's and Brinder's story for you. Up next is my new series, The Red Wine Supper Club. Honor's brother Bash is in for a life-changing experience with a remote, prickly orthopedic surgeon Arabella "Remy" Remington. Curious about the dynamic between Benny and Grayton? You should be! I can't wait for you to read their love story. And will divorced baseball legend Gideon O'Grady get his happily ever after? His rehab nurse, the sister of a much-loved side character, has something to say about that. I'm also excited to introduce two new couples.

SECOND CHANCE AT LOVE SERIES

Heartstrings

What happens when you bury your heart with the love of your life—but someone gives its strings an unexpected tug?

Tiercy Somerville is quite sure you only get one love of your life. But just as she was building a life with hers, he was torn from her forever. Five years later, the popular high school English teacher and single mom has healed to a place of grief-tinged acceptance and peace, but her love of a lifetime still very much fills her heart, leaving no room for any other really big love. Or so she believes.

John Sims "Cole" Colburn is tired of playing the field. The construction firm CEO longs for the harmony, partnership, and deep abiding love his parents had. The problem is...his standards are probably impossibly high.

When their paths cross, the chemistry is instant, but neither is prepared for the intensity and passion of the journey ahead of them.

As their love deepens, Tiercy finds herself emotionally torn, questioning what she's always known. How can one person have two soulmates? And having found the love of his life, Cole must decide if he can bear not being the love of hers.

Arches

A sexy summer fling. A tangled past. A second chance at love.

Ross has a plan: pack up her grandmother's farmhouse, avoid old wounds, enjoy a little no-strings bedsport, and move on in Manhattan. She doesn't expect to rekindle the scorching chemistry with a hot, opera-singing single dad—or confront the shocking family secrets buried long ago.

Single dad Xander Grace has sworn off serious relationships—until Ross Beaufort, the unforgettable one-night stand who's haunted him for months, shows up at her grandmother's farmhouse...next to the property he's renting. She's only there for six weeks. A perfect summer fling.

As desire turns into something deeper, Ross must decide if she can let go of the past and fight for the future she never saw coming.

Stardust

A beloved silver screen star

A playboy doctor

Two scandals

One solution—fake date your long-lost first love

When two scandals unexpectedly reunite long-estranged first loves almost two decades after their painful breakup, can they put hurtful bygones aside to help each other? Will their surprising alliance lead to lost love found?

Honor Wheatley's world has just imploded. A decorated film actor, the beloved "nepo baby" and darling of the silver screen flees to the Shenandoah Valley to escape the fallout from a devastating scandal. When Honor's arranged lodging floods, she finds sanctuary in an unexpected place—the home of her first love and the man who shattered her surgically repaired heart years ago. And when Brinder agrees to be her personal guide on a sexual exploration journey as preparation for a film role—what could go wrong with that?

Dr. Brinder Desai has a well-earned reputation as a player, earning him the nickname Dr. Desiiigh. A fabricated scandal jeopardizes his dream job. Brinder needs to show stability or risk losing the position he loves. Having Honor Wheatley—the woman who broke Brinder's heart a lifetime ago and ruined him for relationships—in his home is a prescription for chaos he doesn't need. Except—fake dating the woman he lost could be the very thing he needs to keep his job.

Stardust is a steamy, emotional, and witty contemporary romance about lost love found, healing, redemption, and second chances.

Coming Soon!

Late Harvest—**Red Wine Supper Club book one!**

About Cathryn Lyons

Cathryn Lyons loves novels. Seriously loves them. Especially romance. This includes reading (often devouring) them...and writing contemporary romance novels of her own. She has been writing since before she could even properly hold a pen.

She is married to her real-life HEA and they share three sons and the world's best and derpiest rescue Golden Retriever (from Turkey!). She is a lifelong Marylander, but wonders if her short stint in London counts as being cosmopolitan (the attribute, not the drink; although those are quite delicious).

Cathryn fills her creative bucket by writing stories she hopes bring as much joy, laughter, escapism...and sexy feelings...that she herself has experienced through the gift of others' words. She hopes you love her stories, and welcomes hearing from you. You can email her at cathrynlyonsromance@gmail.com, or follow her on Facebook at https://www.facebook.com/authorcathrynlyons, and Instagram. Want to have a bit more unfiltered fun? (Sorry, Mom.) Join her Facebook reader's group, Cathryn Lyons' Romance Den, and connect with other lionesses and lions who roar for joy at romance.